Colliding Worlds

Colliding Worlds

Vivian M. Bivins

Writers Club Press
San Jose New York Lincoln Shanghai

Colliding Worlds

Writers Club Press
an imprint of iUniverse.com, Inc.

For information address:
iUniverse.com, Inc.
5220 S 16th, Ste. 200
Lincoln, NE 68512
www.iuniverse.com

ISBN: 0-595-14471-3

Printed in the United States of America

Cover Illustration by Timothy L. Porter

This book is dedicated to my family.
"You Are The Wind Beneath My Wings."

Preface

Candace Brooks is a young, beautiful, aspiring model. When she walks into AFLAME, one of the nation's largest ethnic modeling agency, lead executive, Austin Kawissopie greets her. Their hearts declare love at first sight. But, for Austin it is the memory and pain of a past relationship that holds him in limbo. Candace's innocence and charm entices him and causes him to break the vow he made to never fall in love again. Family intervention and haunting dreams endangers their affection but they find strength to overcome. Then a force stronger than anything Austin has ever experienced threatens his promise of commitment and fidelity. Will their love be able to sustain the future turbulence? Will the mysterious shadow lurking in the dark prove fatal for the perfect love affair? Colliding Worlds will tell you in a voice that is compelling, suspenseful and heart gripping.

Acknowledgements

I THANK YOU, GOD! FOR YOU ARE THE CORE OF MY EXISTENCE.

Thanks to my gang—The three S's, Sammie, Samantha & Senora. Thanks y'all, for giving me space during the creation of "Colliding Worlds". I Love You Guys!

Thanks to my sister, Marsha Griggs—my biggest cheerleader. Thanks for reading and critiquing each and every page enthusiastically. I can honestly say that without you, this book would not have been possible.

A big thanks to my parents, Moses and Vivian Williams. You believed in me and encouraged me on.

A shout out to my girls—Pages Book Club, Devetta Blount, Diane Booe, Pam Chisholm, Marsha Griggs, Melanie Marshall, Kay Purcell, Sarah Stephney, Omega Wilcox

And…A special thanks to Joan (Jo) Dawson for her editorial guidance and friendship.

Special thanks to Timothy L. Porter for giving Colliding Worlds a face. I'm sure his artistic abilities will take him far.

PART ONE

1

This Old House

It was 95 degrees in the shade and the sun was shining with a mighty force on everything and everybody brave enough to stand its intensity. Sable cocked her head sideways and squinted from the sun as she took another look at the high gables on the old 18th century farm house. Her beautiful cocoa-colored skin glistened with beads of sweat. She fanned herself with the Century 21 data sheet. She had already made up her mind about the house. She would buy it, but she would keep that intention to herself until she could negotiate a better price. She had heard the house was inherited property. The heirs were antsy and hurrying to sell so they could get their hands on the money. If she had to, she would gladly pay the exorbitant price. This was her dream house and it had all the features she ever wanted and then some. For starters, it was 50 miles away from rustling, bustling Manhattan. That was far enough away from the, as she put it, "madding crowd," yet close enough if she had urban matters to attend she could jump in her car and be there within an hour or so. She was tired of the fast-paced life the inner city offered. Five years of living in New York was enough for her and she longed for a quieter setting with a picturesque view. Across the Housatonic River, eastward, was the little town of Torryville, Connecticut. That was where she would find the solitude she needed and satisfy the nostalgia for her hometown in Germanton, North Carolina.

Torryville was similar to Germanton in many ways. It was a small neighborhood town with a population not more than 10,000. Everyone knew and kept a watchful eye out for his neighbor. The working class of Torryville commuted into the surrounding metropolitan cities to their jobs. Most used mass transportation instead of their own automobiles. Sable liked the thought of being able to drive her sleek 500 SL Mercedes on the tame streets of Torryville. Her friends and neighbors considered her quite lucky that her car had not been vandalized, stolen or wrecked in a city where every other driver became manic once situated behind a steering wheel. But luck had nothing to do with it. The car was spared from such atrocities because it sat motionless most of the time for fear of the aforementioned.

She had had the car for one year and could count on both hands the times she had taken it out to drive. Each occasion had been a bad experience. Once she reached her destination, there was no place to park and if she was lucky enough to find a parking place, the fee was outrageous. Weaving in and out of traffic was a mandatory New York driving skill that she had not yet acquired. She knew it was a matter of time before a dent claimed its rightful place on the expensive car.

Shamell Anderson, her editor and best friend, had talked her into trading the station wagon in on a more glamorous automobile. Shamell said she needed something in her life that was evident that she had arrived and the Mercedes would be just the thing to make the statement. Two days later and $60,000 shorter, the car sat in her apartment complex garage.

The house had three attached garages with ample space in each to slide the car in and out without fear of scraping a wall. Unlike her New York apartment, the kitchen was a spacious 20-by-20 square feet with cabinets and counter space galore. The feature she liked most about the kitchen was the bay window. It protruded from the side of the house with a perfect view of the main road. There were double French doors that led out to a barbecue-pitted, flagstone patio. The house was almost perfect. Of course, there were a few minor changes she'd have to do to make it feel like it was really hers. She would have the outdated yellow tile that covered the working area of the kitchen removed and replaced with a warm colored brick tile. She thought it would go perfect with the hardwood floor. She'd opt for recess lighting instead of the wagon wheel light fixture that hung above the island cook-top. It was a little too country-western for her liking. Sable thought the previous owners had odd taste. The entire house contained mix-matched decor. There were green carpet and orange walls in one of the bedrooms; in another miniblinds that were three inches shorter than the bottom of the windowsill. But what really left her dumbfounded was the five-foot stuffed gorilla standing in a corner of the den. Its prominent sagittal crests and canine teeth made it come to life. When Sable first spotted it, she was so frightened she screamed to the top of her lungs. The real estate agent chuckled and said it wasn't real. He'd told her the previous owners were safari excursionists. The gorilla was one of their many trophies. Sable wondered what kind of people could sleep in a house with a stuffed monster standing watch.

The house sat on five acres of land surrounded by white oak, elm and sweet birch trees. One acre had been cultivated into a flower garden. It had every kind of flower imaginable that the Connecticut climate would grow. There were carpeting daisies, lilac shrubs with their sweet fragrance, and a wide variety of petunias. There was a section exclusively for roses, roses of every kind. Tea roses of yellow, red, pink and white, and a wide variety of dwarf roses. Sable closed her eyes and visualized her mother smiling down from heaven on the verdurous garden, especially the roses, which had been her favorite. As far back as she could remember, her mother, Loretta Brown, had kept rose bushes planted alongside their A-frame house. Her roses were the talk of the neighborhood. On Sundays she'd cut several stems to place in the vase on the kitchen table. Sable pictured herself spending hours upon hours in the garden, breathing the sweet thick fragrances the plants produced. It would be there in the garden among the flowers where she'd do her editing. She hated editing with a passion, but it was a vital liability in her line of work, so she would do it in a pleasant environment.

Standing there viewing the grand splendor of the house was exhilarating. The third floor attic was where she'd do her writing. It seemed like an inspirational place to depict characters and situations inside the setting of a plot. She thought she would hire a carpenter to come and do the necessary changes she wanted done. She would have the studded walls closed in with sheet-rock. The ceiling would stay as is, beamed with knotted pine, giving the attic a rustic look. The walls would be painted a light color to attract the brightness that shone in through the six-foot wide balcony doors. Then if she needed more natural light, she'd have skylights installed. It would be the perfect work place. Maybe she would put a daybed and a small refrigerator up there for her intense writing days, when she had a deadline to meet. Then she could catch a quick nap or snack without ever having to leave the studio.

"Ms. Brooks, what you think?" asked Mr. Mason, the pudgy Elvis wannabe real estate agent. Mr. Mason's hair was dyed jet black, slicked back with a curl just over his flat forehead. Sable figured someone forgot to tell him the polyester leisure suit he wore had been outdated since the '70s. He had a constant twitch in his upper lip that was beginning to annoy the dickens out of her, not to mention his more physical approach, the touching and close standing. The first touch raised suspicion when she extended her hand for a handshake and he, instead, rubbed his hand up her bare arm and caressed her shoulder. Wanting to give him the benefit of the doubt, she accepted it as a greeting. She would have insisted on another agent, but she knew Mr. Mason would be good riddance after the transaction.

"Oh, forgive me, my mind was somewhere else. What did you say?" she asked, still looking up at the double glass doors of the balcony.

"She is a beauty isn't she! I can write you up a contract today if you want. Your credit is commendable. You won't have any problems at all." Mr. Mason opened his leather-bound notebook and pulled out a legal size sheet of paper. Sable assumed it was the contract. She placed her index finger vertically over her lips pretending to be in deep concentration.

"Hmm, I just don't know. The price is a little steep for me. I mean $400,000 is a lot of money. I've got to take in consideration I'm the sole breadwinner here." She sneaked a quick glance at Mr. Mason, who was looking at the ground and nodding his head as if in complete comprehension. But she knew better. She had just thrown out a wildcard and wondered what Mr. Mason would counterattack with.

"Well," he said as he looked around at the immaculate yard. "You're getting a lot of house for the money. A lot of house. 4,500 square feet to be exact."

"Yeah, I know and I wonder if I really need so much space. I mean, after all, two people living in a house this big. Candace, my 22-year-old, will want her own place soon and I'll be stuck with this pink elephant. Oh, I just don't know, Mr. Mason. You know, my father doesn't want us moving all the way out here. He thinks it dangerous."

"You gotta be kidding me, Ms. Brooks. It's safer than New York. I mean, when is the last time you heard of a crime being committed out here?" he asked with a toothy smile.

Ace in the hole, she thought. He was slicker than she gave him credit for. He was right; she hadn't heard of any crimes in Torryville. Sable was tired of all the crimes being committed in the place she had chosen to make home. Home, that is, as long as she was writing, which was the only reason she had moved from North Carolina to New York. It was more practical to be closer to her editor and publisher. She had removed herself from the country, but the country had not been removed from her. She still had hopes of one day, maybe in her golden years, moving back to North Carolina where her roots were. When she wrote her second bestseller, she decided a house would be a good investment. She was spending $3,000 a month in rent for a three-bedroom two-bath high-rise, money she would never see again. The $3,000 she was paying in rent could go toward a house. After all, she could very well afford it.

"You wrote about a dozen of those best-seller mystery novels, didn't you?"

"Come on now Mr. Mason, You know how to make a woman blush. There's only been two," she beamed.

"Heck, I hear it only takes one best-seller to set you pretty much straight for life, and here you got two!" He let the end of the statement lift in crescendo, "Plus they made a movie out of one of them, didn't they?"

Mr. Mason was partly correct in his thinking. She was wealthy—not rich, but working on it.

"Do you like to cook, Ms. Brooks?" he asked.

"What?" Sable wondered what he was getting at.

"Most women do like to cook. I'm asking because I just remembered the herb garden around the back of the house right next to the kitchen. C'mon." He took off in the direction to the back of the house with Sable in tow. "It's got all the herbs you'll ever need right here."

Sable looked at the rich greenery growing out of the ground and got a whiff of the amalgam of smells. She could distinguish fragrances of the peppermint, onions and garlic but could not place the other sweet smells coming from the small garden. She used to love cooking and experimenting with new dishes, when she had someone to cook for. She would have to buy a book on spices, herbs and their uses.

"I must say, Mr. Mason, this house and property get more impressive by the moment. There's a surprise around every corner. But, I tell you what I'm going to do. I'd like to bring Candace and my father back out here for another look before I make a definite decision. I need to ponder the price, you know, weigh the pros and cons."

The agent fidgeted with the contract a moment before putting it back into the notebook. He shook his head reluctantly. His commission was dependent on the sale of the house. If he could move this property, that would mean a one-percent commission for him, simply put a cool $4,000. "I only hope one thing, Ms. Brooks."

"What is it?"

"That this house doesn't get away from you before you decide whether you want it or not."

Sable gave a calculating chuckle. "At $400,000, Mr. Mason, I wouldn't bet on it."

2

The Indisputable Wilson Brown

Wilson Brown opened the Dutch oven and pulled from it an exquisite golden brown pound cake. It was Sunday and he had chosen not to go to church with Sable and Candace. He told them he was exhausted from yesterday's shopping spree and drive to Torryville to visit the house. He wanted to stay home and rest up a bit. What he really wanted was to catch the Dodgers and Braves baseball game on television. The game had turned out to be a major disappointment, with the Dodgers beating the Braves by 10 runs at the bottom of the fifth inning. That's when he had turned off the set and begun cooking. Candace was a picky eater and would not eat anything with a fat content higher than six grams per serving. The girl was constantly dieting. Wilson had two more weeks before going back home to North Carolina, and he was determined to put some pounds on Candace. He contemplated chocolate vs. cream cheese icing, but decided against icing altogether, knowing Candace would have a reason for not eating any of the cake. He knew the child could not resist pound cake, so he'd leave it plain. The barbecue chicken, corn bread, corn on the cob and potato salad were ready. Of course, they would fuss about the big meal he had prepared; yet eat every bit of it.

First, Candace would say he was trying to make her fat and ruin her dreams of becoming a high fashion model. She certainly had the height, standing at five feet nine she appeared thin enough but in actuality, she was 10 pounds over the weight requirement for the more reputable modeling agencies. Candace was a striking girl who had acquired most of her looks from Sable, including skin the color of rich mahogany. Unlike Sable, who wore her hair cut short and natural, Candace had her thick coarse shoulder length hair relaxed and in an abundance of cascading curls. Her large doe eyes were hypnotic, much like Sable's. Her most complimentary features were her full sensuous motherland lips and dimples that penetrated deep into her satiny dark cheeks.

Wilson remembered Sable's love for cooking when she was married to Jonah and living back in North Carolina. She had been the perfect housewife¾for the more traditional man. Her life had changed from domesticated to sophisticated, dependent to independent, and introverted to extroverted. The transformation was extreme, but admirable. Wilson attributed her newfound sovereignty to her realization that she was capable of doing anything she set her mind to. Jonah and Sable were good for each other. Sometimes he hated she ventured into writing because it had opened up avenues that led to dissolution and eventually divorce.

Jonah worked for a pharmaceutical company. He started as a sales representative and years later progressed to district manager. His job required him to travel often, leaving Sable and Candace alone. When Candace grew into adolescent and formed her own identity, she no longer needed or wanted the constant attention Sable was giving her. She structured new friendships and began to spend more time away from home. For Sable, the emptiness and boredom were too much to bear. She got a job as an office assistant at a marketing firm. All the pieces were coming back together in her life. She looked forward to going to work, being around mature-minded individuals with similar interests. She enjoyed engaging in stimulating conversations, listening to opinions and philosophies, giving her own, and knowing in return she was being heard and acknowledged. All was going well until Jonah decided her working outside the home was putting too much of a strain on the family. Being the decorous wife she was and not wanting to threaten the sanctity of their vows, she abandoned her short-lived career and returned to the apathetic boundaries of her home.

Jonah sensed the vivaciousness Sable once possessed was gone. Because he felt to blame, he tried pacifying her with gifts. Sable had outgrown the simple "mistress of the house" role. She needed more. There was something inside her wanting to bloom and flower into a potential realness. What it was, she did not know. All she knew was this something was burning to get out.

She would never forget the day Jonah brought the computer home. Sable watched his 940 Volvo pull into the driveway after one of his three-day trips. He smiled as he spotted her watching him from the living room window. Instead of coming straight into the house as usual, he went to the trunk of the car and pulled out a big box. Sable knew immediately it was another present and she wondered when he was going to learn that she didn't need or want all of his gifts. He brought the huge box into the house and sat it on the floor. He gave her a peck on the cheek and made a mad dash back outside to the trunk of the car to retrieve another large box. He spent most of the evening hooking up the computer while Sable prepared his favorite meal, country-style steak, mashed potatoes and string beans.

After the excitement of the day had worn off, Jonah and Sable lay in bed, limbs entangled and bodies spent from passionate lovemaking. He remembered how she used to love writing, especially poems, and thought maybe she could recapture her passion for it. He told her the computer might inspire her to start writing again.

Sable did recapture her love for writing. She began writing short stories and before long it became a diversion from her loneliness. It quickly turned into her favorite pursuit. She thought her writings were quite good and was often told so by family and friends. It was through her mother's coaxing that she entered one of her stories into a contest and won grand prize. The grand prize had been her passage into the literary guild of novel writing.

Jonah's account of their problems was she had no more time for him and Candace. She was always at the computer working on her book, or if not that, then she was at the library doing some book-related research. Jonah felt ostracized and frivolous. It used to be when he'd come home from a three-day business trip; Sable would be all over him. She couldn't wait for Candace to retire for the evening so she could physically show Jonah how much she missed him. Now, they had become second in her life and she was quickly outgrowing them. He soon regretted ever buying the computer.

Sable's version was Jonah could not handle her independence or success and would not give her the support she needed from him. Their problems only escalated until it reached the pinnacle of divorce.

Wilson still put a plug in for Jonah every chance he got, even though Jonah was not aware of his doing so. The two men remained close after the divorce. Jonah had a few women friends, but he never let it get as serious as they wanted it to become. Of course, Wilson was delighted. As long as Jonah didn't fall head over heels for some woman, Sable still had a chance of getting her husband back. His gut instinct told him their paths would cross again and their hearts would entwine once more in love. Wilson would never give up on trying to reunite the two. After all Jonah was the son he'd never had.

*　　　　　*　　　　　*

"Mmm, Daddy you shouldn't have. This chow is too good for words," said Sable, licking barbecue sauce off of her fingers and sucking traces of it that settled under her sculptured nails. "I know I've gained at least five pounds since you've been here."

"Yeah, Papa, this grub ain't nothing but the truth," Candace mumbled, with her mouth full of potato salad.

"Miss aspiring model, you better watch it," Sable warned. After Daddy leaves, you'll be crying about all the weight you've gained."

"Ha! I don't see you pushing your plate aside, Ma."

"Yeah, but I'm not wanting to strut down a runway showing all my stuff for the world to see," Sable joked.

"Both of y'all can stand to put on a few pounds here and there. Been so long since y'all ate some down-home cooking, I bet your mouths in shock," Wilson pushed himself up and went to get the pound cake he was hiding in the strawberry ceramic cake plate that had once belonged to Loretta.

"Oh, Lord!" cried Sable, as Wilson sat the delicious looking cake down on the table. "I know I'm gon' have to take me three Correctols now."

"Sable, you ain't still taking synthetic laxatives are you? You know that stuff ain't good for you. Y'all need to start keeping more nutritious food in this house, for one thing; then you won't have to worry 'bout cleaning ya'self out when ever you go on them food binges. You don't keep nothing but junk in them cupboards," Wilson started naming all the unhealthy foods stored inside of them. "'Tata chips, chocolate chip cookies, candy bars, peanuts. Y'all ever drink water 'round here? All I ever seen ya drink is soda. Just a wonder y'all ain't stretched out over there at First Regional Hospital in a diabetic coma. You know, that's what took your mamma 'way from here," he paused a moment to pay homage to his dearly departed. "Sweet Loretta. Lord rest her soul." For a moment, Wilson looked lost and Sable knew he was lost in thought. She imagined he was feeling a sea of loneliness right now and she wished she could make it better for him. When Loretta died, she thought she would never be able to function again, but time was a magnificent healer. Yet, sometimes it seemed time had forgotten to cast its healing powers on her father. In the six years she had been dead, there wasn't a day she talked with Wilson that he didn't mention Loretta.

"Daddy, why don't you come and live with us? The house has a room with your name on it. And, Daddy, you got to admit the kitchen is to die for. You know how you love to cook."

"Yeah, papa! C'mon. Then we can take care of you," Candace begged.

Wilson gave them a "have you lost your mind" look, "Y'all know I can't come live up here."

"Sure you can. You don't have any real responsibilities. You're retired. We are your nearest family and we're 600 miles away. Now if something happens, like you get sick or something, who's going to take care of you?"

"Girl, I ain't 'bout to get sick. I eat right, walk two miles a day and take care of my body." Wilson pushed up the sleeve of his shirt and flexed a muscle for them to see. "Look-a-there, I'm 63 years old and still got it," he teased.

"If you still got it, why don't you use it and catch one of them fine, well-seasoned widow ladies back home? I know I'd feel a lot better if you weren't living alone, Daddy. You still got a lot of life left in you."

Wilson plopped his long, lanky body into a kitchen chair and began cutting and serving the cake. "What makes you think I ain't already living? Just because a person is single don't mean he's lonely."

Sable and Candace passed curious glances at each other as he continued.

"Speaking of widows, Ms. Ruthann King sends her best regards. You remember her, don't ya Sable?"

Sable remembered Ms. Ruthann quite well. She was eight years old the night her parents got into a heated argument. It had been over Ms. Ruthann. Wilson had come home late one evening and Loretta accused him of being with her. Ms. Ruthann was a beautiful woman. She was widowed in the prime of her life, lost her husband in an automobile accident and she vowed she would never marry again. She was flirtatious to a fault and most of the married women in Germanton shunned her and wanted their men to do the same. But easier said than done. There were more than a few that strayed off the pathways of righteousness with Mrs. Ruthann. Sable remembered pots and pans flying across the kitchen that particular evening and Wilson telling Loretta if she couldn't trust him, then the marriage was over and he was leaving and never coming back. His last words before he slammed the door shut were "crazy woman."

The first two days of Wilson's absence, Loretta called her job claiming illness. She spent the days moping around the house in the same housedress, listless and inattentive to Sable's needs. Luckily for Sable, she knew how to spread jelly and peanut butter over bread, and there was always an ample supply of milk on hand.

Sable had come home from school three days later to find Wilson in the kitchen donning one of Loretta's aprons and preparing dinner. She jumped into his arms, encircling his neck with her tiny arms. She remembered begging him to never leave again and he promised that he wouldn't. He'd kept that promise.

It was strange after all those years, she never thought of Ms. Ruthann much. Now, after Wilson mentioned her, her memories came rushing back in full force. She even remembered the khaki pants and brown pullover crew neck sweater Wilson had worn that evening. She also remembered how nice Ms. Ruthann had been to her after the incident and how she'd routinely asked about Wilson in hushed tones. She was only eight years old, but she suspected there was a secret bond between her daddy and Ms. Ruthann.

"Yeah, Daddy I remember her. Is she still pretty?" she asked, winking an eye at Candace.

"Yeah, she still a nice looking woman, but of course, you know she can't hold a candle to your momma. Sable, you remember how your momma used to fix up for church on Sundays? You gotta give it to her, that woman could dress when she wanted to. But then, when she was feeling downright evil, she could look like the devil too," he chuckled. "She was the seasoning of my soul. Naw, they'll never be another 'Retta. You know, ya momma never did like Ruthann. She wasn't a bad person like everyone made her out to be. She really was a kind person, just misunderstood is all." Wilson forked a piece of the cake into his mouth. "Mmm, I do believe this is the best pound cake I ever made."

He was doing it again, Sable thought. She could never get anything out of him concerning companionship. She realized that if she wanted to know she would have to come right out and ask him point-blank.

Wilson wanted to tell the whole story to Sable. He wanted her to know that Ruthann was more to him than just a friend. He wanted her to know that they shared each other's joys and sorrows and he wasn't lonely because she gave him fulfillment. But how could he tell his daughter that the very woman her mother disliked so much when she was living was now the woman keeping his bed warm most nights.

Wilson and Ruthann's initial meeting was right after the death of her husband. They'd met formally at Billiards and Spirits, an eminent pub located in the heart of downtown Germanton and patronized by the black community. Wilson knew who she was and most men, black and white, did too. She was hard to miss, with her captivating smile and full, voluptuous figure. She was aware of the power she had over men, and even when she was married she used it frequently as a means of teasing. But what she found in Wilson was a decency that was untouched by lustful overtones. Wilson had heard of the tragic accident involving Bill King. Some people say he was drunk that night his car ran out of control and overturned five times on Highway 66. Others say he was being chased by the police for trying to bootleg liquor in a neighboring town. Whatever the truth, one thing was certain-the man was dead and Wilson was sitting two tables away from his widowed wife. She was alone and her eyes revealed pain. He read in them an invitation. His gut instincts told him to renege, but legends of her willingness to fulfill a man's darkest fantasy aroused his curiosity to the point that without much effort he found himself walking toward her. They started a platonic friendship that later turned to something much more.

Wilson doubted Sable remembered the night he and Loretta had the argument; she was so young then. But if she did, he couldn't bear for her to know the truth and that Loretta was right all along.

"So, Sable, you really are serious about buying this house, huh?"

"I'm as serious as serious can be. It's got everything I need and want. Besides, the last time Candace and I agreed on something was when she was four years old. After that, it's been 'I don't like that and I don't like this'. If I say its black, she says its white. I'm vice and she's versa," Sable chuckled as she pushed herself up from the table and began to clear away the dishes. "So I'm taking advantage of this 'Kodak moment.'"

Candace shielded her plate as Sable reached for it. "Uh-uh, not finished yet," she said, with her mouthful of cake.

"Girl, you better watch it," Sable warned again.

"Well, it's your fault. You taught me to always clean my plate. I'm eating for all the starving children in Africa, remember?"

Sable shook her head pathetically, knowing that after Wilson left, between her and Candace, they would have gained at least 20 pounds. She wouldn't worry about that now but, instead, enjoy the two weeks Wilson had left with them.

3

Retrospection

The phone rang as Wilson sat down to read the morning newspaper. He had just finished washing the breakfast dishes. He was a little tired, but still planned on buffing the hardwood floors before Sable came home from Alpha Publishing, and Candace from the university. Sable and Candace were clearly not thorough housekeepers. They never dusted, cleaned the insides of the windows, or made their beds properly. They pulled the covers to the top of the bed without making the tucks under the pillows. Wilson remembered the Saturday morning cleanings Loretta and Sable would do before Sable was allowed to watch cartoons. Their five-room house would be spotless when they finished, and sometimes Sable would be so tired she'd fall asleep in the middle of "Casper the Friendly Ghost." Wilson agreed with Loretta that the child should know how to do basic housecleaning, but was opposed to working her like a slave.

"Don't no man want a woman who can't do simple house chores. I'm trying to make her into a well-rounded person," would be Loretta's reply to Wison's protest. Wilson backed down, knowing that some things Loretta was definite about and teaching Sable to be a meticulous housekeeper was one of them. Then, that afternoon, to balance out the day on a pleasant note, he would take her to play putt-putt. He never invited Loretta to join them. He knew she would spoil the evening by being too overbearing on the child. Wilson pictured Loretta six feet under, turning over in her grave because all her domestic preparations on Sable had been in vain.

"Hello?" He answered on the fourth ring.

"Wilson?" asked the unsure voice on the other end.

"Uh-huh, this is Wilson Brown at your service,"

"Wilson, this me, this Jonah."

"I thought I recognized your voice. What a pleasant surprise!

"Ran into Ruthann the other day and she told me you were in New York for the graduation."

"Yeah, man, our baby girl graduating from college. Can you believe that? Seems like yesterday when you and Sable brought her home from the hospital."

Jonah chuckled as mental archives played visions of a plump, jolly, cocoa-colored baby cooing into the gazes of two proud parents. He was happy that his only child was doing so well. He knew the past five years hadn't been easy for her. Her metamorphosing into a young lady without his being around was something he never dreamed would happen. Often, he would find himself wondering what went wrong with his marriage? They were so right for each other. Even in high school they were voted as the couple most likely to marry, have a dozen children and live happily ever after. But that was not how it had turned out.

"So, to what do I owe the pleasure of this call?" asked Wilson.

"Well, you know I'm coming for Candace's graduation next Sunday and I just wanted to get some gift ideas."

Wilson laughed as he thought of how Candace had been trying to coax Sable into buying her a new car. The girl had tried everything under the sun to get Sable to buy her a brand new, top-of-the-line, fully equipped Camaro. Midnight black with gold stripes was her choice of color. Sable assured her that there would be no car other than the one she already had. The '91 Toyota Tercel was in good condition and was all she needed for now or until she was able to work and afford her own car. Wilson's choice was something more practical and useful for his only grandchild—like a nice heavy coat for New York's rough winters, but he knew young folks weren't into practical things. Besides, on Candace's special day, he wanted her to be happy. His graduation present to her would be a crisp $1,000 bill. If Sable knew what he intended to do, she would object; she thought his pension was insufficient. Wilson never disclosed his financial information and preferred people believing otherwise. He had worked 35 years with the postal service and had saved a nice nest egg. His retirement check alone was more than enough to sustain him monthly, not to mention the insurance policy Loretta left him.

"What's so funny, Wilson?" Jonah asked, chuckling himself because Wilson's laugh was contagious.

"Oh, I was just thinking about your daughter. You know what she told her momma she wanted for graduation?"

"What's that?"

"She told her she wanted a brand new Camaro. Want it to be black with gold stripes. You can imagine what Sable told her. Told her she was crazy if she thought she was gon' get another car when the one she got in good shape, 'specially for up here, these psychotic drivers. Candace keeps on trying though. Real persistent. She didn't get that from you, Jonah. If you'd been more persistent, maybe you and Sable…"

Jonah knew what was coming next and he cut him short before he could start his agonizing matchmaking ritual.

"Aunt Elvira is coming with me, Wilson." Jonah fought hard to hold back the chortle caught in his throat. He knew this bit of news would dampen the rest of Wilson's visit. He understood why Wilson couldn't stand Aunt Elvira. She was nosy and openly opinionated, the total opposite of what her sister Loretta had been. But in Jonah's eyes, those not so pleasant characteristics were somehow softened by a few finer qualities she possessed. She'd give the shirt off her own back to anyone in need. It didn't matter if she knew them or not. She was known as the helping hand in Germanton. Whenever there was an accident, illness or tragedy in the small community, she was the one who started the chain reaction of assistance.

"Coming where!" Wilson's tone changed from affable to contemptuous.

"I know you and Aunt Vi don't get along, but she wanted to see her grandniece graduate."

"Why did you have to go and tell her Candace was graduating for? You driving?"

"I plan to. Why?"

"Cause, you should have told her you were catching the plane. That ol' windbag scared to fly" Wilson hissed.

"C'mon, Wilson" Jonah coaxed. "She's family, too."

Wilson was pouting, like a child denied candy. There was no pacifying him. "Aw, she ain't family; she just an attachment that we can't seem to get rid of."

Jonah could hold his amusement no longer and he released his deep guffaw laugh. Five years ago, he was legally considered a part of Wilson's family, but now he felt like the attachment. He missed being apart of their lives. He missed it real bad.

*   *   *

Wilson complained all week about Aunt Elvira's visit. Candace was delighted that she and Jonah were coming. It had been three years since she'd seen her father and grandaunt. Although they stayed in touch by telephone and care packages, nothing was quite as nice as seeing them in person. Candace had already begun to make sleeping arrangements. Wilson would stay in the guestroom, Jonah could take her room, and Sable agreed that Aunt Elvira could sleep with her in the king-sized bed that took up most of her bedroom space. If Aunt Elvira insisted on sleeping on the couch, then she would sleep over at Russell's for a few days. She knew he wouldn't mind.

In a sense, Russell was her closest friend. She could rely on him to the bitter end and she wondered why she could not bring herself to like him the way he wanted her to. He was just so normal and convenient. Sometimes she felt guilty for leading him on like she did, but she figured he allowed it, so why worry about it. When Sable and Candace had their semi-annual quarrel, it was Russell who let her stay at his apartment until things got better between them. And, it was Russell who gave her money when Sable told her not to ask her for any, that she needed to get a job and learn responsibility.

Candace and Russell first met at the post office, where he worked as a mail clerk. She was mailing a Christmas package to Aunt Elvira. After Russell weighed the package for postage, Candace realized she did not have enough money to cover the shipping fee. She was exactly two dollars short. The moment had been an embarrassing one. Russell knew Candace was in an awkward situation. There was a long line of other customers behind her waiting for service. Candace probed her pocketbook, found a dime here and a nickel there, but not enough to make up the amount she needed. There was something about her that struck Russell's fancy and he wanted to help her. He told her he'd made a mistake in his calculation and only charged her for the amount she had placed on the counter. Before handing her the receipt, he scribbled on the back of it his name, phone number and a note asking her out to dinner. She quickly grabbed the piece of paper and, without thanking him, waltzed out of the post office.

On Friday evening, two days after the post office incident, Candace sat with nothing to do. Sable was getting ready to go out with Shamell, and Candace would be left alone. This particular night, she felt like sharing her company but she could think of no one. To her surprise, she picked up the phone and dialed Russell's number. On the third ring she hung the receiver up. She thought he would think she was too anxious. That certainly was not the case. She remembered his light skin and muscular build and those particular characteristics did not strike her fancy. She preferred dark men, tall with a slim build. She summoned her courage and dialed the number again. Russell answered on the first ring this time.

"Hello."

"Uh, hello, may I speak to Russell Ingram?"

"Yo, Whazup!"

"This is Candace Brooks, the girl at the post office on Wednesday."

"Oh, yeah, I definitely remember you, luscious lady."

Candace stuck her index finger in her mouth and mimic vomiting. She thought his rap was starting out weak and that Grandpa Wilson probably used the same line on Grandma years ago. But, she thought she'd play along for a while just for fun.

"Can you be sure I'm who you think I am?"

"Most sure. I don't make a habit of giving my number out to just anybody."

"Oh, really. And how you know I'm not just any ol' body?"

"Because I got a six sense about these things. If I close my eyes, I can see you plain and clear. I even remember what you were wearing when you came into the post office Wednesday."

Before Candace could ask, Russell proceeded to tell her.

"You had on jeans. Tight fitting, I might add. You got long legs and I bet they pretty up under them jeans, ain't they?"

"Well, they are long."

"And I like the way you had your lil' shirt tied in the front exposing your belly button. That was real cute. Yeah, I liked that."

Candace had to admit that his rap was improving.

"Now let me ask you something, but you gotta promise me you won't get mad 'cause I know how sistahs can be about certain things"

"Go ahead."

"Was that a weave or the real McCoy. Not that I got anything against weaves, know what I'm saying, I just want to know."

"One thing I can say 'bout you, Mr. Ingram. You are straight-forward."

"Always. There's no other way to be."

"Well, since you're so direct with me, I guess you deserve a truthful answer. It's all mine."

"All yours meaning bought and paid for or all yours meaning growing out ya scalp?"

Candace laughed. She was almost glad she'd call him. He was pretty amusing.

"It's mine, really. You won't have to worry about getting your fingers caught in the threads."

"Now that sounds almost promising."

"Wait-wait-wait, I was talking about the 'collective' you," she laughed.

"Close enough, still gives me some hope."

"What is this thing with black men and long hair anyway?"

It's not a thing. It's just that hair enhances a woman's features. Bald heads are not in vogue, you know."

"Well, I think Tyson Beckford looks pretty doggone good to me," she said sarcastically.

"Let me explain something to you, Candace. His seven figures look good to you; the man's a super model, he rolling in dough."

"Excuse me!" she said, with the revolving head thing going on. "Are you insinuating that I'm a gold-digger? Because if you are, you're way off base. I happen to be attracted to people because of their self worth."

"Yeah, and I'd guess his self worth equals phat cash," Russell laughed.

"You're so cute, you know that. We've been on the phone not even five minutes and you got my blood pressure up."

Russell continued to laugh, "Good. I like a woman with a good debate. So where is your boyfriend? I know he gon' take you out so you can kick up your heels."

"There's no one special in my life right now."

"Oh, girl, now you know I don't believe that a fine looking woman like yourself ain't got no boyfriend."

Candace cringed at his improper English before answering, "No I don't. What about you? Why aren't you out kicking up your heels with a saucy little number?"

"I can't get a woman," he chuckled,

"Now I don't believe that for one second!"

"You know, y'all women ain't into light-skinned brothers no more. Now when you stepped in the door last Wednesday, it was just like something hit me. Wham! There she is the woman of my dreams. Then you got in my line, g-i-r-r-l, I knew it was fate then. You were supposed to meet me."

"I don't know about that fate stuff. All I know is I got in the shortest line I could find."

"You're good, but hey, that's all right, I like a dog-cat chase. Wouldn't have it any other way. Now what time you want me to come over. I already done took my bath. All I gotta do is put my clothes on. Where you live? I can be there in 30 minutes flat."

4

Disappointment

Candace walked into AFLAME Modeling Agency full of confidence and wearing a $150 navy-and-gold imitation Christian Dior suit. She hoped to be discovered, but as she caught sight of the many glamorous photos of the current models gracing the walls, her confidence and hopes started to dwindle. She felt that the suit she so proudly put on that morning looked like what it was, an imitation. She began to doubt herself and wondered if she could compete with the gorgeous girls in the photos. She pulled at the tail of her mid-thigh-length skirt, feeling outrageously stupid for squeezing her 5-foot-9, 140 pound body into the size-nine outfit. She guessed that the girls in the pictures wore size fives, and at that brief moment she felt unworthy for seeking a job with the esteemed modeling agency. Just as she turned to walk away, Phyllis, the receptionist asked if she could assist her.

"Uh, yes, I was hoping to talk to someone doing some modeling," she said nervously.

The friendly tone of the receptionist took her by surprise. She automatically assumed that because she was black and wore her hair in short sprouting dreads that she'd have an attitude, a stereotype that damaged many African Americans. She managed a smile and walked back to the desk.

"You must be carrying a rabbit's foot and have your fingers and toes crossed, because you're in luck. It isn't often that Mr. Kawissopie has time for interviews, especially unscheduled ones."

Candace inched closer to the desk in anticipation. "Oh yeah?"

"Just so happens, Mr. Kawissopie is free for the next two hours. He's one of our executives, but he does a little bit of everything, including interviewing." She whirled out an application attached to a clipboard. "Here, fill this out. What's your name?"

"Candace Brooks," she said, and then blew out a tense puff of air.

Phyllis chuckled at Candace's anxiety, "Calm down. There's nothing to get all worked up about. To tell you the truth, Mr. Kawissopie likes innocence. Most girls come in here 'T and T style' thinking that's gon' get them a job.

"T and T?" Candace asked.

"Yeah, you know, showing tit and tail. You never heard that expression?"

Candace shook her head "No, I don't think I have."

"Hmm, you are green, fresh and green," she said under her breath. But there was something about Candace that she liked.

*   *   *

Austin Kawissopie was a manly looking man, almost rare and exotic in the masculine version. His hair was cut in a fade and his well-trimmed beard and mustache added flavor to his appearance. His skin was smooth and dark, like the color of a candy bar. Candace noticed his thick accent and automatically assumed he was from Africa. As she sat quietly, waiting for him to finish reading her application, she stole glances at his wall. It was adorned with degrees, credentials, and awards. Candace was able to read enough to know that in 1987 he received his MBA from Wake Forest University, in Winston-Salem, North Carolina.

She was impressed with his accomplishments and, the fact that he graduated from a highly accredited and well known university in a town that was only five miles from her own was impressive too. She questioned his age. He looked mid-30s. She guessed if he came out of school in 1987 at 25, then 10 years later would put him in the mid-30s. She surveyed the office some more. The desk he sat behind was of rich mahogany. On the corner of his desk sat a five-by-five framed photo of several people standing arm in arm. Candace leaned forward to get a closer look. There were two women and three men. She could tell that one of the men was Mr. Kawissopie. The women had on colorful head-wraps and smock-style dresses made from Kente-cloth. The older man was gray-haired and semi-bald. He wore a simple white button-down short-sleeved shirt, with dark trousers. Austin and the younger man wore dashikis and khaki slacks. One woman was significantly older than the other and Candace guessed she was the mother of the younger one. She could see the resemblance and concluded that they were his family members. Before she could straighten herself back in the chair, she noticed that Mr. Kawissopie was staring at her.

"Excuse me, I was just…"

Austin held up a hand to protest her explanation. "It's all right." He swiveled his chair from under the desk and got up. "Let me show you," he said as he walked around the desk to where she sat. He picked up the picture and handed it to her. "This is my family." He seemed proud as he spoke of them. This is my father, my mother, brother, and here," Austin affectionately touched the image of the older lady, "this is Lena, my grandmother. She is the oldest and the wisest. Mama Lena is 87 years young," he chuckled.

"She's very active, huh?" Candace asked.

"Active is not a fair description of her. She walks three miles every day, says it is the walking that keeps her young." Austin sat on the corner of the desk where the picture had been. He crossed his arms across his chest. He wore a charcoal, double-breasted Armani suit. His silk tie had multi colors of red, gray and black, and was perfect with the crisp white shirt he wore. Candace couldn't help but notice his dark-gray loafers. She guessed they were Italians and expensive. She liked the way he dressed, among many other things she'd noticed about him. He appeared about six-four. His build was slim and he had deep-set eyes, the color of shining onyx. His smile was warm and inviting, revealing straight teeth that contrasted against his skin like the ebony and ivory keys of a piano.

"I detect an accent. May I ask where you're from?"

"Dar es Salaam."

Candace frowned inquisitively, before repeating the name.

"It is the capital of Tanzania," he said, watching her closely. "I've been in the United States for 17 years now. Came here to go to school and I have been here ever since."

"Why so long? You prefer the States over your home?"

"The opportunities here are limitless."

His consistent stare was making her nervous. Her hand found a dangling lock of curl and she began twirling her index finger around it.

"How tall did you say you are?" he asked, leaning back and looking over his shoulder at Candace's application.

"I'm five-nine, sir."

"Don't call me sir. I'd like to think I'm not that old. Everyone else calls me Austin; you may do the same." Then he smiled, and to Candace it was the most perfect smile she had ever seen on a man. "And your weight?"

Candace was too lost in his forest dark lips to answer immediately. They reminded her of Hershey candy kisses. She wanted to lick her lips but fought the urge.

"I—I'm, I weigh 140 pounds. I know that's a little heavy for my height, but I'm trying to lose 10 of those pounds. If I lose it, that'll put me at 130. I believe that's the right weight for my height," she rambled nervously.

"You said 'if' you lose it. Have you ever had problems trying to shed unwanted pounds before, Ms. uh," he looked once more at the application. "Brooks?"

"My weight fluctuates. I think it's a seasonal thing. In the summer, I tend to weigh less than in the winter."

"It's a few weeks from summer now. So you're telling me that in those few weeks you'll be minus 10 pounds?"

Candace felt a little provoked at his remark and wondered if this was an interrogation type interview. If it were, she would show him that her skin was as tough as the best of them that had come through these doors. She would go along with the interview without breaking.

"If you're saying you'll hire me, yes, I will lose the 10 pounds— before summer."

"It is not a question of whether you can lose the weight as much as whether you can lose the weight and keep it off. You see, Ms. Brooks…"

"Call me Candace," she cut in.

"Thank you. Candace, you say you're heavier in the winter. AFLAME works year-round. Are you familiar with the supermodel Twila Jackson?"

"Why, yes, everybody knows her."

"I'm proud to say she is one of ours. If that phone rings right now and somebody wants her to do a job, I don't have to worry about if I can send her or not because she has a problem with fluctuating weight. I'm going to tell you, Candace. AFLAME clients want t-h-i-n" and basically that's what we give them. All our models sign contracts for however long we agree upon. In that contract there's a clause that states that the model will stay under a certain weight. If they go over, we have the right to terminate the contract. This is not an easy business, Candace. You've got to know that this is what you want to do. Sometimes the situation can get pretty scary. We know most of our clients, but occasionally a nut will slip through the cracks. We don't provide chaperones for our models when we send them out. They're big girls and, for the most part, they do a pretty good job of taking care of themselves."

"Mr. Ka-wo-pos-se—"

"Ka-wiss-so-pie,' he pronounced his name slowly for her. "Now you see why I prefer people to call me Austin" he humored, and they both laughed.

"Austin, by all respect, if I'm given the opportunity to work for this agency, I won't take it lightly. I have a lot of potential. I've always wanted to be a model. You can see from my application that I have attended several prep schools. I also brought along my portfolio." She quickly opened it and pulled out her most recent and best photographs. "Here, take them and you can keep them for a while if you like—"

"Ms. Brooks," he cut in. "you're a very pretty girl indeed and I agree, you do have a lot of potential. But right now we're looking for someone with different qualities."

The words cut through Candace like a knife. She was being turned down by one of the best ethnic agencies in the country. She questioned her abilities and thought that maybe there wasn't a future for her in modeling. She knew she shouldn't give up so easily, but rejection was painful. Candace was unable to say anything. She could not even find the voice to thank him for his time. All she could think of was getting out of his presence as quickly as possible before she started to cry. She nodded her head as she gathered her photos. Candace rushed out of Austin's office and past Phyllis so fast that she did not hear her when she said goodbye. Once she stepped into the empty elevators, the tears started to flow. She pushed the close-door button and held it for a minute.

When the elevator reached the main floor, Candace had composed herself enough not to draw attention. She walked through the corridors and into the main lobby. Her three-inch heels clicked on the red-flagstone flooring. The sun shone through the lobby's glassed octagon ceiling, casting a spider-webbed shadow on the floor. Candace pulled out her shades and put them on. They concealed her tear-stained eyes, but the tears had left streaks on her face. She was grateful she had driven. Normally, she would have taken the subway, but she didn't want to take the chance of getting soiled by a clumsy passenger carrying a drink or smelling like anything other than Bijan when she got off. As she walked the five blocks to the parking deck, she noticed her reflection in the windows of the various stores she passed. She could see nothing wrong with herself. She was tall with curves in the right places. Her hair was any woman's dream; long, thick and full of body. She had the model's trademark, high-cheekbones, which was also her family's trait. Her eyes were large and almond-shaped. She could even see her eyelashes five-feet from the glass. Candace recalled Austin's comment, "*looking for different qualities.*" She thought the brother had to be crazy. Ever since she was a little girl, people told her she was destined to be a model. Why couldn't he see that?

*   *   *

Austin looked at his Rolex watch. He still had an hour and fifteen minutes before his next meeting. He reclined in his high-back-swivel chair and rocked back and forth. It was shaping up to be a long day and it would not end until 9 that night. Austin thought he'd sit and meditate for a while. He closed his eyes and thought of his family back home. Three weeks ago, he'd called to see how they were doing. He made a habit of calling once a month. He was pleased to hear that everyone was doing well. It'd been five years since he'd gone home. Momma Lena was at the open market and had missed his call. His mother had told him they all missed him, especially Momma Lena. She wanted to see him terribly. Austin explained to her that a trip would be virtually impossible right now in the midst of meetings, photo-shoots, and deadlines. He soothed her coaxing with I-love-you's and promises to come home at Christmas. She reminded Austin of Momma Lena's age and how she might not be around come next Christmas. He thought he would air express some gifts before the end of the week. On his way in this morning, he noticed a burnt orange alligator pocketbook with matching loafers on a mannequin in one of the store shops' window. He would get it for Momma Lena. He could hear her now, bragging to her friends in the elders' group at church. "My grandson loves me. He sent this from across the waters." He could see Momma Lena modeling the accessories for her envious audience.

Candace had triggered memories. He was amazed at how much she looked like Maoma. Candace was tall, just like Maoma. Her complexion, eyes, hair, nose and even body structure were the same. It was haunting enough, but he knew Candace was not Maoma. He almost wished he had taken the pictures she had offered him now, but then again he was glad he had not. They would only serve as painful reminders of what might have been if Maoma had lived. Austin kicked his feet on top of the desk and sank deeper in his chair. He let his muscles relax and his mind drift into thoughtlessness, and in less than two minuets he was asleep.

Maoma looked like an African goddess as she stood before the village chief. She wore the traditional African attire. The ensemble was embroidered with gold fertility designs. The sash wrapped around her tiny waist accentuating her hourglass figure. She wore three strands of colorful beads around her neck. Her gele sat exquisitely on her head making her profile look like Nefertiti. She lifted the front of the dress as she walked toward Austin, revealing beautiful legs. Austin also wore the customary wedding attire. He smiled as Maoma reached him and took her place beside him. The ceremony was filled with singing and dancing. When they were declared husband and wife, Austin's lips approached Maoma's. The heat of her breath made his flesh tingle and he wished they were in the privacy of each other so he could unleash his desire in full force. Her full lips invited the sweetness of his own, but before he could kiss her, two large African vultures tore through the sky. Their eyes were bright red and their beaks were opened as if ready to devour anyone that got in their way. Their fierce expressions sent the guests screaming and scampering about. Maoma, unaware of what was happening, saw the terrified look on Austin's face. She followed his gaze overhead and saw the ugly creatures coming toward her. She let out a horrifying scream, but before Austin could shield her from inevitable doom, the predators swooped Maoma up and flew back into the sky. Repeatedly, Austin yelled for the vultures to stop, but it was too late. Maoma was gone forever.

Austin awoke with a start. His heart was racing and sweat was trickling down his forehead. He leaned forward and cupped his face into his hands.

"My Lord!" he said as he tried to collect himself. It was the haunting dream again. Dr. Bernice Edwards, his psychologist, had told him he needed to let go of Maoma, start seeing other people. She felt that dating would be the best therapy for him. Austin wasn't so easily convinced. He felt all he needed was time to heal the pain. He was taught by his father to commit fully to all his endeavors, be it work, play or love, especially love. For that reason alone, he didn't want to get involved with someone if his heart wasn't in it. Five years was a long time to be without companionship. He took a quick assessment of his life as he had done a thousand times before. He was a 35-year-old man without wife or child. He had all the material wealth any man of reason could want; the Jaguar and Manhattan high-rise, designer suits, stocks and bonds in several major corporations, and an IRA account that would max out around $2 million when he reached 59 years old. With all this, his legacy would end if he were to die suddenly. He glanced at his Rolex again. He had 20 more minutes before the meeting. He picked up Candace's application and began to read it thoroughly. *Name: Candace Renee Brooks. Birthday: March 15, 1977,* "Hmm, just a baby," he said. *Place of birth: Germanton, North Carolina.* "I know Germanton. A little town north of Winston-Salem. How coincidental." *Education: Senior at New York University, majoring in journalism. Expected graduation date:*

May 20. "That's next Sunday." *Address: 409, East 22nd Street, Manhattan.* "So, she lives in Manhattan too." *Phone number: 446-9013.*

Austin put the application in his briefcase. He didn't see any reason to have Phyllis file it away since he knew AFLAME wouldn't need her. He gathered his legal pad and 24 caret Gold Cross pen and placed them neatly in his briefcase. He had exactly 10 minutes to get to the staff meeting.

5

Russell

Candace couldn't go home. Sable had the gift of reading her troubles and she was definitely not in the mood for pampering. She thought she would catch a movie. She did want to see the new movie "Life" with Eddie Murphy and Martin Lawrence. She had heard it was comical and she needed a laugh. She turned the Tercel right on East 45th Street and then left on Fortune Lane. She never understood why this stretch of property was called Fortune. The apartments were dilapidated and half of them condemned. Half it's residents were drug users, dealers, pimps or prostitutes. Any given week she could pick up the newspaper and read where a shooting, stabbing or rape had been committed. She'd heard that 30 years ago Fortune Lane was a mecca for black folks and the name had been changed from East 44th Street to Fortune Lane for that very reason. As she drove down the street she could see taletell signs of that fact. To her right was an old building with a weather-washed sign that read Williams Grocery. In smaller caption were the words 'Chitlins Always in Season Here.' Another few yards away was a red, white and blue barber's pole erected in front of another abandoned building. The letters painted on the side of the building read 'Walter and Maxine's Beauty and Barber'. In smaller print, she was able to make out the prices. 'Men haircuts—fifty cents, children—twenty-five, wash, press and curls—two dollars and manicures twenty-five cents.'

"Press and curls," she said as she shook her head apathetically. Then she thought of Aunt Vi. She still used that beauty method. She couldn't imagine herself going through that type of torture for the sake of straight hair. If that were the only way, then she would go au naturel, like Sable. Sable's hair used to be long and relaxed just like hers, but after the divorce and the move to New York, she stopped relaxing it and eventually cut it off into a small hassle-free afro. The only businesses on Fortune Lane still in operation were Wellington's Funeral Home and Mike's Bar and Grill.

"Mmm, it figures," she said to herself, "A liquor store and a funeral home. One is oppressing and the other depressing. I guess the crime and drugs ran off all the other businesses." She had one more block to go before she reached the Carmichael Theater. R Kelly's 'I Believe I Can Fly' started playing on the radio. She turned up the volume and listened earnestly to the lyrics. It was the first thing she heard that morning when she awoke to the alarm clock radio. The song had served as inspiration as she readied herself for her visit to AFLAME. The song made her think of the interview with Mr. Kawissopie. She refused to acknowledge him on a first name basis as he had suggested. First names were reserved for friends and this man who had just rejected her could never be a friend.

"I can fly," she said "just not at AFLAME." As she pulled into the parking lot of the theater she noticed the parking fee was $3 per hour. She only had $8 and some odd change. The movie alone was $7. "Ain't this a trip. The story of my life. Always broke." She tried backing out of the parking deck, but the arm had already come down. She yanked the ticket out of the ticket dispenser and sped around to the parking lot attendant. The attendant was a tall and burly woman. Her hair was bleached to a whitish blond. She wore heavily applied mascara and blood-red lipstick. She chewed gum like it was going out of style, making popping sounds every 10 seconds.

"Ticket, please."

Candace handed her the ticket and waited for her to release the arm so she could pass through.

"That'll be $3."

"$3! I wasn't even in here two minutes."

"That'll be $3 ma'am," the attendant said as if not hearing Candace's protest.

Candace laughed, "Now wait a minute. I don't believe this. I know there is some misunderstanding here. Let me explain. I pulled in here with intentions of using it, but I changed my mind after I realized I didn't have enough money to see a movie. Now, I'm sure you understand my dilemma, don't you?"

Unmoved by Candace's explanation, the bleached blonde blew out a puff of agitated air. "Look lady, I'm just trying to do my job here. I ain't got all day to listen to you try to wheedle out of paying $3. Once that arm goes up and a car passes through, minimum fee is $3. I don't care if you're the president of the United States, you still gotta pay!"

"Your policy sucks, you know that?" Candace reached into her pocketbook and handed the attendant a five-dollar bill. "I hope you're satisfied."

"Lady, as long as you pay, I'm satisfied." She gave Candace her change and flipped the switch for the automatic arm to go up. Candace hit the gas, making the tires squeal, and she flew out of the parking lot.

Candace looked at her watch. It was 10:45. She had plenty of time but nothing to do. Since Russell let her keep a spare key to his apartment, she thought she'd go by and tidy up the place a bit. She knew it could use it. Maybe she'd cook him a spaghetti dinner. Russell loved spaghetti and meatballs and it was one of the few dishes Candace could make. He was always saying how he missed home-cooked meals after he moved from his home in Roanoke, Virginia, to New York. Tossed salad and

French bread would go good with the spaghetti. She knew she would have to buy the lettuce, tomatoes and cucumbers because Russell wasn't into eating healthy. She hoped he had all the other ingredients to make the meal. He kept all kinds of pastas, so she wouldn't have to buy that. There was probably no ground beef in the refrigerator either. She'd go there first and check the cupboards before going to the grocery store. If he didn't have the things she needed, the few dollars she had would not be enough to buy everything. Then she remembered the broken coffee mug on top of the refrigerator. He always kept emergency money there. She would use some of it.

*   *   *

Candace positioned her long lean body in the Lane recliner. She pushed out the footrest and sank back into its soft cushions. She surfed the stereo until she heard the voice of her favorite disk jockey, Mitch Mitchell. He announced himself as "Mitch Mitchell—Mrs. Martha Mitchell's baby b-o-o-y-e-e, y'all! Here to please, tease and satisfy your needs. Slammin' jammin' nonstop or until the clock tells me it's time to stop!" Then he'd play one of the top 10 from the rhythm and blues chart.

Candace closed her eyes and listened as soft jazz started to play. The melody and lyrics crooned her. Out of boredom, she shifted her weight every five minutes being careful not to wrinkle her suit. Although she was not romantically attracted to Russell, she liked impressing him. He knew how to make her feel special, especially when she was down. She hoped he would come straight home after work. He sometimes went to the YMCA after work to lift weights. He was so sweet, the best friend anyone could have. She looked around his tiny apartment and was surprise at how clean it was. The pillows on the sectional were not in disarray as usual and the thick beige carpet had been vacuumed. There wasn't a trace of dust on the coffee tables. He had even put up swags over the mini blinds in the living room. Russell always kept an untidy place. She wondered why it was so clean now. She had notice a small framed picture of a girl on Russell's nightstand that wasn't there when she visited three weeks ago. She'd have to ask him about her. But then again, who was she to question Russell's personal life. She certainly did-n't tell him everything about hers. She hoped that one day he would find the one true love he was looking for. "He better hurry up before the spaghetti sauce simmers out." She picked up the television-stereo remote control and clicked off the stereo and clicked on Montel Williams. Candace was a Montel junkie. She never missed an episode. If she had a class scheduled during the time his show aired, she taped it. Sable couldn't see what she got out of a bunch of people coming on national television to air their dirty laundry. Candace told Sable she needed to watch it herself sometime, that she could get some good material for her books. Today's show was about Women who have cheated on their companions.

"Aw, this is a repeat. I hate repeats." Candace switched the channel to HBO. "Courage Under Fire" with Denzel Washington was on. "All repeats except the ones with Denzel in them, of course," she said.

She heard keys clanging on the other side of the door. The doorknob turned and Russell stepped in. She had to admit, he was well built and nice looking, even though she preferred slimmer men with complexion three or four shades darker than his. She admired him for the way he took care of his body. He was tall with a very muscular torso. His waist and hips were smaller than his upper portion. He had nice chiseled features. His eyebrows were thick, smooth and downright shinny. His thick lashes somehow soften his masculinity adding a sensitive edge to his appearance. He had a gap between his two front teeth that Candace thought was cute. He smiled at her as he pushed the door shut.

"I saw your car parked downstairs. What's up, C?"

"I just thought I'd come by and make my best buddy his favorite meal."

"Naw, Candace, you gotta come with something better than that. I been trying for ages to get you to cook for me. Why today?"

Candace laughed. "You busted me, partner."

"Yeah, I always do. Now come clean," There was a look of genuine interest on Russell's face as he stood with his hands resting on his hips.

"Truth is, I had an unscheduled interview at AFLAME…"

"Talking 'bout the modeling agency AFLAME?"

"That's' the one."

"Cool. How did it go?"

"It didn't go, Russell. Mr. Kawissopie, one of the executives, told me I didn't meet their qualifications." Tears welled in her eyes again and her voice trembled. "He didn't even give me hope. Basically kicked me out the door. Am I that bad?"

"No, Candace, you know better than that. You turned my head didn't you? All I can say is that man must be out of his mind to turn you down."

"Russell, you're just saying that," she sounded modest, but Russell was saying what she wanted and needed to hear in order to save face with her ego.

"You know I'm not."

Candace wiped her eyes with the tips of her fingers.

"Baby, need a hug?" Russell asked, with his arms opened.

Candace got up from the recliner. She smiled and walked to him. Russell wrapped her in his arms and hugged her tightly. He started rubbing her back in small circular motions that made Candace feel uncomfortable.

"Russell, what are you doing?"

"Mmm, this feels nice, " he teased.

"Russell," she warned, "Watch it."

Before she knew it, Russell's hands slid down her back and cupped the roundness of her buttocks. He squeeze them quickly before she broke lose. Candace slapped his shoulders and then shoved him backwards.

"Boy, I knew I couldn't trust you!"

Russell laughed at Candace's innocent act.

"Girl, you know you done done more than hug and smooch," he laughed. "I'm going to wash up, I'm starved." He pulled off his shirt revealing his muscular build and hairy chest as he walked towards the bathroom.

*   *   *

Candace was surprised at how good her appetite was after the events of the day. The dinner had turned out excellent. Russell was on his second serving. He was even eating the toss salad.

"Pass me some more Kool-Aid, C." He held his glass up for her to pour. Candace looked at his face and started laughing.

"What?" he asked.

"Your chin."

"Huh?"

"You got sauce all over your chin,"

"Good thing we ain't at no high class restaurant,"

"Not ain't, there's no such word and you used a double negative in your sentence," she said disapprovingly.

"You know what I mean. Graduate in a few days and think she Einstein."

"Oh, you know about Einstein? I'm impressed."

Russell licked sauce off his fingers. "Yes I know who Einstein was. He was a great twentieth century scientist who developed the general theory of relativity."

Candace got up and started clearing the table. "I know you're smart Russell. You just need to cash in on your intelligence. Go to school and get a degree. Make it work for you. It can take you a long way."

"Well, you do yours your way, and let me do mine my way. I got plans for the future. I don't intend to be a postal clerk all my life," he wiped his hands and mouth with his napkin.

"Where the dessert at, Candace," He asked, looking around the kitchen.

"I didn't make any. It's not good for you anyway."

"Ain't nothing sweet in here to eat?"

"I told you to stop saying ain't, Russell."

"C, you know I can't go without my sweets."

Candace opened the refrigerator and pulled out a snicker candy bar and tossed it to him. "Here child, you're such a baby."

Russell caught the candy bar in mid air. "Thanks mommy," he teased.

6

Friends like Glue

Sable sat at her personal computer brain-frozen. She had just completed chapter six and it had taken her six months to get that far. A chapter a month was a record slow for her. She was facing a deadline and the pressure was mounting. With her other books, she had ideas, plots and schemes popping in her head so fast, she couldn't get them on paper or into the computer fast enough. She was wondering if she had used up all of her talent but just as fast as the thought entered her mind, she dismissed it. She picked up the recent chapter from her out box. The first five chapters each ranged in length from 10 to 20 pages. So far, chapter six was the longest, containing 23 pages. Her main character, Felicia Jessup was trying to convenience the police that her husband did not kill himself but was murdered. On the night of his murder, he was seen in the company of three associates, his best friend, his accountant, and his secretary. One of the three was to blame. Sable was at a first time lost. How was she going to pull this together? She climbed into bed and crossed her legs Indian style. She began reading from the beginning in hopes that it would get her momentum running and start her creative juices flowing. She heard that some writers got writers' block that lasted for years. Her publisher told her that incidents like these were to be expected, but the key to getting over it was to write continuously, anything that came to mind. Right now she knew this wasn't a good suggestion because the only thing on her mind was the house in Torryville. She was in an anxious state. It had been a five days and she had not heard from Mr. Mason. She thought he had spoken with the owners by now. She figured they were cohering not to lower the price. Mr. Mason would benefit as well as the owners. The more money she paid for the house, the higher his commission would be.

Today was Tuesday and if she didn't hear from him by Wednesday, she'd give him a call. The second matter at hand was Aunt Vi and Jonah's visit. Candace was making plans for all five of them to stay in their apartment. She would welcome Aunt Vi, but wasn't too sure about Jonah staying there. She knew it would be an awkward arrangement. They would arrive on Friday. Jonah told Wilson in their phone conversation, he had some business to attend in New York and he might be staying a day or two past Candace's graduation depending on how soon he was able to close some deals. Sable wondered what kind of deals he had in New York.

Sable heard Wilson clinging pots and pans in the kitchen. He was probably getting ready to make some tasty high calorie dish. He was a great cook and since he retired, he was spending more time in the kitchen. Sable put the manuscript down and slid out of bed. The gray jogging pants and oversized Miami Dolphins tee shirt she wore made her look girlish. She walked out of her bedroom and down the short hallway. She stood in the doorway of the kitchen and listened as Wilson whistled.

"What are you concocting now," Sable asked.

"Thought I'd make some fried chicken, biscuits, greens and candid yams."

"You know we don't need all that food. Candace and I usually make a sandwich or salad for dinner. I hate to see you put yourself out like this."

"Aw, it's no problem at all. I enjoy cooking for y'all. Just gives me pleasure watching you eat. When you was a little girl, you use to love to set in the kitchen while I whipped up a cake. Soon as I poured the batter in the pan, here you come, reaching for the bowl. You loved yourself some cake batter."

Sable inched into the kitchen and pulled out a chair. She felt a 'remember when' story coming on. She listened earnestly while Wilson talked. "You always had a good appetite. Loretta had you on table food by time you turned two months old. Milk wouldn't hold you," Wilson chuckled. "Yes sir, you were something greedy. Always ate. We thought you were gon' be big as a house, cause you know, all of Loretta people big. But you didn't turn out to be nothing like them, thank the Lord. One thing I can't stand is a big clumsy looking woman. Now your momma, she was just right. Not too big and not too small. The rest of 'dem, Lord help 'um."

"They just big boned people, daddy."

"Big boned and ugly. Loretta was the baby of the family. I guess Joe and Mamie used up all their ugly genes by time they got around to making her."

"Daddy, you need to stop," Sable was laughing uncontrollably. She was glad she had abandoned her writing. This was what she needed. "I want you to be nice to Aunt Vi when she comes."

"I'm gon' be nice, as long as she stay out my way," Wilson drop pieces of the seasoned chicken into a brown paper bag that contained flour. He folded the bag's opening and shook it vigorously.

"That's not what I mean and you know it. I don't want you acting like Fred Sanford and treating her like Aunt Esther."

Wilson doubled over laughing. "That's a good one, Sable. You got your old man pegged. I promise not to misbehave. I know this is a special time for Candace, and I don't plan to spoil it."

The sound of the doorbell startled both of them. Sable shot Wilson a puzzled look; "I wonder who that can be. I'm not expecting anyone," She got up from her chair and headed for the door.

"Put the chain lock on before you open that door. This New York!" Wilson yelled from the kitchen.

"You forgetting we got security downstairs on the door, daddy."

"I thought the doorman was s'pose to announce visitors before they came up."

Sable looked through the peephole then opened the door. "Girl, no wonder Ed didn't buzz up here to let us know you were on your way. He thinks you're a permanent fixture here."

"You got that right, girlfriend." Shamell gave Sable a light peck on the cheek and stepped in. Shamell had a china-doll face. She accentuated her light brown oval-shaped eyes with eye shadow and mascara. She wore a diamond-studded nose ring in her left nostril, which Sable detested. Her hair was cut short and naturally curly. She wore a pair of leopard-print skintight leggings and a black spandex tank top that revealed honey colored cleavage.

"Where my favorite boyfriend at, with his fine self," she asked as she dumped her shoulder bag on the nearest chair. She switched her jutting, muscular behind into the direction of the kitchen. "Mmmm-mmm, something smells good in here! Is my baby in here cooking?"

"Come on in the house, Charmin." Wilson grinned as Shamell appeared through the kitchen door.

"It's Shamell," corrected Sable.

Shamell made a beeline to the stove and took a golden brown chicken leg from the platter. "Honey, I'll be a roll of toilet paper as long as he keeps cooking like this." She began lifting the lids off pots, spying on the bubbling vittles inside them. "Greens, yams and I know you baking a little som'um—som'um 'cause my nose don't lie."

Wilson beamed as Shamell continued to flatter him about his cooking. "Made-from-scratch biscuits is what you smell, young lady. See Sable, Charmin ain't scared to eat and she looks fine to me."

"Yeah," said Sable standing in the threshold, "she can afford to eat anything she wants. She works out five days a week. I'll do good if I can keep a date with my treadmill twice a week. What are you doing off today anyway?" She stepped into the kitchen and joined them.

"I'm at home sick with the flu," she whispered. "I had planned to stay home, relax and pamper myself but Charles overheard me this morning when I called in sick. Honey, he thought that was an invitation for him to stay home, too. I had to find an excuse to get out of the house. Don't get me wrong, I love him to death, but when I need time for myself, Charles takes a back seat."

Shamell pulled out a kitchen chair and sat down. She crossed her shapely legs. "Daddy Will, this chicken so good it make you wan'na slap your momma. What you put on it?"

"The key to good chicken is milk."

"Milk?"

"That's right. First you soak the chicken in milk for two hours. After it soaks, you season it with pepper, salt, paprika, oregano and a dash of sage. Then you roll the chicken in the flour. Make sure your oil is good and hot. But, don't cook it too fast, otherwise it won't get done near the bone. Ain't nothing worse than half-cooked chicken. It's enough to make a buzzard vomit."

"Daddy!" yelled Sable. "Not at the table."

Unaffected by Wilson's remark, Shamell finished the chicken leg and got up to get another one, this time along with a plate, making it obvious that she was ready to chow down.

"How is your manuscript coming along?"

"To tell you the truth, I wish I hadn't agreed to do another book so soon after the last one. I should have taken your advice about a month-long vacation to revive my body, spirit and mind. Truth is, I'm running out of ideas. This deadline isn't helping at all either. I'm afraid I'm going to have to ask for an extension."

"How much have you written since the last time I edited?"

"One more chapter. This last chapter has 23 pages so far.

"Don't get too discouraged, Sable. You've always made your deadlines. Your books are averaging 20, 25 chapters. Just figure on doing two and a half chapters a month. That equals 50 pages. There is 30 days per month, give or take one. Divide 30 into 50 and you'll get about one and three-fourths pages a day. I think you can pull it off, girl."

Shamell took a big bite out of the chicken. She made a crunching sound that stirred Sable's appetite. She got up from the chair and took a short thigh from the platter.

"Thanks a lot, Mrs. Calculator, for solving my problems. Now what other helpful hints do you have for me?"

"I tell you what I'll do. Before I leave, let me read over chapter six. Maybe we can brainstorm together." Shamell got up and retrieved a can of soda from the refrigerator.

"Get me one, too," said Sable. "This is good. I don't think you added sage last time you fried chicken, daddy."

Sable and Shamell chowed down on their chicken until it was gone. Shamell threw the second bone in the plate, making a clanking sound. Before she could get up for another piece, Wilson set the platter in the middle of the table. He handed a plate to Sable then proceeded to serve them. He heaped a generous helping of greens and yams onto their plates. Then he pulled the hot, steamy biscuits out of the oven and flipped them into a cloth-lined breadbasket. The biscuits were perfectly browned on both sides. Sable and Shamell's mouths were full of food as they watched Wilson at work. He was clearly a master in the kitchen.

"Where you learn to cook like this?" asked Shamell.

"From my Momma. She was one of the world's greatest cooks. She taught all her children how to cook. Boys right 'long with the girls. That woman never used a recipe in her life." After Wilson had finished serving

Shamell and Sable, he got himself a plate from the cabinet and sat down to join them. They talked about Candace's upcoming graduation. Sable suggested that they all go out to one of Manhattan's finest restaurants afterwards. Wilson and Shamell agreed. The ringing of the telephone halted the conversation. Sable reached for the phone.

"Hello,"

"Hey, sweetheart!"

"Aunt Vi!" Sable knew her voice instantly. " How are you?"

"Baby, I'm doing fine. Not gon' hold you long. Just wanted to make sure y'all knew I was coming up there with Jonah."

"Oh, Aunt Vi, yes we do and we can't wait to see you."

"How's my big girl doing? I bet she's excited?"

"Excited and nervous, all in one. I wish she were here to talk to you. I guess she's out running errands and trying to prepare for Sunday. She's looking forward to seeing you, Aunt Vi. You know you're the closest thing she has to a grandmother now." Sable looked at her watch. It was 7:30 p.m. It had just dawned on her that she had not seen Candace since 9 o'clock that morning. It wasn't like her to stay out practically all day without calling to let Sable know where she was. Aunt Elvira was asking her something but Sable's mind was on Candace's whereabouts.

"I'm sorry, Aunt Vi, what did you say?"

"I said what does she want for graduation?"

"Aunt Vi, don't worry about getting her anything. She has plenty and I'm sure your coming is present enough for her."

"Child, I wouldn't think of coming all the way up there and not bringing her anything. Now quick, give me an idea of what she might like. My phone bill is running up."

Sable smiled at Aunt Elvira's candidness but felt she didn't have the money to spare on gifts. She'd never married or had children. She worked years in domestic services and now that she was well in her 70s and unable to work, Sable wondered about her finances. Sable sent her a monthly check of $100 to supplement her income. Because Aunt

Elvira was a proud woman, Sable preferred she think the monthly con-tribution was more a token of love than charity. If Aunt Elvira found out the latter, she would protest.

Sable thought of something inexpensive for Aunt Vi to buy. "She would love some perfume, Aunt Vi."

"What kind should I buy? You know some people funny 'bout the kind of fragrances they wear."

"Get her some Bijan. She spelled it for her. It comes in a bottle with a hole in the middle of it."

"I'm gon' catch the bus out to the mall tomorrow. I sho' hope them sales people know what I'm asking for."

"Trust me, Aunt Vi, they'll know."

"O.K., sweetheart, I'm gon' hang up now. See you in a few days. Oh, tell Wilson I said hello."

"Sure thing, Aunt Vi. Bye now."

"Bye-bye, baby."

Sable placed the phone back into the wall cradle. Even though she hadn't mentioned anything about her book dilemma, just speaking to Aunt Vi eased her anxieties about the deadline. Aunt Vi wasn't a mother, but she possessed a mother's therapeutic gift. Wilson pretended not to like her, but Sable knew he cared for her.

"Aunt Vi says hello, Daddy."

"Hello back to Aunt Vi."

Sable looked at her plate and saw that she had eaten four pieces of chicken, a mess of greens and yams and Lord knows how many biscuits. Shamell was still eating like she had a bottomless pit for a stomach. Her plate was stacked with chicken bones. She had enough to assemble a complete chicken skeleton.

"Where does all your food go?" Sable asked while she scraped her leftovers into the garbage.

"I don't eat that much. This is my first real meal today."

"Yeah, right."

"All I had this morning was grits, bacon, eggs and one slice of toast. It didn't even fill me up."

"Daddy, this is the only person I know who can eat like a Sumo wrestler and not gain an ounce. Some people are lucky."

"Where's that daughter of yours?" Wilson asked.

"I'm getting kind of worried about her myself. It's not like her to be out this late and I not know where she is."

"It's only 7:40. The girl is 22 years old. She knows how to take care of herself. If you're that worried, call her on her cellular," said Shamell.

"Can't do that because her phone is in there on her dresser. The reason I brought it was for emergencies."

Shamell laughed. "Yeah, but you really brought it so you can keep tabs on her."

"If you had a child, Shamell, you'd know the anxiety parents feel for their children."

Shamell held up a hand declaring truce on a conversation she knew would turn into a debate. She had learned her lesson well a few years back. She had tried to persuade Sable to let Candace go to France for the summer with the modeling school she was attending. Sable had told her that it would be a cold damn day in hell before she let Candace go halfway around the world with a bunch of free-spirited liberal heads. As Shamell recalled, that was the first time and, she believed, the only time she had heard Sable curse. When ever the subject turned to the care and raising of Candace, Shamell knew her limitations on opinions. It was 9 o'clock when they heard Candace's key in the lock, and each of them secretly breathed a sigh of relief.

7

Indiscretions

The wicker basket swung in Sable's hand as she picked up items that belonged to her. She found her $40 bottle of Estee Lauder Herbal Essence body oil in Candace's bathroom. She angrily stuffed it into the basket with the L'Oreal Metallic nail polish, Gillette skin sensor razor and eyebrow tweezers that she had also confiscated. She was tired of Candace using her personal things. She wouldn't have minded so much if she had had the courtesy of asking, but whatever Candace wanted she took. She never put the items back where they came from, but instead left them anywhere that was convenient for her. Sable stepped out of the adjoining bathroom. Candace lay sprawled across her double bed, the covers in disarray and tangled around her long dark legs. She slept peacefully as Sable roamed through her room making noise by slamming doors and drawers shut. The room would have been beautiful if Candace took the time to clean it. Sable tried not to judge too harshly because, after all, it was a mother's duty to teach her children, especially the girl child, basic housekeeping practices. The truth was, she had not done that. She was too busy doting and pampering her. Now she was afraid she had spared the rod and spoiled the child.

Sable justified the spoiling on the fact that she had lost two babies to miscarriages before Candace's birth. Growing up an only child was terribly lonely and she had never planned to bring a child into the world without giving it a sibling. She got pregnant a third time and was monitored closely by her gynecologist. Candace was her last attempt at pregnancy. She entered the world weighing eight pounds and seven ounces. Sable and Jonah's world revolved around her. The very instant she made her debut, each felt there wasn't a thing they wouldn't do for her. Here it was 22 years later and Sable wished she could roll back the years and reshape this child into a more responsible adult. She wondered how long it would be before she started looking for a job. Sunday, she would receive a degree in journalism and to her knowledge she had not sent out the first resume. Sable remembered her mentioning something about going to AFLAME yesterday. She wondered how it went. Maybe that explained her sour mood when she came home last night. Sable guessed her visit didn't go as well as she would have liked. Then, a sudden feeling of compassion overtook Sable as she stood watching Candace. She was trying, she thought. Sable reached down and gently pinched her pinkie toe. Candace stirred, lifting her head to see her standing at the foot of her bed.

"Hey Ma. It's morning a' ready?"

"Candace, it's past morning. It's almost noon."

Candace lifted her head higher and peeked at the clock. She fell face first back onto her goose-feathered pillow.

"Ah, man, I got commencement practice at one."

"Well, I suggest you get to rolling and next time you take the notion to use my things, please put them back where you found them."

Candace propped herself up. "Sorry, Ma. I meant to, just forgot I guess."

"How did it go yesterday at AFLAME? You came in last night and didn't have much to say to anybody."

"I don't know why that place has the reputation that it does considering the incompetent jerk that works there."

"Oh-oh, I sense a tinge of resentment. Yesterday morning you were singing their praises. What happened sweetie?" Sable eased down on the end of the bed.

This was exactly what Candace was trying to avoid, an emotional mother-daughter moment.

"That man there. I don't know who he is, but they need to get rid of him. First of all, you can't understand what he's saying. He's from Africa somewhere. Then he has the nerve to tell me I'm not what they're looking for. If he were any kind of a professional, he would have used tact in dropping the bomb on me. He was cold-blooded."

"Child, you've got a lot to learn. This world can be cruel."

"It's not the world that's cruel; it's the people in it."

"Yes, you're absolutely right. You gotta keep in mind that one person can't stop your show. Keep rolling with the punches, no matter how hard the blows get. So what if AFLAME closed its door in your face, knock on another door. Somebody's bound to let you in."

"But AFLAME is the best. I don't want to work for some unknown agency. How can you get good work like that?"

"Sounds to me like you want to run, when you don't even know how to crawl yet. There's nothing wrong with a smaller agency. It may be just the thing to get your career started. And what about your journalism degree? There're a zillion broadcasting and media stations here in New York," she said.

"I know what you're thinking. That you spent good money for my education and now you think I'm going to throw it away. Well, don't worry. I've got some prospects lined out."

Sable patted Candace's feet and got up from the bed. "Good news!"

"What."

"Mr. Mason called about the house. It's ours. The owners agreed to sell it to me for $375,000. I think that's more than fair. By time I get through paying to have it remodeled, it'll be well over $400,000 anyway."

Candace looked at Sable. She was half-attentive to what she was saying. "Mmm, hmm, that's good, Ma. I think you'll like it out there."

Sable looked at Candace questionably. "What do you mean I'll like it out there? Aren't you coming?" she smirked.

"I was thinking that maybe I'd say here in Manhattan, since I'll be working here in the city anyway."

"And where are you going to stay?"

"Here. In this apartment. I'll take over the payments."

"Tell me how you're going to make a $3,000-a-month payment?"

"I may need a little help at first. But with my degree, I'll find a job and be making good money in no time."

No sooner than the words left Candace's mouth, Wilson appeared at the threshold of Candace's room.

"There ain't no way you gon' stay here in this mean ol' city while your mamma way on the other side of the river. You got a chance to get out of this Sodom and Gomorrah and you talking 'bout you want to stay. What's wrong with you, girl?"

"Granddaddy! How long you been standing there?"

"Long enough to hear your foolish idea."

"That's eavesdropping!"

"I don't care what it is. Now, Sable, you too soft on that girl. You need to put your foot down and let her know what's what. Even if she did work and could afford this place, A 22-year-old girl ain't got no business living alone up here."

"Excuse me, y'all need to recognize I am grown." Candace slung back the covers. She angrily pulled her oversized New York University tee shirt down from around her hips and got out of bed. She walked past Sable and Wilson and stood in the entrance of her bathroom.

"You're certainly displaying a mature attitude for somebody who's grown," Sable said. "This idea is preposterous, Candace. I am not going to be footing the bill for you to live here in this apartment and paying a mortgage note on the house in Torryville, too. If you want to be on your

own, I have no problem with that. You'll just have to find a way to provide for yourself. You're right, you are grown. So it's time you start acting like it. I got to get ready to meet Mr. Mason about the house." She
walked out of Candace's room. Wilson rolled his eyes at Candace then
followed Sable all the while fussing.

*   *   *

The transaction was going well. Sable was very impressed with the
way Mr. Mason handled business. He had prepared everything for her.
The tittle search, termite inspection and all the other finalities of closing
had been done. All she needed to do was take the contract to her lawyer
for him to inspect. She guided the Mercedes down 17th street. A signal
light changed to red bringing the powerful machine to a smooth halt.
She could feel people staring at her. This always happened when she
drove the Benz. She had to admit it was an impressive automobile.

A cream colored sectional sofa in the display window of Steinbeck's
Furniture store caught her eye. It had two double-sized ottomans that
made the sofa look like a huge bed. That would go perfect in the new
house, she thought. She had to get a better look. She was lucky enough
to find a parking space on the street and she zipped in quick as lighten-
ing. She stepped out of the coolness of the car into the sweltering heat.
She wore a yellow tank top and a coordinating flower print broomstick
skirt. The temperature had tempted her not to wear a slip, and had the
skirt been less sheer she wouldn't have. The white sandals she wore
revealed perfect size-eight feet. Her toenails and fingernails were
painted with the L'Oreal Metallic nail polish she had gotten from
Candace's room earlier.

*   *   *

She stepped into the coolness of the furniture store. Four salesmen
were standing in a corner talking about a baseball game that had been

on television the night before. She heard the black salesman tell the other three he'd get this one. He smiled as he approached her. Sable noticed his eyes right off. They were deep and dark, yet friendly. He was the color of a pecan and the closer he got the smoother his skin became. She didn't see a blemish anywhere and thought he must take extra care of his skin to get it to look so good. He was tall with a medium build. His hair was thinning on the top and graying at the temples. His mustache was thick and well trimmed outlining the edge of his upper lip. He unbuttoned his double-breasted navy blue jacket as he walked and she noticed that he was slightly bowlegged. He wore pleated tan trousers *(she believed they were Dockers)* and a crisp white Arrow shirt with a navy, tan and black print tie. Sable knew men's clothing well. Jonah never did his own shopping, but left that task to her. The salesman extended his hand and Sable reached for it. His hand was soft and reminded her of Jonah's. She thought of the pleasure Jonah had given her with his hands alone and wondered if this man standing before her smiling so enchantingly and looking so alluring could perform the same magic. She blushed as the thought of sexual acts with this man danced through her mind. The last time was a solid year ago with that man Shamell had tried to hook her up with. She couldn't even remember his name now. He was superficial to the max and talked only of himself. He took Sable out for dinner and drinks and supposedly forgot his wallet. Then on the way taking her home, he insisted on stopping by his apartment to get his wallet to repay her for picking up the dinner tab. One thing led to another and before she knew it she was in his bed getting her groove on. The only good thing about him was his looks and his ability to satisfy. He called several times thereafter but Sable always made excuses not to go out with him. He finally caught the message and stopped calling. She knew he would be more trouble than companionship was worth.

"Hello, my name is Nathaniel Jackson. How can I help you?"

"There's a cream-colored sectional in your window I'm interested in looking at."

"Oh, yeah. I know just what you're talking about. Follow me. That's a very pretty piece of furniture, ma'am. It's large, too. We just got that piece in two weeks ago. Where you thinking about putting something that big?"

"Actually, I just purchased a house in Connecticut. The living room is pretty big and I think it'll go well in there."

"Yeah?"

"Yes. I don't like overcrowded rooms. Maybe two end tables and a nice wall unit will do."

The sectional was even more spectacular up close. The fabric was knotted Herculean and no doubt would outlast the style.

"Try it out, ma'am. See how it feels."

Sable sat down on one of the large ottomans and slid her body all the way back into the sofa.

"Ooo, this is comfortable and very nice."

"I'll say," said Nathaniel, getting a better look at her partially horizontal.

Sable was flattered. "How much is it?" she asked, looking over her shades at Nathaniel.

"fifty-five hundred."

"I wanted something I could sit on, not live in," she said sarcastically.

"I tell you what, ma'am…"

"Sable Brooks," she said.

"Mrs. Brooks…"

"Ms. but you can call me Sable, "she smiled.

"Well," he said as he raised an eyebrow and flashed his award-winning smile.

"Sable—a beautiful name for a beautiful woman."

"I thank you kindly," she said.

"Since you're the most refreshing thing I've seen all day. I'll make you a deal. I'll let you have this sectional for $5,300. How's that?"

"I'm really looking, that's all. I didn't plan to make a purchase today."

"Sable, come with me. I want to show you something I know you'll like." He extended a hand to help her up. He took her to another area where a black leather sofa and love seat were on display.

"I'm not interested in this style of furniture at all, Nathaniel."

"No, not the furniture. The lamps."

"Ooo," Sable gasped. "They're beautiful."

"Aren't they though? Can't you see them with that sectional?"

The lamps were Santa Fe style, cream with tiny specks of gold glitter in them and the largest table lamps Sable had ever seen. She knew right then she had to have them.

"Yes, I can. You're pretty good at this, Nathaniel."

He smiled and nodded his head.

"Have you noticed the end tables they're sitting on?"

The end tables were made of brass with prominent curved legs. They had sturdy glass tops and bottom shelves that were also made of brass with scallop designs.

"They really complement the lamps, don't they? I don't believe I've seen anything like these before, Nathaniel."

"You haven't, because, like I said, they're hot off the designer's desk. The good thing about it is they're limited editions. You won't see a lot of this exact style around. Let me show you something else, Sable. Come this way."

She followed him, all the while checking out his stride. He led her to the entertainment and wall-unit section. Before he could point the piece out to her, Sable saw it. She rubbed the fine crafted furniture with her hands enjoying the feel of it. It was a five-piece white oak wall unit. The two corner cabinets had five triangular fixed shelves; there was a lighted two-door cabinet/bookcase, a lighted five-shelf open bookcase and a home theater video cabinet. The unit was eight feet high by 10 feet wide.

"Ooo, Nathaniel, you are wonderful. This is exactly what I was hoping to find."

He pulled out his calculator and started punching in numbers. When he finished, he looked up at Sable with a negotiable look in his eyes.

"I'll let you have everything for $11,500 dollars."

Sable's bargaining skills kicked in and she offered a counter bid, "$10,500."

"$11,300" said Nathaniel.

"$10,600. Take it or leave it."

"$11,000 even."

"$11,000 it is." This time she extended her hand first and they shook on the deal.

"Nathaniel, I really appreciate your help. Thank you."

"You and your man will enjoy this," he said pryingly.

"Oh… I'll be enjoying this all by myself."

"No special someone?"

"Afraid not," she smiled.

Nathaniel pulled a red and white sold tag from the inside of his jacket and hung it on the knobs of the wall unit. "I'd like to take you out to dinner sometime."

Sable looked at him through hopeful eyes and smiled. Little did she know that charming women into buying furniture was a tactic of Nathaniel's. He had no intention of calling.

*   *   *

So far the day was very productive. The house closing was moving right along. She had found the perfect living room suite for the house in Torryville, and she had met a charming man in the process. She looked forward to him calling. Last night Shamell had given her some good ideas for her book and she felt so good that she decided to treat herself to some ice cream. She pulled into the Baskin Robbins parking lot.

"Boy, I hope they have winter white chocolate."

The bouncy brunette with dancing green eyes talked a mile a minute as she packed the ice cream into the gallon size tub. She talked about anything and everything. Sable liked her personality. She had the perfect job. She was probably a high school student trying to make money during the summer. She mentally commended the girl and wished Candace had had that same initiative.

"This is our number one flavor. We can't keep this stuff in stock," said the girl.

"I'm not surprised. I can eat my weight in it. A friend back in North Carolina introduced me to this flavor. I really have no business getting a gallon of this stuff,"

"Just enjoy it now because we only have it during the spring and summer months,"

Sable tucked the container under her arm, paid the cashier and left the parlor.

*   *   *

She had eight miles to go before she got home. Traffic was horrendous as usual. It would be another 25 minutes before she got there. She felt the ice cream container and turned the air conditioner up to maximum air control in an effort to keep it from melting. She spotted Shamell's red Porsche a few cars in front of her. She had recognized the customized license tag that read 'UGO-GIRL' and immediately knew it was her car. It was darting in and out of traffic. She figured Shamell had taken an extended lunch and was trying to make it back to the office in time for an appointment. Instead of turning left on 32nd Street in the direction of the office, the Porsche kept going straight.

"Hmm, that's strange, she's going in my direction."

Sable followed the Porsche for two more blocks before it turned into the Centennial Ramada Inn.

She chuckled. "Probably meeting Charles for an afternoon escapade." If Shamell wanted to do something, no matter how ridiculous it sounded, she'd do it. Sable liked her spontaneity. She decided to follow her into the parking lot, toot the horn and give her a thumb up. But, as she pulled in behind the Porsche, she saw Charles sitting behind the wheel. He looked like a Billy Dee Williams 15 years younger. He got out and walked around to the passenger side of the car. He opened the door and helped out a striking brown-skinned girl with long braids. She looked to be Candace's age. Sable put on brakes, bringing the car to a jerking halt. She backed the car into a vacant parking space, camouflaging in with the other parked cars. She felt like a spy as she watched closely. They walked toward the entrance.

"Sable, get hold of yourself. This can't be what you think it is. There is a rational explanation for this," she told herself. Sable was beginning to feel ashamed of herself for speculating the worst about Charles. She would make sure they were out of sight before she moved. She wouldn't want Charles to catch sight of her sitting there watching them. That's when she saw it. Charles' hand slipped from the girl's back down to her butt just as they disappeared through the door.

*   *   *

Sable had a well of mixed emotions all afternoon. She was shocked because she thought Charles was the perfect husband, sad because she knew it would hurt her best friend if she found out, and angry because of the downright deceitfulness of it. She even tried to convince herself that the butt part didn't happened but there was no denying it. It was too clear to miss.

Wilson had told her Shamell had called twice and wanted her to call her back soon as she came in. Sable reluctantly picked up the phone and dialed Shamell's office. She prayed the secretary would say she was in a meeting.

"Good afternoon, Alpha Publishers. How may I help you?"

"Hello, Keisha. This is Sable. I'm returning a call to Shamell."

"Oh, yeah, she's been trying to reach you."

"If she's too busy, I can call back."

"No! She definitely wants to talk to you. Hold on."

What in the world could it be? Maybe she knew about Charles' little secret and wanted to vent frustrations. Oh, God, what am I going to say? Girlfriend, I saw him this afternoon going into the Centennial Inn with this young honey. Or maybe I can say, Shamell girl, you tripping. You know Charles is not messing around on you. "Oh, Lord, help me."

"Where have you been? I been calling all morning," said Shamell.

"I had to go see about the house and then I made a couple of other stops. Is something wrong?"

"Now, honey, why would anything be wrong? Things couldn't be better. Charles drove me to work today. Said he wanted to pamper me. He's got something planned for this evening."

Sable sat on the edge of her bed with the phone nestled between her ear and shoulder. She wrung her hands nervously and thought of Charles as everything but a child of God. He had plans all right, and the only reason he drove her in was so she would be without transportation and his chances of getting away with his dirt would be better.

"I can't wait. Sable, you know how romantic he can be," Shamell gave a joyous squeal. "I had another idea for your book that's better than the one I gave you last night. That's why I'm calling. Let the wife find out that her dead husband was having an affair but with his secretary's 16-year-old daughter, not the secretary as everyone suspects. What 'cha think?"

"So, you're saying let the wife think it was the secretary but in actuality it's the secretary's daughter?"

"Yes! Can't you see it? Who would ever think it's the daughter. She has appeared two or three times in the book so far and each of those times she visited her mom unannounced at the office. One of those times the mother had to run an errand for the boss and the daughter was left alone with him."

Sable studied the idea for a few seconds, "Yeah, that might work. Let me play with it and see how I can make it happen. Thanks for the tip, Shamell."

"Anytime. So what other kind of business did you tend to today other than the house?"

"I purchased some lovely furniture that you have to see."

"Oh, yeah? So, don't tell me, let me guess. You either brought Victorian or prehistoric colonial, your old-timey self," she laughed.

"Wrong. How about contemporary?"

"Get out! You? I'll believe it when I see it."

"Believe it, 'cause that's what I got."

She went on to describe each piece of furniture and how much she'd written the check for. She also told Shamell about Nathaniel and how he'd stirred feelings she hadn't felt in a long time.

"Sounds good to me, girlfriend. Go for it," Shamell said.

"I just hope he calls."

8

Satin on the Loose

Aunt Elvira's picnic basket sat in the back seat of the Volvo. The aroma of fried chicken, deviled eggs and sweet potato pie was driving Jonah crazy with hunger. He loved her sweet potato pies and was glad she had not listen to him when he told her not to prepare food for the trip. He simply didn't want her to go through the trouble. He had told her there would be plenty of restaurants they could stop at on the way. They'd been traveling for five hours nonstop. Jonah had plotted the trip, planning rest stops every five hours. In a couple more miles they would reach their first scheduled stop in Alexandria, Virginia. Aunt Elvira was leery about stopping at interstate rest areas. She read and watched enough news reports to know that rest areas were vulnerable places for crimes. Jonah assured her everything would be all right. A reliable source had told her once that Jonah carried a gun for protection whenever he traveled and she thought that was why he was so cavalier about stopping. She was in dire need of a restroom and would have him pull along the side of the road if he didn't come upon one soon.

"Jonah, we 'bout there yet?"

"It's coming up on your right, Aunt Vi."

Jonah signaled right and eased onto the exit ramp. Aunt Elvira took off her thick bifocals and wiped them with a Kleenex. She put them back on and began looking around at the area.

"Look like we 'bout the only ones here. But it looks pretty decent, I guess."

Jonah slid the Volvo into a slanted parking space and turned the ignition off.

"O.K., Aunt Vi, there's the restrooms over there." He pointed to the square brick building that housed the men's restroom on the left and the women's on the right. In the center stood several vending machines.

"Well, ain't you coming?" she asked, looking at him through the bifocals. "I need you to stand by the door in case som'um happens." She swung open the car door and twisted herself sideways. She stood and stretched the stiffness out of her body, then straightened her pastel blue, double knit leisure suit. Her pocketbook swung on her arm as her hand found its way to her freshly done hair and patted the tight, greasy curls. Her beautician kept a supply of Dark and Lovely blue-black hair rinse as well as Dax pressing oil and curling wax on hand. They were for her older customers who preferred press and curls to relaxers. Aunt Elvira went to Pearl's House of Style twice a month. The twice-a-month visit was sufficient because Pearl hard-pressed Aunt Elvira's hair, then put close to a hundred little curls in it. Each curl was set off by crisscross parts making her head look like the grid map of a metropolitan city. She pulled a silk scarf out of her pocketbook, folded it diagonally and put it over her hair. She tied a neat bow under her chin, leaving the back of it triangled and flapping in the light breeze.

"Thank you, Jesus, for bringing us thus far." Aunt Elvira headed toward the bathroom with Jonah not far behind.

"Now, baby, I know you got to go too, but stand there until I get finish. I don't trust this place." She pushed open the door and stepped one foot in. She bent down and peeked under the stalls. She saw a pair of legs in the first one and felt better knowing she wouldn't be in there alone.

"Go on, Jonah, I'll be all right."

"You sure?" he asked.

"Yeah. Some other lady in here."

Aunt Elvira let the door swing closed and went in stall number two. She wiped the seat several times with toilet paper, then covered it with a seat liner she had gotten form the wall dispenser hanging over the back of the toilet. She emptied her bladder and, within seconds, felt instant relief. She thought of the lunch in the back seat of the Volvo and realized how hungry she was. She flushed the toilet, grabbed her handbag that hung from the door-hook, and stepped out of the stall. She looked for a paper-towel dispenser, but instead found an automated hand dryer. She hated hand dryers. They confined her to one spot until her hands were dry. With paper towels, she could pat them dry while walking toward the wastebasket, thus saving time. Also, she liked stuffing a few into her purse in case she needed to blow her nose.

The walls looked like they could stand a fresh coat of paint and the restroom itself needed disinfecting real bad. "O Lord, they call this clean." Aunt Elvira surveyed the basin area and hesitantly began washing her hands. She heard a squeak and the other stall door opened. The occupant emerged. Aunt Elvira looked in the mirror at the reflection coming forth. She wanted to laugh but fought the urge. This was the ugliest woman she had ever seen. Her hair was stringy and long. Her face looked like it hadn't been washed in days. Aunt Elvira averted her attention back to getting her hands clean. She felt the stranger coming closer instead of going to the other basin. She instantly looked at the other sink to see if it was broken. It looked fine and she wondered why this woman was approaching her. The odor coming from her was downright rancid and Aunt Elvira thought that if she didn't hurry and get herself out of there, it would completely ruin her appetite. She looked back into the mirror at the figure standing behind her.

Something was wrong. She squinted to make sure she was seeing right. What she thought was dirt on the woman's face were actually whiskers. Her eyes lowered to the woman's chest. It was as flat as a pancake. Her immediate suspicion was confirmed. This was not a woman. She felt faint in the pit of her stomach and her heart raced. Standing behind her was a tall white man. He was scratching his skin like he had the cooties. He had a neurotic twitched on the left side of his face. His eyes were blue and wild. His lips were merely a tight thin line. He wore cut off jeans and a tee shirt so dingy it looked brown. Aunt Elvira's mouth dropped open from fright. The entrance was only a couple of feet away. Maybe she could run, but with her arthritis, she'd never make it.

"What you doing in the ladies bathroom?" she said nervously.

The smelly man pointed his index finger under Aunt Elvira's nose. His fingernails were long and packed with black grime. She knew that part of the awful smell was coming from his hands and she could only imagine the filth on them.

"Gimme your money," he said in a raspy voice.

"Mister, I ain't got no money…"

"I ain't playing with you. Don't make me haf'ta cut yo' tongue out."

Aunt Elvira was so frightened her knees gave away and she crumpled to the floor. She balled herself up into fetal position all the while protecting her pocketbook. She tried to scream but nothing came out but a hum that turned into the tune of "Leaning on Jesus." The man started pulling at her arms trying to get to the pocketbook. He yanked, tugged and pulled, but Aunt Elvira held tight. The man grabbed her foot and dragged her to the opposite end of the restroom.

"You ain't gonna be satisfied till I cut you, old woman," he said.

Aunt Elvira knew she was doomed and it was about time to meet her maker. The humming stopped and as if she had no control over her mouth, the words to the hymn started flowing out loudly. "What a fellowship what a joy divine—leaning on the everlasting arms!"

The man finally pried the pocketbook from her arms. He bolted out the door and ran toward the parking lot. Aunt Elvira scurried around on the floor of the drab restroom trying to get up. "Lord, have mercy! Jesus, help me, Father God!" She screamed to the top of her lungs. Jonah was washing his hands when he heard her. He shot out of the bathroom with wet hands just as Aunt Elvira came running out and into his arms.

"That man just stole my pocketbook!" She pointed to the man running across the parking lot. Jonah ran behind him, but the man had put too much distance between them. He stopped cold in his tracks and reached in the side of his pants for the .25 caliber automatic. He yelled for the man to stop, when he didn't, Jonah shot three times in the air. The man threw the pocketbook down and dropped face down on the ground. He placed both hands behind his back.

"O.K., man, I'm sorry. Look," he pointed to the pocketbook lying beside him. "I wasn't gonna hurt that old lady. I just needed the money to get me something to eat. See, I ain't even got no knife." He lifted up his tee shirt for Jonah to see that he was weaponless.

"Man, you 'bout to get yourself killed, you know that? You picked the wrong person to rob today! I ought to put a bullet through you for trying some shit like that."

"No, man! Please don't shoot me," he pleaded.

Jonah looked over his shoulder to see Aunt Elvira running frantically towards him.

"Aunt Vi, you all right?"

"Ooo, Lord," she said, holding a hand over her heart. "No, Jonah, don't shoot…help, somebody help!" She looked around the isolated area but could find no one. Her heart raced and every bone in her body shook with fear.

"Aunt Vi, you don't look so good," Jonah said, pointing the gun at the man and watching Aunt Elvira.

"Be careful, Jonah. He got a knife somewhere.

"There's no knife. Calm down now," he said

"Lord ha' mercy! I was in there washing my hands when he came up behind me! I thought it was a woman in there all that time! He dragged me 'cross the floor talking 'bout he was gon' cut my tongue out! Jesus, Savior!" She bent forward with both hands on her knees.

"Take deep breaths, Aunt Vi,"

"Thank you, Father—Oh Blessed Savior. Whew!" she panted. "I —I —believe I'll be all right."

"Lady, I'm sorry. I was gonna leave your pocketbook. I just wanted money to buy me som'um to eat. I'm hungry."

"Shut up!" Jonah yelled. He looked at the man incredulously noticing the track marks up and down the insides of his arms. The man was a drug addict, which was usually the case in situations like these. Aunt Elvira had heard correctly from her source. Jonah never took chances. Most of the time he had his gun with him, especially when he made out of town trips. Jonah wondered how many other people this man had robbed. It wouldn't have surprised him if he'd killed somebody.

"You always target defenseless women for your victims? You punk!"

The man squirmed on the ground half-twisting over to get a better look at his prosecutor.

"This the first time I done som'um like this, man, I swear. I'm so sorry. Please give me a break. Don't call the cops."

Aunt Elvira inched closer to Jonah. "Reckon he telling the truth?"

"Aunt Vi, get real," Jonah said, agitated. "Look at his arms. See all those marks."

Aunt Elvira peeped closer at the man's arms, "Oh, yeah," she said slowly. "He on dope, ain't he?"

"Dope and anything else he can get his hands on probably. Get my cell phone out the car and dial 911."

The man continued to beg and plead for Jonah not to call the police.

Aunt Elvira didn't move. She watched the man, feeling a bit sorry for him.

"Maybe we ought to feed him a little something first. I sho' made enough."

"He'll get food where he's going. Now please go get the phone."

*   *   *

It took 15 minutes for the police to get there. They handcuffed the man they knew as Mike Fletcher. They'd given him the nickname "Fletcher the snatcher." Mike had a police record as long as his arm, mostly misdemeanors. One of the officers told Jonah they immediately knew who he was when they got the description of the perpetrator. The other officer took an account of what had happened from Aunt Elvira. He asked her if she wanted to press charges. Before she could answer, Jonah answered a resounding yes.

"Is that right, Ms. Elvira?" asked the officer as he scribbled in his notebook.

"Well, I'm a firm believer of second chances but, since my nephew thinks it's what I ought to do, I guess I will."

"I'll need a phone number where we can reach you to let you know of the court date."

"Court date?" Jonah asked. "You mean to tell me we gotta be there?"

"The chance of him being convicted is better if you're there to identify him as the person who committed the crime."

"But, that's crazy. I apprehended him. Aunt Elvira gave you an account of what happened. Even you said yourself y'all knew it was him before y'all got here."

"Mr. Brooks, we have no doubt in our minds that he committed the crime. Mike specializes in this type of thing and that's the reason why he targets rest areas. He knew more than likely his victim would be an out-of-town traveler. Out-of-towners are less likely to come back for a court hearing. Mike will be appointed a court attorney and if he's halfway good, he'll get Mike off if you don't show up to identify him. Our fear is next time Mike might end up killing somebody."

"There ain't no way we can come back. We're from North Carolina on our way to New York for my daughter's graduation."

"When are you planning on coming back through this way?" asked one of the officers.

"I got some business I need to take care of while I'm there. It'll be in about four or five more days. Maybe Tuesday or Wednesday."

"Good enough. Give us a number where you can be reached and we'll talk with the judge and see what we can work out."

Jonah wrote Sable's phone number down for the officers. "I don't want to see him go free. What he needs is help. Some kind of drug counseling or rehabilitation program."

"Mr. Brooks, if you come back and testify, I guarantee that's what he'll get."

Mike Fletcher was thrown into the back seat of the patrol car. The officers thanked them and then advised them on being safe for the remainder of their road trip. As they started the patrol car and backed away from the curb, Aunt Elvira walked up to the driver's side and tapped on the window.

"Yes, ma'am?"

"Make sure y'all feed him. I think he's pretty hungry."

The officers burst into laughter. "You hear that, Mike," said one of the officers. "That nice old lady thinks you're hungry."

"Yeah, for food that is," said the other one.

Mike glared at the officers, Aunt Elvira and Jonah. "Screw all y'all," he said as the patrol car drove away.

Aunt Elvira could still hear the officers laughing 50 feet away.

*   *   *

Aunt Elvira would remember Alexandria, Virginia for a long time. It didn't matter if Jonah had 10 guns on him; there would be no rest-area stops on the way back home. When they got ready for breaks, they'd stop at Burger Kings, McDonalds or other restaurants. She couldn't wait to tell Sable, Candace and Wilson about the incident. If Jonah hadn't been there to witness it, Wilson would not believe her. Wilson was so cantankerous. It didn't have anything to do with Loretta's death either, because as far back as she could remember he'd been that way. Even before the night she told Loretta about Wilson and Ruthann's affair. Aunt Elvira knew Wilson was jealous over Loretta's affection and wanted it all for himself but the thing she wasn't ready to admit was that she had some of that jealously too.

Loretta and Aunt Elvira were close, maybe too close for Jonah's comfort. She could make Loretta do anything for her and she'd always been willing to do anything for Loretta. True, there had been times when she overstepped her boundaries. Like the time she took it upon herself to have Sable's ears pierced. Wilson was furious and Loretta was upset also. They felt that was a decision Sable should have made herself when she got older, since pierced ears were a permanent body alteration. Loretta didn't stay mad at Aunt Elvira long before they were back to being sisters and best friends. Wilson wanted the child grounded from visiting Aunt Elvira unsupervised. Of course, Loretta couldn't go along with that. Aunt Elvira didn't have any children of her own and she adored having Sable around, especially the weekly sleepovers. If she could turn back the hands of time, she would do things differently, but she knew you never got a second chance at the past. What you did get was the chance to say I'm sorry. Somehow the opportunity never presented itself for her to say those two words. Whenever she got ready to, Wilson would spoil it by saying something totally off balance, sending Aunt Elvira into one of her stubborn moods.

"Jonah, I believe I'm gon' take a quick nap. You not sleepy are you?"

"I'm fine. You go on to sleep. We're on the other side of Washington. Won't be long now, Aunt Vi."

Aunt Elvira reclined her bucket seat all the way back. She clutched her pocketbook tightly as it sat on her lap. She was so grateful to Jonah for rescuing her pocketbook and the $435.75 she had in it. It was all the money she had until her next monthly pension check came. She'd already thanked him a thousand times, but she would thank him again before the day was out. She closed her eyes and drifted off to sleep. It wasn't long before she was snoring. She snored low and smooth, the way a woman should, if she snored at all. The way Sable snored. Jonah used to lie in bed late at night just listening to her sounds and sometimes he would poke her gently in the side just so she would moan. Her moans were sensual moans and if he were lucky, some of those times she would awake to his mannish stare and know what he wanted. She'd wrap her arms around him, pull him to her and fulfill his desires. Jonah tried to shake the memories of Sable, but they kept returning like waves on a beach's shore.

He was wearing a shirt that she had brought him on their last anniversary together. It was a last ditch attempt to rekindle the flame of their relationship. He'd made a big to-do about the simple knit polo shirt. He wondered if she still had the sterling silver teardrop earrings that he had brought her. She never liked the larger and more fashionable earrings because they were too cumbersome. She liked jewelry she could sleep and shower in. She didn't want her ear lobes sagging by time she reached 60 like so many women she'd seen who had worn heavy earrings most of their lives.

Jonah had negotiated a deal with Phillips Chevrolet in Winston-Salem to purchase a black Camaro with gold pinstripes. He would pick it up at Briscoe Chevrolet in Manhattan. The sales agent assured him there would be no problem in having the car delivered in another state. All he had to do tomorrow was find the dealership, examine and test-drive the car. If everything were to his satisfaction, he would sign the contract. The only other concern he had was putting the car someplace where Candace wouldn't notice it. Twenty-two thousand dollars was what he had bargained. That was a lot of money, yet it was a good deal considering ordinarily he would have paid $25,000 or above for the fully loaded automobile. It had top-grain leather seats, power steering, windows and brakes, dual airbags and climate control, cruise control, cassette/CD players and a sunroof. Jonah had them to install a cellular phone because he remembered Sable complaining to him that Candace often forgot to carry the cell phone she had brought for her.

Sable would have a fit when she found out. It would be a total surprise to everyone, and Jonah really didn't care if everyone else's response was positive or negative. His main and only purpose was making his baby girl happy.

Sometime he experienced a guilty conscience for not being there to help raise Candace, but that was on his own accord because Sable never led him to feel that he wasn't doing all that a father should do by his child. Although Sable was making good money with her writing and didn't need financial help from Jonah, he always sent a check in the amount of $600 every month. Some of it was given directly to her for a monthly allowance. It was expected to last until the next month, but most of the time it didn't. Unbeknown to Candace, Sable started a savings account with the rest of it. She had planned to give it to her upon graduation. Jonah felt good about the visit. He felt something promising was in store for him. He hoped it was reconciliation.

*   *   *

Sable sliced the cucumbers over the garden salad and looked at the finished product proudly. The salad displayed in a large glass bowl and was layered with lettuce, mushrooms, tomatoes, green peppers, broccoli and finally the cucumbers. She covered the top with plastic wrap and placed it in the refrigerator beside the picture of freshly brewed iced tea and lemon meringue pie. Jonah loved home-cooked meals and after the long trip he would appreciate it. The pot roast with potatoes and baby carrots was fully cooked and warming in the oven. Yeast rolls from the corner bakery were sitting on the counter. They would be reheated once everyone sat down for dinner. It dawned on her that she had put nearly three hours into the preparation of the meal. She was taken back down memory lane to the years of her marriage. She used to spend hours in the kitchen perfecting a meal for Jonah and Candace.

The clock on the kitchen wall read 4:45 p.m. and she knew they would be arriving soon. She wore a new sleeveless A-line knit dress that stopped above her knees. It was new and going to be one of her favorites. On the rack at Abraham's boutique it looked like another simple dress. But Sable knew she could make the dress come alive with her curvaceous figure. That was the reason she bought it in addition to the double markdown. It was originally priced at $85. She purchased it for $35. Sable was a bargain-hunter when it came to shopping. She never settled on retail prices. The brown sandals she wore had two-inch heels and were a perfect match with the tan dress. She had her hair trimmed and slightly faded in the back. She wore the sterling silver teardrop earrings that Jonah had bought. Around her neck was an 18-inch sterling silver chain that held a tiny crucifix charm. She made her eyes up with metallic earth tone eye shadows and dark brown liner—just enough to notice. She wore rum raisin lipstick. Her skin was scented with Juniper breeze body lotion. It left a light floral fragrance in the air when she passed. Sable was nervous about seeing Jonah. It had been three years since their last visit and, she had to admit, he looked good then. His hair was wavy and black with sprinkles of gray here and there. His brown skin had aged perfectly for a man of 45 and his light brown eyes were alert and sexy. She wondered if the three years had been as good to him as it had to her. Sable wasn't the type to boast openly, but she knew she had it going on for a 44-year-old woman.

She took a quick survey of the kitchen. Everything was in order and ready for Jonah and Aunt Elvira. Sable walked into the living room and plopped down on the couch. She picked up the remote control and clicked on the television. The "Andy Griffith Show" was on. It reminded her of when she first came to live in New York and how amazed she was at the naiveness of the native New Yorkers. When they found out she was from North Carolina, they wanted to know how close she lived to the town of Mayberry. Sable soon tired of trying to convince them that Mayberry, not like Raleigh and Mount Pilot (*alias Pilot Mountain*), was a fictitious town that was tailored for the show. Soon, she found herself pacifying their curiosity and telling them Germanton, North Carolina, was thirty miles from the make-believe place. Sometimes she would go as far as to say she knew Andy and that he was as decent and moral as his character on television. She would see a glimmer of satisfaction in their eyes, most of them concurring, "I thought he would be." She felt she was giving them a piece of nostalgia. After all, it was what she did best: fictionalize. What more could she give to people who were only accustomed to the opposite of what Andy and the town of Mayberry portrayed.

This was the episode where Aunt Bea bought tonic from a traveling salesman. The tonic was suppose to be a vitamin-enriched cure-all type medicine but it was 80 percent alcohol. Sable chuckled as she watched Aunt Bea playing the piano in a joyously drunken state. That reminded her that Aunt Elvira and Jonah liked to partake of the bottle every now and then and she didn't have a thing in the house except soda, tea and fruit juices. She made a mental note to pick up some Chardonnay and Scotch tomorrow.

Candace appeared at the threshold of the living room and hallway. She nodded her head while looking at Sable. Sable knew why she was watching her so intently and she felt somewhat embarrassed. Candace folded her arms across her chest.

"Mmm, hmm," she said sarcastically.

Sable acted as though she was oblivious to Candace's hints. "Mmm, hmm, what?" she asked, not taking her eyes off the television.

"Oh, don't play dumb with me. You know what." Candace inched into the room and eased down on the other end of the sofa.

"I really don't know what you're talking about."

"Really now." Candace angled her head upward and sniffed twice into the air. "I don't believe I'm familiar with the perfume that you're wearing. Is it new?" she asked, mimicking a British accent.

Sable rolled her eyes at Candace then averted them back to the "Andy Griffith Show" without saying a word.

"Ah, and I do believe that outfit is new, too. May I add that it is indeed smashing."

At that moment, Sable picked up a pillow from the couch and threw it at Candace. Candace fell back on the sofa in laughter.

"What is your problem, child?" Sable asked, part agitated and in jest.

"You!"

"Me?"

"Yeah. For somebody who doesn't care anything about her ex-husband, you sure are dressed to impress."

"Candace, you're right for a change. I am dressed to impress but, not for Jonah. I'm dressed to impress myself."

Candace held up a hand. "Talk to the hand, Ma, 'cause the ears ain't listening."

Sable disregarded Candace with a fan of her hand, "When are you getting dressed?" She looked at Candace from head to toe. The jean shorts and midriff pullover she wore looked two sizes too small and left little for the imagination. The only thing decent Sable could find on her were the Nike sneakers.

"I am dressed," she said nonchalantly.

"I don't think your daddy is going to appreciate seeing you half naked"

"Dad is not old fogy, Ma. He's up with the times."

"You forgetting about Aunt Vi. You need to have some respect for her, you know."

Candace stood up and looked down at herself. "What's wrong with this? It's not like everything is showing. I don't think they'll have a problem with it."

"O.K., don't say I didn't warn you. By the way, Russell called while you were in the shower."

"He probably wants to hang out tonight. I hope you told him I have plans."

Sable glanced at her daughter. She felt culpable for inviting Russell without consulting Candace's first. She ran nervous fingers through her cropped hair. Candace knew Sable's body language all too well and felt something suspicious was going on.

"Ma, you didn't!"

"I invited him to dinner," she said through a pleading smile.

"That's cold-blooded! What made you think I'd want to see him tonight?"

"I just thought it would be nice for him to meet the rest of your family. Besides, we talked a while and…"

"And you felt sorry for him."

"For Christ's sake, Candace, I don't see the big deal here. I thought you two were friends."

"We are, but that doesn't mean we're supposed to be up on each other all the time. I was looking forward to being with just my family this evening. You want to read more into this relationship than what it is. That's your problem, Ma."

"Candace, he's such a nice fellow. He's hard-working, has his own place, a decent job with the government. You know granddaddy use to work for the post office too."

"All the above correct, but one vital thing is missing, chemistry! I feel toward him like a sister would a brother. I wish you'd stop trying to match-make."

"Jonah and I started out like that, too."

"Yeah, and look at you now." Candace turned and walked out of the room.

"Where are you going?"

"To change into something more decent."

Sable watched her walk away and disappear around the corner. Glad she was going to change clothes, she held up two fists triumphantly and whispered, "Yes!"

*   *   *

Sable and Wilson began clearing away the table. Jonah, Aunt Vi, Candace and Russell headed for the living room.

"Just make yourselves at home," called Wilson. "We'll be in there da'rek-da with the coffee and dessert." The two scurried around the kitchen clearing, cleaning and preparing. Wilson nudged Sable in the side with his elbow and whispered, "Don't Jonah look good?"

"I can't lie. Yes he does."

"You look right smart yourself. I'm sho' glad you put on a dress 'stead of them sweat pants you love to wear all the time. You gotta nice figure. Just like ya' mamma. A man likes to see a woman dressed feminine. You know, showing a little legs," he paused a moment to let Sable soak up his offering of wisdom. "Speaking of feminine, Candace look like a lady tonight, don't she?"

Sable thought she looked more like an old maid. She knew Candace was making a clear statement to her for inviting Russell over. She dressed herself in a short sleeved floral dress that reached almost down to her ankles. She even pulled her luxurious hair back into a ponytail. Despite her effortless attire, Sable noticed that Russell could not take his eyes off her. Her heart bled for him. It was obvious he was smitten by Candace, but she wouldn't give him the time of day except when she needed him.

"Yes, daddy. She does look like a lady,"

"And, I like that young man, too."

Sable sliced generous portions of the lemon meringue pie and put them on the dessert plates.

Wilson reminded her so much of herself. She stopped slicing the pie and looked at her daddy as he poured coffee into cups. Moments earlier she was trying to do the same thing with Candace and Russell that he was doing with her and Jonah. Matchmaking came honest she guessed. Wilson looked up from pouring and caught sight of Sable staring at him.

"What's wrong?" he asked her.

Sable smiled, walked over to him and gently kissed him on the cheek. "Nothing. Just want you to know I love you," Sable grabbed her tray and headed for the living room.

Jonah and Russell were getting along well. Sable could tell that Aunt Elvira liked him, too. When Wilson found out he worked for the postal services there was an automatic bond. Sable passed the desserts around. Wilson came in with the coffee and set the tray down on the coffee table. He picked up a dessert plate and took a seat in the corner of the room. Aunt Elvira was telling the story of her robbery attempt for the third time.

"I just knew that man was gon' kill me and I was going home to meet my Lord. I tell y'all that man looked like something outta' horror movie. Hair long and scraggly, eyes all wild. Y'all know the type." Aunt Elvira exhaled exhaustedly while shaking her head. She forked a hefty piece of pie into her mouth.

"What is the world coming to when you can't go to the bathroom in peace?" added Sable.

Aunt Elvira swallowed the piece of pie hurriedly. "Thank God for Jonah, child. He saved the day. I wish I had a camcorder. I would have taped it so y'all could see him in action." She leaned over and patted Jonah's right knee. " Jonah, somebody, and I ain't calling no names, told me one time that you carried a gun around with you. I thought, Lord if that's true, I don't like it one bit. But, child, I ain't got nothing bad to say 'bout you and your gun no mo'. You hear me?"

Everybody laughed at her as she recanted bits of the story with animated gestures. For most of the evening, Jonah sat unusually quiet. He stole glances at Sable when he thought she wasn't noticing. Candace sat on the floor in between Jonah's legs on a huge overstuffed throw pillow. Every now and then Jonah playfully tugged at her ponytail and Candace would slap his hand in exaggerated agitation. He wondered if Sable was seeing anyone. She looked too good to be going solo. He was sure she had a friend. After he took care of the car business tomorrow, he'd take Candace shopping and then maybe he could find out about Sable's personal life. His eyes found Sable again. He always favored long hair, but the short natural looked good on Sable. It made her look more daring and spunky, more like a "today's" black woman. He liked it and hoped he would get the chance to tell her before he left. A smile warmed his lips just as she caught sight of him staring. Like a deer caught in the headlight, she froze and their gazes locked momentarily. Only when Wilson asked if anyone wanted more coffee did they break their concentration from each other.

Aunt Elvira shifted the attention to Candace when she asked if she had any immediate plans after graduation.

"I plan to rejuvenate. Then I'll start pounding the pavement."

Sable practically choked on her coffee. She had the urge to clear her throat and laugh but didn't want her signals read as mockery, which is exactly what they would have been. This child had a rude awakening when she stepped foot into the real world. Rejuvenate, Sable thought. What had she done so exerting to rejuvenate from?

"My baby is going to be a TV news personality," Jonah said proudly.

Candace twisted around to look at him. "That's not first choice, Daddy. You know I really want to model."

"Model? I thought you got modeling out of your system long time ago. Your major is journalism."

"I know, Dad and I haven't abandoned that possibility. I really think my calling is in fashions."

"Oh, baby girl, I heard some things about that business. Most of them gay, on drugs or both. Why you think they so small? Drugs trick the mind as being a false substitute for food. You choose that career and chances are you'll get hooked up with the wrong kind of people. Next thing you know you'll be doing the things they do."

"Jonah, I think you've just made a pretty strong statement. Don't categorize your child. I'm sure that a certain percent of models do indulge in drugs, but you can pick any other profession and you will find drug users, homosexuals, thieves, murderers and many other kind of people. What we have to do is support her decision to do what she feels is best for her," said Sable.

"I didn't say anything about thieves and murderers, Sable, "he said in a voice as calm as he could make it. "Now the girl went to school for four years so that she could get a job in journalism. It would be senseless for me to try and steer her down other avenues."

"People do it everyday. I read somewhere where more than 40 percent of college graduates choose careers outside of their majors, and statistics show that they are more productive and have more self-worth than their counterparts who stay in their field just for the sake of four years invested."

"I don't agree with you there, Sable. I say let her find something in her major. If that doesn't work out, then let her try her hand at modeling."

"Let her! For Christ's sake, Jonah, the girl's grown. You don't have to let her do anything. She was trying to be considerate to you by letting you know of her plans. She didn't even have to tell you."

"Now, what's that suppose to mean?" he asked defensively.

Sable realized an argument was brewing. She held up both hands in truce. "Nothing. I didn't mean a thing. I just…"

"Naw, you meant something. Wouldn't have said it if you didn't mean anything. What? You think 'cause I live way down in North Carolina and y'all up here that I don't have the right to know what's going on with my own daughter–that I'm an outsider looking in?"

"Jonah, look, I'm sorry if I said something that you misinterpreted."

"Sable, the only thing you sorry about is that I didn't misinterpret what you said."

Animosities had begun to grow in the room and not only were Sable and Jonah feeling uncomfortable but everyone else, too. Candace got up from the pillow. She was embarrassed that Russell had to witness this. Russell was from a well-bread wholesome family. His mother and father's relationship was intact and had been for 35 years. He often told loving stories of them, and he had even invited her on many occasions to visit them in Roanoke. What did he think of her and her dysfunctional family now? She thought.

"Dad, Mom, you both had a hand in raising me and you know I got a pretty strong constitution. I am not going to let anybody make me do something I don't want to do or something I know is wrong."

"Well, what ever you do sweetheart make sure you consult the Lord first. Then and only then will you make the right decisions," said Aunt Elvira.

"Amen to that," added Wilson.

Sable felt lower than low. It was she who had invited Russell over without Candace's consent and, on top of that, embarrassed her in front of him. She of all people should have known better than to try to inject common sense into Jonah. The man was still just as bull-headed as he had always been. "Baby, I'm sorry. Your father and I... we just see differently about some things."

"She's right, Candace. We didn't mean anything."

"That's O.K. Everything's cool," she said as she looked at her watch. Hey, the evening is still young. I've been dying to see that movie "Life". How 'bout it Russell? My treat."

"I can't turn down an offer like that. It's not every day I get treated to a movie by a beautiful woman." He lifted himself out of the chair.

Aunt Vi looked at the young couple and began reminiscing about her own life. "Lord, I remember when I was 15, there was this boy named Moses. We use to go steady. He used to take me to toe parties. The girls would paint their toenails, stand behind a sheet or blanket and let the boy pick out the toes he wanted. Old Moses picked my toes every time. I guess he knew them by heart," she snickered like a transformed schoolgirl. "We'd laugh, talk, dance and drink soda pop until it was time for me to get home. We'd have the best old time. Moses ended up marrying a girl from South Carolina. Vivian, Vivian Hamlin was her name. Them was the days." Aunt Elvira stared blankly into space as her memories left her suspended in thought.

"We better get going, Russell, if we want to catch the movie from the beginning," said Candace.

"It's been nice meeting all of you. He shook everyone's hand. "Enjoyed the dinner, Ms. Brooks."

"Oh, anytime, Russell and I hope to see you at graduation," No sooner than the word graduation escaped her mouth than she realized she had done it again. She'd invited Russell to Candace's graduation. No doubt Candace would have another lecture for her in the morning about minding her own business. She looked at Candace apologetically and then back at Russell. "We enjoyed you."

"We sho' did, sugar," added Aunt Elvira, "Y'all chi'ren have a good time now."

Candace grabbed Russell's hand and led him to the door. She held it open as he passed through. She looked over her shoulder at her family with a murderous expression. "Don't wait up for me." She stepped out and closed the door.

Unknowingly, Jonah and Sable had thrown a monkey wrench into each other's plans. Jonah thought if he had kept his mouth shut this whole mess wouldn't have happened. Then again, why should he silence his opinions? Sable was the one to blame. She didn't have to confront him like she had in front of everybody, especially Russell. It was her new image, the more opinionated and outspoken Sable. It was a mistake agreeing to stay at the apartment with the rest of them. He should have reserved a hotel room like he started to. Candace begged him to stay; that's why he had agreed. He rubbed his hands together apprehensively and tried to think of something to say to break the quiet that had filled the room. The very thing that he wanted to say all afternoon would be inappropriate now. He wanted to tell Sable how good it was to see her and that she looked and smelled wonderful.

"I know everybody is feeling a little awkward right now, so let this be a lesson to us from this point on, at least until we get through this graduation. This is Candace's time. Whether we like each other or not ain't important. Now, this child's graduation is one of the things that memories are built on. Lets don't spoil it for her." Aunt Elvira chuckled as she pointed her arthritic finger at Wilson. "You would have thought me and Wilson would be the ones going at it."

Wilson nodded his head and laughed. "She's right. But I can wait until we get back to North Carolina to insult her."

Wilson's light humor was enough to knock the chill out of the atmosphere. Sable stole a quick glance at Jonah. He was running a hand continuously through his wavy hair. Sable knew instinctively that an apology was coming next but an apology she could do without because before the weekend was out he'd say something else that he'd need to apologize for. She thought he hadn't changed much, still that narrow-minded person he was before the divorce. That had been their biggest problem, his stifling her growth. He had tried to hinder her for as long as he could, but thank God, she was able to see through him and had the wits and knowledge to step out of his shadow. She would be doggone if he was going to do the same thing to Candace. Sable reached for the tray that sat on the coffee table. She placed her cup and dessert dish down on it and began gathering the other dishes.

"Anyone need anything else?" she asked as she headed for the kitchen.

"Lord, I don't know when I've eaten so much," said Aunt Elvira. "If y'all don't mind, I believe I'm gon' retire." She pushed herself out of the chair and headed toward Sable's bedroom. Wilson stood up and yawned like a wide-mouth bass. He stretched his arms upward and announced his retirement, too. "When you get past 60 years old, this is about all she wrote," he chuckled. "I'm calling it a night. Y'all young folks can have it."

"Good night, daddy. Night-night Aunt Vi," Sable held the tray steady and stepped into the kitchen. Jonah followed, bringing with him several unused napkins. She knew Aunt Elvira was tired after the long trip, but Wilson wasn't. It was clear to her that he was trying to give her and Jonah time to spend together. Many a night, he'd sit up till 2 in the morning watching a late movie.

"These are still good. Nobody touched them."

"Just lay them on the table," she said coolly.

"Can I help you do something?" he asked.

"Nope."

"Sable, I'm sorry about what happened in there. I'm just concerned about my child, too. I didn't mean any disrespect," he shifted his weight from left to right.

"I know you didn't" was her only reply.

"Look, I can see that I'm an intrusion here. I can get a hotel room if you would feel more comfortable."

Sable shrugged her shoulders, indicating the choice was his. She really wanted to kick herself for allowing stubbornness to get the best of her. This was not the way it was suppose to go. Candace was not supposed to get upset and leave, the little disagreement was not supposed to have occurred and definitely Jonah was not supposed to be talking about staying in a hotel. She wanted him there, as close to her as possible. She wanted to accidentally brush past him in the hallway and feel the warmness of his flesh and he feel hers. Then her new silk nightgown would accidentally fall open revealing her glorious body. Or he was supposed to say something whimsical and she'd fall in his arms from laughing so hard and they would get caught up in the moment. One thing would lead to another and before the weekend was over they would have made love at least once if not more. Those were supposed to be the events of the long weekend. Now, here he was talking about leaving.

"I get the feeling you would feel more comfortable in a hotel room, Jonah."

Her words had confirmed his suspicion that she didn't want him there. "I'll get my things." He turned to walk away but bumped into Wilson. He thought it odd that he hadn't heard him come in.

"Jonah, I just came to tell you I turned down your bed and hung up your suit bag. See you in the morning." He patted Jonah on the shoulder.

Sable shook her head unbelievingly. She knew Wilson was eavesdropping just as sure as he was standing there. Hanging up his clothes was just a decoy.

"Wilson, I think it would be best if I stayed someplace else."

"What!"

"I'm going to a hotel."

Wilson looked at Sable then back at Jonah. "Why plenty of room right here, ain't it, Sable?"

"Daddy, he knows he's welcome to stay."

Jonah rubbed his hands under his chin and felt the day old stubble. "I don't know."

"Now if I have to, I'll go right in there and wake Vi up. I know y'all don't want to get her started this late at night. You gon' stay right here and that's that. 'Sides, Candace wants you here. She don't get to spend much time with you as it is."

*   *   *

Jonah lay in bed with his hands under his head thinking about his headstrong ex-wife in the next room. "She sure has changed," he said. Then he rolled over and closed his eyes to sleep.

Aunt Elvira snored easy as she slept. Sable held up the ivory silk nightgown that she had hoped to wear for Jonah. It smelled of fresh talcum powders. She folded it neatly and put it in the bottom of her chest of drawers. "He will never change," she mumbled to herself. She climbed into bed beside Aunt Elvira with her old Miami Dolphins tee shirt on.

9

The Midas Touch

"On a scale of one to 10, I give it a seven," Candace said as she slid into the passenger side of Russell's silver gray Camry.

"A seven! That's an insult to the fine art of acting. You gotta give Eddie and Martin their props." Russell scooped the hem of Candace's dress from the car door's opening and laid it on her lap before slamming the door shut. Candace reached over and unlocked the driver's side.

"It would have been better if they hadn't overacted."

"People pay to see them overact. You want to pay good money to go see actors half act?"

"I guess you're right. I just hate seeing brothers behind bars, that's all. I don't care if it is a comedy; to me something like that is no joking matter."

"Well, you know sometimes you have to laugh to keep from crying," said Russell.

He guided the car around to the tollbooth. Candace peeped to see if the blonde attendant who was there the other day was on duty tonight. It was a different attendant and Candace rested back into the seat.

"Do you have any Keith Sweat?"

"Nope, but I got something better." He opened the center glove compartment that separated the bucket seats and pulled out a CD. He put it in the player and started bopping his head before the music began to play. Candace waited eagerly for the music to start. The deep baritone voice of Barry White began singing. Candace bolted up from her reposed position. "What is that, Russell?"

"G-i-r-r-l, don't get ignorant on me. That's the maestro. Ain't he smooth?"

"That's stuff my momma listens to. I wanna get my groove on!"

"You can groove off this." He placed his index finger over his mouth and shushed Candace. "Just listen to the words," he said softly. "The music—and his voice. This ain't nothing but the truth."

"Aw man," she pouted a little before surrendering to Russell's coaxing. When the third song played, she found herself tapping her feet to the soft rhythm and Barry's velvety voice. Russell noticed Barry had cast a spell on another unsuspecting soul. He was enjoying Candace's company immensely, probably more than she'd ever know. He wondered how he could get her to take him serious. He looked at the digital clock in the dashboard. It read 11:30. The night was still young and he wanted to hold on to Candace as long as he could.

"You wanna go by my place for a little while?" he asked, looking straight ahead and expecting an excuse, like she was too tired and had a lot to do the next day.

"Yeah, that's all right with me."

Russell smiled in the darkness of the car. He had to play all his cards carefully if there was any chance of this relationship going to the next plateau.

*   *   *

He unlocked the door and clicked on the hall light. Candace walked past him and into the living room.

"What's on this time of night?" She picked up the remote and channel-surfed. Jay Leno was on. Some unknown comedian was doing "your mamma so ugly" jokes. Candace curled up on the sofa and hugged a throw pillow in her lap.

"Can I get you something to eat?"

"No, thank you. I'm still stuffed from dinner."

"A beer?"

"What do you have?"

Russell opened the refrigerator and pulled two bottles of Colt 45 from their cardboard container. He popped the tops off of each and handed Candace one. Russell sat in the Lane recliner opposite her. He rolled the icy cold beer between the palms of his hands while contemplating telling her his true feelings. Of course, he had told her many times before but to no avail. With all jokes and wittiness aside, he had to make Candace know his sincerity. He heard that Cupid always shot two arrows, but that day in the post office, one of them missed Candace. He watched her. She took delicate baby sips from the bottle. A little beer escaped her mouth and rolled down her chin.

"Um," she wiped the drop away with her index finger. "You can't see TV from there," she said.

"I'm not really interested in TV. Besides, I got a good view of what I'm watching," For the first time he could sense her uneasiness and was flattered that he had unsettled her so.

Candace thought Russell was unusually quiet tonight. Most times when they were together, he talked a mile a minute. She had never seen him so earnest. If she had taken three guesses about what was on his mind, one of them would have been right. She was on his mind.

Candace wondered what else she wanted in life besides a successful modeling career? She couldn't think of an answer. Most women included in their dreams a career, husband and children. In that order. As she sat in Russell's apartment enjoying his attention, she questioned how her life would be with only a career to look forward to. Why hadn't she ever thought of this before? She didn't want to grow old alone. Russell was fun. He made her laugh, cheered her when she was down, was always there for her whenever she needed him. She had said many times that he was her best friend and she could trust him with her life. She remembered the girl's picture on his nightstand. She had a cute face. It was the face of a wife and mother, not a career woman. Maybe this girl wanted Russell and if she did, she had every right. Russell was fine pickings. Before she knew it she was asking him about the mystery girl.

"Whose picture is that on your night stand?"

"Her name is Ophelia. Why you ask?"

"No reason, just asked. I noticed it the other day when I was here, that's all," Ophelia, she thought. Her name sounds wifely and motherly. "A friend?" she asked, not trying to be too conspicuous.

"Yeah." Russell detected a trace of jealousy and thought he could have some fun with it.

"That's funny."

"What is?"

"That I've never heard you mention her before."

"Well," he said as he sat his beer down on the floor and got up from the recliner. "I don't tell all my business."

"Oh. What kind of business you don't tell?"

Russell grinned and walked over to Candace. He took the beer from her hands and placed it on the coffee table. He pulled her up and enclosed her in his arms. To his amazement she hugged him back. Her fingers locked around his muscular neck. Russell kissed her forehead softly, the bridge of her nose and her left, then right, cheek. He unlocked her hands from around his neck and took a step back. He lifted her right hand and twirled her under it as if they were ballroom dancing.

"There's no music, Russell," she chuckled.

"Yes, there is. Can't you hear it?"

She shook her head. "No."

"If you're in love, then you can hear it," he pulled her to him again. This time he kissed her lips. Candace pulled back and Russell followed her. His breath was hot and she felt his heart pulsating wildly. He gently pulled the hair clip form her ponytail and her hair cascaded down around her face. They looked into each other's eyes. Russell could see the uncertainty there. He embraced her again and buried his face in her hair.

"I'll never hurt you. Don't be afraid," He found her lips and kissed them gently before separating them with his tongue. He let his tongue explore the recesses or her mouth. He sucked slowly and softly enjoying her sweetness. She pulled away again and quickly, as if trying to keep her from thinking Russell's moist warm tongue found the canal of her ear. He could feel her melting. A soft moan escaped her lips and she moved in closer to him. Russell felt that if she let him make love to her tonight, she might feel different toward him, in a positive way thereafter. He had to be sure this was what she wanted, because he wanted no regrets in the morning.

"Can I have you tonight?" he whispered.

"Oh, Russell," she breathlessly whispered back. Her body trembled next to his as he unzipped her dress. It slipped off her shoulders and fell to the floor. Russell took in the length of her shapely body with his eyes and could hardly contain himself at her beauty. He ran his hands over as much of her as he could.

"You're so beautiful," he said.

Candace lowered her eyes to the floor and blushed.

"I want you so much, Candace." He took her hand and led her toward his bedroom. He unhooked her bra and she slipped her arms through the straps. He pulled her bikinis down past the full part of her hips and they fell to the floor. His hands cupped then massaged her full breast until he felt the nipples hardening. He placed his steamy mouth over her breast and rolled his tongue around her areola. His tongue teased her nipples until she moaned long and low. He walked her backwards to the bed and guided her down gently. His hands ran up the inner parts of her thighs until he found her soft warm spot. Without warning he explored her secret moist garden with his fingers keeping a perfect rhythm with the movements of her hips. He withdrew his wet fingers, then pressed his lips to hers and delved deeper and deeper into the hollow of her luscious mouth. He released her hold and pushed himself off her.

"What's wrong?" she asked as she reached for him.

Russell said nothing but walked back into the living room. Candace sat up in bed and watched him through the opened door. He turned the TV off and popped Maxwell's "Urban Hang Suite" into the CD player. After turning off the living room lamp, he found his way back to the bedroom in the dark. He turned on the nightstand lamp and saw Candace smiling at him. This was the moment he'd dreamed about for a long time. Now it was coming true. He began unbuttoning his Arrow shirt. He pulled it off in a flash, revealing the jungle of hair on his chest. He flexed his muscles as he threw the shirt in the corner of the room. He unbuckled his belt and unzipped his trousers. Candace noticed every movement he made. His hands seemed so powerful, but she knew they were very gentle. She followed the trousers as they slid down his masterful hairy legs. He stepped out of them and kicked them in the corner with the shirt. Candace could not take her eyes off the massive bulge in his briefs. She knew Russell was well built, but had no idea he looked this good underneath his clothes. She could hardly wait for the grand finale. He turned to face her and without taking his eyes off her face, he pulled down the briefs then stood straight and tall like a proud stallion. Candace was so enthralled she wished she had an Oscar, Emmy or Tony award to give him for his magnificent performance. He walked slowly to the bed with his majestic maleness leading the way. Candace lay back on the bed and held her arms open for him. Their lips found each other's again and their tongues stroked and sucked until she felt a wave of pleasure run over her body. She buried her face in his neck. He smelled so good, so manly. She was glad she had come over tonight, glad for the argument between Sable and Jonah, glad Russell kept pursuing her. She was just glad for all the occurrences that led up to this point.

"You know I care about you, don't you?" he said.

"I know you do."

"I want to please you, baby."

"And I want to please you, too."

He kissed her ears, neck and breasts until Candace thought she would go crazy with desire. She reached for his hard shaft and began massaging it.

"Mmm, girl" was all he said as his breathing became heavier. He lifted his full weight on to Candace and she welcomed him. She guided his erection into her secret folds. He was rock hard and she was equally hot. He entered her and she shivered.

"Russell…"

"Ooh, girl…"

Candace panted as he filled every inch of her. She wrapped her legs tighter around his waist as he thrust inward, then out. With each thrust came unimaginable excitement. They became harder and faster until she exploded in ecstasy. Seconds later Russell busted with pleasure he held her tightly then rolled over on his back and pulled her so close their forms looked like one body.

"You've made me so happy," he said breathlessly. He stroked her hair and waited for a reply.

"That was terrific, Russell."

"If you think that was something, I got some more stuff that will curl your toes," he whispered.

10

Confusions

"I wish you would stay with me the rest of the night." Russell made a sad face as he held tight to Candace hands. They stood outside her apartment door, whispering so they wouldn't wake anyone.

"The night is already gone." She held up her wrist so he could see that her watch read 3:30 in the morning. "I wanted to stay too, but my folks are here and I don't want them thinking ill thoughts about me."

"I understand." He hung his head and pretended to cry.

"Oh, cut it out." Candace slapped his hands. "I gotta go," she whispered.

"Can I see you tomorrow?" he asked.

"I just gotta spend some time with my dad," she patted his chest. "Please understand."

"That's cool."

She slid the key into the lock, twisted it open and stepped in backwards. Russell folded his hands in prayer formation under his chin and whispered, "Please stay with me." Candace smiled as she shook her head. She closed the door and locked it. When she looked through the peephole he was still standing there with his hands folded under his chin. She yanked open the door and gave him a quick kiss. Before she could step back in, he grabbed her and gave her a sensuous kiss.

"Goodnight, Candace."

"Goodnight. Drive carefully," she said, then closed the door. Candace got a light blanket from the linen closet and returned to the living room. She stepped out of her shoes and laid herself down on the couch and covered up with the blanket. Her whole body stilled tingled and she could smell Russell's cologne in her dress. She thought Russell was good buddy material, but never in a million years did she think he could turn her on like he did tonight. Russell wasn't Russell anymore; he was someone different now. He was desirable, sexy and he had brought out feelings she hadn't felt since her junior year of high school. Julian Reed had been her only true boyfriend then.

They were inseparable. She had given up her virginity to him and always thought they would marry. Then he went off to Howard University leaving her to complete her senior year. They had made a pact that she would join him at Howard the following year. She thought they would always be together but when the phone calls and visits home became seldom, she questioned him about his lackadaisical attitude. He blamed it all on tough courses. Said if he wanted to stay at Howard, he had to stay in the books, which didn't leave much time for anything else. Of course, Candace believed him. During homecoming festivities, she decided to surprise him with a visit. When she got there, she was the one who got the surprise. It seems that Julian had been spending most of his time studying a girl who was two years his senior and who had just been crowned Miss Howard University. Candace was so infuriated and hurt that she broke it off immediately. Two days later, Julian called apologizing. He said he never meant to hurt her and had planned to tell her the truth.

The transition from being a couple to being single was made easy when Julian decided not to rekindle their relationship.

Candace still remembered the pain and how it had cut her like a knife. It had taken every ounce of her dignity not to beg him to come back, but she was from proud stock and never resorted to begging. It was the hardest thing she'd done when she responded with a defiant "fine with me." After that, she never saw or heard from Julian again.

Now, here it seemed as though she was getting another chance at love. The ball was in her court and the shot was hers. Most women would have jumped hurdles at the chance to grab a prize like Russell. She analyzed her actions and came up with one conclusion, that the possibility of Russell dating Ophelia was a threat and although she didn't want him for herself she didn't want anyone else to have him. He was her spare tire.

"What have I done?" she voiced in the darkness of the room. How could I have slept with Russell of all people? How am I going to face him? She felt certain of losing her best friend now.

*   *   *

"I can't believe you done this," Wilson said as he walked around the car for the umpteenth time. It looked like smooth black gold. He could see an excellent reflection of himself in the sleek body of the car. He was afraid to touch it for fear of leaving handprints on it.

"Well, I did. Nothing's too good for my baby," C'mon, let's take this thing for a test drive." Jonah got in the driver's side and started the engine. The car purred like a kitten. He eased it out of the sales lot and onto the busy streets of Manhattan. It handled superbly. He turned on the stereo and pushed the volume up as high as it would go. It startled Wilson and he covered his ears.

"I don't think it's loud enough, Jonah," Wilson yelled teasingly.

"Just making sure everything works properly." He decreased the volume and tried out the CD and tape player with a disk and cassette he had gotten from Candace's Tercell. "The sound system seems to be pretty good."

"How much this set you back?" asked Wilson.

"About 22 G's."

"Twenty-two thousands dollars!" Wilson was utterly stunned. "Wow!" He rubbed the fine leather seats and inhaled the new-car smell. "You know what, Jonah?"

"What's that?"

"The smell of a new car is about the third best smell in the world."

"Oh, yeah?"

"Second, is the smell of good food cooking on the stove." Wilson watched Jonah, wanting him to ask for the number one best smell in the world. When he didn't ask right away, Wilson coaxed him along. "Go 'head and ask me what the best smell is," he grinned.

Jonah began laughing. "I remember you telling me a long time ago what it is. You don't have to tell me again."

"Naw, I'm 'ma tell you anyway 'cause I don't believe you know."

"All right then, what's the best smell in the world?"

Wilson leaned his head back on the head rest and closed his eyes and said, "The smell of woman right when she's…"

Jonah chimed in and they said the words "hot, bothered and ready" together. They both laughed.

"I guess Sable sort of disappointed you, huh?"

"Naw, why you say that?"

"Cause I know you. And, I tell you something else I know, too—I know Sable." He kept his eyes on Jonah, reading his expressions. She might not want you to know right off, but she was looking forward to your visit up here. You should have seen her last week. She was running 'round town like a chicken with its head cut off. Trying to prepare things for y'all." He fanned his hand agitatedly in the air. "Ah, shoot, she wasn't looking forward to seeing Aunt Vi much as she was seeing you."

He could tell by the way Jonah raised his right eyebrow that he had sparked an interest.

"Is that so?" Jonah replied, knowing that Sable held in her heart high regard for Aunt Elvira and that the remark was suited for Wilson's indifference towards her.

"Of course. That outfit she had on last night—new stuff. Even the perfume was new. I know 'cause I saw her when she was cutting the tags off. I said right then to myself, she was buying that stuff to impress you. You know yourself that you can't get Sable out of them jogging clothes she likes to wear."

"So it would be safe in me assuming that Sable is not seeing anyone in particular?"

"You real safe in saying that, Jonah. She still cares about you."

"She's the mother of my child, I'll always care for her too, Wilson. There's no doubt about that,"

"Personally, I wouldn't have anybody else for my son-in-law. You don't have to ask how I feel about you."

"I didn't know you felt that strongly about me, Wilson."

Wilson placed a hand on his shoulder and gave it two hard pats. "I care more than you'll ever know."

"Perhaps you and I should cut to the chase and marry each other."

Wilson gave him a questioning look before he realized Jonah was teasing. "If you were a little taller, maybe I'd consider it," Wilson chuckled.

"She getting ready to move way out there in Connecticut in that big ol' 10 room house. Don't get me wrong now; I like the idea of her getting out of New York, but what one person need with a house that big for? She don't keep the five rooms clean she got now. Candace don't want to move out there. She said so the other day. Wanna keep the apartment up and ain't even working nowhere. I told her it would be over my dead body if she stayed there by herself."

"All I can say to that, Wilson, is you have to have an acquired taste to want to live in New York. North Carolina is probably not up to her speed now, and inner city is too fast. I guess she found a medium in Connecticut. As for the big house, I can't really blame her for that. I mean if you're making the big bucks, why not spend it on the things you like. Lord knows, you can't take it with you." One thing Jonah could say about Wilson was that he had a knack about reading people. If he said Sable still cared for him, then she probably did. He quickly changed the subject. "I think Candace is going to love this car."

"I 'spect she will," added Wilson. 'It's not everyday a 22-year-old gets a free, brand new sports car."

Jonah traveled another two miles before he turned the car around and headed back to the dealership. The paper work had already been done back in North Carolina and all he had to do was sign the papers and hand over the check. He couldn't wait to see Candace's face tomorrow after graduation.

*   *   *

Shamell sat on the balcony of her four-story apartment overlooking Riverdale Park. It had been a quiet Saturday morning for her, and she thought she would edit some work before going to her aerobics class. She was quite amazed at the speed with which she was working. She took out a sheet of paper from a legal pad and began scribbling on it.

Angela,

Good work, Your last five chapters were written so realistically and with such clarity. You're improving immensely. P.S. If you keep going at this rate, you're going to put me out of a job. Then she wrote her initials under a smiling face. She placed the sheet on top of the first page of the manuscript and stuffed the papers back into the accordion folder labeled Angela Taylor. The next manuscript she pulled out was Sable's.

Shamell was a rare commodity at Alpha Publishing. Most of her counterparts never took the time to write notes explaining improper language usage or the reason why a paragraph, page or whole chapter had to be done over. Nor would they have added a note of encouragement. As long as they had something to correct they, knew they had a job. Shamell's remarkable bedside manner was due to the fact that she had taught English and literature in one of New York's toughest high schools for seven years. She was dedicated to the students and when they realized she had their best interests at heart and wasn't there just for the paycheck, they worked harder to excel. One year she was named teacher of the year. That same year, her students scored higher than they ever had on the standardized year-end test. It was because of her constant praise and morale boosting. She told them often that they could do and be anything they wanted, that they were loved, beautiful, intelligent and worth receiving all the good things that life had to offer. It was her daily affirmations that changed their perceptions about themselves. Shamell wrote a proposal and presented it to the school board. It introduced a plan for major corporations to get involved with high-risk students and provide them with tutoring and mentoring. It was so successful that most of the participating corporations started a scholarship fund for all students in 11th and 12th grades maintaining a "B" average and above. Eventually, the school made state headline news for achieving unexpected high-test scores. The school had ranked on the level with some of the local private schools. Honorable mention was given to Shamell for her ingenuity and outstanding work.

Not long after that, Alpha Publishing began recruiting her to come work for them. She had turned them down twice. The third time, they offered her double the salary she was making as a teacher and a benefit package fit for a king. The temptation proved too great and she accepted. That had been 10 years ago and she was still with Alpha. Shamell loved her job and found it totally gratifying. Even after so many years out of the classroom, she sometime missed the art of molding and shaping young minds, she missed the camaraderie between her and the students, and most of all she missed seeing the joy on her students' faces when they accomplished something they thought they couldn't. She knew she would never make the money she was making now if she had stayed in the teaching profession.

Charles was dean of the business department at New York University and his annual salary was very good. Their cars, a Porsche and Toyota 4Runner, were paid for; the monthly rent on the Manhattan high-rise was easy. They had a fairly decent nest egg put aside, and they had no children to prepare for college. He and Shamell had just purchased a vacation home in the Pocono Mountains. The vacation home had been his choice. Shamell was content with their annual two-week vacation to Hawaii or Bermuda. The Poconos were such an opposite of where they usually went for vacation. They had gone there on their fifth wedding anniversary and, as she remembered, Charles didn't make a big deal out of it then. So, when he started bringing tons of brochures home about available real estate, she questioned him.

"I hope you're not thinking about purchasing property in the Poconos," she said one day. "I wasn't that impressed with it that time we spent a week there. I don't think you were either."

"I liked it," he said, trying to sound convincing.

"Yeah, right, and I gotta a bridge in Brooklyn I want to sell you real cheap."

"C'mon and take a look at these." Charles spread the pamphlets and brochures on the kitchen table.

"I don't need to see them Charles. I've been there, remember?"

"Why are you trying to be so difficult? A second home would be just the thing for us."

"A second home is senseless. Second homes are for wealthy folks."

"We're wealthy. You know we can afford it."

"We're comfortable. That's a far cry from being wealthy. Besides, I don't want a mortgage on a house I'll only stay in two, maybe three, weeks out the year."

"Don't you ever get tired of going to the same place all the time?"

"No. We have fun when we go and there's always plenty to do."

"There's more to life than the Caribbean and Hawaii."

"You may be right, but it certainly isn't the Poconos."

Charles threw his hands in the air. "I see I can't get through to you right now, so when you come around to your senses, we can talk." He walked off to the bedroom. Minutes later Shamell found him in his pajamas lying on the bed watching TV. She hated him this way. She eased in the bed beside him and started kissing his neck. He jerked away from her, rolled over on his side and clicked off his nightstand lamp.

"Good night," he said peevishly.

"So it's like that, huh?"

Charles said nothing.

"Charles, you're acting real childish."

"Shamell, I'm trying to sleep, if you don't mind."

"All right, mister. Two can play your game." She yanked open the dresser and grabbed her nightgown. "I'll be sleeping in the guest room until you get over your little tantrum."

Charles remained distant for two solid weeks. He treated her as if she was diseased. He left rooms when she came in, declined when she offered to make dinner, saying he had plans to eat elsewhere. They became two ships passing in the night. Sunday into the third week of Charles' avoidance, Shamell could take no more. She got up early and fixed his favorite breakfast. Cheese omelets and French toast. She placed the omelets and French toast on the Lenox china and poured orange juice into the Waterford stemware. She placed everything along with a single red rose on a bed tray and took it to the bedroom. Charles was curled up on his right side sleeping soundly. Shamell eased the tray down on her vacant side of the bed and called his name softly. "Charles." He stirred a little. She called him again, this time shaking his shoulders. "Charles, honey, I fixed you some breakfast." He grunted and said something she could not understand. Shamell leaned over and kissed his face. Charles turned himself over to face her. "What," he said, still half sleep.

"I said I fixed you your favorite breakfast." The delicious aroma drifted under his nose and he sat up in bed. Before he could say anything, Shamell began talking. "Baby, I don't want us to continue this way. I'm lonely without you. Let's call a truce."

Charles avoided eye contact and crossed his arms over his chest.

"I've been looking at the brochures you brought home."

Charles sneaked a peek at her. "You have?"

Shamell moved closer to him. "Yes, and I realized that I may have been a little too hasty in dismissing you. I should have heard you out."

"And."

"And, I'm willing to sit down with you and discuss the pros and cons of possibly purchasing property there."

Charles patted her knee. "Mell, you know I wouldn't force you to do anything you didn't feel comfortable with. I really think this purchase would be a plus in our lives."

"I know," she said, as she sat beside him thinking just the opposite. Truth be told, she was being forced. She could either go along with his plans or receive the cold-shoulder treatment from him indefinitely. "We'll talk about it later, but now let's eat before everything gets cold." They ate breakfast and then made love the better part of the morning.

The incident had happened six months ago. In those six months they had purchased a five-room rustic log cabin. It sat on a wooded hillside overlooking a babbling stream that ran from Lake Wallenpaupack. Since it was located in a popular vacation area where fishing, hunting and skiing were accessible, Charles suggested that they rent the cabin out sometimes, especially during the winter months when skiing was popular.

Shamell sat quietly looking down at the people in the park. She mainly paid attention to the couples. Some were jogging together, a few on roller-blades and others walking. She spotted a couple lying on a blanket under a maple tree. The guy had his head in the girl's lap, and it looked as though she was feeding him ice cream from a cone. She remembered the days when she and Charles use to do those things. Here lately everything was work and no play. The newness of purchasing the property had worn off, and Charles was back to his old ways. Last night he didn't come home until 1 o'clock in the morning. She started to question him on his whereabouts but decided against it.

She wondered if he was having an affair. The first time she had asked him that question he angrily denied it, stating that the pressures of the job and the workload required him to work extra hours. So each time the thought came to Shamell's mind, she pushed it out.

She flipped through the pages of Sable's most recent chapter. Other than a few misspelled words and punctuation misuses, everything else looked good. She wrote a quick note:

Sable, This is going to be another best seller. The affair between the boss and his secretary's daughter is just the right twist this book needs. Keep up the good work. S.A.

11

Graduation Surprises

Candace pulled the pin from the last mesh roller. The lock of hair sprang loose and unraveled from around the roller. She picked up the wide-tooth comb and began combing the soft, bouncy jet-black curls until she had her hair styled the way she wanted it. Satisfied with her appearance from the neck up, she had yet to decide between the gold wrap dress that stopped at mid-thigh or the smart-looking cream crepe pants suit. Did she want to look sexy or smart? Since she was receiving her college degree today and that alone said enough about her intelligence, she decided to go with the dress. She sprayed on some Bijan perfume, then picked up the dress off the bed. She slipped it on over her bra and panties. The dress was lined and she was grateful a slip wasn't needed. The graduation gown was to go over that and she didn't want to get too hot. She opted not to wear stockings and slipped her feet into the black patent-leather three-inch pumps. Candace stood before the full-length mirror that hung on the back of her closet door and surveyed herself. She did a mirthful jig and smiled at her reflection. "Now for jewelry." There was nothing she thought suitable in her jewelry box to go with the dress. "Ma! I need to borrow some earrings!" she said heading towards Sable's bedroom.

Sable was busy applying her make-up. She wasn't too keen on lending jewelry out to Candace because, like everything else she borrowed, it rarely got back to its rightful place. But Sable made up in her mind that today would be Candace's day in all rights. She had no intention of going against the grain. "Look on my dresser and see what you can find." She looked at Candace and nodded her head in approval. "You look very nice, dear. You need some large gold earrings to go with that outfit and you know I don't wear large jewelry"

She stomped her foot. "Shoot, what am I going to put on my ears?"

"What about those gold-button style earrings? They'll go good."

"You're right. I'll have to wear them, I guess. They're so old though."

"No one will know they're old but you. They'll go fine."

Candace trotted back to her room and put the earrings on. Sable was right; they looked great. Jonah appeared in the doorway and leaned against the door joist. He said nothing but smiled as he watched his only child ready herself to take the final step from what had been a protected world into the undeniably real and frequently cruel world. He knew she was so cavalier and that she faced a rude awakening. She already had two strikes against her—she was a female and she was black. His heart wrenched and he swallowed hard to hold back the lump rising in his throat. He eased his hands into his pockets and felt the keys to the Camaro. He felt a bit of relief knowing he was going to give her some joy on this day. Candace looked up and found Jonah standing in the doorway.

"Daddy, you scared me."

"Can I come in?"

Candace chuckled. "It's your room while you're here. Thanks for letting me dress in it."

Jonah sat on the edge of the bed. "You look fantastic."

"Thanks, Dad."

"Look just like your momma at that age."

"Yeah, I've seen pictures of her when she was younger, and we do favor."

Jonah looked at the floor not knowing exactly what to say next. "I wish I could have changed things, Candace."

"Changed what daddy?"

"Being here for you." He blinked away a tear.

Candace sat next to him on the bed.

"Oh, Daddy. You were a good father to me and still are. Sure, I missed not having you close, but you were only a phone call away. I always felt lucky. A few of my friends in school don't even know their fathers. I know I wouldn't have turned out any different if you and Mom had stayed together."

Jonah's mind flashed back to his childhood years. He remembered how his mother single-handedly raised five children. At the break of dawn, she'd start work at the cotton mill and many evenings wouldn't return home until dusk. Jonah was living testimony to what Candace had said. He turned out well and was doing fine financially. Jonah stood to leave. "By the way, been meaning to tell you. I like that young man you had over Friday night."

The statement had caught her off guard. She didn't know how to reply.

"He's a good friend, that's all."

Jonah pointed his index finger and shook it at Candace. "He's a good one. I can tell." He whistled an upbeat tune as he left the room.

*   *   *

Austin wore only a tee shirt and jogging shorts as he sat on the top-grain leather sofa reading a dissected piece of the Manhattan Times newspaper. The radio was tuned to WJAM 97.5 FM, and Mitch Mitchell was dejaying his heart out. Austin enjoyed the luxury of reading the newspaper and listening to the radio uninterrupted on Sunday mornings. He was on his second cup of coffee when he heard

Mitch extend a hearty congratulation to the graduating class of New York University.

"May the wind always be at your backs and the sun shining upon your faces. You did it and congratulations. For all interested in attending, commencement will be held this afternoon at 1 o'clock in the Kennedy Civic Center."

Austin jumped from his relaxed position, spilling some of the hot coffee on his bare legs. Even thought it burned, he was too excited about the possibility of seeing Candace again to concentrate on the pain. He knew there was something important he had put on his mental agenda, but had forgotten. He walked to the kitchen and put the mug in the sink. It was 11:30. "I got an hour and 30 minutes," he said to himself as he raced toward the linen closet and grabbed a king size towel from the shelf. It wasn't until he had stepped under the shower of warm spraying water that he realized it might be out of place for him to go to Candace's graduation. She appeared slightly disappointed that day in his office when he had rejected her, but a sixth sense told him she was more than slightly disappointed with him. Austin couldn't blame her. He had not been truthful with her. He had told her she wasn't what they were looking for when in fact she was ideal for AFLAME. Austin knew that if Beverly Houser, the other account executive/talent scout, had been there that day, she would have hired Candace right there on the spot.

Austin could tell at first glance that she had exactly what they were looking for in a model. She was loaded with potential. She could do runway, photo shoots, hand commercial, hair—the whole nine yards—but the problem was she was too much like Maoma. To let her come work at AFLAME would be like scratching at the scab of a healing wound. He just couldn't do that to himself again. Anyway, he was assuming she didn't have a love interest. Someone as attractive as Candace had to have someone interested in her. She would be with her family and that special person on this most important day of her life. It would be better if he not go. He stepped out of the shower and wrapped the towel around himself. He would fix a pasta salad and maybe later on call his family in Dar es Salaam.

*   *   *

Shamell, Aunt Elvira and Wilson sat sandwiched between Sable and Jonah. Russell sat on the other side of Jonah. They each passed happy glances back and forth as the chancellor called the name Alice Brockton. They knew from their programs that Candace would be next. Sable's stomach quivered as she gave thought to the image of Candace tripping over her three-inch heels and falling face first into the floor. She leaned over and whispered her fears into Shamell's ear. "I hope she doesn't fall."

"Girl, she's as graceful as a gazelle," Shamell said. "Stop worrying."

Candace's full name was called and she walked across the stage as balanced and elegant as any prized model would have done on a cat-walk. When the chancellor handed her diploma, she looked over her shoulder and flashed her pearly whites before the applauding audience and the high-powered 35-millimeter camera she knew Jonah had aimed at her. Candace blew a kiss at section G-22 where her family sat, and then she raised both arms in the air and shook the bogus piece of paper that represented the diploma.

From the platform Candace could see her family standing and cheering. She even heard a loud whistle she knew was coming from Russell. Sable and Jonah beamed with pride. Jonah reached across the three in the middle and grabbed Sable's hand. He gave it a tight squeeze and she gently squeezed back.

The corridor was sprinkled with people of all different shapes, sizes and colors. Bodies in long black robes hugged, kissed and congratulated each other in passing. Flashes from cameras lit the narrow passage like lightning in a southern summer sky. Candace family stood in a huddle doting over her, each person trying to hold or touch her. Their voices ran together, lifting above their heads. Each person talked at the same time and no one was really listening to the other. Together, they sounded like a flock of geese.

"Were you nervous, baby?" asked Sable.

"Course she was nervous. All them kids was," replied Wilson.

"Look like a doll baby, sugah," said Aunt Elvira.

"Sable just knew you were going to fall in those shoes. I told her you had it all under control and you sure did, girlfriend," said Shamell.

"I'm so proud of you," said Jonah.

"Me, too," said Russell.

"Candace Renee Brooks," said an unfamiliar baritone voice.

Everyone turned to see the tall, dark, handsome stranger. He was immaculately dressed and held a single red rose in one hand.

Candace was speechless as she looked into the face of Austin Kawissopie. She wore a dumbfounded expression on her face. Austin handed her the rose. She accepted it hesitantly as a thousand questions ran through her mind. She wondered what he was doing here.

Austin read her mind and smiled his heart-winning smile, hoping to ease her tension. He looked from Candace to each person standing in the semicircle then introduced himself simply as Austin Kawissopie. Jonah cleared his throat and came to Candace's rescue. He extended his hand. "I'm Jonah Brooks, Candace's father."

As if queued, Sable extended her hand as well and introduced herself. Then everyone followed suit until it was Russell's turn. He eyed Austin skeptically and reluctantly offered his hand before speaking.

"I'm Russell Ingram, her friend." But, what he really wanted to say was; she's my lady and I'm her man so step off, Jack! Russell knew by his accent that he was the "African Chief in Charge" from AFLAME. He believed Austin had a hidden agenda that included Candace. He sent a subtle warning by gripping his hand tightly and holding it longer than normal.

"I met Candace the other day and I wanted to come by, congratulate her and wish her the best in her future endeavors."

Candace remained speechless, unable to grasp the moment and rationalize what was going on. She thought he had to be a complete idiot for coming here like they were old friends. He was in her territory now, and she had a good mind to curse him out. If her family wasn't standing around, she believed she would have. Her expression turned murderous. Even though she was mad enough to spit fire, she held what was left of her composure as best she could.

"Mr. Kawissopie, I thank you for the rose, but if you will excuse us we have dinner reservations and we must get going."

Acting the part of a teenager, Shamell nudged Sable in the side. She along with everyone else sensed the resentment Candace had for this man and she couldn't wait to hear the whole story.

"Yes, I understand, don't mean to hold you," he said politely. He took a single step backward and nodded his head once.

Candace turned sharply and began walking away. Her family followed mumbling curiously among themselves.

"Excuse me once more," Austin called.

Everyone turned around. Austin's hand reached inside his suit jacket and pulled out a card.

"Candace, I would like you to give my office a call regarding your inquiry on last Monday if you are still interested. Enjoy your day, everyone." He turned and walked down the long corridor and was gone as quickly as he had appeared.

Candace felt flushed. She looked at the card. The mere thought of this tall, dark, exotic African prince wanting her sent excitement rushing through her body. All eyes were on her, but she especially felt Russell's questioning stare. She felt as thought she had betrayed him even thought she'd done nothing wrong—yet.

*   *   *

The Cut Above Restaurant was packed to capacity. Sable was glad she had made the reservations in advance. It was a popular eatery and from time to time some of the tabloids were lucky enough to get a picture of a celebrity dining there. The waiter sat them in the center of the restaurant at a table large enough to accommodate eight people. Sable ordered two bottles of champagne. Sable was the first to stand and make a toast. "Sweetheart, you have been a joy in my life from the first day you squeezed your narrow behind out of my body." Everyone laughed. "We've had our ups and downs and I'm sure there will be many more, but I know we'll work through them as usual. I know you get tired of me babying you, but honey, you are and always will be my little angel. I have something here I want you to have. Great thought has gone into this gift. I hope you will use it wisely as you prepare for your future." She handed Candace the envelope. Candace opened it and pulled out a simple white card with the words "I love you" in bold print. She opened it and saw the check written in the amount of $10,000. The card and check fell out of her hands onto the table. "Oh, Momma! Tears welled in the corners of her eyes. Shamell handed her a napkin to wipe the tears. Candace dabbed at her eyes. She pushed back from her chair and ran to Sable. She hugged her tight and long then, kissed her cheek leaving a trace of lipstick.

Wilson clanged the spoon against his wine goblet to get everyone's attention. "Now it's my turn." He slid the armless chair back and stood. "I remember the day they brought you home from the hospital. Jonah called me and Loretta. Wanted us to meet them at the house. They were bringing you home. Loretta was so excited she had me packing up all these stuffed toys and baby clothes you couldn't even wear yet. When we got to the house you were nestled in your momma's arms all snug and warm. Loretta loved herself some Candy. That's what she use to call you," Wilson told Candace. "Anyhow, I still remember that day like it was yesterday. It's hard to believe that was 22 years ago. Your grandma is so proud. I know she's watching from heaven. You go on and be that model you been talking about. You got what it takes." Wilson pulled an envelope from his pocket and handed it to her. "It can't touch the gift your momma gave you, but I believe you can use this."

Candace tore open the envelope and saw the crisp $1,000 bill. "Granddaddy, I can't take this. It's too much," she said, handing the envelope back to Wilson.

"Now Candace, don't give me a hard time 'bout this. I know what I'm doing. It's the least I can do for my only grandchild."

"But you're on a fixed income, I can't…"

"I'm doing fine, trust me. I got more than I need."

Candace leaned across the space that separated them and hugged Wilson. Aunt Elvira heaved her heavy purse onto the table making it shake slightly. She pulled out a neatly wrapped box and handed it to Candace.

"Mine is simple but it's from my heart. It's from my heart."

Candace opened it and squealed in delight. "Oh Aunt Vi, how did you know? This is only my favorite perfume in the world," She picked up a butter knife from her place setting and slit the cellophane wrap. She sprayed a little bit on her already Bijan-scented body, then sprayed some on Aunt Vi.

"Child, please! I only wear "Here's My Heart.""

Candace knew Aunt Elvira was an Avon die-hard. "This is perfect, Aunt Vi." She grabbed her hand, squeezed, then kissed it. "Thank you."

Russell cleared his throat as he stood. He raised his glass to make a toast. "I just want to say thanks for your friendship and that I'm very happy for you. I wish you all the happiness in the world. I have something I want to give you. He handed her a small gift-wrapped box. She took it, avoiding eye contact with him as he continued to speak. She placed the box down on the table facing her, then placed her hands in her lap. Everyone looked at the box, then at Candace.

"Open it, baby!" said Aunt Elvira.

Candace looked at Russell. He seemed proud of whatever it was in the box. She was afraid to open it. Afraid because she didn't know what was in it and afraid it might be something non-practical. She was afraid that it would tell the secret of their little 'affaire de coeur' the other night. If it was a gift that told the secret, she was afraid that her family would verbally approve of it, making Russell just that more persistent in his quest to make her his woman. Her hands shook visibly. She blew out a taut puff of air and laugh nervously. She opened the box and found a navy colored velvet case. Inside the case was a beautiful gold bracelet. There were two interlocking hearts etched on the outside. She could see that something was inscribed on the inside.

"Oh, how beautiful," said Sable and Shamell simultaneously.

"Look like that sat you back a pretty penny, son." Wilson winked openly at Candace, who wore a faint smile.

"Is it real?" asked Aunt Elvira, looking at Russell through the thick coke-bottle lenses.

"Aunt Vi!" said Sable.

"Well, is it?" asked Wilson.

Russell found no offense and laughed at the humor of Aunt Elvira and Wilson.

"Yes, it's real." He liked Candace's family. They were much like his own home-grown, down-to-earth folks. They didn't chew their words. Candace held the bracelet in her hand as if it had the fragility of an egg.

"It's very lovely, Russell. Thank you." She placed it back in the rectangular velvet case.

"Read the inside," said Russell.

Candace picked it up again and read it silently. It read: To *a woman who has touched my very soul in ways I thought not possible. LOVE ALWAYS!* The bracelet was lovely to her, but she had to dramatize now—had to pretend she really liked the idea of it coming from Russell. She knew without a doubt that Friday night had been a mistake. She had let her libido take charge, and it had landed her in this awkward situation. She had to admit Russell was quite a fellow, but she wanted more out of life than a mere postal worker. It was hard to even look at him without thinking about last Friday night. Her flesh tingled, and she had to concentrate to stay focused on what was going on now.

"What does it say?" asked Aunt Elvira.

"Now, Vi, that's business between these young folks," said Wilson.

"Thank you," Candace said and placed the bracelet back in its case. "It's exquisite."

Discreetly, Sable shot Candace a baleful look. "Try it on dear," she said.

"Not now, Mom." Candace tried to change the subject. "I'm hungry; where is the waiter?"

"This is a fine restaurant, honey, and good things take time," said Shamell. "Anyway, you got two more gifts to open before you can think about eating. Here, girlfriend." Shamell pushed a medium-sized box across the table. It was neatly wrapped with two ribbons that crossed each other and came together into a large bow at the top.

The CHANNEL calfskin handbag was styled in bittersweet brown with bronze hardware. It was a hit with Candace and was one of the things she had always wanted but couldn't afford. Even the really good imitation CHANNEL handbags were out of her range. After the thank yous were said, Jonah stood. He raised his goblet in the air and paused a moment before speaking. Sable thought he was choking on tears, and she lowered her head until she heard his first words.

"What can I say that hasn't already been said?" he asked briefly. "I'm elated and proud. Just like Wilson said, you are model material. A week ago, I called to get an idea of what you might want for your graduation. Wilson laughed as he told me of you trying to coax your mother into buying you another car." He pulled the car key from his pants pocket and held it out to her. "This is the key to your new midnight black with gold stripes Camaro."

Candace's eyes widened and her mouth dropped. She twisted around, hoping to see the car parked outside the restaurant's window. Sable was clearly surprised and stared at Jonah unbelievingly.

"Where is it daddy?" Candace pushed herself from the table and stood.

Jonah chuckled. "Now hold your horses, kid. Maybe we should eat first."

"Daddy! If you make me wait another minute, I'll die from curiosity."

"In that case, I guess I have no other choice but to let you see it." Jonah motion for the waiter then handed him the parking receipt for the Camaro. "Will you have the valet bring this car around front please?"

Candace could not believe her eyes as she sat behind the wheel of the sporty car. "Oh, thank you, Daddy. I just can't believe it! This is the happiest day of my life. Everything is happening just the way I hoped.

Russell watched an ecstatic Candace and could not help but wonder about the mysterious way Austin had appeared and offered her the modeling job he had denied her several days earlier. He wanted to know why—what was the real reason he had come to the graduation? He felt threaten by his grand appearance and status. He was a black man holding a high position at a leading modeling agency. He had to have credentials up the yin-yang. He was a gentleman's gentleman. There was no way he could compete with him and he suspected Candace's last remark included Austin.

*   *   *

Russell and Candace sat at the restaurant table after everyone else had left. Candace looked at the car's remote control key-chain.

"That's a good device. Every woman needs one," said Russell.

"Yeah. I'm going to have to take a course on how to use all of these control switches."

"You'll learn in no time." Russell scooted his chair closer to Candace and slipped his arms around her. "Well, tell me how do you feel now that you are certifiably declared brilliant?"

Candace smiled. "The same way."

Russell said nothing as he stared into her eyes.

"Russell," she said trying to wiggle away from his powerful arms.

"What?" he asked, sniffing her neck. "You smell good."

"Come on, we need to free up this table."

"I can dig it." He winked at her and pushed back from the table. "Let's say we go by my place?" He said letting his voice sound deep, smooth and seductive.

"I don't think so, Russell. I'm kinda tired."

Russell chuckled. "I got a remedy for that." He nuzzled his nose in her ear just before she shrugged her shoulder to fend him off.

"What's wrong with you?" Russell was totally baffled by her actions, which were in absolute contrast to the night before. "The day is young. I know we gon' kick it, just you and me, right?"

"What are you talking about?"

"You know exactly what I'm talking about," then he whispered passionate words in her ear.

Candace broke away from his grip. "Russell, I think we need to talk." She slid her chair away and looked at him seriously.

"Uh, oh. I don't know if I like the way you said that." Russell exhaled loudly, folded his arms and leaned back in his chair. "Lets' have it."

"I think we're moving too fast," she said, averting her eyes from his and feeling guilty for letting it go as far as it had.

"We're moving too fast?"

"Yeah. I mean we slept together. I didn't mean for us to...."

"Wait-a-minute, just hold-up now! What are you saying? I thought you were ready. I asked you that night if you were and you said yes."

"No! I didn't say yes. I—I didn't say anything...."

"You didn't say anything. That's true 'cause you didn't have to say anything; your actions said yes."

"Yes—no—I mean I got caught up in the moment. Russell, our friendship is too precious to lose."

"Our friendship is the bond that will hold us together," he paused, then began laughing. "Oh! I see. Yeah, I see what you did now. You played me."

"Nooo, Russell, no. I wouldn't do a thing like that and you know it!"

"You needed to get yo' lil' freak on, and now that you did you want to diss me off like some worn shoe."

"Please don't say that." She reached to touch his arm and he snatched it away.

"And don't you think I'm so naive that I don't know what Kunta Kente wants?"

"What?"

"You know what. That dude showing up at your graduation like that. Then offering you a job."

"I can't be exactly sure he wants to offer me a job, not until I check it out."

"Oh, so you really gon' check it out?"

"Yes!"

"The dude tells you the other day you ain't got what it takes to cut it in the business; then a few days later he changes his mind. Don't that seem fishy to you Candace, or you just want the job so bad you don't care?"

"Wait a minute now!"

"Naw, sister, you wait. Let me ask you one thing. Do you want to take this relationship to the next level?"

Candace sat dumbfounded, not wanting to blatantly hurt him anymore than she already had.

"O.K., let me put it to you this way then. Do you want to be with me or not?"

Candace closed her eyes and lowered her head. "I'm so sorry, Russell. If I had known our being together was going to cause such a fray, I never would have led you on."

"If everybody had hindsight, the world would be a perfect place, now wouldn't it?" He got up from his chair. "Get your stuff."

Candace hesitantly obeyed. She gathered the gifts in her arms and followed Russell out of the restaurant. The valet brought the Camaro around and Candace slid behind the steering wheel. She stole a culpable glance at Russell.

"Lock up and go home, Candace," he shoved his hands into his pants pockets.

"Russell?"

"Gone on home, Candace."

Candace handed him the small gift box with the bracelet in it. "I guess you want this."

"I'm not an Indian giver. I bought it for you, it's yours." Russell stood expressionless as Candace started the Camaro and pulled away from the restaurant. She was unaware of her fingernails piercing the palms of her hands as she tightly gripped the steering wheel. On the most wonderful day of her life she felt awful.

12

Trapped in This Thing Called Love

Jonah sat opposite Sable at the breakfast table while Wilson and Aunt Elvira fussed over preparing breakfast. Sable looked up from her part of the morning newspaper at Jonah. "Can I get you more coffee while we sit here starving for breakfast?" she teased.

"No, I'm down to one cup a day, believe it or not."

Sable raised an eyebrow. "Hmm, I thought you were drinking less coffee since you've been here. Never thought you'd give up your caffeine though."

"Had to. Started staying edgy all the time. Went to see the doctor and he told me to lay off the caffeine."

Sable laughed.

"What?"

"I use to have to threaten you into seeing the doctor."

"Well, I had you to take care of me then. Now, I have to take care of me."

"Looks like you're doing a good job of it."

"The position is up for hire for anyone who's interested."

Sable averted her eyes back to the paper and pretend to read. "I'm sure you have a lot of applicants waiting in line for a shot at that wonderful job." They both laughed.

"What's so funny over there?" asked Wilson.

"We made a bet who'd die first of starvation," answered Jonah.

"I would've been finished by now if it wasn't for Wilson. He all in my way. Trying to add cheese to the grits while they half-done. You put cheese in grits after they finished cooking; that way they don't turn out gummy."

"I figured since you toothless you'd appreciate my goodwill."

"I got teeth! They may not be original, but they work just fine. I came in here to help you since you can't cook no-how. Mess up everything you touch."

"Vi, don't you know that some of the world's greatest cooks are men?"

"I don't doubt that, but you ain't one of 'em."

Jonah and Sable laughed so hard that Sable wiped away tears and Jonah held his side. They both knew that even though the two claimed not to like each other, deep down inside they did. Jonah and Sable's laughter only fueled their buffoonery and they kept taking cracks at each other until Candace came into the kitchen. She was dressed to kill in an above the knee, magenta, dress and matching sling back pumps. Her hair was in a French roll instead of the cascading curls. She was a bit more conservative than she was on her initial visit to AFLAME, but then she didn't feel she had to sell herself as hard now.

"Good morning, everybody." She pulled the half-gallon of orange juice from the refrigerator.

"Don't you look fine this morning," said Aunt Elvira.

"Thanks. I gotta hurry. I'm running late."

"Aren't you going to eat something first?" asked Sable.

"I don't have time. I'm going to AFLAME. Besides, I been eating too much as it is."

"Oh, Lord, don't start that diet bit again," said Wilson.

"Granddaddy I've gained five pounds since you've been here. Now that's just five more I gotta lose."

Everyone grew quiet. Jonah and Sable went back to reading the newspaper. Wilson and Aunt Elvira busied themselves with finishing breakfast. Each of them secretly felt uneasy about Austin since meeting him last afternoon. Jonah felt this older and no doubt experienced man had a hidden agenda.

"What happened to taking some time off to catch up on your rest?" asked Sable.

"Mom, that was before I knew Austin—I mean Mr. Kawissopie wanted to see me. You know how bad I want this. An opportunity like this doesn't come around every day."

"Honey, I know. I just don't understand why this man all of a sudden is interested in you."

"He came to his senses," Candace laughed. "Gotta go." She blew four kisses and was out the door.

Aunt Elvira stood stirring the pot of grits. She looked at Wilson. "I got a bad feeling 'bout this. I might be wrong, but I got a bad feeling."

*   *   *

AFLAME was busier than it had been last Monday. Tall, beautiful girls grazed the reception area. Some were getting job assignments from Phyllis, others were scheduled for meetings, and some of the girls were there for interviews. Candace could tell the interviewees. They were the ones who sat wringing their hands and looking into their compact mirrors every 10 minutes. Candace noticed that most of the girls she suspected as being AFLAME models were larger than she was. One of the girls received three assignments from Phyllis. She looked as if she wore a size 11 or 12 dress. Seeing these "larger than model" size girls made Candace wonder even more about Austin's intentions. She remembered

Russell's warning and how Sable thought it strange too that he would have sudden interest in her. She remembered the look on her family faces when Austin introduced himself. It was the look of total suspicion. On last Monday he had made such an issue about weight. Candace began to second-guess her being there. She asked herself if this was a set-up for another letdown? Maybe Austin was at the graduation yesterday to see someone else and he'd just happened to run into her. Perhaps out of politeness he invited her to come back for another interview and she wasn't supposed to accept his invitation. Her mind was clouded with questions.

Phyllis' phone buzzed and she heard the dreadlocks-hair girl say her name into the receiver. Soon the door to Austin's office opened and out stepped a brown-skinned beauty in a low-cut blouse and short-short skirt.

"Tit and tail," Candace mumbled to herself. Her eyes were a brilliant blue. And as she got closer, Candace could tell they were contacts. Candace could not understand why women altered themselves. White women turned themselves dark and had their lips and butts injected for fullness and black women bleached their skin, hair and changed their eye color. Once she saw a very dark-skinned woman with dyed blond hair and blue contacts. Candace remembered thinking the woman would have been pretty if she had not changed herself so drastically. Candace was proud of her rich, dark skin and never once considered using bleaching creams.

Austin stepped out of his office. He searched the receptionist area until he spotted Candace. He smiled a broad smile and Candace thought he was more handsome than he was the first time she'd laid eyes on him. With extended hands, Austin walked toward her. Candace raised to her feet and the two shook hands.

"Good morning, Candace."

"Good morning."

"Phyllis told me you called. I'm glad you did. Come this way."

Austin led her into his office. "Have a seat." Austin eased down into his high-back chair. He opened her file and began to read what he already had memorized. Her portfolio rested across her lap as she waited for the first question. Candace thought he seemed a little nervous, a contrast to his demeanor last Monday.

"First, let me congratulate you again on your graduation. It was a beautiful ceremony."

"Thank you."

"I hope I didn't detain you and your family too long."

"No, you didn't. As a matter of fact, our table was ready and waiting when we got there."

"Good. Let's discuss the kind of modeling you're interested in. You know the field is wide. Here at AFLAME, we deal mostly with photo shoots and runway. Occasionally we do other things like advertising. Now, a few of our models do the whole nine yards, photo, runway, advertising, and benefits. Some have even done movies. They are the top models. One to name is Twila Jackson. If you remember I mentioned her last time you were here. She has come a long way. Would you believe she came to us at the age of 15?

Candace was amazed. Austin pushed the button of the intercom system. "Phyllis."

"Yes, sir."

"Would you bring me Twila's file please."

"Yes, sir."

"We like to start all our models out doing photo shoots and let them progress from there."

The door opened and Phyllis brought the thick green hang file to Austin.

"Anything else?"

"That's all. Thank you, Phyllis." He pulled an 8-by-10 glossy from its contents and handed it to Candace.

"Gosh, that must have been eons ago."

The Twila in the photo barely resembled the Twila now. She looked so young. Austin handed her another photo that portrayed a matured Twila.

"Now this looks more like her."

"Would you believe both the pictures were taken the same day? One is with make-up; the other is without."

"Actually that was five years ago. You see, life in this business starts young. Some say the younger the better, but I don't fully agree with that concept. If a woman is 60 years old and looks good, has the qualities to sell beauty to other 60-year-olds, then she has what it takes to work here. I strongly believe that is one of the reasons why AFLAME is as successful as it is. We don't limit ourselves."

"You mean you have models that old?"

"We certainly do, but not many. Let's see," he said, as he reclined back into the chair.

Candace thought he seemed more at ease as he got into the flow of the conversation.

"Our models range in age from six months to 65 years old."

"That is impressive."

"Hold up your hands," he asked getting out the chair and walking around to the corner of his desk.

"Sir?"

He sat down on the corner of his desk facing Candace.

"Give me your hands."

Candace placed her hands into his and waited for him to explain. They were soft and her fingers were long and slender. Her clear nails were not too long but the perfect length.

"Mmm, hmm, beautiful." He pulled a piece of paper from another folder and gave it to her.

"Take a look at that and tell me what you think."

It was a request and contract from a leading soap company for a dish suds advertisement.

"They need a model to advertise their soap product. You will be modeling your hands."

Candace knew he definitely wanted her for the job and a rush of excitement ran over her body.

"The advertisement will be featured in Ebony, Jet and Essence magazines just to name a few."

Candace's eyes widened as she read while listening to Austin talk. She envisioned her hands up against her face in the popular magazines. Suddenly her elation spiraled and she began frowning.

"This can't be right," she said.

"Ah, I see you're disappointed in the salary."

"I thought models made more than this."

"You're partly correct. Models can make a lot of money—some, an awful lot. Those are the ones who've been in the business long enough to make a name for themselves. I couldn't send a high-fashion model to do this job because it wouldn't be worth her time. This shot does not require face capture. That's the reason the pay is not what you'd expected." He studied Candace for a while. "Talk to me; tell me what you think."

"Mr. Kawissopie, I don't mean any disrespect and I don't want you to think I'm an ingrate, but I was hoping for a little more exposure."

"A little more exposure?"

"Yes, because if you read my portfolio thoroughly you'll see that I've been to several schools to prepare me for a career in this business. I never thought about modeling body parts."

"I understand." Austin reached for the paper and slipped it back into the folder.

"Like I told you last time, this is not an easy business. You have to ask yourself how much you want it. Most all our models started with small jobs. Frankly, Candace, I don't know what to tell you other than I wish you'd give it a try. Don't let the money be a deterrent. If you're meant to be in this profession, money will come later."

Candace looked into his eyes and for a brief moment he looked as if he was pleading her to come work for AFLAME.

"Mr. Kawissopie, may I ask you something that has been on my mind?"

"Of course."

"When I came here last Monday, you showed no interest in me. Now…"

"Yes, I know what you're going to say." He got up and returned to his chair. He clasped his hands together with the two index fingers rubbing against his lips.

"People make mistakes. They pass judgments that are totally unfounded. I think I may have done that to you the other day. I'm just grateful that you took me up on my offer and came back for another interview."

They said nothing for a while. Austin studied her movements. He noticed she was not as anxious as she had been on her initial visit. He didn't know if that was good or bad. Either she was not interested in working for a pompous jerk or she had lost interest, he thought.

"What are you thinking, Candace?"

Candace thought that to accept his offer right now would be too hasty, and then he would know she was anxious. If she hesitated, maybe Austin would give her a better assignment. Candace felt there had to be something in the thick folder that requested face-capture. "Truthfully I'm somewhat disappointed. One thing for sure, I can't make any money with the kind of work you're offering me."

"Money should be your least worry right now. I tell you what. Perhaps we can discuss it further over lunch?"

"Candace was flattered by his offer. Here was a man surrounded by beautiful women every day and she was sure he could have his pick of any one, yet he wanted to have lunch with her. A sixth sense told her that he was interested in more than her working at AFLAME, and secretly she hoped so.

"I am free the rest of the day. Sure, that'll be okay."

"Good. I have two other interviews that should take about 30 minutes each." He walked Candace to the reception area.

"Phyllis."

"Yes, sir."

"Make sure Ms. Brooks is comfortable. Show her the lounge. We will be having lunch together today."

*   *   *

Sable was arguing with Aunt Elvira about letting the automatic dishwasher wash the breakfast dishes versus her washing them by hand.

"You just like Momma use to be, Aunt Vi. Jonah and I brought Momma a dishwasher for her 60th birthday because she complained about having to wash dishes all the time. Then she never used it, said the dishwasher ran the water bill up." Everyone laughed and recounted humorous stories about Loretta.

It was not until the telephone rang that the laughing ceased. Wilson picked up the phone. "Hello?"

"Hello. This is Sergeant McDuffie with the Alexandria Police Department. May I speak with Jonah Brooks, please?"

Wilson handed the telephone to Jonah. "It's the police in Virginia. Probably about Aunt Vi's purse-snatching."

Jonah took the phone and placed his free hand on his hip. He looked youthful in his pullover polo shirt and jeans. Sable followed the outline of his body, admiring how he had taken care of himself. She was out of denial and was able to admit that Jonah never wanted the separation. Wilson blamed their separation on high-mindedness. "Making money now and can't stand living in your husband's shadow. The echo was just as loud and clear as it was that day five years ago when Wilson pulled her aside to give her the words of advice. Now, as she sat watching Jonah through peripheral vision, she realized how true her father had been. Her yearning for independence coupled with Jonah's refusal to praise and acknowledge her success caused her to forfeit the things that were dear to their hearts. She had short-changed Candace, too. That was the cold, brutal truth. Every child needs the comfort of a two-parent family and she alone had taken that away from her own child. She thought that explained a lot of Candace's actions—like her sometimes over-rebelliousness, inattentiveness and unsociable behavior? In North Carolina before the divorce, Candace was outgoing. Her independence had begun to bud, then soar to the point that Sable sometimes found herself envious of Candace's friends. It was difficult to accept that she was no longer the main focus in her daughter's life, and she thought she would go crazy from loneliness. Then Jonah bought the computer and it proved to be a lifesaver. She hated to admit that the $10,000 was more of a peace offering than a graduation gift. She didn't have the nerve to tell Candace how sorry she was for screwing up her childhood. She hoped that one day she would be able to find the words as well as the courage to apologize.

She watched Jonah's every move. He was masculine in every way possible, and Sable knew there was truth in the saying that men don't age, they grow distinguished. She was flattered that he had flirted with her only minutes ago. It'd been so long since a good-looking man paid her any attention. Usually they didn't until they found out she was the famous mystery writer, which she imagined spelled M-o-n-e-y in their minds. Of course, there was Nathaniel the other day at the furniture store. He was handsome and at first seemed to be friendship and lover potential, but as the days passed she became doubtful that he'd call.

Jonah's deep laugh broke through her concentration and jolted her back to present tense.

"Good, thanks a million, Sergeant McDuffie. How did you get him to confess?"

Aunt Elvira got up from her chair and inched closer to Jonah. "Did he confess?"

Jonah nodded his head while listening to sergeant McDuffie.

"Get this. He said it was the old lady that did it," the sergeant remembered Aunt Elvira's kind and gentle nature. "Uh, pardon me. I meant your Aunt. Mike Fletcher said she reminded him of his mother. He has agreed to get into a drug program. He used to be a computer programmer for General Motors. Started living in the fast lane, hooking up with the wrong kind of people. One thing led to another until he almost reached total destruction. Talk about your apples falling far from the tree." Sergeant McDuffie chuckled.

Jonah let out a long sigh. "I hope it works for him. I really do."

Aunt Elvira was pulling at Jonah's arm trying to get him to give her the phone. Jonah covered the receiver to muffle her sounds. "Aunt Vi please wait until I get finished."

"I want to talk to that policeman before you hang up."

Defeated by her pleas and tugging, Jonah gave the phone to Aunt Elvira.

"Hey, this Elvira, the lady that was attacked at the rest stop in Virginia."

Sergeant McDuffie recognized her voice right off and he couldn't help but smile. "Hello, ma'am."

"How you?"

"Fine, thank you. I was telling your nephew that we don't need you to come back and identify Mike Fletcher. He confessed."

"Oh, he did, huh?"

"Yes, ma'am."

"Is he going to prison?"

"He won't be going to prison, but he was sentenced to three years probation. If he violates his probation he goes to prison. He has also agreed to go to a drug treatment program where he can get some help for his addiction."

"Praise the Lord. I knew there was some good in him."

"Yes, ma'am."

"Reckon he got save since y'all caught him?"

"Ms. Elvira, that I don't know."

"The Bible says seek ye first the kingdom of heaven and all these things shall be added to you; now that includes healing of any kind, drug healing too."

"Yes, ma'am." Nearly 300 miles away the sergeant sat at his desk, tightly gripping the phone while Aunt Elvira's preaching began to irritate him. He wished she would hurry and finish what she was saying so he could hang up. Had he not been raised by a God-fearing, Christian woman, he would have, but there was a degree of respect he held for the righteous.

"I want you to do something for me, baby."

"Ma'am?"

"Find out if Mike is saved. If he's not, find a Bible from somewhere and turn to Psalm 51: the 1st through the 19th verses. You writing this down?"

"Yes, ma'am," he lied as he plucked his third Krispy Kreme doughnut from the box.

"Tell him to read that, then fall down on his knees and pray—hallelujah!—pray for God's salvation."

The outcry was more than the sergeant could take. He'd had enough of fire and brimstone preaching evangelists when he was a child and wasn't particularly excited about Aunt Elvira's rendition. It had been so long since he'd set foot inside a church, he could not remember. He hurried her off the phone with a made-up excuse. "All right Ms. Elvira. I gotta go. Another call is coming through." The sergeant hung up the phone while Aunt Elvira was in mid-sentence. He nonchalantly reclined back in his swivel chair and swung his legs on top of his desk. "Forgive me, Lord."

Sable ran a hand through her neatly cropped hair, stopping at the back to twist her index finger around a tight curl. She waited for Jonah to explain the conversation, although she had picked up enough to know that they didn't have to rush back, thus strengthening the possibility of seducing Jonah or his seducing her. Chances were slim that opportunity would offer them time alone with Wilson and Aunt Elvira around. Maybe she could get them to go see a movie together. If they knew her hidden agenda, no doubt they would cooperate wholeheartedly, but since they were not discreet people, she would have to hope for the best and wait and see what developed.

Jonah picked up his section of the morning paper before speaking. "The man that attacked Aunt Vi confessed. They don't need us to identify him. I don't mind telling you that's a load off my mind."

"Me, too," said Aunt Elvira. "I've had enough of that place for a lifetime."

Jonah caught a faint smile on Sable's face. Her finger fumbled with the back of her hair and Jonah read the sign clearly. He had been married to her long enough to know when she fidgeted with her hair she was in deep concentration. He had three more hours before his interview with Glaxnus Pharmaceutical. Jonah had kept his interview confidential. He wanted to see how well Sable received his visit. Other than Friday night's little encounter, he felt things were going well. He would only tell Sable about his interview if he felt his chances of getting the district manager's position were good. Since the graduation Sunday, Sable had been sending him flirtatious signals. What she didn't know was that he was one step ahead of her.Because the Cut Above was Sable's favorite restaurant, Jonah had made reservations for two. He picked up his section of the morning paper before speaking.

"When will you be moving into your new house, Sable?"

"All the paper work has been done and I've made arrangements with the movers to get the ball rolling in two weeks."

"Candace and Wilson told me about it. I'd like a chance to see it before I leave tomorrow."

The word 'tomorrow' was like a curve ball that hit her in the pit of her stomach. She began filling up with dread. She was getting used to Jonah. His being around brought the familiarity of being married again. She wished he could stay longer but knew he had a job to get back to. It was good having men in the house once more. Tuesday Jonah and

Aunt Elvira would be leaving and Friday Wilson's flight would have him back in North Carolina before she could blink an eye. All her financial wealth was still not enough to buy her total happiness, the kind that accompanied companionship. She wondered if Candace would move to Torryville with her or try to stay and keep up the apartment. Sable wanted Candace with her but felt she would find a place of her own before long.

"What you say I take you out to dinner tonight at The Cut Above and afterward we stop by to see your mansion?"

"Sounds like a winner to me." Sable looked at Wilson and Aunt Elvira. "Will you two be all right this evening?"

"Don't worry about us," said Wilson. "We may take in a movie. Candace said that movie Life was okay," Wilson looked at Aunt Elvira for support. "What you think Vi?"

"Long as it ain't got a lot of sex in it, 'cause you know I don't approve of mess like that. I wouldn't want you getting no ideas now," she grinned.

"Vi, if you were the last woman on earth, you'd never have to worry about somebody wanting to get fresh with you."

The statement left Sable fighting to hold back the chuckle in her throat. She crossed her arms across her chest and shook her head.

13

A Rose Bud

Candace thought she knew all the greasy, soul-food eateries in Manhattan, but she had never heard of Momma Hamlin's Chicken and Ribs. As they walked through the doors of Momma Hamlin's, the indisputable smell of barbecue chicken and ribs greeted them. It was a smell Candace knew all too well, especially the past two weeks with Wilson visiting. The orange juice she'd had for breakfast was not enough to nourish a gnat. She was starving and to prove it her stomach growled. She tried to conceal its sounds by taking deep breaths and pulling her stomach in, but it didn't help. Candace read over the menu and decided upon a house salad with low-fat dressing and a glass of unsweetened ice tea. She wanted desperately to impress Austin and led him to believe that she was a light eater.

"Is that all you're having?" he asked skeptically.

"Yes, I'm not too hungry anyway," she lied.

The waiter looked at Candace. "You a model, ain't you?" he asked.

Candace blushed and looked at Austin for the answer.

"Yes, she is. She's going to be doing some assignments for AFLAME," he said.

"Girl, you better gon' on and get you some of these ribs. They good, child!" He rest his free hand on his narrow hip and looked at Austin. "Ain't that right Auddy?"

Austin smiled and introduced the well-known waiter to Candace. "I'd like for you to meet Antwan. He's the man in charge here."

Antwan covered his mouth as he snickered. "You bed' not let Momma Hamlin hear you say that. She think she running this place and last time I checked, she was." Antwan diverted his attention back to Candace and boldly began to check her out from head to toe. "And who is Miss Thang here?"

"Her name is Candace—Candace Brooks."

"Sooo, Candace—Candace Brooks" he teased letting the o's roll on his tongue. "What kind of assignment is he gonna send you on first, and please don't tell me he putting you on the cover of Ebony, Essence or some big-time magazine like that. Not that I'm jealous, girlfriend. Its just that for years I've been trying to get him to grace my seductive body on the cover of one of them magazines and he keep telling me no. So I want to know what you got that I don't." Antwan had drawn an audience of laughing spectators.

Candace's eyes bounced around the tiny but packed establishment. She smiled shyly and again looked at Austin for deliverance.

Antwan patted her lightly on the shoulder. "Girl, you know I'm just playing with you."

A sudden burst of confidence swept over Candace. "Well, I think he ought to put you on the cover of Ebony, 'cause Rupaul can't touch you."

Antwan stomped the floor with his Reeboks and doubled over laughing. "Ooo, she's good Auddy. I like her already." He patted Candace's shoulder a second time. "Girl, you all right." Antwan looked at Austin. "Now what you gon' have, my big ol' African prince?"

Austin ordered a large platter of barbecue chicken and ribs with slaw and cornbread on the side.

"Antwan, bring two plates, please."

"No, no, really. I'm fine. I don't need…"

"Aw, just as I suspected."

"What?"

"You said need—you don't need. I know that you want some, though, because I heard your stomach growling. I'm willing to share; as a matter of fact I insist."

Candace blushed and was thankful for his insistence. "Since you put it that way, how can I refuse," she said. She watched Austin as he ate. There was no shame in his game as he took big bites of the tangy barbecue chicken and ribs. Candace pictured him as one of those starving African children Sable used to talk about when she was small. She thought he was probably deprived of food as a child and that was his reason for eating so ravenously. She enjoyed watching him eat almost as much as she loved eating the tasty meal. When she picked up the paper napkin to wipe the sauce off her fingers, Austin burst into a reverberating laugh.

"Not like that," he said, then demonstrated the proper way to rid fingers of barbecue sauce. He licked his fingers greedily while moaning a moan of enjoyment. "Try it," he said.

Candace licked her fingers one at a time until all the sauce was gone. "Mmm, it is better coming off your fingers," she said, trying to mask a ritual she was very much familiar with. Austin's laugh turned into a smile and then staid as he watched her intently.

"Now, Candace, the business at hand is whether you're going to work for me or not. What is it going to be?"

Candace placed her fork down and dabbled at the corners of her mouth with the napkin.

"Honestly, I'd love to work at AFLAME, but the money is a factor. I had hoped to move out into my own place, but…"

"You have a roof over your head and food on the table, don't you?" Austin asked.

"Yes."

"You are with people who love you; they don't beat you, do they?"

"Of course not," she said defensively.

"You are comfortable, you don't sleep on the floor, or have to eat crumbs for food?"

"No, but…"

"Well. It seems to me that you have all you need for the moment. 'The string can be useful until a rope can be found.' African proverb," he said.

Candace nodded and a warm smile brushed her lips.

"I get what you're saying all right. I still feel you must know what I'm trying to say here. You said you were on your own since 17 years ago. I'm just guessing, but I put you in your mid-30s."

"Thirty-five, and I was 18 when I came here."

"Independence at that age must have been great."

"It is strange to hear you call it independence. You see, Candace, I had a chance those many years ago. I had a chance for education in the United States of America." His eyes lit up when he said America. "Yes, there is an education system in Dar es Salaam, Tanzania, but it can not compare to the education here. Many Africans do not get the chance I did. That is why before I left my family those many years ago. I vowed to them that I would do well in my studies and make them proud. It wasn't that I wanted to get away from them, for they were gentle with me. It was because I wanted and they wanted me to have a better life than they had. I can understand your anxiousness to prove your maturity. I am willing to bet you $20 that everyone sees you just the way you want them to and that is a beautiful adult woman who is capable of handling her affairs. In due time, Candace—in due time. Now are you going to come to work for me?"

Candace liked a lot of things about Austin; his looks, his impeccable good taste in clothes and his mannerisms. Now he had shown her a part of him that she thought she would cherish most of all; his commanding, yet charismatic, approach in persuasion. She though he was a lot like her father.

"Yes, Mr. Kawissopie, I'd love to come and work for you." She extended her hand across the table and they shook to seal the agreement.

*　　　　　*　　　　　*

Candace navigated her new sports car down the city streets. She looked around at the asphalt jungle and found beauty she had never seen before. Everything seemed to have a magical glow about it, even a group of homeless who were gathered on a street corner. They seemed somewhat jovial and moved with an added degree of spryness today. She felt light as the air itself and every breath she took exhilarated her more and more. As she got farther and farther away from the heart of town, the full view of the city's skyline became visible in her rearview mirror and she was able to make out the AFLAME building among the other skyscrapers. It was then that she realized that much of her excitement was over Austin rather than the idea of modeling. She was ablaze with joy and she wanted to share her good news with someone. She looked at her watch and saw that it was only 1 o'clock. She thought of Russell and knew he would be taking his lunch break soon. If she hurried she could catch him and tell him her good news. She took the turnpike heading in the direction of the post office. No sooner had she made the exit than she realized she and Russell were no longer on friendly terms and the last thing he'd want to hear was that she would be working for Austin. A grief swept over her as she watched for an exit to get off the turnpike. She would go home and tell her good news to anyone who would listen.

*　　　　　*　　　　　*

Sable had been giggling all evening and she could not remember the last time she'd had so much fun. Dinner at The Cut Above was splendid.

Just being with him made her feel like an impressionable schoolgirl again. Jonah pulled into the driveway of the house that Sable had signed 15 years of her life away on. It was as enchanting as Wilson and Candace had described it. Jonah couldn't help but feel somewhat chagrined at not being able to afford such luxury for Sable back in North Carolina. But, the house she and Candace had lived in with him and the one he still maintained was nothing to denounce. As a matter of fact it was a right handsome brick home situated on a secluded 3-acre tract of land. It had 2,500 square feet of upstairs heated space, a double-car garage plus a full basement that Jonah had turned into his work area, den and office. He had reserved a small section for Candace. He felt that eventually she would want a place to entertain her friends. But before he could get around to renovating the area, he and Sable were separated.

Sable slid the key into the lock and turned. They stepped inside the roomy foyer. The august staircase seemed to look down and welcome them.

"It's beautiful," he said, as his hands felt the staircase railing. He gave it a firm shake and nodded his head in approval. "Sturdy."

"Shall I give you the grand tour, sir?" she teased.

"Yes, I'd like that."

They climbed the stairs and Sable gave him a brief tour of two of the three bedrooms. Each had an adjoining bath and spacious walk-in closets. When she opened the door to the master-suite, it was as if she had opened the door to a miniature house. The room was commodious and the double-hinged arched windows made it appear even more so. Jonah stepped in and moved in a complete circle while eyeing the scalloped molding that outlined the ceiling.

"This is something else," he said. Then he walked further into the room. "It's going to take a mile of fabric to cover that window." Jonah dipped his head in the direction of the window as he spoke.

"Oh, I'm not going to cover it with drapes. I think I'll go with some vertical blinds and leave the arched section bare. You know how I love sunlight.

Jonah opened the closet and guessed it measured 12-by-12 feet. He moved on to the bath and discovered that it was a masterpiece within itself. The color scheme was gold metals and white ceramics. The basin, a clam-shaped pedestal style complimented the double jet spray whirlpool tub. There was a corner shower stall surrounded by waverly glass. The walls were mirrored and reflected images in multiples. Jonah could not help but wonder how rousing it would be to make love to Sable in the bathtub with the ring of mirrors playing back their every move. He stood in the center of the bathroom reminiscing about Sable's power of seduction over him. He watched her standing there describing her plans for decorating. He did not hear what she was saying, instead observed her shapely curves. She was wearing a silk floral tank top and matching slacks. The outfit moved free and easy and revealed every magnificent curve of her body. Her breasts were firm and nipples distended under the soft-cup bra she wore. She was so beautiful and reminded him of the sweet vulnerable girl he had met those many years ago. An immediate urge to ravish her swept over him. He wanted to take her into his strong arms and kiss every inch of her body madly. He was so compelled by the desire that he felt even if she resisted, he could will her into yielding. But Jonah was a gentleman in every sense of the word. His mother had taught her sons that a true gentleman could control his sexual desires and for that reason he kept himself under restraint.

After she had shown him her would-be office in the attic, he followed Sable downstairs to tour the first floor. Jonah was truly amazed at the beauty of the old house. The den was the last room to be shown. Jonah followed closely behind Sable, taking in her delicious smell as she turned the corner into the den. Forgetting about the stuffed gorilla that stood in the corner, Sable dropped her pocketbook and let out a shrilling scream. Instinctively Jonah pushed Sable out of what he thought was harm's way and stood face to face with the hideous beast. It took a few seconds before he realized what it was he was willing to risk life and limb over. Feeling relieved himself, he let out a soft chuckle. He turned around to make sure Sable was all right and found that he had pushed her so hard she'd landed on the floor. He slid down beside her and gently held her shoulders. "Are you all right?"

Sable was clutching her heart and breathing rapidly. "Yes. I knew that thing was still here. I've seen this house three times already, and each time that stupid gorilla scares the daylights out of me. You'd think I'd know better by now," she said trying to get up off the floor. Jonah leapt to his feet and pulled Sable up off the floor and into his arms. Their eyes locked. Without saying a word, Jonah kissed her lips lightly. She kissed him back more carnally. His arms locked around her waist and he could feel her melt in his grip. He felt her nipples hardening against his chest, and he heard the soft moan that escaped her throat. He said not a word and, just like the scene in "Gone With the Wind" when Clark Gable carried Vivien Leigh up the winding staircase, he did as much; up the stairs and back to the fabulous bathroom with the ring of mirrors.

14

Recovery

It was early Saturday morning and normally Dr. Edwards would be preparing for activities with her husband and grandchildren. She was devoted to her profession as much as the next psychiatric therapist, but she was more devoted to family, life and the pursuit of happiness. Austin had called her before dawn and begged her to see him. He'd sounded panicky and on edge. Reluctantly, she agreed and told him to come at nine o'clock that morning. She was not surprised when she pulled up in front of her office building to find him already there and waiting.

Because it was Saturday, Dr. Edwards dismissed wearing her traditional white lab coat and instead, wore a snug fitting tee shirt over a pair of jeans. Today she looked far younger than her 57 years. Her hair was not combed back into its customary bun, but hung freely around her apple-shaped, copper-face. She hoped she would not be detained too long. She wanted to get back to her family. She peered over her spectacles at Austin and wrote notes as he spoke. He was telling her about the recurring dream he had had the night before. The dream was about the giant vultures coming for Maoma. This time, before they swooped her up, one of the birds pecked a piece of flesh from her arm. Maoma was crying tears of blood and she was repeating the word "please." When Austin woke up, he found himself drenched in sweat. He had never been so terrified in his life. Austin didn't know what to make of the dream. It was torment enough just dreaming about the big birds taking her off, but to see them devouring her flesh was more than he could handle. Whenever he had dreams of Maoma, depression followed for several days. Phyllis and his other colleagues noticed it too and they all sympathized with him. Phyllis and Maoma had become close friends and for that reason, she had a special concern for Austin when he went through the bouts of depression. She gave him the same free advice that Dr. Edwards charged an astronomical fee for.

Austin and Maoma were initially married in New York, but because both were from Africa, they flew to Dar es Salaam to have a more lavished ceremony among family and friends. Maoma had been scheduled to do a modeling assignment in Paris. She had insisted on Austin not accompanying her, but staying behind so he could spend more time with his family. She never made it. Her plane crashed on it's way to Paris.

Austin felt to blame because Maoma never really wanted to be a model. Her love was teaching elementary education. Occasionally she would model at Austin's request. He felt that her beauty should be shared and captured.

Austin sat up from his reclined position. "What can the dream mean, Dr. Edwards?"

Dr. Edwards pushed her sliding glasses back up the bridge of her nose. "It doesn't mean anything, Mr. Kawissopie. In myths and ancient cultures, dreams were often regarded as predictions or messages sent from the gods. In this account, dreams would contain so much meaning they would be beyond human comprehension. Dreams do have meanings, but they belong to the consciousness of sleep, making it necessary to translate them into the language of waking consciousness in order for us to understand them. I'll give you a personal example. One night I went to bed and, feeling rather cold, I turned on my electric blanket, only to dream that my legs were on fire. Needless to say, I'd turned the blanket up too high. The heat was an echo to my mind. Once a dream has been decoded, we find that all it is, Mr. Kawissopie, is the fulfillment of a wish or like the example just given you, echoes of the mind."

"So what you're saying, is that my wishing for Maoma to be alive is causing me to have these episodic dreams?"

"That's exactly what I am saying," she said sternly. She laid her pen down and clasped her hands together.

"Then, if that is indeed the problem, how do I get past these dreams? Last night I woke up in a cold sweat, my heart was racing and I was shaking uncontrollably. The dreams are coming more frequently. If I continue like this, it will surely kill me. Is there something you can prescribe for me?"

"Yes, there is, Mr. Kawissopie. It is the same thing I have been prescribing to you for the past two years now. Pursue someone and start dating. I understand that your wife's death was utterly tragic, but five years is a long time to grieve. As I've told you before, you need to get involved with someone. That is my prescription to you. You work in a business where there are lucrative romantic possibilities. Surely you have the advantage over the average man." Dr. Edwards watched him intently.

Austin thought of Candace. "Yes, there is someone but…"

"But what?"

"A couple of things. Number one, she is 13 years my junior. Number two, I don't know if I am ready or not."

Dr. Edwards sighed. "Answer to number one is, age is just a number. If this lady is mature in her mind and you feel the two of you can relate, I see no problem. Number two—I think you're afraid versus not knowing if you're ready." There was a moment of silence that filled the room. "I say you are ready. You've been ready for quite some time. You feel that by starting another relationship you're somehow betraying Maoma. But from what you've told me about her, she was a remarkable woman. A person that special and unique would not want you living your life in the shadows of her ghost. If there is something to this "myth about the gods sending messages through dreams thing," then, perhaps it is Maoma's way of telling you to go on with your life. You're a young man, Austin, and life is for the living."

Dr. Edwards had called him by his given name for the first time. He felt she was discreetly informing him that it was time to bring closure to his sessions. He had been seeing Dr. Edwards since the death. He knew all that she had said was true. It was time to move on and say good-bye. He had found comfort in his weekly visits with her and would miss her. Although she didn't know it, she had become more than just a therapist to him. She had become his tower of strength and formal friend. Now it was time to stand on his own. He eased his wallet out of his hip pocket and opened it slowly. Dr Edwards held up her hand. "No, my office will bill you."

"Yes, I know, but it is not money I want to give you." He pulled out a small picture of Maoma and handed it to Dr. Edwards. "I am simply saying good-bye." They shook hands before he exited the office. He was less burdened now and was going to take her advice.

Dr. Edwards opened the bottom draw of her desk and dropped the picture inside with other memorabilia of closures from former patients.

*   *   *

Austin guided his Jaguar in the direction of downtown Manhattan. He knew of a ritzy shop that sold fresh-cut flowers and exotic chocolates. He remembered Candace telling him at lunch the other day that she couldn't resist chocolates.

15

Suspicion

It had been three weeks since her family returned to North Carolina, and Sable believed she would have gone crazy from missing them if she didn't have the house in addition to her writing to keep her busy. The crew she hired moved at lightning speed. The painting had been done, the carpet changed, and even the kitchen remodeled to her specifications. The only room that had not been completed was the attic. The carpenter in charge of that task had ordered the knotted pine paneling but was waiting for the shipment to come in. Sable walked carefully from the kitchen to the living room balancing two mugs of cinnamon spiked coffee.

"Here you go, dear." She handed the extra mug to Shamell and eased down on the new sectional.

"Sable, I have to give it to you, girl; you did a good job at picking out this ensemble. Everything goes together so well."

"Actually I can't take all the credit; the salesman on duty that day helped me out a lot. I tell you, he really knows furniture."

"He never called, did he?" asked Shamell.

"Naw, but I really don't want him to now," replied Sable.

They sipped on the coffee and there was a moment of silence before Shamell snickered.

"What's funny?" Sable asked.

"I can't believe you and Jonah did the do, that's all."

"What's so hard to believe about that? Two grown, healthy, and attractive adults of the opposite sex, together…"

"Alone," added Shamell, still snickering.

"Yes, and alone. Well, something was destined to happened. Not to mention I haven't had any in eons." She took another sip of her coffee.

"Hmm, so you think there may be a long-distance romance in the works?" asked Shamell.

Sable set her mug on one of the two coasters that had been strategically placed on the new coffee table. She looked thoughtful for a moment before speaking.

"Perhaps," she smiled gingerly. "Jonah must have been thinking about our reconciliation for a while because he scheduled an interview with a pharmaceutical company before he came to New York. He didn't tell me until after the fact. He said he wanted to see if I would mind him living in New York, so close, you know."

"And?" questioned Shamell, looking intensely at her now.

"And I think I might like that. I've grown so lonely without a man in my life. Two years ago if you had asked me that, I would've said no, I don't need him, but after seeing him, smelling him and listening to his sweet voice, I realize how a part of him has never left me."

She picked up the mug again and took another sip before continuing. "Now I know as long as we live we will always have a common bond other than Candace. She thought about Shamell and Charles and wondered how their relationship was doing. Shamell had never once let on that there were any problems. Maybe there wasn't any that she knew of. Sable knew there was, even if Shamell was oblivious to the truth. She knew what she had seen those four weeks ago. As hard as she tried to tell herself that she didn't see Charles walk into a hotel arm in arm with a girl who appeared to be half Shamell's age, she knew she couldn't. She had never intended to say anything about what she had seen that day, but she also wanted Shamell to know that if she had a problem, her shoulder was available to cry on. She thought that Shamell knew she would always be there for her, but now she wasn't so sure. Shamell seemed lost somehow. She wasn't as talkative as usual and she seemed so tired today. If Sable had even suspected she wasn't feeling well, she never would have asked her to come over and help her put the finishing touches on the house.

"You know what, Shamell?"

"What's that?"

"I think if I get another chance with this relationship thing, I'll certainly know how to cherish it. Jonah wasn't that bad. I never told you, but he never wanted the divorce. I just cringe at the years we were not a family, all because of my selfishness. And you know who suffered the most?"

Before Shamell could ask, Sable answered. "Candace."

"Oh, come on now, Sable, Candace seems well-rounded to me. You two have a tight relationship. You're like a mother hen when it comes to her."

"She hates me, Shamell."

"Stop it now," Shamell demanded. "Why do you put yourself through these agonizing rituals? I'll tell you what it is. It's your guilt over a failed marriage that's all. Subconsciously you allow negativism to tell you that because your marriage didn't work that you've failed at raising Candace and that just isn't so." She reached over and patted Sable's hands. Just then Sable noticed a huge nasty bruise on the underside of Shamell's wrist. Sable grabbed her arm and turned it underside up. The bruise was about five inches long and an inch wide. The purple, red and black coloration looked awful against Shamell's honey colored skin.

"My God! What happened?"

Shamell pulled her arm back and tugged down the out-of-season long sleeve.

"Oh, nothing." She waved her hand casually. "Slammed my own arm in the car door." She gave a silly chuckle.Sable looked at her suspiciously, then back at her wrist, which Shamell now had folded under her breast.

"You slammed your arm in the car door?"

"Yes!" Shamell took on a shielding tone and stared at Sable defensively.

"How?" Sable asked, equally ambitious.

"Carelessness. I wasn't paying attention to what I was doing and before I knew it, Wham!"

Sable kept her eyes on Shamell as she reached over her hand. "Let me see it, dear."

"Sable, I don't want you making a big deal over this now."

"Let me see it, I said."

Shamell conceded and handed her arm over.

"That's bad, 'Mell. Have you seen a doctor?"

Shamell laughed. "No, Mother, I haven't because it's not that bad."

"How do you know? You're not a doctor. There may be some internal damage."

"Trust me, Sable. I'm all right. Where's my purse? I need a cigarette." Shamell got off the sectional and walked through the den and into the kitchen where she had left her pocketbook. Sable followed dutifully. She leaned against the door joist and watched Shamell nervously light the cigarette. She exhaled a long cloud of smoke. Sable noticed that she seemed less on edged now. Sable could not hold her suspicions any longer and decided to ask the question that was plaguing her since she'd seen the abrasion.

"Did Charles do that?"

Shamell didn't realize Sable was standing behind her, and she jumped before whirling around like a tornado. "What did you say?" she asked, incensed.

"Shamell, I honestly don't believe you slammed your arm in the door. Now, I know you well enough to know how careful you are. You worry about getting a crack in your finger nails."

"How dare you stand there with your pious self and pass judgment on Charles. You and Jonah may be on the road to recovery, but don't think you got it like that." She snapped her fingers at the statement. She began nodding her head like a wild woman. "Uh huh, you never liked Charles. That's what it is."

"Shamell, what are you saying!"

"You heard me." Shamell took a long drag off the Virginia Slim. She tilted her head upward to release the smoke from her lungs while watching Sable. Her eyes squinted in anger.

For the first time in her life Sable felt she had overstepped an unknown boundary that she didn't think existed between them. Sable shook her head in disbelief. "I want to make sure I heard you correctly. I have nothing against Charles, never have."

"Look me square in the eyes and tell me that," Shamell said.

Sable could not. She flinched more than once, but that was because of what she had seen that day Charles and the girl walked into the hotel. Truth was, she didn't trust him as far as she could see him and, yes, she did believe he was capable of hurting Shamell.

Shamell laughed hysterically. "See, I told you. One thing I can say for you, girlfriend. You sho' in the right profession. You tell tales." She grabbed her pocketbook and threw it over her shoulder and brushed passed Sable angrily. Sable grabbed her arm in an attempt to stop her from leaving. Shamell drew back in pain.

"Ouch!" She fell against the wall and sobbed into her hands.

"Shamell, I'm so sorry. I didn't mean to hurt you." Sable tried to comfort her with a hug, but when Shamell felt her arms encircling her she stepped backward. Sable realized that it wasn't the injured arm that was bothering her, but something deeper than physical pain.

"We're friends, 'Mell. There's nothing you can't tell me. I didn't mean to upset you. It's just that I'm concerned about you. Let's talk about it."

It seemed that Shamell was letting down her guard. When she uncovered her eyes she saw a woman, not her friend, but a woman who had just accused her husband of spousal abuse. Their gazes silently locked. Shamell wiped her face with the back of her hand.

"Charles is an intelligent man. A black man in a white-collar profession. He went to school for years and studied hard to get where he is today. If something like that got out, it would ruin him and his career." Her eyes closed and another tear rolled down her cheek. "I can't believe what you said about him." She shook her head. "I gotta go." She hurried out of the house and jumped into her Porsche.

"Shamell, wait," called Sable. She stood on the front porch watching Shamell's little red car until it got out of sight.

16

Forgiveness

Stuffed lamb chops, wild rice and asparagus tips with almonds was Shamell's favorite meal. Charles had slaved over the stove all that evening preparing it. He had followed the directions from Shamell's piecemeal cookbook. The cookbook was worn, and some of the pages were held together by aged scotch tape. Nevertheless, the book was Shamell's favorite form of cooking reference. Some of the recipes dated back to her junior high school years when she took home economics. She'd never used the "Black Family Reunion Cookbook" that Charles had brought her three Christmases ago, nor her Betty Crocker cookbooks. Charles had been precise in his measurement and seasonings. For dessert he had made chocolate mousse and garnished each parfait with a fresh raspberry. The sweet rosé was chilling in the refrigerator, as were the goblets. The table was set to perfection, adorning the cherished linen and lace tablecloth that once belonged to Shamell's great-grandmother. The sterling silver had been polished and was correctly placed beside the spotless Lenox china. Charles paced the floor and alternately watched the grandfather clock, checking the time impatiently. He looked debonair in the crisp white shirt and Hermes silk tie with burgundy, gray and black colors. His slacks were Ralph Laurens. They fitted easy around his narrow waist and hips and looked magnificent from rearview. Shamell had brought the Versace leather loafers, for his birthday six months ago, but today was his first time wearing them. His body was lightly scented with Obsessions for men. He had done all the things to himself that Shamell liked. He knew he had to make up to her for his actions last night. It was all so stupid and childish. Her jealously had gotten out of hand and so had his. Last night before he'd stepped inside their apartment good, he knew trouble was brewing. She was standing in the foyer with her hands crossed as she tapped her foot. Charles tried to play his tardiness off casually. He aimed a kiss at her lips but she held the palm of her hand flat up against his face.

"Do you know it is one o'clock in the morning?" she asked, as mad as a wet hen.

Charles laughed a cynical laugh and walked around her into the bedroom's adjourning bath. Shamell followed and stood in the doorway sneering at him.

"Charles, I had dinner prepared. You could have at least called me and let me know you were going to be late."

"Look," he snapped. "I'm sorry, okay? I didn't anticipate being this late."

"A call, Charles, a simple phone call. All I ever ask you do is give me some consideration."

Charles began peeling off his clothes; then he stopped suddenly. "Can I get some privacy here?" he asked coolly.

Shamell backed out of the doorway hesitantly. Before she completely removed herself, she realized he was trying to hide something. Charles had pushed the door and it was about to close but Shamell held up her forearm and blocked it from shutting. She pushed the door so hard that it bounced against the interior wall of the bathroom and left a dent. "Wait a damn minute! You got something to hide, Charles?" Shamell was growing angrier by the second. She stepped back inside the bathroom. She inched closer and began sniffing him. "What's that?"

"I don't know what you're talking about." He turned to face her with his hands on his hips.

"You into wearing women's perfume now?"

"Woman, please." He walked out of the bathroom past her. He took a fresh pair of pajamas from the chest of drawers.

"You smell like a whore," she snapped. "Have you been screwing around on me, Charles? Because if you have, you can just pack your stuff and leave. I don't have to put up with a two-timing man. I can do bad all by myself if I choose to. I don't need the likes of you to bring me down."

"You want me to pack my stuff and leave!" he roared. "That's ridiculous. My name is on the lease and I pay the bills in this house, too. I'm part of the reason why you can drive that Porsche parked downstairs and why you can wear the fine clothes you do. Yeah—you can eat thick steaks and lobsters every night if you want to, you know why? Because I bring home the bacon, too. That's right. You can't maintain the lifestyle you live without my contribution. So I don't want to hear that crap, Shamell." He waved his hand to dismiss her altogether.

"You know what, Charles? This apartment, that car and my clothes can go to hell. They're just things, and don't kid yourself for one minute if you think you are sustaining my luxuries. You're the one who has to have the finest of everything. Just like the vacation home in the Poconos. Don't think I'm so in love with this material stuff that I'll put up with your bull just to keep it. You forget, I came from the projects, I know how to make a meal off of neckbones and cornbread. I'm a survivor, Charles. You can take this house, that car, even this two-carat symbol of eternal love and devotion and stick it where the sun don't shine." She pulled the wedding ring off her finger and threw it at him. "If you think you're the only man on God's green earth, you're wrong!" she laughed.

"What's that supposed to mean?" he asked, wondering if she too was having an affair.

"You're a Ph.D. man, you figure it out." She turned to leave and that's when Charles grabbed her by her arm and began twisting it. The pain was so severe that Shamell thought he was going to break it. She cried out in agony and struggled to break away. Charles released her arm and as she walked away he delivered an elbow blow across her back. The hard hit knocked the air out of her and she fell to the bedroom floor struggling for breath.

In the 15 minutes it had taken for the whole scene to unravel, her spirit had been broken, her trust tried and her body assaulted. She never thought Charles capable of doing such a thing to her. She dared not move from the spot where she lay for fear he would hit her again. She knew she had pushed a button of no return when she indicated she might be having an affair. She lay in the floor engulfed in pain. Charles had grown distant with her over the past year. Their lovemaking had become seldom and passionless and it seemed more and more like an obligation on Charles' part. She wondered if he still loved or cared for her at all. She sobbed, not because she hurt physically but because she was relieved that Charles was interested enough to respond against her alleged affair. She felt that any kind of response was better than no response at all.

*   *   *

Charles fumbled with the ring he had in his pants pocket. He planned to drop the ring she had thrown at him in her wine goblet, then apologize profusely. He was feeling awful and kept asking himself what had possessed him to attack her like he had. He'd never hit a woman before in his life and never wanted to. He remembered the dreadful beatings his mother took at the hands of his father. She had endured years of abuse before the marriage ended with his death. When Charles got older, he asked her why she didn't leave. She said he was a good provider and made enough money at the shipyard so she didn't have to work outside of the home. She could devote all her time and attention to raising her children. Charles remembered her telling him that if his father died he would leave them very wealthy with his insurance policy. He never heard her say that she stayed with him out of love. He was always the first of her three children to rush to her side and comfort her after the beatings. It was at an early age that he vowed he would never strike a woman. He didn't want his father's sins following him.

He had never meant to hurt her; it just happened. It was like he couldn't control himself after she had said he was not the only man on earth. He went into a jealous rage and was out of control. He loved her and could not bear to think of another man's hands on her. He cringed at the thought. It was after he had calmed down that he knew Shamell was not the type of woman to cheat. He tried going to her and apologizing but she would not have any of it. She barricaded herself in the guestroom and remained there for the rest of the night. Even at daybreak, when Charles threatened to burst the door down, she still didn't open it. Charles panicked and thought he had hurt her so bad she was incapable of speaking much less opening the door. He asked if she needed a doctor. Shamell knew if she remained silent he would have an ambulance pulling up outside, and she didn't want the attention from the neighbors directed at them.

"I don't want to talk to you," was all she had said. It was Saturday morning and neither had to report to work. Charles moped around the apartment, frequently knocking on the door begging her to come out and asking if she needed anything. By 10:00 he got himself ready, grabbed his golf bag and left the apartment.

*   *   *

Shamell noticed the smell outside the apartment's door and her stomach growled. She slipped her key in the lock and stepped inside. Charles was standing in the middle of the foyer with his hands in his pockets. He wore a look of pure regret. She turned her back to him as she slowly closed the door. The hearty aroma of good food drifted from the kitchen and filtered throughout the apartment.

"Shamell, baby, I'm so sorry." The words fell from his lips like coos from a baby. They were soft and sweet enough to eat. She had to fight to control her emotions. He must not know how weak she was, that she was eager to forgive him and get back on track with their marriage. Shamell stole a quick glance at him. He looked great. He was still handsome after all the years they were together, and his tremendous looks still made her quiver. The Obsession fragrance he wore lingered in the air and she never tired of smelling it on him.

"I'm a little tired right now. I believe I'll take a long bath, then lie down."

"Aren't you hungry? I made dinner," he said pointing toward the dining room. The aroma smelled wonderful, and she was hungry. She had skipped breakfast and although Sable prepared hoagies and fruit for lunch, Shamell could not summon up an appetite. She'd only had a piece of fruit and two cups of the cinnamon spiked coffee.

"No, I'm not in the mood to eat."

"Since when have you not been in the mood to eat? You're always hungry." He tried to humor her, but she made no indication that what he said was funny. She exhaled and peeked beyond him into the dining room. He stepped aside and let her pass through. Shamell was impressed at the layout of the table and was somewhat touched to see that he had gone through the time and trouble to locate her fineries. She kept the lace tablecloth and silver hidden in the bottom of her hope chest. She had no idea he knew where they were.

Charles pulled out her chair and she eased into it gradually.

"I made lamb chops and asparagus tips with slivered almonds," he said with the enthusiasm of a child, "and chocolate mousse for dessert." He hurried into the kitchen to retrieve everything. In less than five minutes Charles had the main course on the table and was pouring wine into the goblets. He sat down in the side chair nearest Shamell. She looked at him oddly.

"You usually sit at the opposite end of the table. Far from me as possible."

Charles lowered his head before speaking and when he finally looked up, Shamell saw that tears had welled up in his eyes. One of them escaped and rolled slowly down his cheek. "Shamell, I can't began to tell you how sorry I am about last night. When you said that you were seeing another man…"

"I didn't say I was seeing another man, Charles." She spit the words out venomously and, as if they were a snake striking at Charles, he jumped back in his chair. He was totally shocked at the low, quick and angry tone of her voice. He lifted his hand slowly to calm her. "I know that now, 'Mell, honey. It's just that last night I wasn't thinking and my anger caused me to jump to conclusions that I now know were absolutely unfounded. I pictured you with someone else and I just…Shamell, I love you too much to let someone else take you from me. I showed my love the wrong way by twisting your arm and…" He couldn't bring himself to say the word hit.

"You elbowed me in the back. You literally knocked the breath out of me. I can't count the many times you told me stories about your father beating your mother and how she stayed with him because he kept food on the table and clothes on your backs." She shook her head. "I could never do that, even if I loved the man." She looked at him, wanting him to read clearly her message.

Charles dropped from the chair to his knees. He grabbed her hands and rubbed them against his face before kissing them. "I won't ask you to do that, baby. I promise you from this day forward that I'll never so much as raise a hand to you unless it is to hold, comfort and love you. Please forgive me 'Mell."

*   *   *

Candace pushed the garage door button of her remote control. She eased the black Camaro in between Sable's Mercedes and the old Toyota. She made a mental note to put an ad in the newspaper advertising the Toyota for sale. Everything had gone so well for her in the past three weeks. Under normal circumstances she would have found a reason to spend some of the graduation money on things she did not need. Since she had met Austin and started working at AFLAME, nothing seemed normal anymore. She'd opened up a savings account at First Manhattan and deposited the entire $11,000. Now she was planning to sell the Toyota and bank that money, too. Austin had impressed her greatly. He seemed to tower over her like a fortress of guidance and protection. He gave her sound advice and in the three short weeks she had been there he had shown her special attention. The office was buzzing with news that there was a romance budding. Whenever some of the other models asked her about their relationship, she told them there was nothing going on between them, which was the truth, although she wanted there to be. Sometimes when Austin looked into her eyes she felt as thought he wanted it too, but nothing ever happened.

Periodically she heard some of the girls whispering about how much she looked like someone Austin use to know. But, she never knew exactly who that someone was because she always caught the tail end of their secretive conversations. She'd just gotten back from shopping and had purchased a very sexy nightgown. It was a sheer, mauve number with French cut bikinis that tied into satin bows at the hips. Candace had never before slept in anything so delicate. Most of the time she chose pajamas or oversized athletic jerseys. They were warm and comfortable and she had no one to dress up for at night anyway. Although she doubted that her relationship with Austin would materialize into anything other than what it was, she hoped there was a chance. She turned the key in the lock and stepped from the garage into the kitchen. The house was quiet and it made her remember three weeks ago when Wilson, Jonah and Aunt Elvira were visiting at their Manhattan apartment. Aunt Elvira and Wilson made sure there was never a dull moment. She missed them.

Sable heard Candace come in. After today's encounter with Shamell, she would be grateful for Candace's company. She headed to the kitchen. "You hungry?" she asked.

"Come to think of it, I am. What's to eat?"

"Shamell came by to help with the decorating. I fixed hoagies, but she wasn't hungry." Sable took the half foot-long sandwich from the refrigerator. She got a plate from the cabinet and placed the cellophane-wrapped sandwich on it. "You want some fruit?" she asked retrieving it before Candace could reply.

"Mom, you don't have to do that. I can do it." She looked at her mother and could tell that something was bothering her. She pulled out a kitchen chair from under the table. "Here, sit down. Let me do it. You want something?"

Sable was amazed and impressed with her unusual concern. It seemed like overnight she had mentally matured into the kind of daughter that she'd wanted her to become. She was more positive, assured and sensible here lately. She hoped it was because of the modeling job and not the person running AFLAME. The seed of suspicion Aunt Elvira had planted was causing Sable not to like Austin, although she knew nothing about him. She remembered clearly the words Aunt Elvira had spoken. *"That old man after one thang. Now Sa-ble,"* she'd said, making the second syllable reach an octave higher, *"you better put your foot down."* Rationally thinking, it was natural to wonder what this man in his mid-30s wanted with Candace after telling her that AFLAME could not use her. Her blood boiled just thinking about the possibility of some man using her daughter. All she could hope was that Candace had learned the roads of deceit from her relationship with Julian Reed back in her high school years. Sable knew she had little experience with men. She could only count two, Julian and Russell, and she wasn't sure what Russell was to her other than a friend. There were times she thought they were an item, and other times when Candace treated him like a redheaded stepchild. She guessed love had to be the reason why Russell put up with her shenanigans.

"No, dear, I'm fine."

"What's wrong? You're not acting yourself, Mom."

"I think Charles may have hurt Shamell," she said candidly, then went on to tell her about discovering the ugly bruise on her arm. She didn't act like the Shamell we know. She wasn't jovial like she normally is."

"I hate to say this, but it doesn't surprise me."

The statement stunned Sable and she looked at Candace. She waited for more details.

"I mean he fits the mode. When I was at NYU, I'd see him from time to time with his cocky-self. It was rumored that he was going with a sophomore. I've seen the girl several times. She's very pretty, sort of flirtatious."

"Why didn't you tell me, Candace?"

"Mom, what could you have possible done? Go and spread hearsay to Shamell? Go confront Charles? All you would have done was worry about something you couldn't change."

"Oh, my God!" Sable dropped her head in her hands.

"What Mom?

"I think I may have seen that girl, too."

"Where? With Charles?"

Sable nodded. "That day you had commencement practice and I went to sign the papers for this house. On my way back I spotted Shamell's Porsche. I thought it was her, so I followed. It pulled into the Centennial Ramada Inn parking lot. Charles got out of the car with this pretty young thing. She looked about 19 or 20, brown-skinned with long braids down her back. She had a shape like an hourglass. They walked arm in arm into the hotel. I wanted to believe it was just an innocent meeting and there was a logical explanation to why they were going into a hotel together, but then his hand slid down and rubbed her butt. Well, I knew it wasn't innocent then."

"I guess the grapevine is ripe after all. You've just described that tramp to a T," said Candace.

"I can just kill Charles myself. To think he would try something like that at the university. He knew you were going there. Didn't he think you would find out and come back and tell me and I would mention it to Shamell?

"Evidently not, Mom. Some men think with their dicks."

"Watch your mouth. You may be grown, but you still watch your mouth," Sable warned.

"Sorry. Anyway, guess we know where Charles' brain is," Candace said, taking a large bite out of the hoagie.

"Candace, she tore out of here like a bat out of hell. I hope she made it home without getting into an accident."

"She's probably all right."

"I don't know; she was pretty upset because I accused Charles of hitting her. She usually calls me to let me know she made it home all right."

"Don't count on her calling this time. Sounds like she has some cooling off to do first."

"Perhaps you're right. I still can't help but worry."

"I tell you what. Why don't you and I find something entertaining to do this evening to get your mind off Shamell. You want to play cards?"

Sable was still finding it hard to believe how much Candace had changed. She was really offering to spend time with her. "Sure, pitty-pat or spades?"

"Spades."

"I'll get the cards." The phone rang just as Sable was getting out of her chair. "That's probably Shamell calling to say she made it. I'll get it," she said anxiously. "Hello."

"Good evening. May I speak to Candace Brooks?"

It was Austin. Sable recognized his voice right off and her excitement dissipated. "Uh, yes, she's right here. Just a moment." She handed the phone to Candace.

"Hello."

"How are you, Candace?"

Sable watched the shocked expression sweep across Candace's face as she realized who the caller was. She thought the evening was taking a turn for the better, but now she had her doubts. She watched Candace and with an agitated look on her face silently asked what he wanted. Candace waved Sable off and when that didn't work, she escaped to the den.

"I was hoping to catch you at home. I was afraid you would be out."

"I was earlier, but I'm in for the rest of the evening now."

"Well. So I gather that you are enjoying your day?"

"Yeah, it's been quite pleasant. I didn't do much except visit the mall. What about you?"

"My day has been terribly boring." He yawned to emphasize the statement.

Candace laughed at his witticism. "Sorry to hear that. You know what they say, all work and no play makes Jack a dull man."

"Are you suggesting I should play a little?"

"If the shoe fits, Austin."

"Hmm, how coincidental, because I was calling to see if you would come out and play with me."

"What do you have in mind?" she asked. She had a smile on her face that reached form ear to ear.

"While I'm on my way over, why don't you decide the perfect evening for us."

"O.k., then. Let me give you directions to my house."

17

First Date

Candace decided to dress casual. She wore a black safari shirt that was tucked neatly into a matching short skirt. She ran a leopard-print belt through the belt loops and buckled it snugly around her waist. The flat, leather woven sandals she wore were a pleasant switch from her normal heels. They made her long legs look comfortable. Her hair had been pulled back into a bouncy ponytail. Sable watched Candace's reflection in the mirror as she expertly applied eyeliner. Sable had never gotten the hang of putting on eye makeup. It always ended in her eyes.

"You don't have to get upset with me. All I'm asking is that you be careful."

"What you're really asking is for me to break this date with Austin, Mom. You know, I just don't get it. Austin has never said or done anything out of the way to make you dislike him. At least wait until he gives you reason before you start judging him." The two women stared at each other defiantly before either spoke.

"Ma, give him a chance, please. At least be sociable to him when he comes over."

Sable sucked her teeth and rolled her eyes away from Candace before speaking. "I'll try."

"No! Do more than try. You didn't know that he was the one who talked me out of moving out on my own. He said I should be here with you. He explained it to me so clearly and made me see how lucky I am to have you." She touched her mother's arm gently knowing it would soften her disposition.

"He said that?"

"Yes," she said tenderly.

Sable exhaled. "Where are the two of you going anyway?"

"Maybe to Arthur's for drinks. I don't know if Austin has eaten yet or not. If not, then he can get something there. Then, I wouldn't mind seeing the Museum of African Arts. I've always wanted to go there but never had the time." She realized that Sable would be alone, which wasn't good since she had the falling out with Shamell.

"Sorry about the card game; maybe we can play some other time."

"Yeah, some other time," she replied dryly.

"Why don't you take in a movie or do something to get yourself out of the house?"

"No, this is prime time for me to work on my manuscript and I'm going to take advantage of it."

"How's that coming anyway?"

"Very good. I've planned the plot and identified which character is suitable to be the killer."

"Who is it going to be?" Candace asked, trying to sound eager for her mother.

Sable was perceptive of her guilt. She had not shown interest in her writing for quite some time now. It used to be that Candace could not wait for her to finish a chapter so she could read it. Now she hardly ever asked about it. Here lately, Sable volunteered and read each chapter to her upon completion. "You're welcome to read what I've written if you like, but I'm afraid you'll have to wait until I get it written down on paper if you want to know who the killer is."

"I'll do that sometime." She took another quick assessment of herself in the mirror and was pleased. The doorbell rung and she ran her hands nervously down the front of her skirt.

*　　　　　　*　　　　　　*

The assorted flower arrangement consisted of daisies, daffodils and carnations. They were wrapped as a bouquet in floral paper. The box of Godiva chocolates were under his arm. Candace opened the door and was surprised to see him bearing gifts. She thought all along he was classy but this confirmed it. She'd gotten flowers and candy on Valentine's Day, but never on a first date. This was something that had been done in the days of yore, and she thought that Aunt Elvira and Grandma Loretta, when she was living, could identify with this type dating ritual. "Are they for me?" she asked, excited.

"Sweets for the sweet."

She received the gifts with a smile. "You shouldn't have, but I'm glad you did. Come in. They're beautiful. I'll eat every bit of the candy, and I don't need it. You want some?" she asked holding the box out to him.

"No, I'm not a big chocolate eater."

"Have a seat while I get a vase for the flowers."

Candace came back and placed the vase with the beautiful arranged flowers in the center of the coffee table. "Thank you, Austin."

"You're quite welcome."

Austin was wearing a dashiki over jeans. Although he looked like a million dollars, she was somewhat surprised to see him in the outfit. "I like this," she said as she ran her hand over the cotton material with its vivid colors and bold asymmetrical prints. Austin sprang off the couch and began modeling his outfit. He turned around and jiggled his hips like a model.

"I'm finding that you're quite a comedian," she laughed.

"Do you have one?"

"A dashiki? No, I never had the inclination to buy one, but seeing how good it looks on you, maybe I will. He looked around at the spacious quarters. "You have a very lovely home."

"Thank you. It beats the apartment we moved out of."

"That's right, you did move from Manhattan. I enjoyed the drive out here. It is so unruffled and serene. I think when I come to a point in my life when I want to settle down, it should be in a place like this."

"It reminds me of back home in North Carolina. Did you like it when you were there?"

He knew his diplomas in his office revealed that he lived in North Carolina for a while. He was flattered that she knew. It showed interest on her part. "I loved it there and I would have stayed if I had been able to find a decent job. All the jobs offered to me were never the ones I initially applied for. They were always beneath my abilities. I worked as a mere manager's assistant at a textile mill. I could run circles backwards with my eyes closed around that manager. When he was promoted, I applied for his job and they told me I wasn't qualified. They gave it to another manager's son who was fresh out of high school and still wet behind the ears. I got tired of their manipulations, so I moved north hoping for better opportunities. The prejudices in the South are quite different from the prejudices in the North. Up here they're a bit more clandestine. The Northerners like to be thought of as crusaders of the African American plight. They really don't like you, but they want you to believe otherwise. And God forbid if you call one of them prejudiced. They will bend over backward to prove you wrong. Don't get me wrong, I don't consider all whites to be prejudiced. It's just that I've run into a fair share who were."

"I can see your point. My grandfather can tell some pretty wild stories about his experience with racism. He and my grandmother attended the March on Washington in 1963. I'm so grateful to all our ancestors for the paths they cut for us. The problem is, we have not kept up their momentum. It seems we have gotten complacent. We don't even vote like we should. Why we don't realize that if we vote it would rectify some of our problems, I'll never know. If our ancestors could see us now, I know they wouldn't be pleased," she said

"I think that for the most part, blacks are conscious of the effects and power behind the black vote. Most of us make excuses about not being able to get to the polls. We sit back and wait on the next brother or sister to do the job. I can't tell you how many times I've heard people say that their vote won't make a difference. So, all African Americans have to suffer just because the majority of our population won't vote. Yet, when things go wrong in the system, the ones who don't vote are the first to cry injustice," he said.

Candace nodded her head in compliance. "You're right."

"You are greatly insightful for someone so young."

"That's because I've always enjoyed American history, especially black history."

"Bet you got all A's in school, huh?"

She laughed remembering her not-so-good grades in high school. "Only in American history," she said.

"So, what are we going to do this evening?"

"Have you eaten?"

"No, and I'm famished."

"I've eaten already, but I know this great place where we can go. It's called Arthur's Place. They serve a wide variety of hearty foods, or if you just want something light like soup, salad, and sandwich…"

"Did you hear me, woman? I said I am starving," he teased.

Candace remembered their lunch at Grandma Hamlin's Chicken and Ribs and how he had eaten with passion. Then he had the nerve to order a take-out for later that afternoon.

"How do you stay so slim, Austin?"

"It's in the genes I guess. I've never had a problem with my weight."

"If I ate the way you do, I'd be as big as a house."

Sable forced a smile as she walked into the living room. When Austin saw her he stood to his feet and extended his hand to greet her.

"Hello, Mr. Kawissopie," she said, keeping her arms tightly folded.

"Good evening." Austin sensed the tension she had brought with her and knew instinctively that she had concerns over Candace going out with him. He knew she was probably thinking that a man his age wanted only one thing with her daughter. He wished he could convince her that was the furthest thing from the truth. He had a sincere interest in Candace and had no intention of messing over her. He would have to prove to her his earnestness. "I was just telling Candace how much I love your house. It is so spacious, and the drive out here was delightful."

"Yes, it does have a way of quickly growing on a person."

"I noticed your flower garden outside. Are you an avid flower connoisseur?"

"No, I'm not," was all she said.

"Well, perhaps you will learn. The garden really adds character to the house and I'm sure you want to keep it."

"Yes," was all she said again.

Candace was growing impatient with Sable and it was also obvious to Austin that she was not going to make this meeting comfortable. Candace cleared her throat and gave Sable a murderous look. "We better get going, Austin. After Arthur's Place, I've planned for us to go to the Museum of African Arts."

"It was good seeing you again, Mrs. Brooks."

"Ms. Brooks," she said. "I'm a divorcee." Sable knew there would be hell to pay when Candace got back home tonight, but that was the consequences she was willing to pay. She'd not planned to act unsociable. It was as if she had no control over her actions. As soon as they left the house she began feeling embarrassed over her laconic behavior.

*　　　　　　*　　　　　　*

Austin opened the passenger door of the Jaguar and Candace eased onto the leather seat. She was impressed with his car. She had thought the Camaro was loaded but it didn't compare to the Jag. The dashboard was mahogany-grained wood and the leather on the seats was not stiff like the leather upholstery in her car. The Jag's leather was supple and soft. The sound system was so realistic you could close your eyes and swear the musicians were right there in the car. Candace could not help but glance at Austin from time to time as he drove. He was already a wonderful looking man, but seeing him behind the wheel of such a stylish and powerful machine made him seem that much more appealing. She knew many females scoped him out when he drove his car. She had caught a few staring at him boldly while they were in transit. That was the thing about the modern woman she didn't like. Here lately, women had no respect for the other woman. They didn't even respect the sanctity of marriage. If they saw something they liked, they'd go after it. The couple of times they were together, he never gave her reason to be jealous. He'd always given her his undivided attention. She liked that about him.

Austin had not said a word since he pulled out of the driveway, and she knew the reason why.

"Austin, I apologize for my mother's behavior. She's a little stressed right now. She and her girlfriend had a falling out this afternoon. She's usually not curt with people."

"I could sense something was wrong and I hoped it wasn't my taking you out. I understand parents can be very protective, and it doesn't matter if their children are grown. If you're wondering, Candace, my intentions are honest. I have never misled or hurt a woman in my life, and I don't plan to."

"Austin, that never crossed my mind," she lied.

"Good."

As usual, Arthur's was crowded. The dance floor was packed with folks dancing to the tunes of Usher, Pattie LaBell, and Luther Vandross, just to name a few. The waitresses and waiters scurried about delivering food and taking orders. Austin ordered a quarter-inch thick T-bone steak, baked potato and salad. For dessert he ordered a slice of German chocolate cake with a scoop of vanilla ice cream. Candace ordered a fruity drink mixed with club soda and rum called an Arthur's lady. They talked about his family. He told her he missed them and planned to visit them during the Christmas holidays. They talked about AFLAME and the other jobs Candace had done since the hands-shoot advertisement. She was finding modeling very satisfying and was glad she took the chance to come and work for the agency. In the three weeks she had been there she'd earned decent money. Austin warned her that this was the fast season and not to expect this pace all the time. She was too thrilled to worry about the future. She wanted to know when she was going to do a swimsuit shoot. She heard the other models talking about their shoots and how much fun it was, not to mention the money they'd made.

"Austin, I was wondering when you're going to let me model swimsuits?" she asked openly.

"It is not time yet. There are other things I want to expose you to first."

"But the other models are asking me why I haven't modeled swimwear yet. They seem to think I have the right body for it."

He chewed the tender steak more vigorously. It was a subject he did not want to talk about. Candace was special to him. He wanted all her better qualities for himself. He'd planned not to make the same mistakes he had with Maoma. He was too free with her, wanted the entire world to see her splendid beauty, and because of that, she had died. He had sent her to Paris to pose in a bathing suit and she had died. He knew that the little jobs he was sending Candace on would not pacify her for long. She had caught him off guard with the question. There was no way he could tell her the real reason why he didn't want her to do swimsuit. "You know, I think there is a request for someone to do a fabric softener commercial. This model will be doing an actual TV commercial for Ivory Snow fabric-softener. It doesn't call for her to say anything and it's about a 10-second, slow motion, body-capture shoot. It shows the model taking the terry cloth robe from the dryer and putting it on. She then feels the softness of the robe and snuggles herself in it. It pays much more than the $500 you've been making. How does that sound?"

"You mean a real TV commercial?"

"Yes."

"Sounds good to me," she beamed. She looked at the couples on the dance floor and wanted to dance. She could not remember the last time she went dancing with a man. She started dancing in her seat.

"When you finish that big meal, why don't we exercise some of it off on the dance floor? That is, if you know how to dance. I'm not sure Africans have the rhythm."

Austin laughed. "I'll show you rhythm."

Austin was a smooth operator on the dance floor. Candace couldn't believe how talented he was. Every dance she sprang on him, he mastered. They were like two children playing at the park. Austin exaggerated some of the dances, making Candace and everyone else laugh. It wasn't hard to find the happiest couple in Arthur's. Austin grabbed her hand and swirled her around until she became dizzy. She fell into his arms laughing. Then the song "You Make Me Feel Brand New" by the Stylistics began playing. Arthur's took on a serious ambience as the men cradled their ladies closer for the slow dance. Candace looked around at the dancers. She felt out of place and didn't know if Austin would care to dance close to her or not. Austin watched her as she looked from couple to couple. He waited for her eyes to find his. He was glad for the slow song. He took her in his arms and held her close and carefully. His moves were gentle, slow, and in perfect tempo with the music. He rubbed his face to hers and sniffed her scent, then nuzzled his nose to the side of her face, bringing it to rest in her ear. He whispered how lovely she was. She consented to his advances and he lifted her chin and planted a soft kiss on her lips. When the song was over they went back to their table. Candace felt weightless, carefree, and downright giddy. She was happy and it showed. She couldn't seem to stop smiling. Austin asked if she wanted another drink.

"Thanks, I'm burning up," she said fanning herself with her hand.

"It will be quicker if I go and get them. I'll be right back."

Candace watched him disappear into the crowd as he made his way to the bar. She picked up a napkin and started dabbling at her moist face.

"Having a good time?" a familiar voice asked. Candace knew it belonged to Russell. She was stunned to see him and ashamed for him to know she was with Austin.

"Russell! She hoped he wouldn't make a scene but as quickly as the thought entered her mind, she dismissed it.

"How have you been?" she asked, feeling guilt-ridden.

"As well as can be expected," he said. "You look good."

"Thanks. So do you, Russell."

"I see you're with the AFLAME guy," he said bluntly.

"Russell…" she warned.

"Candace, I'm just here to say hello. I spotted you on the dance floor having the time of your life…" He chuckled before continuing. "I never made you laugh like that."

"Don't!" Candace warned.

"Naw, it's cool. I'm not here to hassle you. Anyway, I would like for you to meet someone." He took her hand and coaxed her out of her seat.

"I don't think I should right now."

"Don't worry, I'll have you back at your table before he gets back."

Ophelia Myerson, the girl whose picture was on Russell's nightstand was even prettier in person. Sitting, Candace could tell she was not as tall as she was. Ophelia was a busty girl, not fat but more plump than slim. She was wearing a mini-dress. Her shapely legs were crossed. She was brown like creamed coffee and sported a Toni Braxton hairstyle.

"Ophelia, I'd like you to meet Candace Brooks. Candace this is Ophelia Myerson."

Candace saw Ophelia's enthusiasm and guessed the girl got excited about anything that half-interested Russell. She reached over the table in a hurried attempt to shake Candace's hand. She smiled a candy-apple smile revealing a set of perfect dimples and beautiful teeth. She looked like a nature girl. Candace imagined her on the cover of some health magazine with an apple in one hand and a glass of milk in the other.

"Hello, Candace. I've heard a lot about you. Russell says you're like a sister to him. That's really good being that he's so far from his family back in Virginia."

"Candace looked at Russell and wondered if he had told her that after they'd made love or before. "Yes," she said warmly. "Russell's a dear friend. We go back a long ways." She thought Ophelia was genuine or she was naïve; either way, she had charm. She sat there beaming at Candace and talking a mile a minute. Candace was listening to Ophelia but not hearing what she was saying. She questioned Russell's happiness. Ophelia seemed to be the opposite of him. She hoped he had found the girl that could positively make him happy. It was clear that Ophelia adored him. She wrapped her arms around him as she continued to talk.

"Is that your boyfriend you're with?"

Candace noticed that Russell seem to perk up at the question. "We're just friends."

"You two certainly make a striking couple. Don't they, Russell? Everybody was checking the two of you out on the dance floor. He seems like a load of laughs. We must get together sometime."

Russell did not answer but looked as if his mind was in another dimension. Candace noticed his distant look and knew he was thinking of a time that included the two of them together. Ophelia kept talking, oblivious to Russell's melancholy.

"You're a model, aren't you?" asked Ophelia.

"Yes," said Candace. She realized she should at least show herself friendly by adding to the one-sided conversation. "I haven't been modeling for long, though. I'm kind of new at it."

"Oh, really. I think modeling has to be one of the best careers there is. When I was a little girl I dreamed of growing up and becoming one."

"I think all little girls dream of being a model or ballerina." Candace saw that Austin had made his way back with the drinks. He began looking around for her. "I gotta be getting back. It's been a pleasure meeting you, Ophelia."

"Same here. Don't forget about us all getting together sometime," added Ophelia.

Russell eyed Candace longingly as she backed away from the table.

"Good seeing you again, Russell." Then, just when Candace thought she was about to make a clean break, Russell offered to walk her back to her table. He was by her side quicker than she could protest. They maneuvered themselves through the sea of people.

"Are you happy, Candace?" Russell sounded interested.

"Yes, Russell. I'm always happy," she said, trying to soften her answer.

"No, you know what I mean. Is he making you happy?"

"Yes, Austin is making me very happy." There was no other way to be with him but direct. She didn't want him to be hopeful. "What about you? Ophelia seems like a lovely girl." She would not say what she truly thought. She felt Ophelia was a left shoe for Russell's right foot.

"You're filet mignon and she's chopped steak, but since I grew up on ground beef, I can appreciate it," he said seriously. Candace did not respond to Russell's statement. She thought it best not to.

"See you around, Russell." She found her way back to Austin and the drink that was waiting for her.

18

A True Gentleman

"What is it called again?" Candace stared closer at the wood carved mask of an African woman. It was greatly exaggerated with large forehead, high cheekbones, sunken eyes, and filed teeth.

"It is called Mwana Pwo, which translates to 'young woman.' It is a female dance mask that's used by the Chokwe people of Zaire. This mask incarnates a feminine ancestor. The ancestor encourages and watches over the fertility of future generations. It represents young women who have been initiated and are ready for marriage." Austin pointed to the teeth. "The filed teeth of the mask are considered a sign of beauty."

"Do they really file their teeth?" she asked, bewildered.

"Yes. It is their custom." He smiled at her amazement and took delight in answering her questions. It thrilled him that she was so interested. "It is strange to you just as your beauty rituals would be to them."

"I guess you're right."

"See the incisions below the eyes?"

"Yes."

"They represent tears of painful experiences or death."

The next exhibit was of a Nimba mask. Austin explained how the Baga people of Guinea believed that it represented the goddess of fertility to their people. "It portrays the Baga notion of a woman at her finest moment of power, beauty and presence. She appears at weddings, funerals, and at times of planting and harvesting."

Candace had learned so much in the time they'd been at the museum. The African culture itself was rich and vast. The more she discovered about it, the more she wanted to know. She asked so many questions Austin could not keep up with them. She was astonished to learn that many of the tribal customs had not changed much in hundreds of years. In tribal societies the mud or clay houses consisted of one large room where all activities were performed. They were usually built directly against neighboring structures and were often close to the tribal meeting house or church. Most of the houses were circular with conical roofs.

"What kind of house did you live in, Austin?"

"A house very similar to the ones here," he laughed. "Not all Africans live in huts, my dear. In my home there were two bedrooms, a bath, kitchen and living room. We even had a barbecue in the back yard. My brother and I shared a bedroom until my grandfather died and Momma Lena came to live with us. My mother and father gave her their bedroom because it was the nicest, and they took our room. We slept on blankets on the living room floor until my father added a third bedroom"

Candace sighed longingly. "I would give anything for the chance to see Africa."

"Anything is possible. Africa is remarkable. It is a place where every African American should visit to find out more about their roots. Centuries and distance could not destroy our sonorous culture. When I left my native home to come here, I was so homesick I thought I would die. After a while I began to see Mother Africa all around me. I saw her in my stolen brothers' and sisters' faces, in their body designs and movements. Even though our language is different I was able to hear her in their voices. I see her in you," he said, smiling his smile of wisdom as Candace hung on his every word. "I see her in your lips." He touched his index finger against them. "I see her in your hair. And, Lord, I see her in your hips. Have you ever heard the expression, 'the proof is in the pudding'?"

"Yeah, I have."

"Well, I say the proof is in the hips and lips." They both laughed.

The museum was five minutes from closing. Austin grabbed Candace by the hand and pulled her alongside him. He took giant steps and walked quickly. Candace was thankful she'd worn the flat sandals.

"Austin, why are you in such a hurry?"

"We have one more stop before the museum closes."

"Where are we going?" She paced beside him, taking two steps to his one.

Austin said not a word but laughed. Whatever the secret was, it was amusing him. They rounded the corner and came to the gift shop. Austin led Candace to a rack that was loaded with a wide assortment of African garments.

"Pick out what you like."

"Austin, what are you doing? Flowers, candy, now this. This is too much."

Austin fished through the garments and chose a dashiki with warm earth tones. It was embellished in shimmering gold trim. He held it up against Candace's shoulders.

"Ah, now this is you. Quickly, go try it on."

"I don't know," she said reluctantly.

"Don't argue with me. Do as I say," he teased, then clapped his hands making a crackling sound that made Candace jump.

"Yes, sir."

She stepped out of the dressing room and Austin knew she was nothing less than a true African goddess. She looked so much like Maoma.

*   *   *

She was surprised to learn that Austin lived 10 blocks from her old apartment in Manhattan. She knew the apartments were ritzy and the occupants were in the high-income brackets. Candace was impressed with his spacious, five-room apartment. The foyer and kitchen floors were gray-marbled. The living room floor was hardwood with a thick lamination that shone brilliantly, and was adorned by beautiful Persian rugs. The cream stucco walls illuminated the light that filtered in through an eight-foot, arched window, and the stone fireplace added to its drama. The living room was tastefully furnished with black leather furniture. The coffee and end tables had gray-marble tops supported by four marble legs. A zebra skin hung on the center wall above the couch. Two 7-foot African spears stood crisscrossed in a corner of the room. In another corner was an African drum made out of ebony wood and goatskin. Over the stone fireplace was a large picture of an African chief sitting on a tree stump. Laymen surrounded him. Candace guessed they were his army, and he was in conference with the men. The kitchen was decorated with hand-woven straw baskets and wooden bowls with carved design that told stories of African life. On his king-sized bed was a quilt that had been made by his grandmother. Its design showed an African village with the roundhouses and their straw pitched roofs. Strips of green material represented vegetable gardens. The dark brown swatches were cut into the shapes of people. Some of the women carried baskets on their heads while others tended children. One woman was nursing a baby. On the outskirts of the village was a leopard. He stalked lowly in nearby grasses, ready to pounce upon a gazelle. Hunting the leopard were African warriors with their mighty spears.

"It is the most beautiful thing I've ever seen." Candace ran her hands over the masterpiece.

"I am quite fond of it. When Mamma Lena learned I would be coming to America, she decided I should have something to remind me of home. It took her several weeks to make it."

"The workmanship is superb. I can even see the expressions on he warrior's faces. She could make a fortune making these and selling them here."

She is commissioned by one of the local art dealers in Dar es Salaam. I'm sure it is not what she would make here, but whatever she makes she is satisfied. She never discusses finances. I know if the dealer bargained to pay her $100 per quilt, she would have persuaded him to pay for the cost of supplies, materials and $200 for labor. She is shrewd."

"Does she work at a factory making these?"

"No. They have what is known as markets. Some are outdoors others are situated under roofs. They're usually located in the heart of town where tourists can come and buy souvenirs, and see the art being made. Some of the workers rent the space and give a certain percentage of their sales to the art dealers who own the space. Others are merely workers for the dealers. They are paid whatever the dealer wants to pay them. Momma Lena refuses to work without dignity. She calls her own shots."

"She sounds like a self-assured woman."

"She is. She is the best quilt maker in Dar es Salaam and everyone knows it. That is why she is able to work independently like she does."

"Now I see where your determination comes from."

"Do you feel like some wine?"

"Sure, what do you have?"

"What about some red Zinfandel. It has a very unique taste. I think you will like it."

Candace lounged on the comfortable sofa listening to Austin's whimsical stories about his childhood. The wine had relaxed her out of her sandals and she wiggled her toes whenever she laughed. Austin sat inches from her on the sturdy coffee table with the near empty wine bottle at his side. He could not remember when he'd had so much fun with a woman. He wanted the evening to go on and on. They had learned so much about each other in the past hours. Austin had learned that Candace grew up an only child, and for that reason she wanted many children. She had no qualms about putting her career on hold to be a full-time wife and mother. She did make it clear that she wanted to model for a few years before settling down. She told him about Julian Reed, her first love, and how after their breakup she concentrated on her studies. If Austin had not asked about Russell, she wouldn't have mentioned him, not because she felt he wasn't worth mentioning, but because he was an extraordinary person, and she didn't want Austin to have tainted impressions of him.

"Russell is a dear friend, Austin."

"Something tells me that he would like more from you than mere friendship."

"Why do you think that?" she asked, trying to convince him that their friendship was and had always been platonic.

"It doesn't take a genius to see when a man is in love with a woman. I saw it the day of your graduation. The way he looked at you, the warning signal he sent to me in our handshake. I saw it tonight at Arthur's Place, too. When you turned and walked away from him, he looked like a broken man."

"You sound as if you're rallying for him."

"I should say not. I just need to know how you feel about him."

"Like I said, he is a dear friend. Nothing more."

"Good. I wouldn't want to be the cause of breaking up something." Austin slid off the coffee table and onto the couch beside Candace. He rubbed the back of his hand against her smooth, dark skin, then he bent slightly and kissed her cheek.

"You taste wonderful," he said.

The wine had taken effect and Candace felt warm and mellow inside. She circled her arms around his neck and drew him closer to her. She planted a soft slow kiss on his lips and when she felt him smile she slid her tongue across them until he opened his mouth and she entered. She tasted the sweet wine on his tongue, and began sucking softly at first. Her body was heating up, and Austin felt her suggestive moves underneath him. She began kissing him passionately, letting little moans escape her throat. She was like an inferno now and could not hold her desires any longer.

"Austin, take me." It was almost like a plea.

Austin pushed himself off her but she was like a human magnet. She clung to him and rose up off the couch, tightening her grip around his neck.

"Ca-Ca-Candace, wait."

"Austin, what's wrong?"

"To move slowly is sometimes more advantageous than to go speedily."

"Is that another one of them African proverbs?"

"Yes, it is."

"Don't quote me 'nair 'nother proverb. Talking is not required for what I have in mind."

"You're not in the right frame of mind. We can't do this now."

"Aw," she wined. 'C'mon Austin. I promise I'll be good." Then she giggled.

Austin looked down at her and couldn't help but laugh. She was stoned drunk and unaware of the comical faces she was making.

"I gave my baby too much wine," Austin said, not intending for her to hear the remark.

"Am I your baby, Auddy?"

Candace's muscles relaxed and she sank completely back onto the couch. She was like a puppet and he the master. He could get her to do anything he wanted, but this was not the way he wanted her. He wanted both of them to be consciously consenting. He wanted their first time to be cherished memories. He tried to control his laughter but found it difficult. "Yes, you are my baby." He slipped his arms around her waist and propped her up on her feet. "Do you think you can walk?"

"Of course I can walk. I got two feet, don't I?" She laughed more hysterically. She was like rubber in his arms and flopped back down on the couch.

"You need some strong coffee to sober you up."

"I don't want coffee. I want some more wine." She was quick as lightning as she reached for the bottle of wine and turned it upside-down before Austin could stop her. The remaining wine gushed out of the bottle, missing her mouth and spilling all over her clothes.

"Oops, sorry about that, chief."

"Oh, great," he said agitatedly. "Stay there. I'll be right back."

Candace slouched back on the sofa and laughed herself to sleep before Austin could return with a towel.

*   *   *

The third ring woke Sable up. She looked at the neon-lit clock. It was 2:00 a.m. "Who in the world could be calling this time of morning?" She picked up the receiver. "Hello."

"Ms. Brooks."

Sable knew the voice. "Austin, is that you?"

"Yes, ma'am."

"Oh, my God! What happened? Where is Candace? Is she all right?"

"Nothing is wrong with Candace. She is fine."

"Put her on the phone."

"I can't do that because she's asleep."

"She's asleep? You call me at 2 in the morning to tell me my daughter is at a man's house, no doubt in his bed, asleep?"

"Candace had a little too much to drink. She passed out. I didn't think it appropriate to bring her home in her present state. I just didn't want you to worry about her. She is in good hands."

"Good hands, huh. Good night, Mr. Kawissopie." Sable slammed the telephone back down on its hook.

At 3 in the morning Sable found herself not able to sleep for worrying about Candace. She wished she had gotten a telephone number from Austin but hadn't thought of it at the time. She started to dial Shamell's number and then remembered the conflict they had earlier. She felt as though she would go out of her mind with worry if she didn't talk to someone. For all she knew, Austin could have been lying about Candace being all right. What if she wasn't all right? She dialed Jonah's number.

"Hello," answered a female voice.

Sable immediately thought she had dialed the wrong number. She started to hang up and redial when Jonah came on the line.

"Hello."

Sable was speechless. Every emotion she possessed presented itself. She was angry, embarrassed, and sad. She felt used and foolish. She thought of the promise they had made to each other on their last day together. He told her he hoped the district manager's position would come through so he could be near her and Candace. He'd told her how much he still loved and needed her, and there would never be another woman who could take her place.

"All lies," she whispered.

"Hello, is anyone there?"

Sable hung up the phone, turned off the lamp and sat staring in the dark.

*   *   *

A ray of sunlight filtered through the closed blinds, and warmed Candace's face. She opened her eyes and looked around at her unfamiliar surroundings. She propped herself up in the bed, then saw the handmade quilt she admired so much draped over her. Her head throbbed, and her recollection of last night came back to her in bits and pieces. She lifted her quilt and saw that she had on the dashiki Austin had bought her. "What happened to my clothes?" She tried to remember every detail about last night but could only remember Austin bending over her and kissing her cheek. Everything else was a blur. She wondered if they had made love last night. She didn't picture Austin to be the type to take advantage of a woman. She threw back the quilt and stepped on the plush carpeted flooring. She heard the rattling of pots and pans coming from the kitchen. She stood silently in the doorway watching Austin scramble eggs. He had on an Orlando Magic jersey and gray sweat pants. For an instant he looked like Jonah, and vivid images swirled in her head from her childhood. Jonah had been such a good father and she loved him for it. A part of her was still angry at Sable for ending the marriage. She felt she did not put forth hard enough effort to make the marriage work. She knew if she ever married and had children, she would do everything in her power to make it work. A child of hers would never grow up without the presence of two parents in the household if she could help it.

Austin turned around to find Candace staring at him.

"Good morning."

"Good morning, Austin." She walked into the kitchen and gestured at the dashiki she was wearing.

"I seem to have lost my clothes."

"They're not lost. I had to launder them."

Candace looked puzzled, not knowing weather to ask about the complete details of last night or be patient and hope he would divulge more information.

"Oh," she said as she pulled out a kitchen chair and eased into it. She cradled her throbbing head in her hands.

"Don't feel so good this morning, huh?" he asked.

"My head is killing me."

"I got just the thing for you." He placed a plate of eggs and toast in front of her. Next he poured a glass of orange juice and a cup of strong black coffee.

"Eat up and I guarantee you'll feel better in two shakes of a lamb's tail."

Candace forked at the eggs and nibbled on the toast. She didn't have an appetite for the breakfast.

"Austin, I don't remember much about last night. I don't remember putting this on."

"That's because you didn't. You were drunk as a skunk," he laughed. "You spilled wine all over your clothes. I had no choice but to change your clothes and launder them before the wine set in. The stains would have never come out if you'd kept them on a minute longer."

"Oh." She sipped the coffee and frowned at its bitterness.

"Don't worry, Candace; we did nothing. But I have to admit, you are quite tempting."

19

I Go to The Rock

Sable dialed Aunt Elvira's number. It was 8 o'clock in the morning and Sable knew she would be getting ready for church.

"This is the day that the Lord hath made; let us rejoice and be glad in it. Good morning."

"Aunt Vi!" Sable's voice was panicky.

"Sable, that you?"

"Yes Aunt Vi. Its me."

"Baby, what's wrong? You don't sound right?"

"Maybe it's nothing, but Candace didn't come home last night after going out with Austin, that African. I know she's grown, Aunt Vi, yet I feel so uncomfortable about him."

"Lord, ha' mercy! No baby, you got a right to feel the way you do. I felt the same way first time I laid eyes on 'em. Me and Jonah talked about it on the way back. He don't like 'em neither, but he thinks it's just an affair that'll blow over with the wind. But I'm like you; I'm not so sure."

"He called me at 2 o'clock in the morning to say that Candace had too much to drink. She passed out, Aunt Vi."

"Oh, sugah, I don't know what to tell you other than not to worry, and I know that's hard to do. Pray for her, baby. Take it to the Lord. He'll work things out. Look, sweetie, I'm getting ready for Sunday school. The church van gon' be pulling up soon. I 'ma put her on the alter, hear? The whole church gon' be praying for her. The Lord gon' fix it, you watch and see. It might not be our way but it'll be the best way; his way."

Sable thought about church. With the confrontation with Shamell, Candace's staying out all night doing God knows what, and the woman at Jonah's last night, she needed a spiritual uplifting. She walked into the spacious bathroom and drew a tub of bath water.

*   *   *

It was a beautiful Sunday in June. Parishioners were making their way from the parking lot to Rising Star Baptist Church. Devoted little girls followed their mothers willingly, while fathers struggled with their rambunctious little boys. As Sable drove the Mercedes into the parking lot, she could not help but marvel at the scene. It all looked like something from a Norman Rockwell painting. Sable swung her navy and white pumps with the gold bows onto the asphalt. She stepped from the car feeling better than she had earlier. She straightened her navy sailor-dress with the row of white and gold buttons, then tilted the wide brim of her white hat over her right eye. She walked confidently up the steps and through the double-arched doors and into the crowded church. One of the ushers greeted her and led her to the third pew from front. The choir swayed from left to right in their colorful robes. It wasn't long before Sable felt the rhythm and joined in by clapping her hands to the harmonious sounds of the pure gospel singing. Reverend Montgomery took the podium and started his sermon off with a song. "It's a highway to He-a-ven, none can walk up there, none but pure in heart…" His deep baritone voice vibrated through Rising Star, bouncing from the high tech surround sound system, then touching the congregation's souls. He hit each note perfectly and halfway through his singing the members started jumping out of their seats like popcorn. They raised their hands in the air and started praising the Lord.

"If the Lord has done something good for you, then ya' ought to stand to your feet and praise him," said the reverend. The whole congregation stood and started making a joyful noise unto the Lord. Sable was burdened with the occurrences of the day before. Her eyes clouded over and the tears began to flow down her face.

"The Lord tells us in his word that if we trust in him that he would fight our battles. All we need is faith the size of a little bitsy mustard seed, and he said he'll fix it didn't he?"

"Amen! Hallelujah!" said the church.

"But you know, some of us don't believe that, do we, church?"

"That's right, pastor!"

"In our darkest moments is when we ought to have the most faith. When the doctors tell us they've done all they can do, that's the time we ought to trust the Lord the most. When friends fail us, that's the time we ought to call the Lord's name a little louder. When that son or daughter strays, that's when we s'pose to cry J-E-S-U-S! I know you still there. I know you haven't left me! In Psalm 121 verse 3 he said he would not suffer thy foot to be moved: he that keepeth thee will not slumber. Jesus doesn't sleep on the job, folks. He doesn't need caffeine to pep him up, does he? He's always working miracles."

"Amen!"

"He's always wake ain't he y'all? I think about old Job and how he was confronted with tragedy after tragedy. But Job kept holding on? Even when his wife called him a fool and told him to curse God and die, he kept holding on didn't he?"

"Amen!" church

"I don't believe y'all hear me in here this morning!"

"Amen! Hallelujah!"

"Even after he lost everything he owned, he kept right on holding on." Reverend Montgomery strutted across the pulpit stretching his hands towards the heavens and re-enacting the part of Job in torment. "Our trials and tribulations don't even compare to what Job went through, yet time we get a little headache we want to give up. We serving the same God today that Job served back then. The same God that locked the lions' mouths so they couldn't hurt his child Daniel. We serving the same God that parted the Red Sea so Moses and the Israelites could escape old Pharaoh and his army. The same God that put a child in Sarah's womb at the ripe old age of 91! The same God can cure cancer—huh! The same God can cure AIDS—huh! The same God can mend a broken heart—huh! The same God can make that spouse straighten up—huh! The same God can get your children off drugs—huh! We serving THE SAME GOD! THE SAME GOD! THE SAME GOD!"

The music started playing, the choir singing and the whole church was in a joyous uproar. Sable was standing with her hands extended in the air. She was crying tears of relief now. At this moment she felt she could take on the troubles of the world. She was glad she had come. Her soul had been fed.

20

Guilt

Charles rolled over on his side to discover that Shamell had already showered and was dressing. She bent slowly like an old woman and stepped into her panties. As she pulled them up over her hips, Charles noticed the bruise on her back. It was the diameter of a grapefruit. He remembered the elbow blow he had given her the night before last. A lump rose in his throat as he watched her pull the housedress over her shoulders then down past her knees. He closed his eyes pretending to be asleep as she turned around to leave the room.

Shamell fixed herself a cup of coffee and grabbed the inch-thick stack of manuscripts. She balanced the cup of coffee in her right hand and managed to open the balcony door with her left. She stepped out into the warm sunlight and took her place at the patio table. The sun felt stimulating to her after being inside an air-conditioned apartment all night. That was one of her pet peeves with Charles; he loved running the air 5 degrees above the comfort zone and it always chilled her to the bone. She took a sip of the sugared and creamed coffee and rested her head back against the exterior wall. She was growing lazy fast, but she was determined to edit the writings before evening. But first, she enjoyed the coffee and the warm sun. She knew Charles would be leaving for the golf course soon, and the solitude would be greatly needed. She edited Sable's work first. She halfheartedly read through the two chapters in no time. It was almost perfect with the exception of two mistakes; subject-verb agreement. She didn't bother to write a note like she usually did; instead she circled the errors with a red marker. She was still upset over Sable's remark yesterday. Even though every bit of it was true, she still thought Sable had a lot of nerve to verbally accuse Charles. It would have been another thing if she had thought it and kept it to herself, but she had embarrassed her and that had been painful.

After clearly rethinking the events of Friday night, she could see how Charles had gotten upset. Why she pounced on him like she had was beyond her. It wasn't the first time he had come home late and probably wouldn't be the last. His tardiness didn't mean he was being unfaithful any more than she was being unfaithful when she had to work late. The only difference was she made a habit of calling when she was running late. Of course, men were different in that respect. You couldn't expect them to be conscientious about everything. Thousands of men around the world were committed to their jobs and that's all it was, ordinary job commitment, she told herself. She knew that was something she'd just have to deal with if she wanted to keep Charles. If Charles knew of Sable's accusations, he would be livid. He didn't care much for her anyway. He was always trying to drive a wedge into their friendship. He'd told her often that he thought Sable was pretentious, high and mighty. She was just sorry it had taken so long for her to see it. Shamell quickly tossed the manuscript aside and grabbed the next one. She took more time with this one, highlighting the errors in a soft fluorescent yellow instead of the bright red. She wrote in corrections and gave advice along with friendly little jokes so as not to dispirit the author.

She had been editing for quite some time and was getting through the pile when the patio door creaked opened. She looked up to see Charles standing before her with a tray of food in his hands.

"It's 12 o'clock, aren't you hungry?"

Shamell smiled slightly. "I've been working so hard I haven't had time to think about food, but I guess I can take a break. She pushed the papers aside to make room for the tray.

"I've got something good." Charles said. "Cheeseburgers with chopped onions cooked in the burgers just the way you like them. And homemade cottage fries."

"It smells wonderful." She squeezed a little ketchup and spread some mustard on the thick cheeseburger. She didn't realize how hungry she was until she sank her teeth into the sandwich.

"Mmm, this is good."

"You just eat up; you need it. I notice you didn't eat breakfast."

"I had a cup of coffee."

"A cup of coffee! That's not breakfast. You decided not to go to aerobics today?"

"Yeah, just wanted to get started on my editing."

"How's it coming?" he asked.

"Okay."

He picked up a manuscript and began reading it aloud. He chuckled "Who writes this stuff?" he flipped over to the last page and discovered it belonged to Sable.

"Sable Brooks," he said sardonically. "How she doing? Haven't heard or seen her around lately"

"She just moved into her new house. That keeps her pretty busy."

"Out in Connecticut, right?"

"Um hmm."

"Maybe that'll keep her from loafing around here so much," he said.

"I'm going to ask to have her reassigned to another editor."

"Oh, yeah?" He was clearly interested.

"I'm overloaded and overworked."

"Sure there's not more to it than that?" Charles wondered why she chose Sable to be the one to have reassigned.

"We haven't been seeing eye-to-eye lately."

"I tried to tell you a long time ago, Shamell, that the two of you are like oil and water. She so bourgeois and you—you're conventional. When you're around her, you pick up her persona. You know I've told you a thousand times I don't like you acting like Sable."

"I didn't see it then, Charles, but now I do."

Shamell sipped on her cola. The coolness of the drink flowed through her body, bringing rejuvenation from the sun's glow. Now, if she could persuade herself to believe what Charles had just said, she would be all right.

*   *   *

Sable had found the courage to pick up the phone and call Shamell. She figured she had calmed down by now and come to her senses. She rehearsed what she was going to say, but when Shamell answered the phone Sable went blank.

"Hello?"

"Shamell, this is Sable. I'm calling to see how you are."

There was a moment of silence that seemed to last an eternity. Doubt began to surface and as the seconds grew, Sable realized she had made a mistake in calling her so soon. She was finding it hard to believe that her concern for her best friend had brought their years of friendship to a halt. The situation was turning ridiculous, and she was not about to let Shamell walk out of her life without a fight.

"I'm fine. Why wouldn't I be?"

"Of course you are…"

"Listen, I'm in a bit of a hurry. Charles is taking me to a Broadway musical and I don't want to be the holdup."

"Oh, certainly. I won't keep you then. Maybe we can talk later?"

"We'll see." Shamell's tone was cold and distant. The phone went dead. What Sable had thought would be one of their infamous long conversations turned out to be a three-minute quickie. She remembered the church service and what Reverend Montgomery had said about withstanding your trials. These were no doubt trying times she was going through. Somehow she had to find the power to endure. She decided to give it until Wednesday. If Shamell didn't call back by then, she'd pay her a visit at the office.

*   *   *

It was 3 in the afternoon before Candace and Austin returned to Torryville. They found Sable sitting in the flower garden working on her manuscript. The engine of the Jaguar was so quiet that Sable didn't hear them pull into the driveway. It wasn't until the car doors slammed shut that she turned around to see them walking slowly toward her. She removed the shades from her stern face. She wanted to make eye contact with Austin and Candace, stare them square in their eyes and watch them squirm.

"Hi, Mom."

"I see you decided to come home," she said

"If you would allow me," Austin said. "It was certainly not either of our intentions to disrespect you in anyway. Like I explained to you last night, Candace had a bit much to drink and I didn't think it proper to bring her home so late, especially in her condition."

"Mr. Kawissopie, I don't think you're the one to justify ethics to me. If you knew the least thing about it, you would have considered your age difference before pursuing my daughter."

"Mom!" Candace was outraged. She couldn't believe what she was hearing coming from Sable. "How dare you talk over me like I'm a child. I'm 22, grown as I'll ever be and quite capable of making my own decisions about who I want to go out with. Austin has been nothing but a gentleman to me. He does not deserve the treatment that you're giving him and I won't allow you to continue disrespecting him." Candace looked at Austin, "I knew it wouldn't work, my moving in with her," she mumbled the words softly but loud enough for both to hear.

"Well," Sable said as she lifted herself from the chair and began gathering her papers. "I can see I'm not needed out here, so I'll just leave you two alone."

"I am sorry for everything," added Austin.

"I'm sure you are." Sable made her way past them, then turned around as if forgetting something. "I appreciate your effort in trying to sway me over. I don't mean to seem overbearing or harsh, but you have to consider my position here. I'm a mother, and my love and concern sometimes get in the way."

Candace and Austin watched Sable strut hurriedly across the lawn and into the house.

Candace was a little calmer hearing the reason behind Sable's hostility; still it was not an excuse she could accept.

"Now do you see why I want my own place?"

Austin eased his hands in his pants pocket and looked around at the assortment of beautiful flowers. He spotted a section of daisies with bees swarming around them.

"Candace, do you see the bees traveling back and forth from the daisies?"

Candace gave him an incredulous look. She could not believe his mind was elsewhere after what had just happened.

"Austin, we're not talking about flowers."

"Do you like bees, Candace?"

"What?"

"Bees? What do you think of them?"

"They're bothersome and especially if they sting you."

"Actually, the bee is very useful. They make honey, you know."

"I know that Austin."

"Do you like honey?"

Candace knew now where the conversation was going. She was beginning to get the message behind his speech, and the revelation eased her anxieties.

"Even though they're a bother and can be threatening, their benefits greatly outweighs their cons. The same thing applies to your mother. Her words and actions disturb you, but they're only for the good of your preparation. Your finishing. True, your mother has a sting. I have felt it too, but it is a sting that is medicinal in purpose. It is a sting that tells the truth, and is based on old-fashioned morals and respect. I can't harbor ill feelings for her, because she is sincere. I respect her for that." Austin pulled out one of the patio chairs from under the table and sat down. He reached for Candace's hands and rubbed them gently.

"You're almost too good to be true," she said.

"And believe me when I say you are a godsend," he replied.

"Can I ask you something personal?"

Austin knew the questions would be very personal, and he was ready to answer almost anything she wanted to know.

"Sure, you may."

"Why in heaven's name aren't you married? Why hasn't some woman snatched you up yet?"

He blushed and was grateful for her delicate and flattering form of questioning.

"I was married for a short while. Her name was Maoma Ngare. She was from Tanzania, too. Like me, she came to the states for educational reasons. She was an elementary school teacher. I met her in Central Park one afternoon when I was having lunch. It was in the summer and she was free from teaching. She was sitting on a park bench reading a book. Her hair was in braids and she was wearing a tee shirt with a picture of the continent of Africa on it, and the caption underneath read Habari Hujambo."

Candace tried to pronounce the words. "Ha-ba-re…"

"No." Austin helped her with the pronunciation. "Habari Hujambo, which means 'hello, how are you?'"

"Ha-ba-ri hu-jam-bo," she said again, this time near perfect.

"When I saw the inscription on her shirt, I figured she could speak Swahili so I answered 'Sijambo,' which means I'm fine. Maoma looked up from her book at me. She said 'samahani,' which means excuse me. It was at that moment that I knew she was from my home. We began to converse in Swahili." Austin smiled at his warm memories as he told the story to Candace. "Upon our departure that day we said our good-byes and never uttered a word about meeting back there the next day. We just knew we would. Sure enough, the next day we met at the same place and time. A year later we were married in a small ceremony here and a grand ceremony in Dar es Salaam. While we were there, Maoma traveled to Paris on business." Austin felt it was too soon to tell her the nature of her travel. He would tell her when he felt the time was right. "She was only supposed to be gone for a few days. I stayed to visit with my family. Her plane never made it. It crashed and she was killed."

"I'm so sorry, Austin. I never would have asked if I'd known."

"It's okay. I'm glad to say that the healing process is over. Maoma was very beautiful, soft-spoken and so lovable. She was kind and giving. She loved teaching and more than that she loved children. You look so much like her. That day you walked into my office I thought I was seeing Maoma's ghost. Seeing you brought back so many memories."

"Man! I don't know if that's good or not, Austin."

"What do you mean?"

"Do you like me for who I am or the person I remind you of?

"For who you are. I have to admit the reason I rejected you was because you reminded me of Maoma. I mean, a fool would've known you were model material. I was afraid, that's all. Afraid to be reminded of what I had and afraid to move on without it. So, I've been in limbo since her death five years ago."

"You chose a life of celibacy for five years?"

Austin's expression was serious yet kind. "No, I did not practice celibacy. I am a man of needs. I chose to fulfill my needs without choosing love. Do you understand what I'm saying, Candace?"

She knew exactly what he was saying and she certainly didn't like the idea of his dalliance. She wondered if it was one woman or many women. What kind of relationship did they have now? Did they practice safe sex? Was he carrying a sexually transmitted disease? Candace shook her head in confusion as the questions raced through her mind.

Austin squeezed her hands tightly. "What are you thinking?"

"So many things right now."

"I am not a complex man to figure out. I would not keep anything from you that you should know."

"Do you still sleep with them?"

"It was only one and I haven't seen her in quite some time now. We were always careful when we were together intimately and not every time we were together we had sex. Sometimes we went to dinner and dancing or to a show or we just got together for conversation."

"A call girl, huh?"

"Yes, a call girl. Does that bother you?"

"It's something I wouldn't do, that's for sure."

"That is refreshing to know," he chuckled.

They sat in the flower garden talking for hours before fat droplets of rain started to fall. They made a mad dash to the front porch. Candace pulled Austin closer to her and planted a long wet kiss on his lips.

"I should have kept you with me instead of bringing you back home," he said.

"Yes, you should have."

He held her tighter and Candace could feel him stiffening. Her breath came in short pants and her nipples hardened as she pushed herself closer to him.

"C'mon," he said as he led her off the porch and to the car. He opened the passenger door and helped her in. He turned the key in the ignition and the Jaguar started quietly; so quietly it was some while before Sable knew they had left.

          *   *   *

The drive back to Manhattan was quiet as each anticipated what was about to happen. Austin drove with one hand on the steering wheel and the other caressing Candace's hand. Periodically they shared glances at each other. When they pulled into the garage of Austin's complex Candace's heart skipped a beat. Even though she was more than ready to make love to Austin, she was equally nervous. Once the elevator doors closed they clung to each other like magnets.

Austin followed close behind Candace as she stepped through the threshold. He pushed the door closed behind him. Austin reached for Candace's arm and turned her around to face him. He kissed her full lips making sucking sounds as he released them. She buried her face in the side of his neck teasing him with her tongue. She licked tiny circles then larger ones until she reached his ear. She flicked her tongue against his earlobe. He moaned low and the sound of it aroused Candace. She inserted her wet warm flesh in the canal of his ear and he shuddered as he called her name. Austin unbuttoned the buttons of her black safari shirt then pulled the hem out of the skirt's waist. He unbuckled the leopard-skin belt with familiar fingers as he had done the night before when she had passed out. He let each article of clothing drop to the floor. She stood before him in French cut panties and bra. She was to him a vision of beauty. For the first time in a long time Austin didn't think of Maoma, but only of Candace.

Candace peeled away his clothes as delicately as she could. She tried to conceal her ravenous desire for him. Her mind reverted back to Russell when she looked at Austin's body, and for the life of her she didn't know why. There was nothing similar about the two men. They were different, intellectually as well as physically. Russell was light-skinned with a muscular build, while Austin was lean and dark. But, as she discovered the large bulge in his briefs she knew there was one thing they did have in common. Austin eased down on the leather couch bringing Candace down and straddling her across his lap. He explored her back with his fingertips while gazing in her large brown eyes. He unhooked her bra and slid it off of her arms. She had gorgeous breasts. They were full, round and smooth. Her nipples were perky and perfectly shaped. He cupped each with both hands feeling their round pliable form. When he covered them with the warm wet heat of his mouth, she melted a little more and called Jesus. Her head rolled backward and she arched her back inward to give Austin more leverage. As she reveled in her rapture, she began rotating her hips over Austin's massive swell, and when she began to feel on the verge of insanity, she grabbed his temples with the palm of each hand and guided his mouth away from her breast toward her mouth. Their tongues played tag as his hands tugged and pulled at her underwear. Candace lifted her body enough for Austin to peel away her panties. When she eased back down he felt her juices moisten his thighs. He kneaded the inner parts of her thighs moving closer and closer to her secret garden. His index finger traced the lips of her opening, then tickled her. She trembled with excitement and her kisses grew frantic while baby-cries seeped from the corners of her mouth. She ran her hands down his hairy chest, stopping only to massage the cavity of his navel, then down to his family jewel. She slipped her hands under the elastic of his briefs and pulled them far enough down so that Austin could get them completely off. He was anxious and erotic as his scepter greeted her with full eloquence. She massaged him, and when Austin could take no more, he lifted her buttocks and slid himself slowly inside her. Candace used every muscle in her thighs and legs to seesaw herself above him. Their passion grew, and the two of them were quickly becoming one. Austin thrust deeper and faster. He felt Candace's arms tighten around his neck.

Her perspiring face stuck to the side of his own as they moved in undulated motions on the couch.

"Austin!" She called his name quickly as the amorous tingles promised to explode in her body. And then, she called it once again. This time slowly, releasing with it gushes of hot breath that emphasized each syllable as she relished in the final notes of ecstasy. "Au-stin!"

He held her close to him and was drunk with rapture and the knowledge that she had taken of him what she wanted and hopefully needed. He steadied himself as Candace tightened her feminine muscles around his maleness, then relaxed them slowly. She continued the cycle, adding to the drama by circling her hips. It wasn't long before Austin too had exploded in rhapsody.

"Nakupenda!" he said breathlessly. "Nakupenda Malaika!"

She could not know now that the words meant "I love you, I love you angel." She was too wrapped up in the experience to ask, but she would hear them many times to come.

It had been years since he had known such happiness. He was so overcome with bliss that he could not say anything more. He looked at her face beaming down on him. He buried his face in the center of her breast and released his tears, letting them camouflage with the sweat of their bodies. Austin had taken her to a place where Julian had never taken her but she had to admit, Russell had come close, pretty darn close.

21

Can't Shake the Feeling

Sable was surprised to see Russell standing on the other side of the screen door. He was drenched from making his way from the car up to the front porch without an umbrella. She hurried and opened the door to let him in.

"Russell!" she said with sincere excitement. She hugged him before he stepped all the way inside. "This is a pleasant surprise. Look at you. You're soaked through to the bones. Where is your umbrella?" she said with a maternal chime that reminded him of his own mother.

"Aw, I didn't think the rain would amount to anything. I was out riding around and decided to come out and pay you and Candace a visit. I hope I'm not intruding."

She grabbed him by the hand and led him into the kitchen. "You need to stop. You know you just like family. You have to settle for me, because Candace is not here. I'm sorry."

"You'll do just fine, Ms. Brooks."

Sable filled the kettle with water and sat it on the eye of the stove. "I'm going to make some tea. You'll catch your death of cold. Now you sit right there while I go get a towel."

Sable came back with an oversized beach towel. She handed it to Russell and he began drying himself.

"I haven't seen you since the graduation dinner. Where have you been hiding?"

The muscles in his jaw tensed. "Ms. B, I haven't been hiding. I don't want you to think that. I don't know if Candace has told you everything or not, but for the record I want you to know I love your daughter and probably always will. I know she has something going with the African."

Sable poured boiling water over the tea bags. She placed a cup and saucer in front of Russell and the other at her setting. The ill at heart got her sympathy every time and it seemed that Russell had his fair share of broken hearts. She had to commend him though; he had a great determination to win Candace over. She hoped he would but feared he wouldn't. She reached over and patted his hand. "Good things come to those who wait."

"You're right," he said with a paltry smile. "Thing is, I can't wait too long because I've met someone too. Her name is Ophelia and she is a good girl. She's kind, pretty, smart, has a good job, and I know she cares for me but…"

"But there is no chemistry there, is it?" Sable added.

"Right." Russell took a sip of the tea.

"You know, Russell, it's rare that in the beginning two people will have the same kind of attractions for each other, get together and stay together for life. That just isn't the norm. Usually one will like the other more. Personally, I don't want you to give up on Candace, yet I don't want Ophelia to be hurt either. There aren't any easy answers for you. The best advice I can give you is to let God decide for you. Entrust everything to him."

"I'm not a very religious person. I mean I was raised in the church and everything, but since I moved up here I sort of strayed."

"Russell, as long as there is life in your body it's never too late to reinstate your faith in God."

Russell shook his head. He felt somewhat relieved just talking to her. "I saw her at Arthur's Place last night—with him."

"Yes. They did go out last night. He came by the house to pick her up."

"What kind of person is he? Did you get to talk to him much?"

"He comes off like a gentleman and he may very well be but, there is something that makes me uneasy about the whole thing. Aunt Vi felt it too and she is very in tuned to her sixth sense. Jonah and Daddy don't like it either, but they think it's something that won't amount to anything and I sure hope they're right for Candace's sake. I just don't want to see her get hurt. There was once a guy in her life named Julian Reed. She was so in love with him. When he decided he wanted to start seeing other girls it nearly killed her. She retreated and withdrew from everybody and everything. Then you came along. You were a blessing, whether you knew it or not. She eventually started coming out of her shell. She didn't take an interest in any other guys but you. But then I noticed how slow your relationship was moving so, I chalked it up as friendship. I still think that if it's in the cards the two of you will get together."

"Where is she now?"

"They're together, Russell."

"I was afraid of that," he buried his head in his hands and took a deep breath before continuing. "I thought if I came by to talk to her for a while maybe I could find out how deep she's in with this guy and maybe steer her away from him. I guess the thought was demented, huh?"

"Oh, honey, you're only doing what any normal man in love would do." Again, she had to admire him for his courage. He was a remnant of a fast dying breed of men who stilled believed in chivalry. "Just don't let yourself get obsessed with this pursuit. Give it a reasonable amount of time, but don't put your life on hold waiting for her to come around because, honestly speaking, she might not. If you see that Candace has made her mind up about wanting to be with Austin, move on."

They sat at the kitchen table talking for a solid hour. Then Sable gave him the grand tour of the house. Russell decided he had to go and get ready for work the next day. Sable loaned him one of her umbrellas and walked him to the door.

"You keep in touch with me now and remember what I said about faith."

"Sure thing, Ms. B." He stepped onto the porch then turned quickly. "Tell her I came by."

"Certainly."

Russell had done his homework well. He had already found out a lot about Austin. Working for the postal service was convenient when you wanted to find out personal information. He traced Austin's home address via AFLAME. He used a bogus name the day he called the agency and asked for an employee directory. He'd told the person that he worked for the post office and that the directory would be helpful in tracking and sending incomplete mailings going to the agency. The naïve employee complied and within four working days Russell received the directory.

He circled the block that housed Austin's condominium complex three times. There was not much he could tell from the outside of the building. He parked and dimmed his headlights across the street form the underground garage. He knew Austin drove a gold Jaguar and that was the car he was looking for to come driving out. He looked at his watch. It was 11:57. He knew spying on them was underhanded, but he could not go back to his apartment with anything but memories of the times they shared and that special night they lay together.

If only Candace had driven her own car he could have followed her and signaled for her to pull over by blinking his lights. Of course, this late at night it might have frightened her and caused her to speed, thus causing an accident. He certainly didn't want that to happen. If only he could talk to her alone where there were no intruding ears or prying eyes, he knew he could convince her that he was the only one for her. He had to make her see that. He heard Sable telling him to move on with his life if Austin was the one she chose. He shook his head at the voice. "She doesn't know what she wants," he said in the darkness of his car. "I'll have to show her."

Two round beams of light surfaced from the underground garage and Russell crouched lower in the Camry so the light would not shine on him and give him away. As the light of the Jaguar rolled past the abandoned looking car, Russell sprang up. He quickly started his engine and with the headlights still turned off, he turned the car around. He waited for them to get barely out of sight before he turned his lights on and began trailing them.

22

Strategies

The senior staff members of AFLAME had just adjourned a meeting to plan for the fifth annual Blacktravaganza Fashion Show that was to take place in October. It was one of New York's biggest ethnic black-tie affairs of the year. All the dignitaries of New York's society circle would be there. The timeline for the Blacktravaganza event was on schedule and running smoothly.

Hardin Ferguson was Austin's closet friend and confidant. He had known Maoma and was deeply sadden over her death. He also knew about Candace and how much Austin was taken with her. There were several reasons why Austin liked Hardin. He was a down-to-earth person who didn't have an ounce of pretentiousness about him. He was supposed to be an inner-city statistic that ended up in prison or dead but he'd beaten the odds by playing his way through college on a basketball scholarship. He was one of few players who didn't expect basketball to pave his road to success. He knew the odds. No matter how good he thought he was or how good his coaches told him he was, he knew there were better players. When he finished college he took a job with

AFLAME as a technical assistant. Ten years later he was the director over AFLAME's marketing department.

His ability to think quickly on his feet was another reason why Austin liked him. He had brilliant marketing and strategic ideas that, when put into action, had saved AFLAME tens of thousands of dollars. But his humor and jollity were the other reasons why Austin liked him. Austin was walking side by side with Phyllis, giving her instruction for the day. Hardin took double steps to catch up with them.

"Austin," called Hardin. "Just wanted to say that I think your idea is great. Having the new designers' creations modeled by our newest models is a wonderful idea. You know how our veteran models feel about modeling garments by unknown designers. Your plan will keep everyone happy. The new models will be grateful for just being in Blacktravaganza and the veterans will get to keep their superior complexes." The three of them laughed.

"This will be the first time that inexperienced models grace the runway at Blacktravaganza. If it's a success, then we should try it every year," said Phyllis.

"Every major media station and paparazzi in New York will have their cameras aimed at the new models. Are you sure Miss Brooks doesn't have anything to do with this?" asked Hardin with an insidious smile.

Austin blushed a broad grin. "I promise you she doesn't. Matter of fact, she knows nothing of it." He walked briskly while Phyllis and Hardin hurried alongside him.

"Phyllis, I need to see the garments that will be modeled. I'm especially interested in the new designers' creations. I also want to get with the fashion coordinators and discuss with them who will be wearing what."

Hardin eyed him suspiciously. "But Austin, that's the coordinators' job. I mean, we never intervene with the selection of garments or decide who wears what. The coordinators are the experts. I say let them earn their salaries."

"They are the experts, but there is nothing wrong with diversifying ourselves through cross-training. A strong company is one that knows the ins and outs of the operational structure. That is something I'm going to recommend to the board members. I think it's a sensible and sound idea."

"I agree with that, but why try to fix something that isn't broke? Upper management knows enough about every department here. We have our books to prove it. For the past three years our capital gains have been 15 percent higher than expected."

"Excuse me, but is that all, sir?" Phyllis interrupted.

"Yes, Phyllis, and thank you," said Austin.

Hardin was grateful for the privacy. He knew Austin all too well and wasn't buying the diversification bit. They had been friends for a long time, but when it came to business, which in terms meant his bread and butter, he didn't view it lightly. "What you're going to do is disrupt the regimen, and we don't need that right now this close to show time. The fashion coordinators and the models are the ones who make us look good. Trust me you don't want to upset them. You know over 50 percent of our accounts are based on how good we look at Blacktravaganza."

"I hear what you're saying and I appreciate it. I still say this is for the betterment of the company."

"You want to put too many biscuits on your plate, dear friend. Why don't you just admit it?"

"Admit what?"

"That you want to keep close tabs on Candace."

Austin said nothing but gave Hardin a culpable look.

"You can't protect her, Austin. You can try with all your might and that still won't be enough. I know you're still dealing with Maoma's death and you feel part to blame, but truth is?" he paused before continuing. "It was her time. When it's your time, my time, or even Candace's time to go, all the protection in the world won't save us."

"I'm over Maoma now," he said persuasively.

"I hope you are. If this is something that you feel you must do, there're other ways you can manipulate without upsetting everyone."

"Manipulate! I'm not manipulating!"

"Okay, I'm sorry. Poor choice of words. Talk with Madame Yvonne. She's cooperative. Tell her the style of garments you want Candace to wear. Honestly speaking, Austin, I wouldn't want my wife bearing all either."

Austin shook his head and patted Hardin lightly on the back.

*　　　　　*　　　　　*

Sable walked up to the doors of Alpha Publishing Company with her latest chapters under her arm. The cool air greeted her as she pulled opened the entrance door and stepped in. She stepped on the elevator and pushed the 5th floor button.

"Hello, Keisha."

The cute girl in her early 20s looked over her glasses at Sable "Hi, Ms. Brooks. It's been a long time."

"Yes, it has. How have you been?"

"Busy as ever."

"Is Shamell in?"

"Yes, let me buzz her for you."

"Yes, Keisha?"

"Ms. Brooks is here to see you."

There was silence and then Shamell's office door opened. Sable looked at her with apologizing eyes. Shamell crossed her arms defensively across her chest.

"Hello, Sable," she said icily.

"Hello, Shamell." Sable's tone was warm and cheery, which was an absolute contrast from Shamell's.

"I was just about to give you a call and inform you of some changes."

"Changes?" Sable was thinking she meant changes that had to be made in her manuscript.

"Yes. I won't be your editor anymore. You've been assigned to Marsha Griggs."

Sable was speechless. Her mouth dropped opened and hung for a full 30 seconds before she was able to speak. "What are you saying, Shamell?"

"I'm overloaded, overworked and can't handle the weight anymore. I needed help, so I asked the senior editor if he could take some of the pressure off."

Sable looked around at the staff, who had grown quiet. Some were purposely avoiding eye contact while others stared openly. The two women stood formally. Sable felt sick and had the impulse to grab her stomach but fought the urge. Humiliation swept over her. She felt like she was being fired in the presence of the whole world.

"Can we talk in the privacy of your office?"

Shamell looked around to see that all eyes were suddenly on her now. She stepped aside and let Sable pass through. She pushed the door closed and walked around behind her desk. She remained standing as Sable began to talk.

"What has gotten into you, Shamell? I cannot believe what you just said out there in front of everybody. Are you that upset with me to discard me off like that?"

Shamell exhaled. "I'm sorry, but the arrangements have already been made."

"And Marsha Griggs of all people. You could have done better than that, Shamell. You know how she is. She doesn't understand slang jargon, she is as proper as they come, and I'll never get my book completed on time. Besides, how could Mr. Easton assign me to her anyway? She's not a fiction editor. She edits histories, and you know that's a total contrast to my style of writing."

I had no control over who Mr. Easton assigned you to. Maybe you need to talk with him. I'm sure he has the power to give you to someone else."

"I can't believe you. It is obvious that our friendship means nothing to you." She waited for a reply from Shamell, who instead eased down in her chair. Sable thought she saw signs of weakening.

"Shamell," she said pleadingly and softly. "I'm sorry for what I said on Saturday. But I said it because I love and care about you. You're too good a person to let someone take advantage of you in any kind of way, especially abuse. There's support groups that can help you."

"You something else! You're still clinging to your wild accusations. I didn't mention it to Charles because he would have been livid. Being accused of beating his wife, of all things! You call yourself my friend, yet you call me a liar! If that's what you think of me, then it's better we end it."

"Look, Shamell, I didn't want to have to tell you this, but Charles is being unfaithful to you with a NYU student. She is brown-skinned and wears her hair in long braids. I saw them together that day I purchased the living room furniture. Even Candace has seen them together. She says they are an item on campus."

Shamell said nothing but busied herself with papers on her desk.

"Listen, Shamell, I didn't want to believe what I was seeing, but he took her to the Centennial Ramada Inn. At first I thought it was you driving the Porsche and I followed, but when Charles and this girl got out and he rubbed her butt…" she paused and looked at Shamell, who seemed unaffected by what she was saying, "well, I knew it wasn't innocent then."

Shamell picked up the phone and buzzed Keisha.

"Yes, Mrs. Anderson?"

"Keisha, get my husband on the phone and let him know that I will be meeting him for lunch."

"Yes, ma'am."

"Thank you, dear."

After everything had been said and done, Sable swallowed the lump in her throat. She looked at Shamell, who pretended to be editing. She thought things were supposed to be looking up. She'd prayed and entrusted everything to God like Reverend Montgomery had preached, yet Candace was still coming in late every night after being God knows where; though she suspected with Austin, and she hadn't heard Jonah's voice since the last time she called and the woman answered the phone. He had promised to call her daily until they could be together again. He was clearly not living up to his promises. Last, her best friend had just called it quits and on top of all this she was being assigned to the Attila the Hun of editors. No, things weren't looking up; they were taking a spiral downward. Talk about the trials of Job, what about the tribulations of Sable?

*   *   *

Marsha Griggs sat upright at her desk reading over Sable's latest chapters. Sable sat nervously as the monarch read her work. She showed no emotion as she sat stern-faced with her glasses half on the bridge of her nose. Her salt-and-pepper hair was styled in an outdated mushroom. Her simple white blouse was buttoned up to the neck and adorned with a Madonna broach. It was neatly tucked into a maroon colored skirt. She wore support hose and laced Hushpuppies. Sable looked around at her office trying to find an indication of personality and character. There were no family portraits, flowers or knick-knacks on her desk or credenza. Her office was so unlike Shamell's; it was clutter-free and spotlessly clean. Sable guessed that her office was a reflection of her personal life, plain and boring. She felt kind of sorry for her as she sat in the antiseptic looking room waiting for her to finish reading. Marsha lifted her head from the manuscript and peered over her glasses at Sable. She gathered the stack of papers in her hands, aligning them together by tapping them against her desk. "This is quite good, Ms. Brooks."

Sable was shocked. A compliment was the last thing she'd expected to hear from her.

"Well, thank you," She said almost breathlessly.

"I encountered only minor errors, but with a careful eye I'm sure you can clear them out."

Sable looked into the woman's eyes and for a brief moment she didn't see the harsh person everyone made her out to be and she thought she was probably misunderstood by a lot of people. Sable would prefer things back the old way, but if that could not be then she would have to make this work.

"I understand that the agreement date for completion is Christmas?"

"Yes, Mrs. Griggs, it is."

"Do you think you will be on schedule?"

"I think I will. I've recently moved to the suburbs where there is a lot of peace and quiet. It has proven to be a focal point for me. My creative juices have been flowing like crazy," she said with a friendly chuckle trying to warm her.

"Well, yes," she said without reciprocation of the slightest smile. "You just keep your juices flowing and you will make a lot of people happy: your readers, Alpha Publishers, and naturally you." She stood and extended her hand to Sable.

"I thank you for taking the time with me and I think maybe you and I will do fine together."

"I'm not particular whether we hit it off or not, Ms. Brooks. The only thing I'm concerned about is that your writing is good and you get it to me on time."

"Uh, yes, I understand. Good day." Sable closed the door behind her ever so carefully. As she waited on the elevator she noticed that Shamell's office door was still closed.

*   *   *

Jonah spoke clearly into Sable's answering machine. He was on the road and calling from his cell phone. He knew how bad the reception could be to the receiving party. He hoped that when she listened to it, she would be able to understand his message. He was on his way to Philadelphia to a pharmaceutical sales convention. He had agreed to fill in for a co-worker who had taken ill at the last minute. And, the only reason he had agreed to come was because it was close to New York and he hoped he could persuade Sable to drive or fly down so they could spend some time together. After years of working basically on the road, he was getting tired of it. The job in New York would be perfect. Regional manager meant less travel than what he was doing now and that meant more time with family. "Hello, Sable, I'm just leaving Richmond. I'm on my way to a convention in Philly. I was thinking how lonely it's gonna be. I wonder if you'd like to take a few days' hiatus from your writing or bring it along to work on while I'm in meetings? You could drive it in no time or you can jet it in less than an hour. I'll pick up the tab, of course. I'll be staying at the Ivory Arms Holiday Inn. I don't have the number right now, but information can give it to you. I should get there by noon. The convention doesn't start until tomorrow. There's a flight that leaves Kennedy at 3:30 this afternoon. It could have you here by dinnertime. I'd love to take you to dinner, some place. We can share the whole evening uninterrupted. What do you think? Call me."

Sable stood over the answering machine as it played back Jonah's message. His voice was so seductive. She began to grow weak in the knees just listening to him. He knew how to do that to her still. She wrote down the name of the hotel. Of course, there was no way she was going to meet him now. She looked at her watch. It was already past 1:00. He would be there by now, she thought. She flopped down on the four-poster bed and contemplated calling him. What would she say? I'm not coming because when I called you Saturday night a woman answered the phone. I know you're whoring around? She fell back on the bed. It felt good and she realized how tired she was. She decided she'd take a nap to release herself momentarily from her problems. She started drifting into slumber land when the phone rang. She rolled over and picked it up. "Hello?"

"Sable."

"Jonah."

"Did you get my message?"

"Yes. I just got in and was resting a bit."

"So I take it that you're not interested in my proposition?"

"Jonah, I don't think this is a good idea."

"Yeah, I know it was a bit short notice. I just thought since you're on your own time and don't have to punch a clock that you would be able to come. But I understand."

Despite what she thought he was doing behind her back, he sounded genuine. She could not allow herself to be played the fool. She knew she had to uncover his little deceit.

"Jonah, I'm not busy. I don't have any plans preventing me from jumping on a plane and coming to Philly. Truth is, I don't want to come."

"What?"

"Look, let's not insult each other's intelligence. I called you before day Sunday morning and a woman answered. Now that annuls every promise you made to me before you left. I don't have time for foolishness. I'm a 44-year-old woman who hasn't time for a man who doesn't know?"

She was cut off by Jonah's laughter.

"What's so funny?" She was growing angrier now.

"That wasn't another woman who answered my phone the other night." He roared some more with laughter. "I mean, yes she is a woman but not like you think."

"If you're going to tell me I dialed the wrong number, forget it. You picked up and I heard your voice!"

Jonah was laughing so hard he could hardly talk. "That was Betty."

"Who?"

"You know my sister, Betty."

"Betty? Are you sure?"

"Yeah, I'm sure, I ought to know my own sister. She had a fight with her husband, came to stay with me until he cooled off. When you called we thought it was him trying to get her to come back home. I took the phone from her because I was gon' tell him a thing or two about hitting women." He broke into laughter again. "And you thought I had another woman in my bed? To tell you the truth, I'm kind of flattered, but you know I've never been the playboy type. You remember what we said to each other on the floor of your bathroom?"

"Yes."

"I meant it. I want my wife back. Now how serious are you?"

"What time did you say that plane leaves?" she asked.

23

Judging a Book by Its Covers

Sable scurried around the house trying to remember if she had packed everything for the three-day stay. She wished Candace were there to drive her to the airport. She decided to take the Tercel. She didn't trust leaving the Mercedes on the airport grounds for three and a half days. She wrote a quick note to Candace telling her where she was, that she had taken the Tercel and when to expect her back. She lugged the medium-sized suitcase into the trunk of the Tercel and threw her pocketbook on the passenger-side seat. She checked her makeup in the rearview mirror one last time before backing out of the garage.

*　　　　*　　　　*

Shamell finished her club sandwich and slurped the last drop of Sprite through the straw. She wondered what had kept Charles from coming. She laid a $5 tip on the table and picked up the bill. Just as she lifted herself out of the chair, Charles came in.

"Going somewhere?" he teased.

"What happened to you? I was about to leave."

"I'm sorry, got detained by a colleague." He smiled his million-dollar smile at her and kissed her hand. "You've eaten already, huh? I'm starved. You don't have to go right away, do you?" he asked.

"Charles, I've been here an hour and a half waiting for you. I have to get back."

"Please stay," he whined. "I gotta work late tonight and I want to spend as much time with you as possible."

"You're working late tonight?"

"Yeah." He picked up the menu and started reading it. "The roast beef and provolone looks good."

"But school is out, the students are gone. What could you possibly have to do to keep you after hours?" Shamell was growing frantic. She thought about what Sable had told her in her office earlier.

"Preparation and planning for summer-school. You know it starts in two weeks."

He had already prepared for his summer-school classes three weeks before school ended. It was obvious he'd forgotten. She knew because she had helped him with it. Shamell wanted to cross-examine him but knew that would be a bad decision. His temper flared easy, and she didn't want to be embarrassed in the restaurant. For the sake of peace she decided to let it go and take him at his word.

The waitress came back to the table and set a glass of ice water before Charles. "Are you ready to order, sir?"

"Yes, I'll have the number two." From behind his menu, he eyed her body guilefully so Shamell would not see him.

"Okay." The girl was used to provocative stares and ignored him. "Roast beef and provolone. Anything to drink?"

"Coffee with cream and sugar."

"Ma'am can I get you anything else? Maybe some desert?"

"Nothing else for me, thank you."

Charles eyed the waitress as she sashayed back to the kitchen.

"So, what have you been up to today?" Charles asked.

Her mind was on the mystery girl with the long braids. She asked herself what would a twenty something girl want with an older man like Charles but after looking in his face the answer came so clearly. Even though he was probably 20, 25 years this little spring chicken's senior, he was without a doubt very handsome, well positioned in his career and earned a good salary. He was a charmer, had been from day one. She realized that the young girl saw in him the same thing she had seen those many years ago and still saw today. The girl had to know he was married. Her pictures adorned every corner of his office, and he wore his wedding band religiously. Perhaps he was buying her things to allure her, or maybe she was just a common slut, the type of girl who loved upsetting marriages. Some women were like that; they found pleasure in conquering challenges. What if this young girl truly loved Charles? Even worse, what if he loved her? Where would that leave her?

She thought about the property in the Poconos they had just purchased. Was it just some kind of decoy or getaway for him to take his women? He had wanted the property so bad for their use, but they hadn't used it yet. She remembered the weekend workshop he had to attend several weeks back. Now she wasn't so sure if it was a workshop or a romantic getaway.

"Charles," she grabbed his hand. "Let's go away for a while. I'm so tired of being in New York. I've got some vacation days that I need to take. We can take a long weekend and go up to the Poconos."

"I think we can do that, but not this weekend. I got that golf tournament this weekend, you know."

"Oh, yeah, that's right." Shamell looked disappointed. "Maybe I can come with you?"

Charles grinned. "That's a switch. Why all of a sudden an interest in golf?"

Shamell shrugged her shoulders questionably. "I don't know. Maybe our problems stem from us not spending quality time together. You remember how we were in the beginning? We were like Siamese twins, always together. I miss those times."

"Yeah, I know what you mean. It's the demands and stress of our jobs that's got us distant."

"Well, what about it?"

"Baby, it's not a good idea. We're going to be out there all day. It'll be hot; the bugs will be biting. I don't want to subject you to all that."

"It won't bother me, Charles. My physical endurance is great thanks to my aerobics classes and I can put insect repellent on."

"I tell you what you do—make plans for us in the Poconos the first week in August. It'll be just like a second honeymoon."

"But Charles, August is so far away."

"No, it's not baby, It'll be here in no time."

The waitress returned with Charles' order and placed it in front of him. The aroma drifted to his nostrils.

"Umm, this smells good. Thank you, honey." He winked at the waitress unaware that Shamell was making mental notes of his dalliance.

*   *   *

Sable stepped off of the Boeing 747 and found Jonah standing at the end of the corridor. He grinned as he waved his hands and proceeded to walk past the attendant to greet her.

"Sorry, sir. You can't cross the boundary." The attendant smiled courteously.

Sable was wearing a sky-blue, soft cotton tunic with matching pants. Her white espadrille sandals matched great, not to mention their comfort. She walked gracefully and when she reached him he took the luggage, then wrapped the other arm around her waist and kissed her sweetly.

"How was your trip?" she asked.

"Long, tiresome, but I managed to take a long nap when I checked into the hotel. What about yours?"

"It was fine."

"You look so good."

"So do you." Sable planted a kiss on his jaw.

"Are you hungry?" He asked, eyeing her.

"Yes, but not for food," she said alluringly.

*   *   *

Sable was thoroughly enjoying herself with Jonah. On Thursday evening after dinner they visited Longwood Gardens. They both took pleasure in walking through the flower gardens, woodlands and meadows. Sable picked up some valuable tips on raising plants. Some of the plants were the same kind as those in her garden. Before leaving, Jonah bought her a bouquet of roses from the gift shop. On Friday evening they visited the Elmwood Park Zoo. She loved looking at the animals, especially the American bison. Ever since seeing the movie "Dances With Wolves," she had a secret devotion to the animals. They had provided so much to the Native Indians and without their existence the Indians would not have survived.

She had updated Jonah on everything that was going on in her life from A to Z. She had told him about her and Shamell's estrangement. He agreed with her that it sounded like spousal abuse. She told Jonah about Austin and her uneasiness about him. She confessed to him that her attitude toward him was shameful. She vowed to treat him better and would start by inviting him to dinner when she got back. Jonah thought that was a good gesture for reconciliation. They hadn't gone many places but mainly stayed to themselves in the confines of their hotel room. They tried to make up in the few days for the lost years spent apart. Late that night they lay in bed talking about their futures.

They made promises sealed by kisses. She apologized for accusing him of cheating. He laughed it off nonchalantly.

"What if you don't get the job in New York? What will we do?"

"We've got love and love is the answer in itself. We'll find a way."

"Maybe I can move back to North Carolina, but then Candace…"

"Candace is grown. She can take care of herself."

"But I can't leave her in New York unsettled. I mean, she doesn't have a place to stay. The house in Torryville is too big for her and she wouldn't even want to live out there. You know how young people are. They want to be where the main attractions are. I'm afraid Torryville would be too slow for her. Something told me I was moving too fast when I purchased that house."

"Hold on a minute now. I love that house. What about me moving to New York and finding another job?"

"You would do that?" she asked.

"I would walk around the world and swim the ocean twice for you," he said.

"But Jonah, you can't swim," she teased. They both laughed.

*   *   *

Sable pulled the casserole of macaroni and cheese out of the Dutch oven and set it on the baker's rack. It was golden brown with bubbles of cheese simmering in scattered puddles. It looked delicious. Candace worked diligently on a side counter making a six-item garden salad. She cut the tomatoes in perfect slices, not too thick or thin. The radishes were garnished to look like miniature roses. Sable was amazed at her culinary ability.

"Didn't know you were so handy in the kitchen."

"It comes from years of watching you."

"Never knew you were paying attention."

"I was," she said, smiling all over herself. "I can't tell you how happy this makes me, Mom. I couldn't believe the message you left inviting Austin to dinner. I have to confess though…" she laughed.

"What, dear?"

"I waited until you got back before I invited him. I wasn't sure if you meant it or you were caught up in the euphoria of seeing Dad again."

"That's why you asked me about 50 million times yesterday if I was sure about having him come over?"

"Um hum. I knew if I asked him he would come, and I didn't want him to be slighted by you anymore."

"I understand. I have been acting like a horse's behind, haven't I?"

"Yes, you have."

"From this day forward I promise to do better. Of course, you know how I feel. I don't approve of the age difference and I still can't help but think he has an ulterior motive."

"You make me feel like I'm not worthy of someone like Austin. Like he's got better things to do than to find interest in the likes of me."

"Of course, I don't mean that!" she declared. "If anything, it's the other way around. I know you're grown and must make your own decisions," She paused before continuing, "Just be careful honey."

The table was immaculately sat. The Lenox china, Waterford stemware and Oneida silverware were a perfect combination. Sable had picked fresh flowers from the garden and arranged them skillfully in a crystal vase. She set it gloriously atop the fine linen tablecloth in the center of the dining room table. Ice tea, baked veal cutlets and crescent rolls were on the menu with the macaroni and cheese and salad. For desert, Sable had made strawberry shortcake. The trio bowed their heads and Austin led them in prayer.

"Most gracious Father, we humbly thank thee for the bounty of your harvest. We are sincerely thankful for the hands that prepared it. I ask your continued blessing upon this house and its occupants. In your precious name, amen."

"Amen," said the two women.

Sable was impressed with Austin's grace. They passed the dishes of food around to each other until everyone had some of everything on their plates. Austin took the first bite of macaroni and cheese.

"Oh," he said earnestly. "Ms. Brooks, did you make this?"

"Yes, how is it?"

Austin closed his eyes and the look on his face read sheer pleasure. "There aren't words to describe its scrumptious taste."

Sable blushed and forked some macaroni into her mouth. "I should have added more cheese," she said. "It would have really been good then."

"I can't imagine it being any better," he praised, then winked at her.

Sable blushed again this time to the point of giggles. She was beginning to see why Candace was so taken with him. He had charm, charisma and was pleasing to look at. He was winning her over fast.

"Your cooking reminds me of my grandmother," Austin said.

"I gather she's a wonderful cook."

"She is more than wonderful. She is extraordinary. One of my favorite dishes is peanut stew. She taught me how to make it. Have you ever tried it?"

"No, I haven't. Does it actually contain peanuts?"

"Ah, yes. It is a dish from Ghana and is called Hkatenkwan. It's quite delicious. Many good things go into the stew." He proceeded to tell them how to make it:

3-lb chicken, cut into pieces

1/2 of a whole onion

2 Tbl. tomato paste

1 Tbl. peanut oil or other light cooking oil

1 cup onion, well chopped

1 cup tomatoes, chopped

2/3 cup peanut butter
2 t. salt
2 t. grated fresh ginger,
2 hot chilies, crushed,
or 1 t. ground ginger
or 1 t. cayenne powder
2 cups fresh or frozen okra
1 eggplant, peeled and cubed Serves 4-6

"Soups and stews made with peanuts are main-meal foods in much of Africa. I must warn you that it is a spicy dish. If you want it less spicy, you should start with only half a pepper. Boil the chicken with ginger and the onion half, using about 2 cups water. In a separate large pot, fry tomato paste in the oil over a low heat for about five minutes. Add to the paste the chopped onions and tomatoes; stir occasionally until the onions are clear. Remove the partially cooked chicken pieces and put them, along with about half the broth, in the large pot. Add the peanut butter, salt and peppers. Cook for five minutes before stirring in the eggplant and okra. Continue cooking until chicken and vegetables are tender. You can eat it just as it is or serve it over rice."

"That sounds good. I believe your grandmother taught you a lot about cooking."

"Yes, she did. One day soon, I will invite you to my house and make the soup for you and Candace."

"Oh, Momma, you gotta see his apartment. It's loaded with all these African artifacts. They're not just decorations either; they have deep meaning behind them. Austin, tell her about the quilt your grandmother made for you," she said anxiously.

Austin began telling Sable all about the quilt and the reason behind his grandmother making it. Before they knew it, they had sat at the table for two solid hours talking about his family, childhood and country.

Sable found Austin delightful. She was inwardly embarrassed for her earlier treatment of him. She wanted to tell him how sorry she was but found the words difficult to say. But, from the way he smiled at her and talked with her like they were old friends she was certain he knew.

24

Truce

Sable and Candace were sitting in the garden talking cheerfully about how the Sunday dinner went with Austin and the move Jonah would be making to Connecticut. Although he did not get the job at Glaxco Pharmaceuticals, he was sending resumes left and right to companies in the New York area. Russell pulled his silver Camry into the long driveway. He spotted them in the garden and waved from his car. He got out and walked casually to the flower garden where they sat. Candace was annoyed by his presence and sighed heavily as he approached.

"Candace, I know how you feel but please let's try to keep this as civil as possible," pleaded Sable.

"Who invited him?"

"Honey, no one invited him, he probably just wanted to pay us a visit. Now be nice."

Russell was wearing a Chicago bulls tee shirt that was tucked neatly into a pair of Docker shorts. The baseball cap and sunglasses added to his sporty look. He pulled the sunglasses off as he got nearer.

"Hello, ladies!" he said.

"Hello, Russell. It's good to see you. How have you been?" asked Sable. From under the table she kicked Candace's foot in an attempt to get her to respond to his greeting.

"Been doing good." He kept his eyes on Candace. "Candace, how are you?"

"Hi, Russell. I'm good. What brings you out?"

"Actually, I just got back from Virginia visiting my folks. They loaded me down with vegetables. I'm not one for doing a lot of cooking, especially vegetables. I very seldom eat the things."

"Tell me about it," Candace said.

"Anyway, I know how you two love vegetables, so I brought them by."

"That's mighty sweet of you Russell. Sable looked around at her flower garden. "You know I've been thinking about starting a small vegetable garden myself, maybe some tomatoes, squash and cucumbers. It's a shame to let all this good rich soil go to waste."

"Momma packed some corn, tomatoes, and stuff. I'll go get them."

"That can wait. Sit down and talk to us for a while."

"If you're serious about that garden, I'll be glad to help you out. I know a lot about it since I was raised on a farm myself."

"I will certainly take you up on that offer."

Candace relaxed in her chaise lounge and crossed her legs one on top of the other. "So," she said, "when did you go to Virginia?"

"Last week. Took a few days off from work to go see them."

"Bet they were glad to see you, huh?"

"Yeah," he lowered his head as if there was something else he wanted to say, "I took Ophelia with me."

A wave of panic washed over Candace. If Russell took Ophelia down south to meet his family then their relationship must be serious. She tried not to show shock as she forced herself to relax. A part of her thought Russell would always be available for her. She hoped he would find someone to settle down with but thought it would be after she had settled down herself. Now the idea of his possible marriage didn't seem so romantic. She was happy with Austin and felt he was her soul mate; still, there was the chance that he did not feel as strongly about her.

Sable knew where the conversation was leading. This was Russell's last attempt to see if there was a chance that he could win Candace. His bringing the vegetables was just an excuse. She knew Russell would appreciate her absence. "Excuse me, folks, but I've got an errand to run." She pushed herself out of the chair and disappeared into the house. Ten minutes later she left in the Mercedes.

Russell exhaled and relaxed a bit as they watched Sable drive off.

"So I take it that you're pretty serious about Ophelia?"

"I asked her to marry me," he said.

Candace looked at him and she did not see total bliss. She saw a man who was unsure about the step he was about to take.

"I guess congratulations are in order then." She extended her hand to shake Russell's. He took her hand in his and held it with both hands.

"I guess so," he said solemnly.

"You don't sound too enthused."

"You know the real reason why I'm here. I love you and it's hard seeing you with him…"

"I can't take this Russell!" she said. She jerked her hand from his and bolted from the chair.

Russell stood to face her. "Wait, Candace. All I want to do is talk. I won't touch you anymore. I promise. I don't want to see you get hurt."

"Russell, I don't want to talk about this. I thought we cleared this up weeks ago at Arthurs."

Russell broke his promise and inched closer to Candace. She took a step backward but he grabbed her and enclosed her in his arms.

"Russell, stop it! You're scaring me!" She struggled to get loose from his powerful arms. Russell ignored her insistent pleas and began kissing her madly. He tightened his grip on her until she stopped squirming. When he felt her relaxed in his arms, his kisses became tender. To her own surprise, she began kissing him back. Russell felt her passion and her arms went around his thick neck. He rubbed her back, then pulled away from her.

"I knew it."

Candace was embarrassed at her actions. She said nothing. She stepped back from him again. "You knew what?"

"You love me; you just don't want to admit it."

"That's ridiculous"

"Deny it," he challenged her, "You wouldn't have kissed me like that if you didn't."

"That was purely physical, so don't flatter yourself."

"Yeah, you said something like that last time, right before you gave me the boot, but it's funny how quick you warm up. Either that or homeboy ain't keeping your pilot lit like he should."

"You're a fine one to talk. You're the one who's engaged to be married but you're here kissing me."

"You know the deal, C. I'm here FOR you. That dude might be educated, suave and sophisticated. He's probably able to put you up in his 5th avenue penthouse, buy you a Lexus, hell, even buy you a gold Jag to match his, but one thing he can't do and that's love you as much as I do."

Candace looked at Russell suspiciously. "Hold up. How do you know where Austin lives and what kind of car he drives?"

Russell shrugged his shoulders before stumbling on words. He could not tell her that he had been spying. "It doesn't matter how I know. The fact remains that I know."

"That was you!"

Russell didn't try to deny anything. He knew there was a good chance that Candace would detect his spying and now it was evident that she had.

"That WAS your car parked across the street from his apartment that night; and that was you again outside the Luther Vandross concert. I had this strange feeling like I was being followed. You've been spying on us!" Candace was growing hysterical.

"Wait!" Russell said.

"No! What kind of freak are you?" She turned and tried to run to the house but Russell caught her.

"Let me go!" she said frantically "Oh, God!"

"Candace, calm down!"

"Don't hurt me!" she cried.

"CANDACE!" Russell shook her. "What's the matter with you, girl? You know me! I'm not capable of hurting a fly! Get yourself together!" He relaxed his grip, held both hands up and took two steps back from her. "Okay, I was following you around but that was for your protection not my curiosity. I admit I was wrong."

"I can't believe you!"

"I didn't know if this man could be trusted. To be honest, he came off real shaky at first. Everybody thought so. I had to be sure you weren't in any kind of danger."

"I'm not in danger with Austin, never have been. I want you to stop this craziness, Russell. I hate to terminate our friendship, but if you don't stop I will."

The threat made Russell mad and from this point on, he considered their friendship terminated. "Go ahead and end it then!" he yelled in anger. "You think I can be friends with you now? I'll back out of your life for good. I guess I was in denial about you and him. You're capable of making your own damn decisions, and it's clear to me he's who you want. You don't have to worry about me no more. Musta' been a fool coming out here." He retrieved the bushel of vegetables from the car and placed them on the patio. Still slightly shaken by the ordeal, Candace stood transfixed in her spot until he left.

25

I Do

Autumn was Sable's favorite season. The trees always looked like they were in a fashion parade, dancing to the wind's music, each tree imperiously displaying its own bold, vivid colors. She sat in the fading flower garden working on her manuscript. She had proudly presented the last of the 37 chapters to Marsha only to have them returned with instructions to change the murderer to a character she felt was less of a suspect. Sable disagreed, saying the change would make the story line too weak. Marsha contended that it would be more realistic with the change. Of course, Marsha won and Sable had to start from chapter three making changes. Shamell would never have done a thing so demeaning. She had been four months without the friendship of Shamell. She missed her and wondered how she was. She hoped Charles was behaving and keeping his hands to himself. The thought of him hitting Shamell brought on a chill that penetrated through the thick wool sweater she wore. If she had it to do all over again, she never would have accused Charles of abuse, at least not so bluntly. She would have hinted at the subject, leaving Shamell with dignity. She was crying over spilt milk now. After trying unsuccessfully many times to rekindle their friendship, she decided to let Shamell go and move on with her life.

Her days were lonely since Candace moved in with Austin. She tried to talk her out of it. Moving in with a man without matrimony went against her morals. She was raised the old-fashioned way and was taught that marriage equaled commitment equaled sex. Although she suspected Candace had lost her virginity dating back to Julian, she still wanted her daughter to marry and then live together, in that order. "A man won't buy the cow if he can get the milk free" is what her mother would have said if she had still been living. Lord knows, she had heard it enough when she was growing up. She had given the milk away before she had married Jonah and once after their divorce, but somehow she viewed her case as being different from Candace's. She felt more mature and wiser, plus she didn't have to contend with all the STD's being spread around nowadays.

At first Candace started staying with Austin on Saturdays and coming home early Sunday mornings to ready herself for church. Sable knew the child was feeling guilty and going to church with her was her idea of redemption. Then, the weekends started to grow from only Saturday nights to Friday, Saturday and Sunday nights. On Monday morning she'd come home, dress herself for work, eat a bowl of cereal and leave for work. One particular Monday evening when Candace returned, Sable asked her why she bothered to come home at all. One word led to another and before long an argument had brewed. The next day Candace packed all her belongings that would fit in the Camaro and moved in with Austin. Two days after she was settled, she called Sable and apologized for not living up to her standards. She had told her that she and Austin loved each other and couldn't stand being separated.

"If he loves you that much, why doesn't he marry you?" she had asked.

"Because we're taking it one day at a time."

"Candace Renee Brooks, let me tell you one thing. A man will never buy the cow if he can get the milk free. Marriage equals commitment equals sex." She was preaching the same words her mother had years ago and she suspected Candace would reserve those exact words for her daughter in the years to come.

It was early September when Candace moved. A month later Sable still couldn't get used to the idea she was gone. She was grateful for their regular visits on Wednesdays and Sundays. Their actions indicated they loved each other. She had never seen a man so attentive to the needs or wants of a woman. If Candace said she wanted a glass of water, he'd be out his chair heading toward the kitchen to retrieve it before she could count to two. No sooner than she'd say her shoulders ached than he would be right behind her massaging them. At first Sable thought Austin was putting on airs, but she began to see the genuine devotion he had for her.

"Candace," she said one time when the two of them were alone, "I hope you are as good to him as he is to you." Candace smiled wickedly. "Oh, I am, Momma."

But the best news came one Sunday evening when Austin and Candace took her out to dinner. The two of them had been acting strange all evening and Sable knew they were up to something. Right before the main course was served, they sprang the news on her that they were engaged. Sable was speechless.

"When did this happen?" she asked.

"Officially, last night. We wanted you to be the first to know, since you're the closest one in our lives," said Austin.

Sable reached her hands across the table and squeezed Austin's hand.

"Candace is what I need in my life. When I'm with her I feel complete. For years I was lost, but not anymore. We are good for each other."

"Momma, you already know how I feel about him. He is everything I ever wanted in a man. He's considerate, kind, handsome and very sexy."

"That is enough, young lady. I don't mind hearing about his other qualities but that last one is a bit personal." They all laughed. "I can't tell you how relieved I am to hear this news. Candace knows how I feel about living together out of wedlock. Why so soon though? You've only known each other a few months"

"Yes. But, in that time I have found out all I need to know about Candace."

"Are you both sure this is the thing you want to do?"

The couple shared a concurred looked then nodded their heads.

"Well, have you set a date yet?"

"We have decided on May, since it will mark the anniversary of when we met," said Austin. "We have both agreed on a simple ceremony with family only. My family will fly to the United States to take part in the ceremony and I trust Candace's family will be present also. We hoped you would allow us to marry in your flower garden."

"You're more than welcome to use it. Oh, I can see it now," she babbled on in excitement. "It will be so beautiful. The archway leading into the garden is perfect for the occasion and by that time it will be covered in beautiful roses. We will need about two 12-foot tables for the food and a much smaller one for the cake. Oh, Candace, I know just the cake for you. I saw a picture of it in Better Homes and Gardens. It was garnished with real flowers. You are going to be an exquisite looking bride. You're tall and slender. Honey, with your long neck you simply must wear an off the shoulder gown—with pearls, thousand of little pears all over it, and your hair, it will look better in an upsweep, don't you think? You'll need something old, something borrowed, something blue and something new. Of course, the gown will be new. You can borrow my pearl earrings; that'll kill two birds with one stroke. Not only will they be borrowed, but old too. They belonged to your grandmother, you know. Most brides wear blue garter belts. Oh!" she almost screamed, "An orchestra! An orchestra will be perfect for the garden…"

"Mom," Candace cut in, "I know you're excited, but we want something simple."

"But, honey," she said disappointed, "this will be your first and only wedding. If you have a small insignificant ceremony, you'll regret it when you get older. Austin, you've been married before and I can understand your lack of excitement. I think it would be an injustice to ask Candace to settle for anything less than grand. After all, she is my only child and I'm sure her father would want to give his only daughter away nicely. If you're worried about the expense, don't. I'll foot the bill."

"Money is not a factor, we just…"

"That's settles it then. We can have a small but lavish ceremony with family and maybe just two or three close friends. Is that a deal?" Sable had her hand above the table ready to shake and seal the deal before Austin could protest. Austin raised his hand slowly above the table and shook hands.

*   *   *

"Aunt Vi, I just couldn't wait to tell you. Candace will be calling you soon but don't let her know I already told you; act like you're surprised."

"I sho' will baby. But I still feel a little funny 'bout this whole thing. Like Austin gon' cut up 'fore its all over with."

"We just have to face it, Aunt Vi. We had him pegged wrong."

"Well, maybe we did. I reckon it just goes to show that you can't judge a book by its cover. I'm glad things are looking up. I ain't gon' worry 'bout it no mo'. I'll put everything in the Master's hand and if anything is wrong, he'll fix it."

"I wish Momma was alive to share in this joyous occasion."

"She'll be there, sugah, just not in human form. Her spirit and presence will be all around us."

"I wish I had your strong constitution, Aunt Vi. You are always so positive. You never let life's problems get in your way. I don't know what

I would have done without you after Momma died. You stepped right in and have been more than an aunt to me. You have become my mother."

"Child, that's the way your momma would have wanted it. You know, you always was my favorite niece. Them other nieces and nephews of mine ain't no count. Two of them live in Charlotte, just an hour and a half's drive away. You think they ever jump in their car to come see me? No! They don't care nothing 'bout me. Yeah, they call once a year to see if I'm still living. Somebody done told them I got money stashed away somewhere. Well, I got news for them. I'm leaving all my money and thangs to you and Candace. Y'all my chi'ren. And after I'm dead and gone, watch and see won't they start coming around. They'll be trying to find my money. You know I keep all my important papers in a JC Penney hatbox under my bed, don't you?"

"I know."

"Don't y'all give 'em nothing. You hear me, Sable?"

"Aunt Vi, you shouldn't be like that."

"I'm serious, Sable! I don't want them to have none of my stuff, and another thing, I don't want y'all putting big money in the ground on me either. Just make sure I'm put in a nice enough casket where water can't seep through. Never could stand dampness."

Candace was laughing uncontrollably. "Sure thing, Aunt Vi."

*   *   *

The 12 regular models and the three new models, including Candace, listened attentively. Madame Yvonne, the lead fashion coordinator explained how Blacktravaganza was going to run this year. The 6-foot-3 wo/man (*No one really knew what Madam Yvonne was. Some said she was born a male and had undergone the sex change operation; others said she was a transvestite.*) floated as she walked around the boardroom. The coffee-bean-colored woman was paper-thin and wore her hair pulled back in a tight controlled bun. Her false eyelashes and heavily applied makeup only drew attention and gave hints of concealed masculinity. In ballerina formation, she stood in first position with her heels together and toes turned out. It wasn't uncommon for her to perform pliès in the middle of a lecture or conversation. She suffered from a mild form of rheumatoid arthritis and did it to reduce pain by keeping her blood circulating. She passed out a single sheet to each model.

"Listen up, girls," she commanded, "It has come to my attention that more than a few of you have put on a considerable amount of poundage. This is not good. When you walk down that runway three weeks from now I don't want to see any Jell-o asses. This is a four-day diet that I want each of you to try. It's guaranteed to take off five pounds if you follow it exactly. You get on it for four days, off four days, then get back on it. My calculations tell me if you follow these instructions you should lose 15 pounds by show time. For you newcomers, this is a ritual we do every year this time to get ready for the show. The thinner you are the better you're going to look and the better you look, the more accounts for AFLAME."

"This diet is the pits; I can certainly do without it," said Twila Jackson as she slung the piece of paper across the table.

"Excuse me!" responded Madam, "You may be Miss Thang in front of the cameras, but you're in my domain now and, frankly, I don't care how high you are on the totem pole. It doesn't make a bit of difference to me. I'm in charge now and when I'm in charge I will have your respect. I have been assigned to make sure you girls look good at Blacktravaganza and that's what I intend to do. Is that clear, Twila?"

Twila shuffled in her chair before answering. "It's clear, Madam Yvonne."

"Thank you!"

Madam Yvonne went over the fashions each model would wear. The show would be divided into four sections representing the four seasons. She explained that the new models would wear the garments by the new designers. The experienced models would wear garments created by the veteran designers. Candace noticed that all the other models including, the male models, were assigned swimwear except her. She was assigned 10 garments and most of them were office and casual attire. She didn't want to complain because the garments were beautiful and she was grateful just for being in Blacktravaganza. But without the right kind of exposure, her modeling career would never take off the way she wanted it to. There were two other girls hired around the same time she was. They had already done swimwear and now they were getting requests left and right, sometime two and three assignments a day, while she was doing simple things like hand soap or nail polish shoots or modeling choir robes.

Her most recent assignment was a Betty Crocker cake mix commercial where she portrayed a mom making a delicious looking chocolate cake for her family. Whenever she asked Austin about more exposure, he would say the time wasn't right. Then he'd do something to take her mind off of it. She was aware of what he was doing but didn't know the reason behind it. She thought he felt that if she got too much exposure she would leave AFLAME for one of the larger European agencies. She was growing sick and tired of getting the menial jobs.

*   *   *

Austin noticed Candace's aloofness. He had never seen her this way before and didn't know if he should say anything or give her space. She cleared the dinner dishes from the table and loaded them in the dishwasher without saying a word.

"Dinner was scrumptious." Austin said, trying to warm the cool atmosphere.

"Thanks." Her body jostled as she wiped the table down vigorously.

"I don't believe you've made that for me before, have you?"

Candace was thinking how medieval he was. Why did he assume that her effort in making dinner was done solely for him? Had he forgotten that she had to eat, too? Typical, she thought. She questioned herself for expecting more from a man who was raised in the bush by a domineering father and submissive mother who no doubt believed that their assigned roles shouldn't be questioned, challenged or altered. She cut a quick glance at him out the corner of her eye. She looked at him while she decided if she wanted to answer the question or not. Was this how life was going to be married to him? She would stay at home tending the children and house. The table would be eloquently set with a five-course meal awaiting his arrival every evening and she was supposed to wait anxiously, then sit attentively while he told her about his day at the office. She wondered if this was why she wasn't getting the better assignments? Truthfully, she had no objections to staying at home and tending her family. She wouldn't have it any other way. But the choice had to be hers. She didn't want things simply assumed upon her. She was intelligent and educated and she had a voice. The sooner Austin realized that the better off both of them would be. She was reminded of her own mother and how she had struggled for years to get out from under her father's shadows. When he had refused to give her some of the sun, she left. For years she thought her mother was being selfish and had blamed her for it. Now, she was beginning to see the light. She couldn't imagine living a life in a man's shadow. A wave of grief swept over her as she thought about Sable's plight. How could she have been so insensitive to believe that her mother wanted to break up their family?

For so long she had been looking in from the outside. It had taken coming in to see that the view was entirely different.

The humility from the events in the boardroom today, Austin's insensitivity about dinner and the fact that he didn't bother to lift a hand to help her with the dishes gnawed at her. Plus, her PMSing didn't help the situation either. Her eyes clouded over with tears. She thought about Russell. He was in tune and sensitive to her wants as well as her needs. The first tear that rolled down her cheek was for her mother; the second one was for the pity party she was having. She was tired of

Austin trying to stifle her career. The third one was for Russell; she missed her friend and knew he would never try to overshadow her. She wiped the tears away with the back of her hand.

"It's pot roast, Austin. I've made it plenty of times before. How can you not know?"

"Are you crying?"

"No!"

"What is bothering you then, Candace? I sensed something was wrong all evening." He took the dishcloth from her hand and led her into the living room. "Let us sit and have a little chat about your problems," he said gently.

"Austin, I have always wanted to be a model for as long as I can remember. You know that."

"Yes, and you are doing a fine job of it."

"No, I'm not! I'm not modeling at all. I'm doing nothing but penny-ante jobs."

"But Candace, you're trying to put the cart before the horse."

"Why am I the only one of the three new models who's still doing these two and three hundred dollar jobs?"

"Is it money that you cry about? Candace, I can give you all the money you need…"

"No!" Her voice was louder than she intended, "No, Austin. It's not the money."

"What is it then? I don't understand. I thought you were happy."

"I am happy. I'm just disappointed. I feel you're not allowing me to be all that I can be at AFLAME. I want whole-body capture and I want to wear exotic fashions. I want to be seen and discovered. I want to make it in this business. I feel you're trying to hide me. Everybody is wondering why I'm not doing more. They think I have the right qualities. Even some of the designers have asked me to model their fashions. When I think I'm going to get that chance, there is always a change of plans. Personally I think the changes are coming from you, Austin. Now you tell me what's up with that?"

"Why would I want to hide you, Candace? I am so proud of you. Do you know how you make me feel when I have you on my arm? I don't want you to think that I would keep anything that's good from you, because I wouldn't."

Candace was beginning to feel silly now. "I believe what you're saying, Austin; I just want to do more."

"I know you do and you will. Right now I need your patience." He cooed the words to her. "You are subconsciously nervous about our wedding ceremony and your mind is telling you all sorts of things that are of no importance."

"Maybe you're right."

"A trip is just the thing for you," he said matter-of-factly.

"A trip?"

"Yes. After Blacktravaganza, you and I will take a trip to Dar es Salaam."

"To Africa! To your home! We're going to Africa?"

"Yes," he laughed.

Candace planted kisses all over his face. "Nakupenda Austin!"

"Nakupenda Malaika."

26

The Whole Truth and Nothing But...

It was a star-studded event. The well-known of Manhattan came out in masses for the annual fashion show. Blacktravaganza was an appropriate name for the gala because most of the attendees were African Americans. The older, powdered-faced women with their coiffed hair and mink-draped shoulders walked arm in arm with their tuxedo-wearing husbands. The attires of the younger women were more daring. They wore cleavage-revealing, glittering, dresses that clung to S-shaped bodies. Some had weaves down their backs; others wore their hair in scrunches, upsweeps and various other styles. They were coupled with spouses, boyfriends or escorts. A few came solo. The rainbow collation of BAP's (*Black American Princesses'*) was spectacular. The reception area was wall to wall with classy looking people sipping from champagne glasses with their pinkies in the air. They pulled drags from cigarettes held in long decorative cigarette holders. The older men sneaked provocative looks at the younger women and they reciprocated with a flutter of their eyelashes, a wink or sly smile in hopes of catching themselves a sugar daddy. Soft jazz flowed from the orchestra pit and filtered throughout the civic center.

Sable and Jonah stood cornered by several of her fans. She smiled and talked warmly with them before signing her autograph on hors d'oeuvre napkins. She reminded them that her new book would be released around Christmastime. The music ceased and a sultry voice laced with a French accent announced that the show would begin in five minutes. The patrons assembled and singled-filed into the six entrance doors. Sable had sent Shamell a ticket but doubted she would come. Once everyone was seated the exotic, cinnamon-flavored commentator with the mile-long legs stood before her captive audience and extended her hands grandeur style. "Welcome, ladies and gentlemen, to the fifth annual Spectacular Blacktravaganza Fashion Show. My name is Shayla Depew and I am you commentator for this evening." Her bedroom eyes twinkled as the words rolled off her native French tongue. The audience applauded. The women sat with pleasant smiles on their faces while the men seem to instantly come to life at Shayla's beauty. "Before we begin I would like to introduce you to the key figures instrumental in getting Blacktravaganza under way. They are AFLAME's top management team. Shayla's hand followed the spotlight as it shone on the runway and four figures appeared from behind the props. Shayla called each name as they strolled down the runway. The first to appear was Madam Yvonne. Since she was working the show and would be on her heels and toes all evening, she wore a black pullover turtleneck and gray wool-blend trousers with leather loafers. Beverly Houser, the talent scout, was next; then Austin and Hardin Ferguson. Beverly was decked out in a black-sequined, haltered gown with a slit up to the thigh. The men wore black tuxedos. Austin's cummerbund and tie were Kente print, while Hardin wore the customary black and white. They bowed, waved to the crowd and each, except Madam Yvonne, took a seat down front. The jazz started up again dominated, by cool low notes from the bass guitar.

"Let's give them a generous applause," said Shayla, as she sashayed over to the director-style chair and perched herself lovingly. The show got under way and some of the most beautiful garments in the world were modeled. Austin, Hardin and Beverly beamed as the girls and guys strutted before the mesmerized audience. They switched, pranced and even danced down the catwalk, bringing the clothes to life. Fashion photographers were all around flashing their cameras. Sable and Jonah were beside themselves seeing their child perform in front of thousands of spectators. They were happy knowing she was finally doing something she always wanted to do. She was a natural at modeling and Jonah knew this was her calling. He was glad she hadn't listened to his argument about her pursuing journalism. Besides, if she tired of modeling then she could try her hand at journalism.

Madam Yvonne noticed Candace's natural ability to mesmerize the crowd. She was sorry Austin had persuaded her to let the girl model only the more conservative designs. She was talented and the spectators couldn't get enough of her. She was outshining Twila by leaps and bounds. Madame Yvonne knew she could easily become a supermodel if only Austin would loosen his grip. If she had known the girl had this much talent, she never would have agreed to Austin's request.

The half-naked models scurried around the dressing room changing garments, hairstyles and make-up. They bumped into their counterparts without a second thought to their nudity. Madame Yvonne was thoroughly pleased with the expeditiousness of her staff. There wasn't much supervising she needed to do. They were up to summer wear now and the girls and guys had more time to laugh and talk with each other since they had fewer clothes to change into. Candace sat in the corner wrapped in a robe and taking a sip from a can of Pepsi. She was finished with her runway stint until the last act, the wedding attire. She along with five other girls would be modeling bridesmaid's gowns. Twila Jackson would be modeling the wedding gown designed by the late Gianni Versace. It was an off-the-shoulder satin gown with gold and silver trim. It had a snug-fitting bodice and waist with a gathered skirt. One of the assistants handled the gown with extraordinary care. She hung it up carefully, unzipped the garment bag and removed the gown. Madam Yvonne clapped her hands to get the models' attention.

"Listen up, everybody," she said, easing into her commando mode. "You all have done excellent thus far. Let's try to continue throughout the remainder of the show. I want you to oil your bodies down so you can have that fun-in-the-sun look."

The orchestra changed from romantic to upbeat jazz.

"That's our key, folks. Assemble yourselves."

Just then Madam Yvonne felt someone's hand clutch her arm and whirl her around. It was Twila. She looked as if she was about to collapse. She stood before Madam in a cream, two-piece, thong bathing suit.

"What's wrong with you, child?" Madam asked, afraid to hear the answer. She knew Murphy's Law would not allow her to get through the show unblemished. She had been in this business long enough to know that behind the scenes there was no such thing as a perfect fashion show.

"I'm sick." Twila said in a horrible voice, still clutching Madam's arm.

"Sick! What do you mean, you're sick? You're the second to go out…"

Then without further warning, Twila bent forward and began throwing up.

"Oh, my God!" said Madame. "Quick, somebody get me a towel. Twila, take off that bathing suit!" Madame was moving with lightning speed. She helped Twila shed the bathing suit without getting vomit on it. She spotted Candace sitting in the corner and quickly realized she was the only one who wasn't modeling swimwear. "Candace, come here and put this on!" she barked, "You're going in Twila's place."

"What?" she asked, not comprehending what Madam had said.

"Move!" she ordered again. "Twila is sick. You'll have to take her place. Now, here, put this on. You're going out second."

Candace grabbed the suit. She dropped her robe and quickly stepped into the bikini thongs; then she slipped on the eye-patch bikini top that only covered a fraction of her breasts.

"Put some of that oil on your body and get in line."

"But, Madam, I didn't rehearse for this. I don't know what to do."

"If you're a true model, it will come natural. Now go, we haven't time!"

Candace rubbed the oil into her skin as quickly as possible and jumped in line. Everything was happening so fast. She didn't have time to think about how Austin would react to her wearing the suit.

"You go, girl!" said a voice behind her.

She turned to see smiling faces looking at her.

"You look great," said another.

"Can I have a date?" teased one of the male models who was undoubtedly gay and proud of it. "Girl, you almost make me wanna' straighten up." Everybody laughed. Even Madam Yvonne chuckled at the joke.

"Now don't get too excited, y'all. I said almost," he teased again.

Candace's hair cascaded around her face and she stepped from behind the props in the cream color two-piece. She moved with the music as Shayla commented on the creation.

"Isn't she lovely?" asked Shayla, and the orchestra began to play the Stevie Wonder tune in cool jazz tempo.

Sable and Jonah watched Candace as she strutted down the runway. Neither was thrilled with her modeling in such skimpy wear but they held their breath and prayed for this part to end quickly. As long as they didn't dictate for her to go au naturel, they would continue to support Candace's career choice. She reached the end of the runway and turned to make the walk back. The Civic Center buzzed with startled comments, mostly from the older women, tasteful cat whistles and applause from the men, and approving laughter from the younger women. Every five steps Candace looked over her shoulder and teased the spectators with her eyes and lips. Her body moved divinely with not too much or too few jiggles. When she reached center stage she faced the audience. She looked for Austin, thinking that because the audience was so receptive to her appearance, he would be too. He would see that she was ready to model big-time. She searched for Austin only to find that he was gone.

Austin's was the first face Candace saw when she stepped backstage. She smiled, anticipating his approval.

"What the hell are you doing?" he blared at her.

The remark was unexpected. She had never heard him raise his voice before. All eyes were on the two of them as he seized her arm.

"Take it off!"

"What has gotten into you, Austin?" she asked, totally perplexed.

"How dare you go against the program? Where is Twila? Why isn't she wearing this? Who gave you permission to do this?"

The questions were far too many. She tried to answer Austin, but when he continued to talk over her she became engulfed with anger.

"Twila got sick and Madame Yvonne needed someone…"

"So this is Madame Yvonne's concoction, huh? Where is she?"

Madame Yvonne was standing a few feet behind Austin patiently listening. "I am right here, Mr. Kawissopie."

It was very uncommon for Madame Yvonne to address anyone by his or her last name. Everyone knew when she did that meant she was incensed. "Yes, it was my idea to put Candace in the suit. I sense you have a problem with that," she said as she walked slowly yet confidently toward him.

"Yes, I have a problem with that, Madame. We have an outlined program that we were supposed to follow, but I see you want to play God back here."

"Mr. Kawissopie, behind the scenes I am God. I was hired to do this job so let me do it. Didn't you hear the girl tell you that Twila got sick?"

"That's besides the point…"

"No, my dear, that is the point. You see we work as a team; we have to in order for the show to run smoothly. You knew the thonged swimsuit was one of the highlights of the show. Tell me, what would you have suggested I do? Omit the suit all together?"

"You could have found someone else to do it!"

"But I found the best qualified person to do it. Candace is a jewel. Didn't you hear the response from the audience when she turned and walked back to center stage? Come Monday morning AFLAME's phones will be ringing off the hook with requests for her. I tell you, this girl is going to push AFLAME up another notch. You need to lighten up on her."

Austin inched closer to Madame and whispered, "You and I had an agreement."

"All agreements go out the window when I'm in a crisis. I had to make a judgment call. I did and it worked. Now if you would excuse me, I have a show to run." Madame Yvonne walked away from Austin. "Candace," she called. "You're taking over for Twila. Get ready for the grand finale. You're going to model the wedding gown."

"Candace, you're forbidden to put that gown on!" Austin roared.

Madame looked at Candace. "The choice is yours, Candace, not Austin's. Now AFLAME needs you in that gown in less than 10 minutes. What will it be?"

Candace knew what she had to do. She could feel a bit of liberation coming on as she stripped out of the suit and stood butt-naked before Austin and all the other models. It was crystal clear to her now why she wasn't getting the better jobs. Her assumptions were true about Austin holding her back. She looked at him defiantly. "Forbidden," she said. "Last time I heard that word I was a child."

Two of the attendants rushed around Candace preparing her for the final scene.

Austin turned to Madame Yvonne, who had dismissed him entirely.

"First thing Monday morning I want to see you in my office," he ordered.

"First thing Monday morning I'll be there," she challenged.

*   *   *

The show was a major success. The models celebrated backstage with champagne while they changed into their regular clothes, mostly jeans and tee shirts. They helped the assistants pack up the garments. Madame Yvonne had planned a big bash at her place and all of the models and executives were going. Candace held a bouquet of roses in her hands, compliments of Sable and Jonah. She listened as they commended and then hugged her. Austin waited patiently in a far-off corner for the threesome to finish. When they departed, Candace caught a glimpse of him standing alone. She walked over to him. She was still angry about his actions but decided not to say anything about it for the sake of peace. She was thinking they would go to the party, have a good time and forget about all that had happened. "Do you want to go home and change or are you wearing that to the party?"

"We're not going to the party."

It was obvious that Austin wasn't going to put this past him. Candace was seeing a side of him she didn't like. She could have been just as stubborn, but she didn't want to play those games. She loved Austin and wanted their relationship to stay on good terms.

"Okay," she said calmly. "We'll do whatever you want then." Candace said her good-byes and left with Austin.

After three hours of Austin giving her the silent treatment, Candace could take no more of it. She was trying to be as obliging as possible. When she offered to fix him a snack, he said he wasn't hungry. Fifteen minutes later he went in the kitchen and popped a bag of microwave popcorn. She ran him a warm tub of bath water but he opted for a shower. When she peeled off her clothes and slipped into the shower with him he got out quickly as if she was plagued with a disease, wrapped himself in a terra-cotta bathrobe and went to the bedroom to watch TV.

"Let's talk, Austin," she said, wrapped in an oversized towel and standing in the doorway.

"There is nothing to talk about since it is obvious you want to parade around in front of everybody ass-out."

"I'm a model, and that's what models do. You of all people should know that. Look, the way I see it, if my parents can deal with it then I see no reason why you can't."

Austin rolled his eyes at her and continued to watch TV.

"You're acting so possessive and childish."

"Is a man childish for not wanting everybody looking at his woman? Would you want me to stand before the world showing all my secrets?"

"Austin, it wasn't that bad!"

"Well, if left little for the imagination."

"I guess you had a problem with Maoma modeling too, huh?" she asked sarcastically.

The question cut through Austin like a razor and his emotions began to bleed. He raised off the bed and look at her with terror in his eyes.

"The life I had with Maoma is none of your business. Don't you ever speak of her again! Is that clear?" He hurried past Candace into the spare bedroom and slammed the door.

Candace could not believed what had just happened. Could this be the same amiable man she had fallen in love with several months back? He was turning into Dr. Jekyll right before her eyes. He was still in love with Maoma. She was dead, had been for more than five years, and he was in love with her ghost. She was filled with anger. She slammed her fists against the locked door. "Open up, Austin. I want to talk to you!" she demanded.

There was total silence.

"I was humiliated by your actions at the board meeting three weeks ago, then again tonight at the show, and now you tell me you're in love with a ghost! I can't compete with a ghost, Austin. I'm not about to play second fiddle to anyone living or dead!" She hurried into the bedroom and pulled her suitcases from under the bed. She yanked opened the drawers and began pulling her clothes out. She stuffed them in the suitcases. She raked all of her toiletries off the bathroom counter into her overnight case. It took only two trips to load up the Camaro. She laid the key and the engagement ring on the kitchen table, let herself out and locked the door behind her.

Austin yanked open the drawers to find them empty. She had left him but he wasn't too worried. He felt confident she would be back. He would give her time to reach her mother's house, then give her a call to make sure she made it safely. He decided on a cup of hot tea. He spotted the ring and apartment key. It was then that he felt a sense of panic. Candace was serious. He darted to the bedroom and changed quickly into a pair of jeans and a sweatshirt. He slipped into his sneaks without bothering to put socks on.

Austin raced the Jaguar out of the underground garage and onto the streets of Manhattan. He looked at his watch; it read 1:00 a.m. In about an hour he would be in Torryville.

*   *   *

If she went home, Austin would either call or show up there. She was not in the mood to see or talk to him. He was such a good persuader and she needed time to think and clear her head. She had to find a place to go where he or Sable didn't know anything about or least suspect.

If Sable knew where she was she would surely tell him if just to keep him from worrying. She could go to Madame Yvonne's place, but she was having the party and that would be one of the places Austin would check. Russell's was out of the question; they weren't friends anymore, plus he had his new life with Ophelia. She drove past the public library. The billboard read "Read a Book Today." The answer came easy then. Within 15 minutes she was standing in the lobby of Shamell's complex buzzing herself up.

*   *   *

"I can't thank you enough for putting me up for the night. I had no place else to go."

"You know you're always welcome here, but I wish you would call your mother so she wouldn't worry," said Shamell.

"I will, Shamell, just not tonight. If she knows where I am, she will tell Austin. I need a few days away from him."

"A few days? I thought you only needed room for tonight."

"Charles won't like my being here, will he?" she asked with apprehension.

"He won't have a problem with you staying here for a few days; neither will I. I just don't think it's good for your family though. You know, mothers are prone to worry, and I know your mother enough to know that she is probably climbing the walls right about now."

Candace sighed and reclined on the guest bed. "My head is so jammed right now I couldn't think if I wanted to. Just give me until tomorrow, please, Shamell?"

"All right. But tomorrow I expect you to call Sable." Shamell got up to leave, "I know you're tired; get some rest."

"Wait."

"What, honey?"

"Let's talk for a while. I've missed you."

Shamell smiled as she sat back down on the bed. "I've missed you too."

"The show was marvelous tonight, wish you could've been there. Momma said she sent you an invitation."

"She did, but don't think I didn't want to see you. I thought under the circumstances it would be better if I didn't."

"But why? You and Momma go back a long way. You're closer than any friends could be. That's why I don't understand this rift. You gotta know Momma would never say or do anything to hurt you, Shamell."

"Oh, Candace, you're so young and there're a lot of things that you don't understand."

"I might surprise you. I'm wiser than you think."

"I'm sure you are," she said, "I have to admit, I have a lot of pride. You know, pride is a good thing but too much of it is harmful."

"I wish you would swallow it for the sake of you and Momma's friendship."

"Sometimes swallowing pride means accepting harsh realities, and I don't know if I'm ready to do that yet."

Candace looked at Shamell with aged-old wisdom. "You know, I love Austin like I've loved no other man, and I'm sure I want to spend the rest of my life with him, but I'll give him up first before he makes me less than what I am." She was referring to Charles' cheating and abuse. "One time I thought modeling was the source of my happiness, but after I met Austin that changed. If I had to choose between Austin and modeling, I would gladly choose him. I have no problem with giving up my career periodically and staying home to raise a family, but it will have to be my choice. Austin has old ideas about how things should be done. More or less, he believes that women should be seen and not heard."

"Probably his culture," added Shamell.

"Oh, I know it is. He's in a different world now and he has to adjust if he wants us to be together." She went on to tell her all about Austin's life, the loss of Maoma and the incident tonight. It was 4:00 in the morning when they finished talking and decided to go to bed. Shamell walked into her bedroom and closed the door. She picked up the telephone and dialed Sable's number.

"Hello!" answered a frantic voice.

"Sable, this is Shamell. I'm calling to let you know that Candace is all right. She's with me."

"Oh, thank God! We were all worried to death!" Sable began to cry.

"She just needs a little time to think. I promised her that I wouldn't call you, but I know how you worry." She chuckled. She could hear a smile in Sable's voice.

"Thank you so much, Shamell."

"I've asked her to give you a call tomorrow. She doesn't want you to know where she is."

"I understand. I won't let her know you called me."

"Try to get some rest."

"Okay."

The two women hung up the phones. Shamell pulled back the covers of her bed and slid underneath. Her hand ran across the smoothness of the sheets to the empty side of the bed. She wondered where Charles was. His staying out late had become so routine that she didn't worry as much as she used to. When he did come home she never asked where he had been. Candace's voice played back in her mind. *"I'll give him up first before he make me less than what I am."* It was probably the wisest thing she had heard in a long time.

*   *   *

As soon as Sable hung up, she dialed Austin's number to put his mind at ease. He wanted to know where she was, but Sable would not give him that information. She assured him that all she needed was time and afterward she would come back to him.

On Tuesday afternoon Candace showed up at his office. He had given Phyllis instructions to interrupt him if Candace called. When she walked into the receptionist area, Phyllis gave her a broad grin. She buzzed Austin and announced Candace's arrival. Immediately he stepped out of his office and seized her in his arms. Their reconciliation was a sweet one. He told her he was the reason that Maoma was on that plane and that he felt responsible for her death. Maoma had agreed to do the swimsuit shoot in Paris because he had asked her to. The guilt and pain he felt was the underlying reason he didn't want her doing swimwear. He felt that God was giving him another chance at love and he would cherish this opportunity. He admitted that he was too protective of her.

"If you hold an egg too firmly it breaks; if you hold it too loosely it drops. How shall I hold you, Candace?"

It was the dearest thing she had heard from him. It was more than just a statement or question, it was an intangible symbol of willingness to conform for her sake. She knew it wasn't easy for him to change after years of strong African beliefs and moldings. But she would not ask him to change completely. She would meet him halfway because there were things about her that needed adjusting too.

"We will hold each other gently," she said with sympathy and understanding in her eyes.

They made promises that they would be considerate and open with each other. Austin agreed not to be so domineering and Candace agreed not to model anything that would make Austin feel uncomfortable.

These are the things that good marriages are made of. Austin and Candace were well on their way to a wholesome and happy life together.

27

Christmas Holidays

Sable hugged Candace and Austin.

"This will be our first Christmas apart," said Sable.

"Don't worry, Momma, we'll be fine." Candace kissed her cheek, "Tell the family I love them. I'll send them a post card from Africa."

"You call me as soon as that plane touches down, you hear me?"

"We will," said Austin.

Sable walked through the terminal to the plane heading for North Carolina. She was going to spend Christmas and New Year's with Jonah, Wilson and Aunt Elvira. She turned one last time to wave at the pair. It was four days until December 25th. This time tomorrow Candace and Austin would be boarding a plane for their trip to Dar es Salaam.

          *   *   *

Besides the two tote bags there were six pieces of Louie Vitton luggage between them; two contained Austin's personal items and one was filled with gifts for his family. Austin tried to persuade Candace to pack light, but she packed two changes of clothes per day. Of course she would never wear some of the things, like the silk dinner dress and the wool pants suit. Dar es Salaam was seasonably warm year-round. Too hot for silks and definitely too hot for woolens. The only thing she'd wear would be cotton shirts, loose-fitting slacks and dashiki-style dresses.

It was to be the vacation of a lifetime for Candace. Austin had even planned for them to go on a safari in Kenya. Austin had the luggage checked. The ticket agent handed him the claim stubs and he tucked them away safely in his pockets. Candace flipped through the pages of one of the five magazines she had brought along. The trip would take two and a half days, with stops in London, Frankfurt, and Lagos, Nigeria, before arriving in Dar es Salaam on Christmas Eve. She looked snazzy in her 501 jeans and black turtleneck. The black Baldi Nini shoes were stylish, comfortable and suitable for the walking they would be doing between terminals. Austin wore a pair of Edwin Italian jeans, a beige pullover cardigan and Sebago loafers. They had packed an extra set of clothing for the 13-hour lay over in Frankfurt.

The terminal buzzed with people of varied nationalities, race and backgrounds. Each seemed mindless of the others as they scattered about the airport in their own worlds. After years of living in New York, neither Candace nor Austin could get use to the unfriendliness of its inhabitants. They were both from places where folks made their pleasantries in the form of smiles, greetings or small talk. Austin had told her that friendliness was contagious in Dar es Salaam and everyone spoke whether they knew each other or not.

Dar es Salaam being Tanzania's capital, Candace expected to see a grand airport when they landed. Instead, it was a fraction of the size of Kennedy International. When she stepped off the plane the heat swallowed her. The air was humid, heavy and dominated with a sweet yet sour, fruity-spice smell. She would soon come to know the smell as Dar es Salaam's national anthem of scents. When they reached luggage claim, most of Austin's immediate family were waiting. Candace recognized each of them from photos. Momma Lena had on a colorful flowered-print dress and a matching headpiece. She looked younger than her picture and moved with nimbleness and grace. His mother wore a dashiki over a simple beige skirt and his father, a white cotton shirt over slacks. They too looked far younger than their pictures. They smiled and when they got in arm's length of each other Momma Lena was the first to embrace Candace. Austin was rushed by his parents and showered with hugs and kisses.

"Habari *(hello)* Hujambo *(how are you)*," said the old woman.

"Habari. *(hello)* Shikamoo *(I touch your feet)*," replied Candace.

"Marahabaa *(I acknowledge your respect!)*,"said Momma Lena and she loosened her grip and inspected her for what seemed like an eternity to Candace. She mumbled something else in Swahili and looked at her daughter and son-in-law for a response. They nodded their heads and smiled, as they looked Candace up and down. Austin had taught her quite a few Swahili words and phrases, but she was baffled by what Momma Lena had just said. She looked at Austin uneasily.

"They said you are beautiful," he told her. They did say she was beautiful but they also commented on how much she looked like Maoma. Austin chose not to mention that part. The night of the argument she accused him of being in love with Maoma's ghost. He wanted the relationship between his family and her to grow healthy without any indifference. He felt that telling her of the close bond his family had with Maoma would be an unwise decision. Given her personality, he was certain his family would take to her in the two weeks they would be there just as they had Maoma.

"Welcome to our country," said the father as he let go of Austin and reached for Candace. He surrounded her with his large arms.

"Thank you," she said. She didn't expect to hear English spoken from his family or many of the citizens but she would later learn that most Tanzanians were bilingual, English being one of the spoken languages.

"Yes, we are honored to have you visit with us. Momma Lena and I have made a large feast for the both of you in honor of your engagement," said Austin's mother. "Everyone is at the house anxiously awaiting your arrival. We will have a big celebration. She looked at Austin again. "It's good to see you, my son. You look well."

*   *   *

There was food in every corner of the kitchen. Golden pieces of fried chicken stacked high on a large platter sat on the kitchen counter. A large pot of the Hkatenkwan stew Austin loved so much sat atop the stove simmering on low while two generous pots of rice were on the other eyes ready to accommodate it. There were squash, pineapple nut and chapatis breads. Corn, tomatoes, turnip greens and peas could be found in pots and dishes around the table. Momma Lena's specialty was desserts. She'd made jam cake, yam cake, candid yams, puff-puff and chin-chin cookies. There were doughnuts that Candace thought were a hundred times better than the doughnuts in the States. They weren't as sweet and were filled with spices, nuts and fruit. The five-room house could not hold all the people who were invited. Some stood in huddles outside laughing and talking. Rows of people sat on the two couches in the living room, balancing plates of food on their laps while they ate. The kitchen flowed with a steady stream of people coming for refills. Austin and Candace sat at the table with mouths full of food, greeting family and friends in between bites. Candace took big spoonful bites of the Hkatenkwan stew and found it delicious. Austin had promised to make the stew for her and Sable but had never gotten around to it. Had she known it was this good she would have insisted upon him making it sooner. Momma Lena patted Candace lightly on the back and began speaking to her. Some of the words Candace picked up, but not enough to know what she was saying. Candace smiled at her and looked to Austin for help.

"She wants to know if you're getting enough to eat," Austin translated.

"Sijambo asante *(I am fine, thank you),*"

"Nzuri *(good)*." She said and walked on to the next guest.

Austin was proud of Candace for picking up as much of his language as she had, and he saw the pleased look on Momma Lena's face when she greeted her professionally at the airport.

"Austin, why doesn't Momma Lena speak English?"

"When she was growing up she did not have the educational advantages that allowed her to learn. Although we spoke it in the house from time to time, she insisted on us speaking Swahili in her presence. I guess part of the answer, too, is that she didn't want to learn. Older people are peculiar about new ways and find it hard to stray from old customs."

She met his brother, John, his wife, Tasha, and their three children. John and Tasha were schoolteachers in Dar es Salaam. They lived a pretty comfortable life compared to most of the residents. They had one car between the two of them, a 1988 Audi, and lived in the heart of town in a five-room townhouse loaded with modern amenities. John was the flip side of Austin. Almost everything that came out of his mouth was comical. He was well known and liked among everyone. He, Tasha and the children accepted Candace with open arms and immediately started referring to her as family. Later that night the family gathered in the living room to laugh and talk and familiarize themselves with Candace. They found her delightful and Candace adapted to them easily, too.

*   *   *

The next day they all celebrated Christmas at John's house. They exchanged gifts. The toys, clothes and especially the Play Station were big hits with the children. Austin gave his mother and sister-in-law 24-carat gold necklaces, his father and brother Rolex watches and Momma Lena a new outfit for church on Sundays. He bought Candace a one-carat diamond necklace to match her engagement ring. Candace gave him a solid gold bracelet inscribed with the words "I love you for a lifetime and a day." The next five days were spent visiting some of Austin's friends, buying souvenirs for Candace's family and touring the city and farmlands. On the fifth day Austin had Momma Lena to pack a light lunch and he took Candace on a picnic in the countryside overlooking a scenic valley of undeveloped grasslands. The view was spectacular. They lay on the blanket laughing, talking and nibbling the lunch for hours before making love under the blanket of the warm African sky.

Austin and Candace spent the last day of their visit in Dar es Salaam at home with his family. Tomorrow they would travel to Kenya for a three-day safari and then head back to the United States.

Momma Lena took Candace under her wings and shared with her the ways of a good Tanzanian wife while Austin's mother translated. Of course, her views on marriage were patriarchal and Candace would never submit to some of them, like allowing Austin to put her aside and take another woman if she was barren. But she listened eagerly anyway, curious and bewildered at the subservient role of the African wife. If they knew how liberal her ideas on the subject were they'd no doubt denounce her right then and there. Candace had fallen in love with Africa, but living there would require too much alteration of her personality and beliefs. Momma Lena gave her a tribal mask called Mwana Pwo. She told Candace the mask had inside it the spirit of her great grandmother, who had had 12 healthy children. She remembered the mask from the museum Austin took her to in New York. She knew it was an ancestral mask used for guarding and strengthening the fertility of young women who were preparing for marriage.

When Momma Lena finished, she hugged her warmly and gave her blessings. Candace extended a warm welcome for them to come and visit her and Austin in New York. Candace hoped she could visit them again in the years to come, but if she didn't get that chance she would remember Dar es Salaam and Austin's family for a lifetime.

*   *   *

The safari camp base was at the Ol Tukai Lodge at the foot of Mount Kilimanjaro. The first morning Austin and Candace had breakfast on their private balcony, watching the tallest mountain in Africa. The view was spectacular. They could see the snow-capped peaks hovering over the blue sky and white clouds. Just the sight of the cool mountain brought a bit of relief from the horrendous heat. They ate croissants with jam and drank coffee that had been grown and cultivated on the lower slopes of the mountain. They both thought it was the best coffee they had ever tasted. The first day the guest was broken up into five groups. Each group consisted of 10 people including two tour guides. Candace and Austin were placed in Group A, which included a couple from Cambridge, England, celebrating their 20th wedding anniversary. The other four were oilmen from Texas. They were in Africa on business but found time from their busy schedules to do the three-day safari. After lunch, Group A loaded into the custom-built Land Rover, each equipped with cameras, complimentary half-liter bottles of water and binoculars. They traveled 40 miles away from the lodge out into the remote areas. The ride was quite bumpy, but Candace held on tight to the handgrips on the rear of the facing seat and endured the roughness. The men seem to enjoy the jarring. When the guides came upon a dip in the road they would yell "bump!" to forewarn the passengers. Each time the vehicle jolted, the four oilmen burst into uncontrollable laughter. Their laughter was contagious and soon Austin and the Englishman were laughing, too. Candace and the other woman looked at each other and smiled wearily. They said not a word but communicated with their eyes, each wishing the driver would slow down.

The first animals they saw were a herd of gazelles grazing in an open plain. They were grayish tan with black markings on the upper legs, face and tail. The male had long, pointed horns. The Rover came to a halt and one of the guides began his speech on the animal.

"These are called damas. They are from the gazelle and antelope family. The damas are very elegant and graceful. The males are also quite territorial. During breeding season, they fight off any other adult males that come near the receptive females. The male damas fight by butting their head close to the ground. It is one of the largest gazelles, reaching 3 to 4 feet in height."

The guest snapped pictures and looked on in awe. The Englishwoman commented on how beautiful they were.

"Will we see any of them get eaten by a lion?" asked one of the oilmen as his buddies laughed. It had become apparent by now that the oilmen had been drinking and this was reason for their constant laughter. The Englishwoman looked at him with disgust.

"What a horrible thing to ask!" she responded.

"Actually, it is not," said the guide, "It is the cycle of life in process. The gazelles are plentiful. The lion and other carnivorous predators keep their population in check. The gazelles eat the vegetation; the lion eat the gazelles, thus fertilizing the earth so more vegetation can grow for the non-carnivorous animals. So, you see, all things work together for the good of the ecological system."

"I understand that totally but the very thought of him wanting to see the dear sweet animals being savaged by those beast is unthinkable."

"The jungle can be too graphic for the weak at heart. We are not likely to see a kill this afternoon, but for those who would like to see one, it is possible that you will before your adventure is over."

They traveled 10 more miles further, finding giraffes and zebras. After the guide had done his spiel on the two animals, the Rover turned around and headed back to the lodge. After dinner Group A loaded back in the Rover and headed for Ngong Hills. They enjoyed refreshments while watching a traditional Masai tribe display dancing, fire-making and even a wedding ceremony. The guide explained that the Masai people were herdsmen who devoted their lives to the raising of livestock.

"The women of the Masai tribe are considered as less important than the men. In most African tribes the women are not allowed to speak their minds and must follow the orders of their husbands. The Masai women play a significant role in all aspects of the Masai lifestyle. The men go out and hunt the cattle and retrieve some of its blood, but that is only half of the job. The women are then expected to milk the cattle. The blood and milk are mixed together and the Masai drink it. It is crucial that the Masai work together because the cattle serve numerous purposes, all which greatly contribute to the success and survival of the Masai tribe. The overall expectations of the Masai women are greater than most of the other tribes in Kenya and throughout Africa. They have a wide range of responsibilities, many which would be considered as jobs for men. In Masai society, women do most of the work, at home and in the field. By doing these challenging and rigorous jobs, the Masai women are gradually realizing that they deserve equal treatment for everything. The women have started speaking their opinion on some very serious issues. The Masai tribe has some very strong beliefs and rituals when the Masai girls and boys are initiated into adulthood. The main part of this induction is circumcision. The male circumcision symbolizes manhood and is nothing compared to the female circumcision, which is extremely harsh. For that reason an increasing number of Masai women are speaking out against it."

"Female circumcision is a much more involved and drastic procedure," the guide went on to say. "If the Masai women continue to speak their minds, they have the ability to make some permanent changes in the Masai traditions and customs."

Candace watched the colorfully dressed Masai women with their heavy ear and neck ornaments go about their daily routines. She searched their faces looking for pleas for deliverance from the brutal practice. But they seemed happy and she guessed if she was born in this culture and it was all she'd known, she would be happy too. She had heard about the female genitalia mutilation rites of passage and also knew that there were a lot of outside intervention groups trying to stop it. Part of her felt it was an intrusion upon these beautiful people and their way of life. The civilized culture always tried to inflict its own beliefs and way of life on others it felt were less fortunate. Of course, she didn't agree with this custom, but she would be the last person to try to change a way of life and heritage. For a moment, as she stood surrounded by hundreds of people, she felt alone, dissected and dismembered from them; yet she was never happier to be born American.

When they returned to the lodge it was after midnight. The guide told them they would be going out even farther tomorrow and they would encounter lions, elephants, rhinoceros and other carnivorous species. He warned the English woman that she might want to reconsider coming along, that the chance of seeing a kill was great.

"Breakfast starts at six; we leave at seven. Have a great night," said the guides and retreated to their quarters. Candace and Austin walked up the rustic staircase to their room. Once inside they collapsed on the bed and drifted off to sleep with their clothes on. They both had had a full, enjoyable and educational day.

The clock's neon light read 5:45. Austin shook Candace, "Wake up, sleepy head. We'll be late for the safari."

"What time is it?" she asked groggily.

"It's 5:45. If you want to make breakfast you have 15 minutes."

"I'm not hungry," she said and rolled back over.

"Okay, suit yourself then. You can lay in the bed all morning if you like, but I'm going on the safari." Austin jumped in the shower and was out in no time. He left the water running for Candace. He came out of the bathroom wrapped in a towel. Candace lay in bed still sleep. Austin phoned down for pastries, juice and coffee. Without warning he lifted Candace over his shoulder. He had taken her by total surprise.

"Austin, what are you doing?" she said in alarm, and before she could comprehend what was happening the cool water from the shower was trickling down on her, clothes and all.

*　　　　　　*　　　　　　*

It was 5:00 p.m. when they spotted the first lion. His bushy brown-orange mane bopped above the thicket as he walked. He watched the familiar Rover come to a slow halt and then roared, signaling to the female lioness that were walking in front of him. The females nudged at their cubs and roared a warning toward the Rover.

"The lion is a member of the cat family. Their size, power and bearing have captured human imagination since earliest times. The mane covers the head and neck sometimes extending to the shoulders and stomach area. It varies in length and color, from black to tawny. The well-fed, healthy lions have fuller manes. The smaller, equally muscular females are of the same tawny color except without the mane. Both male and female have hooked claws and wide, powerful jaws. The lion's roar can be heard up to five miles away and is usually uttered before the animal's hunt in the evening or in the early morning. They spend two to three hours a day hunting and the remaining hours resting and sleeping."

The guest snapped away with their cameras as the Rover slowly trailed the animals.

"We may be in luck," said the guide. "The lions are heading toward a watering hole the blue wildebeest frequent."

The oilmen laughed delightedly and gave each other high-fives. Two of the lioness crouched low as they zeroed in on a wildebeest and her calf. One of the lionesses crept to the left and the other to the right, encircling the mother and calf. The herd of animals scattered in different directions while the mother tried to lead her baby out of harm's way. The lioness picked up speed and shortened the distance between them. The mother knew that they were doomed. She led the baby toward a scattered group and when it was close enough she slowed her pace and let her calf run past her and into the ark of safety. She zigzagged in the other direction across the dusty plain trying fruitlessly to confuse the vicious hunters. But their synchronized calculations were exact as one of the lions followed the jagged path and the other cut across it. The mother took one last look at her calf as it disappeared into the mass of wildebeests before the lions pounced upon her. One grabbed her by the neck, suffocating her, while the other clawed and bit her hind legs. Five minutes later the animal lay gutted with the pride of lions tearing at her lifeless carcass. A group of hyenas lurked close by, licking at the blood-scented air and hoping for a taste of the fallen animal. Candace and Austin clicked their cameras at the ravenous lions. The Englishwoman buried her face in her husband's chest throughout the whole ordeal. One oilman who had been so thrilled about seeing a kill stuck his head out the window and began throwing up.

*   *   *

Sable tore open the envelope and smiled at the $20,000 check. The royalties would start rolling in around the middle of January. She titled her latest mystery "Murder at Corporate Level." Her agent had done an excellent job of promoting the book and the first printing was over 100,000 copies. Sable was content at this point in her life—Candace's upcoming marriage, her and Jonah's reconciliation, and his moving to Torryville the end of February. He'd found a job with another pharmaceutical company, which had negotiated his salary $10,000 more than his current salary and agreed to match his benefits, add on his years of service and pension plan. Sable had met Mrs. Ruthann and found her to be everything she hoped she would. It was very clear watching Wilson and Mrs. Ruthann together that the two cared deeply for each other. She felt at ease knowing that after Jonah left North Carolina there would be someone back home watching over her father. In all her happiness there was one thing she would change if she had the power and that was her relationship with Shamell. Shamell had given her hope the night she called to tell her Candace would be staying with her for a few days. The next week Sable called and left a thank-you message on her answering machine but Shamell never acknowledged it. When Jonah moved up, most of her loneliness would dissipate and she would be able to close that chapter of her life and stop worrying about Shamell. Sable flipped through the cookbook, looking for a scrumptious dessert recipe. She was putting together a menu for tomorrow night when Candace and Austin returned. It would be a welcome-home and a book finishing celebration. She decided on barbecue spare ribs, potato salad, collard greens, and cornbread, and for dessert she would make a pineapple upside down cake. She wrote out a list of the items she needed for the dinner and then got in the Benz and headed to the grocery store.

*　　　　　*　　　　　*

The photos lay spread out on the coffee table beside the cups of coffee and saucers of cake. Sable looked at them as Austin and Candace described each shot to her. Candace talked continuously about Africa, Austin's family and especially the safari. Sable forked a piece of the cake in her mouth before shuffling to the shot of the lions eating the wildebeest.

"Ugh!" she uttered before spitting the cake into a napkin. "What are they eating?" she asked, disgusted at the gory picture.

"Um, that looks like the wildebeest's intestine," said Austin nonchalantly.

Sable slapped at his hands. "You both are so vulgar. How can you eat while looking at that picture?"

"It was much worse live. The lions were covered in blood and bowels," added Candace. "Momma, I'm glad you weren't there. You could not have taken it. You would have been like a few others on the trip," she laughed, thinking about the oilman and English woman.

Sable's appetite was ruined. She eased her cake down on the coffee table and listened to Candace describe in gory details how the lions captured, killed, devoured and fought over the last remains of the wildebeest. She told her about the Masai tribe and how the women did most of the work, yet were submissive to the men. She showed her the Mwana

Pow mask Austin's grandmother had given her. "This mask has powers, Mom. It's going to help give you 12 grandchildren." Austin and Candace laughed at the joke while Sable stared blankly at the mask.

"Help give me twelve grands, huh?" she said, flipping it over to inspect the other side, "I'll settle for two. I've heard about this tribal mask. Aren't they suppose to perform a dance over you first?"

Austin laughed even harder at Sable's quick wit. "Don't take it so lightly, Sable. The powers are real and it really works. Candace and I will have to be very careful not to give you more than two grandbabies."

"Well," said Sable, handing the mask back to Candace, then wiping her hands to rid the mystic powers, "as long as it doesn't work on me. You know your daddy will be moving here in several weeks." A smile warmed her face.

"You are delighted aren't you, Sable?" asked Austin.

"I am."

The ringing of the telephone halted their conversation. Candace eased out of her chair to answer it.

"Hello? Oh, hi, Daddy. Yeah, we got back early this afternoon. Yes, it was wonderful. I can't wait to show you the pictures. Yes, she's right here. Daddy, is anything wrong? You don't sound right."

Sable was off the couch in an instant. She peeled Candace's fingers from around the phone.

"Jonah?"

"Hello, Sable." Jonah's voice was solemn and at that moment the bottom of Sable's stomach fell. She gripped the receiver so tight the color rushed out of her knuckles. She waited for Jonah to say he had a change of heart, that he didn't want to marry her again. She braced herself for him to tell her there was someone else. She remembered the night she'd called him and "Betty" answered the phone. She couldn't be sure it was Betty. It hadn't sounded like Betty. She felt foolish for acting gullible and like a charmed schoolgirl. If her marriage didn't work the first time, why did she think it would work a second time? Candace stood nearby staring into Sable's face waiting to know what was happening.

"Sable, you need to come home. I've got bad news."

28

Good-byes Forever

New York University's second semester normally started two weeks after the Christmas holidays. Shamell couldn't imagine why Charles had so much work to do on campus. She was still out for the holidays and did not have to report back to work until Monday, four days from now. She packed the ham and Swiss sandwiches in the thermal sack and tucked the thermos of coffee under her arm. The surprise snack would be a welcoming break from the monotonous life she and Charles had been living and could possibly rekindle some romance. He was still coming home late and complaining about not having enough hours in the day to do the things he needed to. He'd been tired a lot too, not wanting to make love or talk for that matter. He'd say what he had to to keep her from asking questions about his day and on the rare occasions when she did he wouldn't feel like talking. Shamell loaded everything in the Porsche and drove to the University. Parking spaces at NYU were scarce to none. The handful available was reserved for the chancellor and a few department heads. Charles was lucky enough to have one. Since it was the holidays, Shamell knew she would be able to find someplace to park. She spotted Charles's Toyota 4Runner and pulled in beside it. The campus was isolated except for four other cars. She recognized Professor Dillon's 1969 Cadillac. It was nicknamed the mad bomber because of its age and the fact that Professor Dillon had a lead foot behind the wheel of his car. He was a respectful gentleman in his late 60's and came out of retirement to return to his first love, teaching. The faculty and staff had a great deal of respect for the NYU icon. Shamell liked him and his wife too and realized it had been over a year since she had last seen Mrs. Dillon. She made a mental note to stop in and say hello and invite them to dinner in the near future. She entered O'Grady Hall and trekked down the long, deserted corridor toward Charles's office. The classrooms reminded her of her years with the New York school system. There were times when she missed teaching and thought about re-entering the profession if and when she tired of publishing.

From the end of the hallway, she saw a female figure walking toward her. As she got closer, Shamell noticed how pretty the girl was. She was wearing a sea-breeze type fragrance that smelled wonderful. She wore her hair in long braids and had large almond-shaped eyes that twinkled when she smiled. She said a cheery hello to Shamell as they passed.

"Hello," Shamell replied. The girl looked like a student, and Shamell wondered why she wasn't home with her family during the holidays. She turned the knob to Charles's office and stepped inside. The office was empty. There wasn't a sign anywhere indicating that Charles was here to do work. No papers, books or lesson plans. Charles's belt lay across the clean desk. The adjoining bathroom door was ajar, and Shamell could hear running water. She started putting two and two together, but they weren't adding up to four. The girl she had just passed was the same girl Sable was trying to warn her about. She smelled the familiar perfume she was wearing still lingering in the office. She took another look at Charles's belt lying on the desk. This is the kind of work he's been doing, she thought. Her heart sank and she dropped the lunch bag and thermos on the floor.

"Leticia," called Charles from the bath, "did you forget something, baby?"

"Baby?" said Shamell softly. She couldn't remember the last time he called her sweet names and meant it. The anger rose in Shamell. She said not a word but bolted from the office in the direction the girl was going. The girl was crossing the campus lawn when Shamell exited O'Grady Hall. She got in Charles's 4Runner and started the engine. Shamell's fast pace turned into a trot. She wanted to catch the girl before she got away. Just before she closed the car door, Shamell called the name she'd heard Charles call only seconds ago.

"Leticia, wait up!"

Leticia watched Shamell run toward her. She stepped out of the 4Runner and waited as she approached. Thanks to the aerobics, Shamell was only slightly out of breath when she reached her.

"Hello," she said casually, checking the girl out from head to toe. Shamell had to give her credit. She was a beauty standing at 5-foot-7, about 130 pounds. She was two shades darker than Shamell's own honey color. Her make-up was applied expertly. Shamell looked into her face and saw a young girl who'd undoubtedly grown up too fast. She couldn't be more than 20 years, yet Shamell suspected she knew as much about life as any 40-year-old woman did. Leticia slung her braids back over her shoulder before speaking.

"Do I know you?" she asked with an air of arrogance.

"Well, you should. I'm the wife of the man you been screwing for God knows how long."

Leticia's mouth dropped and her eyes widened. She quickly jumped back into the 4Runner but before she could close the door, Shamell was right behind her. She blocked the door with her arm.

"What are you doing?" demanded Leticia hysterically.

"Get your ass out of my husband's car." Shamell stared at the girl murderously and when she didn't move Shamell reached in grabbed the keys out of the ignition and threw them behind her. They slid on the smooth pavement, then into a manhole. She yanked Leticia out by the collar with both hands.

"I'm Shamell Anderson, Professor Charles Anderson's wife." She watched the expression on Leticia's face change from frightened to defiant.

"I know who you are. Charles has told me all about you, how you won't give him the time of day because you too wrapped up in your career and that dyke friend of yours, the-the writer."

Shamell was shocked. She swallowed a gulp of air and listen to Leticia babble on about all the lies Charles had fed her. Shamell had heard enough. She raised her opened hand in front of the girl's face.

"Hold up. You mean to tell me Charles told you I was gay?"

"Yes, he did. Look lady?"

"Lady! You called me Lady? I am Mrs. Charles Anderson! You don't seem to get it. You're messing with a married man. My man and I want it to stop. There's plenty of nice guys on this campus who I'm sure would love to date you. Why don't you get out of the big league and get on a race track that's more your speed."

"I seem to be giving you a run for the money."

Shamell was past being civilized; she was mad. Four-letter words began flying from her mouth and before she knew it she had grabbed Leticia by her braids and swung her around in a full 120-degree circle. She yanked the artificial hair and Leticia slipped away from her frenetic grip and went tumbling across the lawn into a puddle of melted snow.

"You don't know who you're messing with, little girl. I will beat you back into infancy."

Warm moisture dripped from Leticia's head. She reached up to examine it and found that a plug of hair the size of a 50-cent piece had been pulled out and she was bleeding. She looked at Shamell's hand to see several of her braids clutched in her grip. She began to scream.

"My hair! Oh, God! Charles, help me!"

Charles had witnessed the whole scene and was now running toward them. He knew he had to reach them before the chaos got any louder and drew attention form the few other faculty who were there working. He did not need this incident to go on his record. If board members knew of his affair with the sophomore, he would surely be dismissed. He grabbed Shamell around her waist and carried her to the Porsche. "Get in, Shamell," he said calmly.

"This is work, huh, Charles?"

"Shamell, we'll talk about this later."

"No, we'll talk now!" She got louder.

"You don't have to yell, Shamell. You don't want the attention and neither do I."

"I'm sure you don't, Professor Anderson!" She cupped her hands around her mouth like a bullhorn and screamed his name. "Your little two-bit, fake tramp thinks I'm a dyke. I wonder where she got that from?"

"I don't know?"

"Yeah, right. You could have been more realistic and told her I had a boyfriend."

Leticia got out of the puddle and went to Charles. "Charles, what do you mean you don't know? You told me she was Butch?"

"Shut up!" he snapped, then averted his attention back to Shamell, "C'mon." He grabbed her arm again, trying to calm her. Shamell jerked away.

"Oh, no, you want me to be a good wife, go home and wait for you to come and reason this thing out with me in the privacy of our house. And when I don't agree with you, you can sock some sense into me. Well, I don't think so." She looked at Leticia. "That's right. Professor Anderson beats his wife, but don't worry, dear, I'm sure he's got a few hard punches reserved for you."

"Shamell, that's enough!"

"I was gon' buy your sorry ass a bottle of Viagra, but I see that Leticia is your Viagra. You want this two-bit whore, Charles?" She threw the braids in his face.

"No. Baby, you know I love you. She doesn't mean anything to me."

Shamell looked at Leticia triumphantly. "You hear that little girl? Your Professor Anderson is turning out to be a real dog."

Leticia's eyes clouded over with tears. "Charles, you don't mean it. You said you loved me and you were going to divorce her so we could be together."

"I said no such thing. Every time I turn around you're in my face, teasing me with your body. I did what any full-blooded man would have done."

"Oh, my God!" cried Leticia. "You lied to me. You said you were going to marry me."

Shamell looked at her competitor and then at the trophy she'd supposedly won. They were both sorry sights. Leticia and Charles deserved each other. She had been so afraid of losing him and being alone, but standing there amidst his deceit, betrayal and lies she was able to see that she deserved more than what Charles was giving her. If she never found the man of her dreams, being alone would be better than being with him. She had given up her self-respect and a friendship for the sake of keeping Charles. He stood before her pleading. Memories of the night he'd beat her came flooding back and it was the pleading and crying that made her forgive him that time. She would not be played a fool a third time. He'd promised her he would never do anything to hurt her again. It was too late, because from this point on all his promises were void.

"Leticia, if you want this scumbag, he's all yours. I have no use for him anymore." Shamell got in her car and locked the doors so Charles could not get in. She sped off toward what she knew would be a new and better horizon.

"Where my car keys!" Charles yelled at Leticia.

She pointed to the manhole; "She threw them down there."

"Oh, great!" Charles rushed off to his office with Leticia running behind him in fervent tears. The few faculty members there had come out of O'Grady hall to see what the ruckus was all about.

*   *   *

Shamell knew she couldn't stay around, because Charles would be coming home soon. She suspected he had found a way to get the keys out of the manhole and was on his way now. She packed the things she would need to carry her over for a few days until she could get a court order to restrain Charles from the property. Then she would file for divorce. The answering-machined blinked furiously. She pushed the message button and heard Candace's voice. She was crying.

*   *   *

The Germanton First Baptist Church was packed with people who had come to pay their last respects. The scent from the hundreds of flowers drifted throughout the church. The funeral director led the family down the aisle to the front of the church where the body lay. Sable gripped Jonah's hand tight and steadied her wobbly body against his as they walked slowly toward the open casket. Onlookers reached out to touch her and utter words of comfort as she passed their pews. She acknowledged them with a forced smile and nod of the head. Everything was so familiar, the church, the flowers, the smell and the pain. They stopped in front of the casket. Sable looked down upon her loved one's face.

"Are you satisfied with the preparation, Ms. Brooks?" asked the director, "Turned out good, I think. Don't look dead, just sleep."

Sable hated when people said that. She knew it was a remark to soften the ache, but it didn't. It didn't paralyze the sting of losing someone you loved. Dead was dead and nothing about death resembled sleep to her. Aunt Elvira looked just like Loretta lying in the coffin. Her high cheekbones and full lips were a family trait. Sable thought they put too much powder on her face and the blush and lipstick were out of character because she never wore them. Nevertheless, she looked good. Her beautician had taken the time to dye her hair with the blue-black color she liked and put the tiny curls in. Sable knew that if Aunt Elvira could see how they laid her out she would be fussing, "*Got me looking like Jezebel laying up here. Lord, they got me on a white shroud. They know I can't stand dead-people clothes. I wanted to be buried in my navy polka-dotted suit.*" Sable looked at the rich mahogany casket with its pure silk lining and she imagined Aunt Elvira protesting it too. "*I hope y'all didn't spend up all my money on this thing. How much money this box cost anyway?*" Sable's tears turned to a smile and then a snicker. The funeral director looked unexpectedly over his bifocals at her.

"You all right, baby?" asked Jonah and he tightened his grip around her shoulders. She peeked at him through her black veil.

"Aunt VI and I were sharing a last-minute joke, that's all." She winked at him and they moved on to the first pew. Wilson, Candace and Austin crowded around the coffin next.

"I'm gon' miss you, Vi" said Wilson. "When you get to heaven tell Loretta I said hello."

Aunt Elvira was lucky. She had died suddenly of a stroke. During the Christmas holidays she'd cooked up a storm. She had prepared ham, turkey and dressing, sweet potato pie, chitterlings, turnips (heavy on the ham hocks) greens, macaroni and cheese, potato salad and three different kinds of cake. Sable warned her about her high blood pressure and that she shouldn't be eating the rich foods. It was after Christmas dinner when Sable was helping her clean the kitchen that she discovered her bottle of blood-pressure medicine. The seal had not been broken and the refill date read November 5th. Sable warned Aunt Elvira that she was playing with two evils, eating rich foods and not taking her medication. Aunt Elvira assured her that she never felt better and eased her worries by promising to start back taking the medicine. Gut instinct told her that Aunt Elvira would probably die of a stroke or diabetes like her mother, but she thought it would be a long time coming and there would be warning signs first, like a bout of illness and hospital stays. Never in a million years would she have guessed she would die instantly like she had. Since Aunt Elvira's death, she had been preaching to Wilson about his health and although he had no apparent problems she still worried. She scheduled an appointment with his doctor to give him a complete physical and a nutritionist to put him on a good healthy diet he could live with. He was all she had left in the form of guardianship and she was going to take extra good care of him.

The church listened to the dear stories a few of Aunt Elvira's friends shared. The choir sang up beat spirituals that put everybody in a shouting frenzy.

"This ain't a funeral!" announced the minister. "This is Sister Elvira's home-going celebration. She fought a good fight and won the battle; now she's resting over on the other shore. A place where I'm striving to get to—where we all wanna go." He looked down on Aunt Elvira's peaceful face, "No more sickness, Sister Elvira, 'cause God is your doctor now. We all know how you loved to dress, but you ain't got to worry 'bout what kinda clothes you gon' put on cause God is your tailor. He got a Holy Ghost robe adorned with diamonds, emeralds and sapphires that won't ever go out of style. You won't have to worry 'bout transportation cause God's got a pair of 24 karat golden wings up there waiting for you that will fly you anywhere you want to go. You don't even have to worry 'bout what you gon' eat, 'cause God is your chef now. You can eat all the chitterlings, pork chops and fatback you want, and it can't hurt you now. You all right cause God 'got your back,' Sister Elvira!" Then the Reverend began to sing; "One Fine Mor—nin' When this life is o—ver I—'ll Fly A—way. To a place on God's celestial shore, I—'ll Fly A—way." The choir chimed in and the shouting started again and Sable witnessed something she had never seen before. Wilson jumped from his seat and began shouting. He hollered "Hallelujah!" Here was a man who seldom went to church. He believed in God and the hereafter but never devoted even a small part of his life to church. Sable's religious persuasion came from Loretta and Aunt Elvira. They were the ones who'd taken her to church, read her the Bible and kept her feet on the straight and narrow. A warm feeling spread through her soul and in the midst of sorrow, she gave thanks. Thanks for the birth of a new family member. The procession made its way around to comfort the family. Sable was impressed at the many lives Aunt Elvira had touched and inspired. Everyone had something kind and positive to say about her.

"Sho' gon' miss her," said an unknown who had bent over to whisper in Sable's ear. As soon as one person moved on, another came. They touched, rubbed, sobbed, hugged and kissed Sable. She was quickly growing tired and wished deeply for it all to be over. Then a familiar touch stirred her. It was soft yet firm, friendly but refined. Sable looked up to see her dear friend staring into her grief-stricken face. She lifted herself from her seat and encircled her arms around Shamell. They stood there for a full 10 minutes saying not a word, but just hugging each other.

*   *   *

Sable and Jonah put Shamell in the guest bedroom. Austin and Candace insisted on staying with Wilson. Shamell and Sable talked into the wee hours of the morning. They played catch-up on all the things they had missed over the past few months.

"What are you going to do with this fabulous house when Jonah moves to Torryville?"

"I really don't know, Shamell. We thought about renting it out, but then that's still a lot of responsibility. Candace will soon be anchored in New York, so giving it to her is out of the question. We really don't want to put it up for sale—too many memories and one day we might want to move back here. It's a hard decision."

"Do like the movie stars do, child. They have several homes across the world. When they get tired of one, they move to the other one for a while."

"You're too much, you know that? I'm a long ways from being rich"

They grew quiet for a moment before Shamell spoke.

"I'm sorry, Sable."

Sable looked at her and placed her index finger across her lips. "You don't have to apologize to me, Shamell."

"Yes, I do, at least I want to. I was such an idiot. A part of me knew what was going on with Charles. I just didn't want to believe it. After he hit me that time, I was more embarrassed than frightened. People always thought my marriage was ideal, and I wanted to believe it was too. Over time I did grow afraid of Charles, especially when he'd come home late at night in one of his sour moods. I knew he had been with another woman. I could smell her on him. Yet I just stayed there like a fool and endured it, hoping and praying things would get better. I grew up in the projects dirt poor and without a father figure. Somehow I felt Charles was everything I missed while growing up. I watched my mother work and slave to take care of her children and, Sable, she always told her girls that we needed a man in our lives to make us complete, that we would not be successful without one. That woman stressed the importance of keeping ourselves beautiful. She never said anything about education. She was mad at me for a long time because I chose college over marriage. She wanted me to marry my high school sweetheart. He got a job working in a factory right after high school. I remember it so clear the night he came to my house and asked my mother if he could marry me. They had my life all planned in a matter of minutes before I knew anything about it. I said no, of course, said I was going to college so I could be a schoolteacher." She looked at Sable through tears. "You know what my Momma said after I told her that?"

"What did she say?"

"Said I ain't gon' give you one dime to waste on college. This boy here wants to marry you and you talking about going to college. College for rich white folks."

I think that's partly the reason why I didn't want to let Charles go. I didn't want to disappoint my Momma up in heaven. Don't get me wrong, I don't blame her, because that's all she knew. She worked so hard by herself I guess she thought having a man had to be better and easier than going it alone. She just wanted the best for her girls."

"You never told me anything about you childhood before."

"After hearing you talk about yours, I was ashamed of mine. So I said nothing."

"I can't tell you how many sleepless nights I've had worrying over you, girl. I'm so glad you got away from him. I just hope he doesn't sweet-talk his way back into your life. I hate to say this, but a leopard doesn't change his spots."

"Let me tell you that's one leopard I don't want." Without reason or warning, Shamell burst into laughter.

"What's wrong with you?" Sable picked up a pillow and threw it at her, hitting her on the head.

"It felt soooo good, Sable."

"What?"

"Beating Leticia's ass. You should have been there. When I finished with her, she was crying like a baby. If I ever decide to change professions, I might just go into boxing, I'm pretty good at it."

29

Confrontations

Candace sat passenger as Twila Jackson drove her car through the heart of New York City. They were on their way to Tugg's Studio to do an assignment for Maybelline cosmetics. The shoot would later be advertised in Cosmopolitan magazine. They would be modeling along with five other girls of different nationalities. The caption underneath the photo would read: "Beautiful Colors of the Rainbow."

Although Twila did a good job of masking her true feelings about Candace taking over her position at Blacktravaganza, there were times when Candace picked up on her resentment. The two girls walked into the building and were directed to suite 530. The cosmetologist and photographer greeted and led them to a dressing room where the other five girls were already changing. The five models consisted of a Native American, an Asian, a Hispanic, and two Caucasians—one a redhead and the other a blonde. The girls were friendly and talked excessively. The blonde and the Asian knew each other and they talked openly about their personal lives. Candace could not believe some of the things they had done. The blonde talked about her use of drugs and invited the Asian to a party her boyfriend was throwing that night. The Asian said she couldn't make it because she had a hot date. The blonde extended the invitation to the rest of them. When she said there would be free liquor and drugs, the Native American and Twila accepted. Candace was shocked that Twila would even consider going to a party where the main attraction would be drugs. She nudged her in the side.

"What?"

"You're not really going to that girl's party, are you?"

"Hell, yeah," she laughed. "Didn't you hear her? She said the snorts are free, and I don't pass up no free smack."

"Twila!"

"What, Candace?" she said, annoyed over her simple innocence.

"You know that stuff is bad."

Twila laughed, "C'mon girl, you can't be for real. Everybody do drugs."

"Not me."

"That's part of your problem," Twila said as she struggled to free herself from the spandex pants.

"Part of my problem? I didn't know I had a problem."

Twila rolled her eyes toward the ceiling and exhaled a puff of air that blew her bangs out of place. "You better step into the new millennium with everybody else. You ought to try it. It just frees you, girl."

"No, thank you. I feel pretty good without the help of drugs. Why you need them anyway? Your life is good, you got the upper hand on most people."

"Pressures, child, plus it gives you a good feeling." She had gotten her clothes off and wrapped herself chest down in the towel. She went to one of the sinks and began scrubbing off her makeup. Candace was curious now and wanted to pinpoint the reason behind her using drugs.

"I can't imagine what kind of pressures you would have to make you turn to drugs. I mean, when you come off your high your problems are still there."

"Oh you wouldn't understand. Austin got you so cushioned and protected that you'll never have problems in this business as long as you stay with him."

"What kind of problems are you having? Maybe I can get Austin to help you."

"Girl, I wish I had a joint or something right now," Twila laughed. "You a trip, you know that? C'mon, they waiting for us."

It took the cosmetologist an hour to make up the girl's faces. They were told to lie down, making a circle with their heads in the center. He placed yellow and white daisies and carnations on each girl's neck and chest. Then the photographer positioned himself on top of his stepladder and started taking pictures of the girls.

"Perfect!" he said. "This is just the effect I wanted."

It had taken three hours to complete the session. The girls changed back into their clothes and left.

*   *   *

Candace pushed the grocery cart down aisle 9. She stood in front of the huge selection of coffee, trying to decide which brand to buy. Since tasting the mountain-grown coffee in Kenya, their tastebuds had become spoiled and the brand they were used to didn't measure up anymore. She scooped two spoonfuls of the gourmet coffee beans into the grinder and flicked the button. She watched as the beans turned to grounds. "Maybe this will taste close to what I want," she said to herself. She was amazed at how her life had changed over the past 10 months. She had gone from a person with limited cooking skills to almost a gourmet chef, at least that was Austin's nickname for her in the kitchen. Austin was an eater and Candace soon realized that one of the ways to keeping him happy was keeping him well fed. Her cart was armed with the necessary provisions for fighting his hunger pangs. Two gallons of ice cream, one Rocky Road, the other butter pecan. Three 32-ounce bags of potato chips, nachos and pretzels, Famous Amos cookies, Orville Redenbacher microwave popcorn, beer and soda. Then there was her stock, the foods that were absolutely vital to her existence in the world of modeling. Nonfat yogurt, lettuce, tomatoes, nonfat salad dressing, low-fat bread, tons of frozen vegetables, fruits galore, fresh fish and poultry and the leanest of lean meats, brown rice and gallons of Dannon bottled water.

She guided the cart out of the aisle and collided smack into another shopper. She covered the overloaded buggy with both hands to keep its contents from falling out, but an apple escaped and rolled to the center of the aisle.

"I'm so sorry," she said, stooping down to pick up the apple. When she got up she was looking into the face of Ophelia Myerson.

"It's a small world," said Ophelia. "Now what are the chances of me meeting you here?" she asked in her usual bubbly character.

"Probably one in a thousand," said Candace, suddenly sorry she chose Food Galaxy to do her shopping. It was not the grocery store she normally patronized, but since she was in the area she decided to stop. She knew she would have a hard time getting away from Ophelia.

"More like one in two thousand, I'd say. So how are you and your cute friend?"

"We're doing fine, thank you."

"My, you've got enough in that buggy to feed an army," she said, surveying the contents of the cart.

"No, not an army," she smiled, wishing someone would come and rescue her.

"I see you got a lot of junk food in there. Girl, Russell loves junk food, too. He can eat his weight in candy bars if I let him. I'm shopping for him. He tells me not to worry about it but to be truthful I love doing it. You know how men are. They don't know how to grocery shop."

As Ophelia talked on, Candace couldn't help but notice the large cans of Chef Boyardee spaghetti, Vienna sausages and about half a dozen frozen dinners. Russell must have changed, she thought, because he would never touch a frozen dinner when she knew him and he detested anything that came from a can. Somehow, she thought Ophelia was one of those old-fashioned girls who could throw down in the kitchen.

"Well, I see you've got enough to keep Russell's tummy full."

Ophelia laughed as if she had just heard the joke of the week. "Oh! Russell and I are engaged." She extended her hand to show off the engagement ring. Candace thought the ring was a bit small, but Ophelia seemed delighted over it, so who was she to complain.

"April is the magic month."

"Congratulations," said Candace, opting not to tell her that she too would soon be getting married in May. Ophelia was probably the nicest girl on the face of the earth, but still she felt sorry for Russell because she knew Ophelia was not his match.

"Give me your exact address and I'll send you an invitation." Ophelia fished through her shoulder bag for pen and paper.

"Russell has my address out in Torryville," she said, hoping Ophelia would settle for that.

"Oh!" she said, eyeing Candace suspiciously, "I thought you would want it sent to your Manhattan address."

"My Manhattan address?" she asked, suspecting that Russell told her about her living arrangements with Austin. "How do you know I live in Manhattan?"

"Russell told me. He talks about you all the time. He personally thinks you should move back in with your mother instead of shacking up with that man. Now, Russell and I have decided not to live together before we're married. I know to each his own, but right is right and wrong is wrong. I'm traditional myself, I haven't let Russell..." she blushed before continuing, "you know, go all the way with me. I want to be exciting and new to him on our wedding night."

Candace directed her anger at Russell. There was no reason for her getting mad at Ophelia when Russell was the one telling her business.

"Like you said, Ophelia, to each his own. It's been real talking to you but I've got a busy schedule ahead of me and must get going." Candace pushed the cart toward the checkout counter. She hoped she didn't run into Russell before her temper cooled off because she would give him a piece of her mind.

*   *   *

Candace fingered the adding machine with lightning speed. She had totaled her net worth to the tune of $44,000. She was thrilled and proud at the amount of money she had put into her account in such a short period of time. The $11,000 in graduation gifts, the $3,000 for the sale of her Toyota, and the $30,000 income from modeling had really mounted up. Austin was financially literate and was constantly telling her to put her money into tax sheltered accounts with high interest rates. Candace was hesitant about taking that route because the money market accounts tied your money up and the penalty was great if you needed it before the maturation date. He'd told her time and time again that she didn't need to touch a penny of her money, that he would provide her with what ever she needed. She was going to take his advice but kept putting it off for one reason or the other.

Austin was sitting at the kitchen table reading the Wall Street Journal. Candace sneaked behind him and planted a kiss in his soft hair. "I'm out of here," she said grabbing her coat and pocketbook. "Where are you going?"

"I've got a fitting for my wedding gown. Then Mom and I are meeting the consultant to go over and discuss some ideas for the wedding and reception.

"I thought we were going to have a simple but elegant wedding. By time your mother finishes the whole state of New York will be invited."

"Honey, I know, but you know how Momma is. I'm her only child and she wants to do it right. Don't worry, I'll persuade her to keep it as simple as possible."

*   *   *

Sable and the attendant marveled at Candace as she stood before the full-length mirror inspecting herself in the gown. It was exquisite. The bodice was strapless and covered in tiny pearls and sparkling crystals. The belaro jacket with its pearls and crystals matched the bodice. The A-line dress was made of shimmering French silk and followed by three feet of train. Her headpiece was a tiara and had gathered and ruffled white chiffon that trailed from the back. Candace smiled at her reflection. "It's flawless."

"Almost," said Sable, reaching to close the jacket so it would hide Candace's cleavage.

"I can honestly say I don't believe I've seen a prettier bride," said the attendant. "Does it feel comfortable?"

"Yes, you've done an excellent job of altering it."

"Well, are you ready to take it with you now? Of course, we can keep it in our non-wrinkling storage facilities until the wedding. The fee is only $2 a day."

"No, thank you," said Sable, "$1,200 is enough for this gown, we don't want to pay a penny more."

"Three months is a long time for this gorgeous gown to sit. You've got to think about moths eating this delicate fabric too, you know," said the attendant.

"I'll lay it down on one of my spare beds. It'll look fine for the wedding, thank-you." Sable wrote a check in the full amount minus the down payment. The attendant carefully placed the gown in its garment bag. Sable and Candace were on their way to meet with the consultant.

AnnaMarie walked around the flower garden and snuggled inside her warm coat against the cold February weather. Sable and Candace walked on either side of her.

"This is a perfect place to have a wedding. Candace, you will walk down the stone path here up to the rose-covered archway. Your groom will be standing there awaiting you. How many attendants are you planning to have, dear?"

"Only two; one maid of honor and one bridesmaid."

"Oh!" Sable shook her head and rolled her eyes in agitation. "AnnaMarie, I've tried to tell her that she needs more attendants. I mean, that gorgeous gown; it needs to be enhanced by at least half a dozen bridesmaids. If Candace plans this wedding, there won't even be a flower girl or ring bearer."

"Mom, I'll carry my own flowers and Austin's ring and he will carry my ring. Besides, Austin doesn't want a big wedding."

"I just don't understand it. Most girls would kill at the opportunity to have an elaborate wedding like the one I want to give you, *free of charge,* mind you, and you don't want it."

"I'm not most girls, mom. My joy is just becoming Mrs. Austin Kawissopie."

Sable waved her hands in the air. "AnnaMarie, try to talk some sense into her, please."

"Candace, your mother is right. Years from now you can look back on this special occasion with rich and fond memories. Your gown is so pretty and it deserves an entourage of bridesmaids. Having only two attendants would be like serving caviar on paper plates. It just isn't done. A garden this magnificent calls for a storybook wedding, my dear. Take it from an expert, you won't be sorry."

"Oh, boy! I know Austin is going to kill me but I guess I can add a few more attendants."

Later, the three women sat at the dining room table drawing up pre-agendas for the special day. When they had everything planned, Sable excitedly called Jonah in to go over the plans. Jonah came in wearing his Charlotte Hornet sweats and nothing on his feet but thick white athletic socks.

"Yeah, baby?"

"We're finished!" she said eagerly.

"Good. Can I go back to my ball game?"

"Jonah, aren't you the least bit excited?"

Right now Jonah was more concerned about the basketball game between the Hornets and the Bulls. The game was tied in the fourth quarter with only 20 minutes to go.

"But the game..." he said, pointing back in the den where the 51-inch-screen TV played the most exciting game of the year.

"This won't take long, I promise."

AnnaMarie described every detail of the wedding and reception right down to the releasing of the two white doves.

"Sounds nice." Jonah patted Candace on the head and gave Sable a quick peck on her cheek. He disappeared back into the den to finish watching the ball game.

*   *   *

Shamell unlocked the three locks on her door and stepped inside. She dropped her purse on the side chair, kicked off her heels and peeled herself from the cashmere coat before heading straight to the kitchen. She was famished and all she could think about was the leftover fried chicken and potato salad in the refrigerator. She didn't know what it was about church that made you so hungry. She smiled as she thought of Sable's church. The service was delightful and uplifting. She was glad Sable and Jonah had invited her to come. She didn't attend church regularly mainly because she didn't belong to any church. After visiting Rising Star Baptist Church she knew she would visit again, maybe even join. She pulled the chicken and potato salad out of the fridge. She was so hungry she didn't bother to warm the chicken. She grabbed a fork and began eating the potato salad straight out of the bowl.

"My, but you're hungry," came a voice from behind her. Startled, Shamell jumped and dropped the bowl on the floor, cracking it into large pieces. She screamed to the top of her lungs before turning around to be face to face with Charles.

"What are you doing here?"

"Just came by to visit my house and to see you."

"How did you get in here? I had the locks changed."

"Shamell," he laughed cynically, "you know you can never lock me out of your life." He walked toward her as she backed away.

"Now Charles, I don't want any trouble."

"Funny you should say that when you caused enough trouble for me to last a lifetime."

"We've outgrown each other, Charles. There is no use in trying to patch up something that's not going to?"

"Shut up!" he shouted. "Who said anything about patching up anything. I'm here to let you know how bad you screwed up my life. I have nothing now."

"Charles, I—I?"

"You have cost me my home, my job, us." He looked like a madman as he glared at her.

"No, no, no, Charles. I didn't?"

"They fired me, Shamell! You came down there and made a big scene and they found out about me and Leticia and they fired me. I spent my whole life in school learning, then teaching. I got tenure and they still fired me. Don't you understand that teaching is my life?"

Shamell could see that Charles was not thinking rationally. She knew she had to say something, anything, to pacify him and make him believe she still cared. He looked as if he could kill her this very day. She had to save herself. She wasn't ready to die when her life was just beginning.

"Fired you? Well, they can't do that," she said with believable concern in her voice.

"Well, they did and it's all your fault."

"I didn't mean for them to fire you. All I wanted was for Leticia to leave you alone. I wanted her to get out of our lives so we could be loving like we use to be."

Charles looked at her through tear-stained eyes, "Really?" he asked innocently.

"Yes, Charles. I mean all the lonely nights I spent here without you made me realize that it wasn't you."

"What?" he asked, now sniffing and wiping away tears.

"No, it was me, me all the time. I wasn't being the wife I should have been for you. I-I wasn't understanding or loving enough the way I should have been. You had every right to go out and find love the best way you could and I guess you found it in Leticia. But, Charles honey, I just couldn't handle being rejected by you. You know how much I love you."

"But-but you said you didn't want me anymore, that-that Leticia could have me if she wanted me."

"Yes, I did," she said self assuredly, "but you have to understand, Charles, I was angry. You say all kinds of things when you're angry."

Charles stared into space absorbing her words. "Yeeaah, I-I suppose you do."

Shamell moved easy around the kitchen so she would not upset him or break his hypnotic state of mind. "I don't think you should worry about your job though."

He looked at her and a spark of anger resurfaced, "Not worry about my job? Did you hear me, woman? I told you that they fired me!"

"I know what you told me," she said authoritatively, banking on gut instinct that Charles needed a commanding voice right now. "I think if we both go down there first thing in the morning and talk to the board they will see the whole picture and reinstate you."

"Do you really think so, Shamell?"

"Yes, I do. They can't fire you because of your personal life. If that's the case, half of the faculty staff over there would be out of a job right now for something immoral they've done."

"Yeah, you're right." He chuckled.

Shamell pulled out a kitchen chair, "Here, sit down and let me get you something to eat."

Charles eased down in the chair and watched Shamell as if she was a stranger. A large object fell from his pocket and hit the floor with a loud thump. It was a gun and at that moment she knew he had come there to kill her. Her heart broke out of fear and the realization that Charles had fallen so far from grace. The little calm that she was holding on to dwindled and her hands began to shake. Her whole life flashed before her eyes in a matter of seconds. She thought of Charles 20 years ago. He was young and even more handsome then. His loving and caring personality only added to her attraction to him. She looked at the person he was now and wondered what had gone wrong. She stared at the gun on the floor. It was like staring at death and she realized she had not done all the things she wanted to do in her 43 years. She was never able to have children, but she had hopes of adopting a little boy one day. Up until their estrangement she had been waiting on Charles to agree on adoption. She had given up on the idea of being some little boy's mother until this morning in church when she decided to take the first steps toward adoption. Reverend Montgomery's sermon on "helping someone that needs you" had prompted her decision. She envisioned a sweet little baby boy cuddled up in her arms and the two of them sharing a lifetime of love. The thought of the baby calmed her nerves and she began to think shrewdly again.

Charles looked at the gun that was only inches away from his dangling and trembling hand. Shamell held her breath and prayed that he would not do anything that they'd regret. Charles bent down and picked up the gun and pointed it at her. Shamell held her breath as he blinked away the last tear from his eye. The sound of the gun going off was earsplitting and made Charles jump from his seat. The blast brought him to cognizance. "Oh, my God! Shamell!" he cried, with the gun clutched tightly in his hand. "Lord, what have I done? Oh, Shamell I'm so sorry!" Charles fell to the floor with the gun lifted above his head.

"It's okay, Charles," she said soothingly, "It was an accident. I know you didn't mean to fire it. But I think you better put it down before one of us gets hurt. Now we don't want that, do we?"

Charles shook his head like a confused child. "Here, baby, will you put this away for me?"

"Yes, Charles." She steadied her shaking hands as she took the loaded gun away from him. She took it into the bedroom and dialed 911.

30

The Limelight

When the police arrived, Charles did not put up a fuss or fight. He extended his wrists so they could cuff him. He looked at one of the arresting officers and whispered in his ear but loud enough for Shamell to hear.

"I think I may need psychiatric evaluation."

The officer looked at Shamell and she nodded her head in concurrence.

"Do you want to press charges, Ma'am?"

Shamell knew what had to be done and it hurt her to the core to have to do it. She had to send a message loud and clear to Charles that she didn't want him anymore.

"Yes, sir. I want to press charges."

Charles looked at Shamell beseechingly. "Does this mean it's over, Shamell?"

"No Charles," she said softly. "It's not over for you. It's just over for us."

Charles hung his head as they led him to the squad car parked downstairs.

      *   *   *

Austin sat at his big mahogany desk, reading the request for the 15th time. He knew this day was coming and dreaded it. There was no way he could work around it. He could not send someone else in her place. That would be deceit. And even it he did have the indecency to hide the assignment from her, he was sure she would find out about it in the long run. He had promised her he would not be too overbearing and protective of her and he meant every word of it. California was such a long distance away and 501 Jeans wanted her specifically for a whole week to model their line of jeans. She would be traveling to Palm Springs and various other parts of California for photographic back-drop purposes. The frightening part of it all was the new line of jean swimwear 501 had created and wanted her to model. It was all so famil-iar. The getting on a plane, going away for days, and modeling the swimwear. He had a bad feeling about it and had tried unsuccessfully for the three days since he had received the request to reason himself out of his superstition. He buzzed Phyllis and asked her to get Candace for him.

Fifteen minutes later Candace walked into Austin's office wearing sweatpants and an oversized sweatshirt.

"Yeah, boss, you rang?" she teased.

"Have a seat, Malaika. Let's talk."

"I don't know if I like the sound of that. You sound so serious."

"It's nothing to get alarmed about." He managed a smile and wished he could believe that himself. He handed her the request and rested back in his chair with his hands clasped under his chin. He watched her expression as she read. Even though she was thrilled, she held her excitement until she could know how Austin felt about it. She loved him now and he took priority over her modeling career. If he asked her not to go, she wouldn't.

"So how do you feel about going to Palm Springs, for a week?"

"I think we both know how I feel. The question is how do you feel?"

What she had just said was answer enough. He knew what he had to do. He said an internal prayer before speaking. *Lord, please take care of her. Bring her back safely to me. Steady the wings and sure the engine of the plane she will be flying. You be the real pilot of the airplane, guiding the hands and minds of the operators.* "I think you should go." He smiled. She came over and hugged him.

*   *   *   *   *   *

The mid-March weather was unseasonably warm for New York. Temperatures rose into the mid-70's. Candace dressed light in a gray pair of Anne Klein slacks and a gray short-sleeved crew neck sweater. She checked one large piece of luggage and kept a carry-on shoulder bag with her personals in it. She and Austin walked toward the corridor hand in hand. He had been praying a lot here lately, mainly for Candace's safe passage.

"You call me as soon as the plane lands."

"You know I will."

They gave each other a goodbye kiss. Austin stayed until the plane lifted off into the sky.

That night Austin showered and readied himself for bed. Candace had arrived safely and he could rest soundly now. He pulled back the covers of the king-size bed and got in.

The chief pronounced the couple husband and wife. He circled the ceremonial shaft in the air to represent unity. Austin leaned forward to kiss Maoma and he heard an awful screeching sound. He looked toward the sky and saw the two horrible birds. His heart began to race. It had been close to a year since he last had the dream. Still he knew it by heart. The vultures targeted Maoma and just like before in all the other dreams she was gone. He stood screaming at the birds as they flew away with her.

Austin bolted upright in bed. The sweat trickled off his forehead. His pajamas clung to his wet body and his heart beat wildly. He didn't know if the dream was an omen or forewarning for Candace. Did it mean she would not have a safe flight back home? Austin threw the covers back and got out of bed. His instinct told him to call Dr. Edwards. He picked up the phone but returned it just as quickly when he realized it was 3:00 in the morning. Besides, he was no longer a patient of hers. She had finished her therapy with him and had basically told him there was nothing more she could do. The answer to his problem was to drive to Palm Springs, get her and drive her back to New York himself. He calculated the time it would take him to drive to California. Including rest stops, he figured two and a half, three days tops. His adrenaline was pumped and there was no way he could go back to sleep now.

He went into his office and pulled out a travel atlas. He highlighted the route from New York to Palm Springs. The yellow fluorescent line traced interstate 78 to Pennsylvania then I-70 to West Virginia all the way through Indiana, Illinois and all the states in between until it came to I-40 in Arizona and finally Interstate 10 to Palm Springs. He thought the drive might not be so bad. He had never visited that part of the country before, and Candace would be surprised to see him. He began to feel better at his spontaneous plans. He laid the map on his desk and went into the living room to watch a little TV. A John Wayne western was on. Austin loved westerns. He nestled back in the leather recliner. Ten minutes into the movie he had put the nightmare behind him.

Things were quite different the next morning when Austin awoke. His head was clear and he had convinced himself that the dream was only *(as Dr. Bernice Edwards would have put it)* a fulfillment of a wish, a wish for Candace to have a safe return home. His underlying fear of the plane crashing had triggered it. He smiled as he thought of how proud Dr. Edwards would have been of his educated opinion of the dream. He tightened the necktie around his shirt collar, grabbed his suit jacket from the hanger and walked into the kitchen. The coffee was ready. He poured a strong black cup and took a sip of it. He spread jelly on toasted English muffins and placed the bacon and eggs in between. Yes, he was feeling much better this morning.

*   *   *

Candace felt she could easily get use to this kind of life. Today was her third day on assignment. She was now in Napa Valley, where she was modeling casual wear. She modeled mostly jeans and cotton shirts. She and the cameramen had eased into a relationship filled with camaraderie and jokes, which made the working environment easy as well as amusing.

Napa Valley was well known for its wines. They toured a real vineyard and did a two-hour session there. The photographer thought she was a jewel and played with Candace's appearance a hundred different ways. The first series of shots were with her hair in an upsweep. The others were with her hair down, in ponytails or French braids. The pose she liked best was one of her wearing a peasant-style, off-the-shoulder dress. It had ruffles around the shoulders and tail. Her hair cascaded around her shoulders and she held a huge cluster of grapes in one hand and dangled a stemmed grape over her opened mouth.

"Act natural, baby—That's it—I love it—You're wonderful—Play with it now." The photographer sang her praises as he snapped away with the camera and she swung from pose to pose. Although it was loads of fun, she would be glad when the session was over. All she wanted to do was get back to her hotel room, take a long hot bath, relax for a while and then call Austin.

The last day they went to El Paso (the Rodeo Drive of Palm Springs). She went to Iris of El Paso, a shop that featured exclusive designs by Harari, Hino and Malee, Donna Jessica, Flax and V.C. Torias. She had modeled her fair share of the designer's clothes and knew them well. She bought Sable a three-piece silk pants ensemble by Donna Jessica. It had cost a pretty penny but she was glad she could afford it for Sable. The kimono jacket was loose and comfortable. The shell was a pullover and hung just below the hips. The loose-fitting pants had slouch pockets and an elastic waist. It was dressy enough for Sable to wear out to a show and dinner or comfortable enough to recline at home. Because Jonah liked to thank his clients via notes for trying out a new drug or placing a big order, she brought him a pen and stationary gift set with an Iris of Palm Springs insignia inscribed on it. For Austin she bought a palatable pair of briefs. She knew they both would get a kick out of them.

*   *   *

Austin stood at gate 47 of Kennedy International Airport waiting for Candace's flight to get in. He was growing anxious because it had been due to arrive 10 minutes ago. He paced back and forth, periodically looking at his Rolex. An announcement came over the terminal's intercom saying that flight 107 would be delayed. Austin went into a panic and rushed the information desk.

"What is causing the detainment of flight 107?" he asked, trying to sound as unruffled as possible.

"Sir, I'm sure it's nothing to get alarmed over," said the agent behind the desk, and went back to tallying tickets.

Austin was growing irritable fast. He felt the woman had more information than she wanted to give. Usually when that happened they were trying to hide something. Could there have been an accident and she was waiting on the proper authorities to come and make the tragic announcement? He was an avid flyer and knew about these things. The woman looked doubtful; she couldn't even keep eye contact with him, pretending to be counting tickets. She must have counted those same tickets three times. Austin thought the woman might want him to disappear, but he wasn't going to give her that satisfaction.

"Can you tell me why the plane is late? Did it leave the other airport late or is it having mechanical problems or what?"

"Sir, I'm absolutely sure it's nothing."

"How can something be nothing? If it was nothing they never would have made the announcement."

The woman was on her last nerve. She kept her voice low as not to upset the other travelers. "Why don't I get someone on the phone who can better answer your questions."

"Yes, why don't you?" he demanded. He ran a nervous hand through his hair.

"Sir, I have one of the air traffic controllers on the phone." She handed Austin the phone.

"Hello. I'm concerned about flight 107. Can you tell me why it's late?"

"It's very common for planes to get detained for one reason or another. There could have been a hundred or more things to happen to delay the flight—a late passenger, mislabeled luggage, maybe the planes needed restocking at the last minute. One thing I can assure you of is that the plane is not in any danger of crashing or not arriving here in New York within the next several minutes. I spoke with the pilot and he gave us a 10-4. Take it easy and don't worry. The plane will be here before you know it."

Austin handed the phone back to the woman. "Thanks," he said and drifted over to the observation window to watch the planes take off and land.

When Candace walked off the plane and into the terminal, Austin was all smiles. She walked into his arms. They kissed each other tenderly.

"I missed you," she said sweetly.

"I missed you too.

PART TWO

31

The Efe

Underneath the thick, green canopy of kombokombo trees, nestled between sprinkled raffia palms, fig trees, bamboo and vine sweet potato plants were large clearings containing five to 10 huts each. Every few miles the shaded forest was interrupted by another cluster of huts. The people who lived here were descendants of the ancient and legendary Africans known to outsiders as Pygmies. Although the total population of Pygmy people spread throughout the vast Ituri rain forest of Zaire was over 5,000, this particular section was home to 300 or more scattered in a 50-mile radius. They stood less than five feet tall and lived a seminomadic life style. Their tradition dictated for them to hunt and gather, little affected by the modern world. The only contact they had with outsiders was an occasional missionary who would visit their villages once every three years. At first, the visits were common, but the missionaries were discouraged from coming around when they learned that the Efe people did not want their religion or modern influences forced upon them. The only other outside contact was with a group of Africans who lived 10 miles away. They were called the Lese people. The Leses were taller than their neighboring Efe. They were more tolerant of the missionaries and had come to rely on the white tradesmen who frequented the forest. The Leses lived up and down a dirt road that had been cut in under the Belgian colonial administration in the 1940s. This road ran parallel to the Ituri River. The Efe remained close enough to the Lese people so they could trade their forest products or labor for produce, iron and cloth, but far enough away so that their life style would not be affected by modern society.

On a hot humid day a little dog named Jut followed the smell of monkey meat cooking on an open fire. He traveled the four-mile dirt path that led to his neighboring thorp. He hoped he would beat the other dogs that lived in the neighboring villages and be rewarded with a big juicy bone. He liked coming to this little commune of only six huts. The woman named Muzungu was kind and she always had soothing words for him. She was not like the others who threw scraps and leftovers at him. She always pinched off a portion of what she was eating and fed it to him out of her hand.

A special event was approaching and the women were cooking an elaborate feast for their dinner. They were hopeful that the men would be successful on the elephant hunt tomorrow. Gimiko, the village leader, his son and four other tribesmen sat in a semicircle preparing their arsenals for the hunt. They tightened the strings on their bows and sharpened the metal arrowheads. The elephant hunt was a rare event and such hunts required great stealth and courage on part of the hunters. It was a dangerous venture, but if they were successful in their quest, then, it would be well worth the risk, energy and time. Many hunters did not survive an elephant hunt and more than a few refused to hunt the colossal creatures. The Efe thought that if a man was brave enough to hunt elephant then he was a man in spirit also. Before daylight tomorrow morning, the six men would kiss their families and set out on their journey while the women and children stood behind singing and calling to the spirit god to protect them and help them kill the elephant.

Jut entered the circled clearing. He saw the men and women with their bare chests and cloth-wrapped bottoms. The women were bent over the fires, poking at the meat and stirring in big black pots. The men sat on the ground holding a conversation and fidgeting with their tools. He sneaked closer, sniffing around the smoking meat. Gimiko's wife, Tifu, picked up a warm ember that had rolled off the fire and threw it at him.

"Get out of here and go back to your own house!" she yelled in Swahili.

Jut backed away from the scolding woman but did not leave the commune. He had come too far to go back without tasting some of the meat. He heard Muzungu's voice followed by children's laughter coming from one of the huts. He inched closer and peeked inside. One of the children spotted him and motioned for him to come in.

"Hello, my friend Jut. Come to me," said a little girl who had spotted him first.

Jut looked around at the other children and then at Muzungu for approval. Muzungu smiled a broad smile and patted her thigh lightly. Jut wagged his tail and ran to her.

"You have come a long way. What brings you here?" she laughed knowing that the smell of the food has brought him to their place. She rubbed his head and scratched behind his ears. "Aw, yes. It is the smell of the monkey meat that brings you."

Jut howled as if understanding her words, and Muzungu and the children laughed louder.

"I will share with you, Jut," said the little girl who had come closer to rub his back.

Muzungu ran her fingers over the little girl's tight hair. She took delight in anyone who showed kindness to animals. Jut went from child to child, sniffing their hands for hidden treats.

"It will not be long Jut. Be patient as we are being," said Muzungu. The dog lay down on the dirt floor and looked at Muzungu with impatient, sad eyes. Muzungu smiled at him before continuing her story to the children.

*　　　　　　*　　　　　　*

The 23-member clan sat on bamboo mats enjoying the lavish feast. They pulled hot pieces of meat from the tender monkey and dipped their fingers repeatedly in the three large communal bowls of yams, turnips and stewed peanuts. The children took more pleasure in eating the honey-sweetened yams than anything else. Their overzealous hands were slapped often for taking more than what their parents thought they needed. The mothers chewed the food to a mush, then fingered it into their infant's mouths. Their stomachs bulged as they talked excitedly about the upcoming hunt and told found stories of past hunting experiences.

Jut walked from person to person gobbling up discarded pieces of scraps. When everyone had finished the women and children performed a dance to wake the spirits of their ancestors. Then, they sung a song asking the spirits to accompany the men tomorrow morning on the hunt. The men mixed tobacco and marijuana together and stuffed the ground mixture into a pipe fashioned out of banana rib. Marijuana was a high trade item. The Efe could only afford to smoke it ceremoniously, and the upcoming elephant hunt was occasion enough for them. The men sat lazily watching the women and children dance late into the night.

*　　　　　　*　　　　　　*

Gimiko led the five men through the brush. The only sounds were the boisterous calls of the startled hornbills high in the canopy of trees. They looked down on the half-naked men trekking single file and barefoot through the thicket. With bows, arrows and spears strapped to their bodies, the men were ever so quiet as they walked and looked for signs of the great elephant. They knew that the slightest unfamiliar sound would disrupt the order of things, and like a chain reaction send the animals running throughout the forest. They had been in the forest all morning. Gimiko looked at the sun sifting through the awning of leaves. It was nearing noon and they had not eaten since they left their commune at 5 that morning. The leftover monkey meat and stewed peanuts had long left them. Their stomachs growled with hunger. Suko, Gimiko's eldest son, tugged at the back of his father's loincloth. He knew it was forbidden to speak on a hunt such as this because in addition to not frightening the animals they had to keep their senses keen and focused. To speak would break the concentration and could cause them to miss a sign like a leaning tree, large impressions in the ground, or dried elephant dung. But not only was Suko famished, he was tired. He could not understand his father's endurance. He was more than twice his age and seemed to never tire. Gimiko turned around to face Suko. The look on his face was total agitation. Suko uttered not a word, but instead gestured that they were hungry by rubbing his stomach. Gimiko looked at the other four men behind him. They shook their heads and pointed to their mouths. Gimiko motioned for the men to sit down on the ground. He opened the antelope skin pouch that was tied around his waist. He pulled out two bundles of meat and turnips wrapped in mongongo leaves. He opened the leaves carefully and divided it up evenly among the six of them. Suko bit into the savory meat. He tasted hints of the mongongo leaves and thought the added flavor made it taste just that much better than the night before. The men ate ravenously and no sooner had they finished eating they were up and pacing through the brush again.

Gimiko hated defeat, especially when his family was depending on them to find elephant meat. The word had spread throughout the Efe villages that they were going on the big hunt. The Lese people had gotten ear of the news and some of the men came to make fun of Gimiko and his clan.

"We hear you are about to go on an elephant chase," teased Jabusa, the Lese chief's only son and heir to the throne, "There has not been elephant in these parts for years now. You will throw away two days in the forest hunting the beast and come home to your family with empty hands. Why don't you settle for a nice monkey or a gentle antelope? I hear bush rats are plentiful this time of year." Jabusa's followers laughed as he made joke. The Lese believed that eating bush rats was like feeding the body filth. Although the Efe people felt the same way about the lowly creatures, the Lese accused them of eating the scavenger type rodents anyway.

Gimiko didn't care for Jabusa at all. He and most of the Lese people thought they were above the Efe because of their connection with the outside world, their semi-domesticated lifestyle and their taller size. By the same token, the Lese men were quite fond of the Efe women, and often chose them to marry because of their ultra subservience to men. In addition to that, marrying an Efe woman was economical. The Lese man did not have to pay the bride's family for taking her away because they were from different tribes. If a Lese man took a Lese wife, he had to pay the bride's price to her family, usually in the form of livestock, labor or other material worth. The Efe believed that if an Efe man married an Efe woman then the man had to give one of his sisters to the bride's family for a full year in exchange for taking their daughter. The Lese men could not exchange their sisters because they refused to live among the Efe people.

Jabusa's wife had died of malaria a year earlier and since her death, Jabusa had his eye on Muzungu. Gimiko was the guardian of Muzungu, and Jabusa often brought gifts to Gimiko and his family in attempts to win her over. Gimiko's dislike for Jabusa was never shared with Muzungu. Whether she chose to marry Jabusa or not would be of her own will. He did not want to influence her one way or the other. He sensed that Muzungu did not care much for Jabusa and he hoped she would not choose him. He also knew that she was feeling the pressures of being a single woman way past the age of 20, the required age for Efe women to marry.

Gimiko was growing weary. They had been in the forest for the better part of the day and had not seen one sign of the elephant. He thought about the dream he'd had several nights ago. His grandfather had come to him and told him that the great creature had come back to the forest. He had told him to travel toward the river and he would find the elephant there. Gimiko was beginning to believe that the dream was only a dream. He stopped in his tracks and turned to face the men. He was about to tell them that they would discontinue their hunt for the elephant, and instead, hunt the smaller game when his peripheral vision showed him a bark-stripped acacia tree. Gimiko knew that elephants loved to eat the bark off various trees, but the acacia were one of their favorites. He had the men's full attention but walked past them toward the tree. It did not take the men long before they too saw the tree and followed Gimiko. Ten yards away they spotted another bark-stripped tree. The six men smiled at each other and looked below them to find the large footprints in the soft moist earth. They single-filed behind Gimiko as he followed the prints. They were quiet as they stepped, over, under and around branches.

Four of the men, including Gimiko's sons, had never gone on an elephant hunt before. Gimiko could sense their fear, and he knew they had every right to be because the African elephant were very aggressive and had the ability to move rapidly over rough ground. Their ferocious disposition coupled with their high intelligence made them tremendously dangerous. Gimiko felt he had enlightened the young men well on the rules of elephant hunting. He told them that the elephants were extremely social among their herds. "The elephant has a sense of devotion, loyalty and love among themselves and they will protect each other the same way man protects his family. You must never let him see, hear or smell you. If possible try to stay down wind of him so he will not catch your scent. We only want to target the isolated elephant; that way when he falls it won't alarm the other elephants." Those were the words he had preached to the men the past few days. Gimiko began to smell their prey in the thick humid air. It was a smell of musk and feces mixed. A loud beastly noise penetrated through the silence of the forest. The four younger men looked at each other. The odd sound was similar to the great horns the Lese people blew from time to time during their wedding and funeral ceremonies. They knew it had to be coming from the elephant. Gimiko turned to face his men. His eyes were wide and sweat gathered on his forehead. Suko had never seen his father so aroused. He thought he saw apprehension on his face but decided that it was the thrill of the hunt. Suko wanted to be brave like his father but he was finding it very difficult to keep up the pretense. Gimiko nodded his head, and each man knew that his test of manhood was shortly forthcoming. He ordered the men to crouch low in the dense under-brush. Their hearts pounded so powerfully against their chests, that the sound echoed in their ears, making it difficult to concentrate. Gimiko pointed beyond the brush at the dark-gray mass that stood before them. The bull stood alone feeding on tree bark. Suko looked at the illustrious creature. He admired the elephant and for a brief moment, dreaded having to kill him, but he quickly put his sentiments aside and thought of his wife, child and villagers. Their survival depended on the forest creatures, and the elephant meat, which once smoked, would keep their stomachs full for a long time. From behind the brush the hunters looked for more elephants. When they felt confident that the bull was alone, they looked at Gimiko for further instructions. He nodded his head at the men, raised, stepped out of the brush and aimed below the elephant's left shoulder blade where the heart was. The other five men followed his lead, but picked different targets. The elephant continued to eat, pulling away at the bark, oblivious to his fate. Only when he heard the rustling of leaves did he step back from the tree and look in the direction of the noise. Before he could comprehend what was hap-pening, the force from the strings pulling away from the bows sent the arrows flying. They pierced through the air with a shrill sound. Within a fraction of a second, the men's arrows found their targets.

The contact of the arrows made the elephant lift his front legs in the air. He made the loud trumpet sound again, this time angrily and then charged toward the men.

"Run for cover!" shouted Gimiko. The men scattered as the bull approached them. They ran to the safety of the thick forest trees. All of the men were excellent climbers, and with their bare hands and feet, scaled the trees within a matter of seconds.

"Is everyone unharmed?" Gimiko yelled to his men above the animal's tumultuous cries.

"Suko! Where is Suko?" asked one of the men frantically.

Gimiko balanced himself with one hand holding an overhead tree limb and stepped farther out on the limb supporting him. He had to get a better view of below to see if his son was all right. He searched furiously for Suko, then spotted him lying a few feet from the tree. He had slipped on elephant dung and was trying to regain position on his feet. The bull saw him. With blood trickling down the side of his body, he lifted his trunk, shook his head angrily and charged at Suko. Gimiko saw that his son was overtaken by a paralyzing fear. He knew if something weren't done immediately, the elephant would kill him.

"Your spear, Suko! Use your spear!"

"I've lost it," he yelled back with absolute panic in his voice. The elephant ripped up intercepting bushes from their roots and slung them behind him as he made his way toward Suko. Spit foamed at the corners of his mouth and his eyes squinted in fury.

"The spear is in your hand, Suko," shouted Gimiko.

Suko looked at his hand to find that the spear was locked in his tight grip. He saw the faces of his wife and baby daughter and knew they would have a hard life without him. He heard the moans of his mother grieving over his dead, tusk-ripped body. He could not let the elephant kill him. He had to live for his family if not for himself. Courage chased away his fear and he positioned the mighty spear between the ground and atmosphere. The elephant raised his trunk against Suko and struck at him. Suko rolled to the left, dodging the blow. The elephant began lowering his head, aiming his tusk at the 90-pound warrior, but Suko steadied the spear with all of his weight, and as the elephant's head came down on him, the spear pierced him directly between the eyes, exiting through the back of his head. Blood spilled onto Suko's face. The bull crumpled to his knees. Suko rolled out of the way as the elephant came crashing down on the ground.

Gimiko was the first to descend from the trees. He ran to his son and patted him on the shoulders. "You killed him, my son," he said, then wiped some of the blood off of Suko's face and tasted it. He laughed in exultation.

Suko stared blankly at the animal, absorbing in all that had happened in the past few minutes. He panted for breath and smiled wearily at his father. Gimiko walked around the fallen beast, examining him. "Now we will eat for a lifetime." He directed the remark at his son.

The men praised and honored Suko for slaying the elephant. The story of how the elephant was slain and Suko's bravery, would be the talk of the forest. Gimiko was proud of his son. He couldn't wait to see the look on the Leses' faces when they found out Gimiko's son killed an elephant. Gimiko sent two of the men back to camp to get the women. They would come with their knives to help butcher, pack and carry the elephant meat back to camp. The trip would take half a day going and coming back again. He gave them the remainder of the food. He and the other three men would carve up some of the elephant meat to make a meal.

32

Jabusa

Jabusa carried a rooster under one arm and held the bridle with the other hand. He sat high on the mule as they made their way to Muzungu's village. The rooster was a gift to Muzungu and her family. He knew the men were away hunting and this was prime opportunity for him to visit her without the interference of Gimiko. It was no secret that the two men did not like each other. Gimiko tolerated Jabusa because it was the law of the Efe people. They respected all creatures and did not insult or inflict pain on another human being. With the men away, Jabusa thought, he could persuade Muzungu to marry him. Muzungu was a peculiar woman to him. She didn't flirt or chase after him like the other single women did. Her appearance was completely different from the Lese and Efe women. She refused to cut her hair and wore it in long, coarse braids. Jabusa had never even seen her breasts. She always had a piece of cloth tied around them. He was dying of curiosity to see, touch and taste them. They looked round, perky and well proportioned in the center of her chest through the clothing she always wore. They were nothing like the Lese or Efe women's breasts, which drooped and sagged and were always exposed. Her stomach was flat because she had not borne children and she refused to go in her bare feet. She made shoes out of animal skins and wore them religiously. Jabusa was mesmerized by her height¾she was as tall as he was. Her look was odd to him, yet enticing. Muzungu never acknowledged him except out of politeness. Whenever he came to the Efe village, he brought her contributions but the only ones she would accept were the edible ones. Muzungu didn't want to take any of his offerings because she didn't want to be indebted to him, but her village was poor and she never turned down a gift that would soothe a hungry stomach. Jabusa was growing tired of Muzungu's games. Today he would give her an ultimatum. Either she agreed to marry him or the food gifts would stop and he would not pursue her anymore. The children's laughter greeted Jabusa when he entered the circular clearing where the six huts stood. The children saw Jabusa and they ran to him. He always brought candy he had gotten from the traders. He knew Muzungu was fond of children. He thought supplying the children with sweets could do nothing but improve relations between the two of them.

"The candy man!" The children yelled and jumped up and down around Jabusa. The Efe people had a fondness for sweets and it was on rare occasions that they got candy. Certain times of the season the men in the village would go hunting for honey, but they never brought back enough to go around, mainly because they would have eaten most of it themselves before returning to camp. The women stopped their daily chores and gathered around Jabusa, too. They held out their hands and he placed a lump of the hard sweetness in them.

One of the Efe women held her stomach that was full with child. She whispered in one of the other women's ears, "That Muzungu is a fool. This man travels a long distance to bring us gifts just to win her heart and she pays him no mind. She will wither up and blow away with the wind. She will not even leave behind a child to mourn her. Her spirit will be lost forever without the love of children or husband."

"You are right," said the other woman. "She is lucky to catch the eye of Jabusa, the chief's son and inheritor of the throne. What he sees in her the Almighty only knows. But who am I to question his desires? The Lese men are strange enough. I do not wish to comprehend them."

Muzungu sat on a bamboo mat outside the hut's door. She was sewing mukluks for the children. She had persuaded Gimiko and his wife Tifu to let her have the animal skins so she could make them to protect the children's feet. It took a foot injury of one of the village children before Gimiko agreed to Muzungu's request. Muzungu had seen Jabusa when he first entered the village. She did not stir with excitement over Jabusa as the others because he simply did not excite her. Of course, she loved sweets and yearned to have a piece of the candy, but if it meant asking Jabusa for it she would do without. Perhaps she was harder on him than she should have been. She was told this often by the Efe women. They wanted her to marry him and become wife of the soon-to-be chief—that way she would have their best interests at heart. They knew with her sitting at the feet of the king; she would make sure they received fair trade from the Leses for the animals they hunted. The two women went about their chores.

Jabusa spotted Muzungu sitting crossed-legged outside the door of her hut. His shadow slowly crept upon her, shading her legs, then consuming her entire frame. She did not bother to look up at him. Her fingers worked quick and diligently, pushing and pulling the threaded needle through the thick skins. A pile of finished mukluks lay next to her. Jabusa picked up one of the finished slippers and examined it carefully before tossing it back into the pile. "Efes in shoes." He chuckled at the absurd notion. He thought Muzungu had not heard him but she had.

"So, what is it that brings you here?" she asked as she continued to sew. Muzungu knew the answer before he could answer. She knew the rooster was intended for her. She knew the candy for the children was to impress her, and she knew he was there because the men were away. He thought he could gain headway with her in their absence. She tilted her head upward and glanced at him quickly. Although she did not care much for his personality, she had to admit Jabusa was pleasant to look at. His long braids hung down around his head, accenting his chiseled face. He had prominent cheekbones and strong jaw lines. He was dark like the forest night. His teeth were as white as the clouds in the morning sky. His nose was strong and broad. His lips full, eyes analytical, quick and alert, seeing everything and missing nothing.

"I brought you a cock to cook for your supper tonight. Since your men are away and no one is here to do the hunting, I thought you would appreciate it."

Muzungu put her sewing aside and stood to her feet. She accepted the rooster and looked it over once. "He will make a fine meal. My family and I thank you deeply." She knew she should invite him to stay for supper and knew that if she did he would graciously accept. She did not want to deal with putting Jabusa off tonight, especially without Gimiko or Suko to intercept his advances. When it was clear to Jabusa there would not be an invitation coming from her, he snatched the rooster from her hands. He enclosed his powerful hand around its head and began wringing him furiously in the air. He loosened his grip on the twisted bird and he went flying around the yard. The rooster landed on the ground where he danced nervously around with his broken neck dangling at the side of his dying body. Muzungu looked at Jabusa in horror. The Efe never intentionally killed an animal in a way that would cause needless suffering. She would have struck the back of the chicken's head with a hard blunt object or chopped its head off. Either way would have been less inhumane than Jabusa's method. Jabusa laughed as the rooster continued to scurry around in the dust.

"I could have killed him, Jabusa,"

"I have done it for you and I will also pluck and clean him."

Muzungu had never known a man to kill and then prepare an animal for a meal. Jabusa would be the laughingstock of his village if word got out that he killed and cleaned a rooster for Muzungu, and even worse if they found out he had not eaten any of it. He was making it difficult for her not to invite him. She went inside the hut and got the pots. She had seen a banana tree with ripe bananas on it at the edge of the clearing. The eggplants in their tiny garden would make a tasty stew. Muzungu gathered wood to make the fire.

*   *   *

Jabusa licked all eight fingers and his two thumbs. He rubbed his stomach and moaned gratefully. "You are a great cook, Muzungu. You will make a splendid wife to some lucky man."

Muzungu knew Jabusa again would ask her to marry him. She didn't know if she was more tired of him asking the question or her trying to dodge him altogether. She gathered the pots and stacked them on top of her head for washing in the nearby stream.

"I hope you enjoyed your meal, but now I have work to do."

Jabusa got up off the ground and took the pots from her.

"I will help you."

"No! Jabusa, you have done enough already. I'm sure you have matters at your village to attend."

"But I do not," he grinned. "I am free for the evening to do whatever you want me to."

Muzungu ignored his smile and walked briskly to the stream. She tried to distance herself from him by taking large steps, but he kept up. He enjoyed watching her rear end wiggle underneath the leopard print wrap. When they reached the stream Muzungu took the pots from his hands and began washing them in the cool, rushing waters. When she finished she collected each piece, turned and walked back through the path that had brought them. Jabusa stayed behind. It was clear that she wanted him to leave but he didn't care about that. All he wanted was to win her over.

"Muzungu," he called. His voice was deep and commanding. It permeated through her soul and questioned her doubts that he was qualified to be a ruler. Even if he hadn't the mental strategy to command, he surely had the voice.

She turned to find him standing unmoved near the stream's edge.

"Yes, Jabusa?"

"How much longer will you refuse me?"

"What do you mean?" she asked, all the wiser to his question.

"You are no fool. For months I have tried to charm you. I bring you beads, cloth and food. You will only accept the food and then you run like a frighten duiker being hunted by a hungry lion. I mean you no harm; in fact, I'll bring you protection. If you become my wife, you and your village will never have to want for anything again."

"You speak promising for a man who is not yet in charge."

"I speak what I know. My father is in his 80s. His walk has become slow, his hair white, and his sight poor. His blood runs cool in his veins and he spends most of his time in his hut under the covers of a warm blanket. He is chief only in name. I am the one who gives the orders and makes the decisions. It is I who bargains with the white man when they come to trade in the forest. If you marry me you will have the finest silks, beads and the thickest skins to lie upon. You will have real shoes made from the western world, much better than what you wear now. You will never have to carry water from the stream to the village again. You can rest all day and have milk and honey whenever you like." He looked at her intensely and waited for a reply.

"I see," she said. "And how do you expect me to gain the respect of your people if I am to be a lazy queen?"

"Surely no one expects you to work. It has always been our custom for the queen of the Lese people to live a pampered life.

"If that is the case, Prince Jabusa, then I am unsuitable to be your wife. I don't lie around waiting to be waited on. I earn my way." Muzungu turned and began walking away.

"You place yourself on an imaginary pedestal that no one else sees but you." Jabusa's words were thunderous and startled Muzungu. Her blood tingled at the icy statement.

"You think you are too good for me, the chief's son! You are strange to all of us—the Efe as well as the Lese. I think you should count yourself lucky that I even look your way."

"My appearance may be strange to you, but I believe there is something about me that holds you captive." She began hearing the voices of the Efe women's chorus behind Jabusa's hard words. The voices were telling her to be kinder to him and that he would supply them with good things to eat and make their lives easier. They told her that she would grow to be an old lonely woman without the love of children. Tifu was the only one who didn't pester her about getting married. She was patient with her and had never said she should marry and make a family for herself but instead made subtle references to how good a catch Jabusa was. Muzungu knew that marriage was inevitable. She only hoped that it would be with someone she loved or knew she could grow to love. With Jabusa she wasn't so sure. Muzungu forced a slight smile across her lips. "I will discuss the possibility of marriage to you with my family when Gimiko and Suko return from the elephant hunt."

Jabusa watched her disappear into the foliage before his lips turned into a broad smile.

*   *   *

The four men had already begun butchering the elephant when they arrived. The women and children gasped in awe at the huge animal. They had never come this close to one before, and many of them had never even seen an elephant. At first the children kept their distance, fearful that it would awaken and snatch one of them with its trunk. After a while they made a game of seeing who would go nearest the elephant. When one of the children got close enough to touch it, one of the men startled the child by making a loud roaring sound. The children screamed and ran for cover behind surrounding bushes and trees and the adults burst into laughter. After the game ended, the children were told to go find mongongo leaves. They would be used to wrap the meat in. They placed the meat on a huge rack built out of bamboo and hard woods. They lit a fire underneath and smoked the meat to keep it from spoiling. The Efe worked long, backbreaking hours on the one and a half tons of meat. Every part of the elephant was saved, from the trunk to the nutritious marrow in the bones. The women and older children fashioned several sleds out of tree limbs and animal skins to transport the meat back to their village. It took two days and two trips back and forth between village and campsite before they had gotten all the meat.

The women prepared a tremendous feast and invited the neighboring Efes to share in their good fortune. They sang, danced and recounted how Suko had brought down the elephant. When the celebration was over, they gave some of the meat to their neighbors. They still had more than enough for themselves and some to trade with the Lese people.

* * *

Muzungu sat in the hut staring into the fire as her family waited for her to tell them her news. Gimiko poked a stick into the fire. He knew something was troubling her and he was trying to give her time to present the situation to them all. He was growing anxious and tired.

"Jabusa has asked me to marry him." She dropped her head and said nothing else. She waited for their response.

Suko's wife clapped her hands once. "This is good news!" she said excitedly. "Now we will be favored by the Lese." She looked at Suko, who had a sullen look on his face and seemed embarrassed by her actions.

Gimiko looked at Muzungu sympathetically. "Are you sure you want to do this?" he asked her.

Muzungu didn't answer his question but smiled at him and Suko. She was grateful for their concern over her. She lowered her head again and remained silent.

"If it is love you worry about, Muzungu, that will come in time," said Tifu. "Jabusa has his faults, but overall he will be a great provider for you. He will give you sons who will rule over the Leses. Your children's future will always be secure. What more can a mother want for her children? When we found you several years ago, we had no intention of letting you stay here with us. We did not know you or anything of the tribe you came from. To this day we still do not know of your ancestors. We called you Muzungu because it means foreigner and stranger, but over time we found your soul to be kind, your service generous and your spirit sweet. You give of yourself freely. The children have found in you true friendship. You have even showed them how to have compassion for the hornbill that falls wounded from the sky. A soul such as yours is easy to love. That is why you are still with us to this day. Even though your name implies that you are a stranger, you know you are not a stranger to us anymore. We have grown to love you. The same way you will grow to love Jabusa." Tifu rubbed Muzungu's hands to comfort her.

"You know my feelings for Jabusa," said Gimiko. "It is no secret that the two of us do not see eye to eye, but Jabusa is a big man in these woods and I guess you could do a lot worse. Maybe with you as his wife, he will gain respect for the Efe people."

"I am thankful that you found me. I don't remember much after the crash. I remember crawling from the wreckage and into the thicket. When I awoke I was here and you," she looked into Tifu's eyes, "were attending me. I don't know where I have been or where I was going on that day the plane crashed here in the forest. I don't even know who my people are. In the beginning I worried about not knowing my background. I prayed that my people would find me and make me remember them and my past, but now it does not bother me that much. You all have become my family and I love you very much." She looked from one face to the other as they all sat around the warm fire. The love in the small hut filled the atmosphere and penetrated each of their hearts.

"I have been having these strange dreams in the middle of the night. In the dream there is a man who is trying to catch these two large birds but he never catches them. The dream always ends with him crying." The man in my dreams has a handsome face and I believe he is a kind man. His face alone has captured my heart. Sometimes I pray that the birds will bring him to me and save me from a life with Jabusa. Muzungu sighed before continuing, "No, I do not love Jabusa, but I know that it is time for me to start a life for myself. I will marry him and I promise you he will change his heart toward the Efe people. I will see to it that he does."

33

The Trade

The next day Gimiko's tribe packed 200 pounds of meat on sledges and made their way to the Lese village. Tifu hoped she could trade some of the meat for cooking pots. Gimiko needed new hunting tools, an ax and machete in particular. If they could get these things, they would be grateful. Muzungu knew her days were numbered with the Efe. She would soon be leaving them and living among the Lese. She was about to do something that had never been done before. The things she would ask for would not be for herself but for the Efe. When they entered the village Gimiko and his followers stopped at the entrance. To go beyond the first hut was an insult to the Lese people. They stood for several minutes waiting to be acknowledged. An elder named Osun approached them. He looked at the sledges packed high with the meat.

"You come to make trade, huh?"

Gimiko came forward. "Yes, we have fresh elephant meat."

"I heard about you going on the elephant hunt. So you were successful after all." Osun peered at the meat.

"We want to see the chief."

"The chief sees no one. Besides, he is not very well and must rest to save his strength," said the man, hungrily eyeing the leaf-wrapped meat. The Lese who were watching from their huts gathered up cheap notions and useless items in hopes of trading.

"It is happening again," whispered Tifu. "Every time we come here to trade they never let us see the chief. They will cheat us again,"

Muzungu had heard enough and could stomach no more. She towered through the short Efe clan and stepped forward, "Since your chief is ill, then we want to see Jabusa. He is next in charge."

Osun and the few who had gathered laughed at Muzungu's request.

"Jabusa is much too busy to come and oversee your trade. Besides, you don't need him; we will see that you are compensated fairly for the meat," said Osun.

"Where is Jabusa?" Muzungu stood face to face with Osun. The crowd behind him mumbled disapproval at her actions.

"As I've said, if you want to do business with us, let us get on with it, otherwise be on your way."

Muzungu pushed past Osun and into the crowd of Lese. The crowd gasped in shock and Osun whirled around.

"It is forbidden for you to enter the village without invitation."

"You step foot in our village anytime you want without invitation. You take food from our pots without asking; you ask us to help you work in your gardens and give us one turnip as payment. Your men take the Efe women as wives and offer no bride price to her family. Now you stand before me and say that we are only welcome by invitation!" Muzungu was angry. Her words were loud and had drawn more of the Lese out of their huts.

"I demand to see Jabusa!" she screamed.

Jabusa heard the commotion and exited from the chief's quarters. He wore an angry expression as he walked briskly toward the crowd. "What is the meaning of this ruckus? You know that your chief is ill!" He saw Muzungu standing amidst his people and the Efes in the background with haunting expressions on their faces. His anger ceased and rolled away like dissipating rain clouds.

"Muzungu," he said, surprised.

She walked out of the crowd and up to him. "Jabusa, my people and I have come in the spirit of kindness. We have elephant meat and only wish to share our good fortune with you and your people. I asked for you only because I think you are the one wisest enough to decide what is fair for the Lese to give us in exchange." She looked at Jabusa without blinking an eye. She stood tall, strong and self-assured, yet there was an air of submissiveness about her. Jabusa found favor in her courage to stand up to him and the Lese and again he thought what a splendid queen she would make. For a while neither of them spoke but observed each other silently. It was like a battle of strengths to see who would back down or speak the first defiant word. Both clans watched eagerly, wondering what would happen next. The Efe were fearful for Muzungu. Never before had an Efe taken such a firm and direct stand against a Lese, much less a woman to a future chief. On the other hand, the Lese were shocked at this woman's boldness and anticipated Jabusa's punishment for her disrespect.

"What is it that your people want?" he asked.

Muzungu's heart skipped a beat. She could not dare believe that their transactions could be this easy. Was he insinuating that he would give them the things they asked for, or was he preparing her to be the brunt of a cruel joke? She kept her composure. "The Efe men have risked their lives in bringing down the elephant. Their quests were not only for themselves and their villagers but also for you as well, for if it was not so we would not be here today. We will trade the meat for a rooster and four hens, three axes, three machetes, five cooking pots, smoking tobacco, two water jugs, 10 yards of cloth and three bundles of furs. Oh, yes," she said half forgetting the Efe children, "and some candy for the children."

The Lese people's protests buzzed around Jabusa's head. Some laughed and some shook their heads in disbelief. Gimiko could not believe what he'd just heard. Now he wished he'd left the women at home. He was certain they would leave the Lese village with nothing in hand and Muzungu's actions here today would be held over their heads for a very long time. Jabusa turned to Osun and nodded his head. The old man's mouth dropped.

"But, Jabusa, surely you do not mean to give them these things. The things they are asking for warrants exchange of the whole elephant, certainly not the small portions of meat they've brought."

"Get these things for them now!" ordered Jabusa. He took Muzungu by the arm and led her out of ear range. "So you are making me pay a bride price, I gather?"

"I have not given the word that I will marry you," she said.

"I feel in my heart that you will." He smiled.

"If I decide to marry you, the price you pay will far exceed what you have given today." Muzungu smiled a never-before-alluring smile at Jabusa. She turned and walked away letting her rear end switch shamefully.

*   *   *

Tifu brought supper for Muzungu and three other unmarried girls who were confined to a hut during their menstruation. The Efe believed that when an unmarried girl or woman shed blood she became weak and was shedding impurities from the body. During the period she was allowed to rest, performing only light work such as basket weaving or mending. Their hands were never to touch food unless it was for their mouths only. They were forbidden to interact with others for fear of spreading the impurities. Tifu sat the hot pot of couscous cooked with elephant bone marrow in front of the three women.

"Mmm, it smells good," said Muzungu.

"It will help to restore your energy" answered Tifu.

The three women put aside the baskets they were weaving. They washed their hands with water from one of two jugs that was kept in the hut for the purpose of cleansing and drinking. The cleansing was ritual and done several times daily. Tifu dipped portions of the mush into each woman's bowl and they began eating. She sat beside Muzungu. "Jabusa came by the village today asking for you. You will have to give him an answer soon."

"Does he know it is my time and I am in the hut?"

"Yes. He has counted and I suspect he will be back in a few days."

"When he comes back, I will give him the answer he wants to hear." She sighed. "I suppose this arrangement will be for the best."

"Yes," replied Tifu. "You know we are thankful for what you did yesterday at the Leses."

"You do not have to thank me for anything, Tifu. You are my sister, you know."

Tifu smiled. "I will miss you terribly. You are the closest friend I've ever had."

"We shall always be friends and the Efe will always be my people. You must let the chickens multiply. They will help to make you self-sufficient. They will bring you meat and eggs. After Jabusa has fallen madly in love with me, I will get him to give you some goats. Then you will have fresh milk to drink anytime you want."

"You have big plans for us, Muzungu. If you had said these things to me a week ago, I would have called you foolish. But after seeing the power you have over Jabusa, I believe you can do them. Your people must have instilled great confidence in you. Whoever they are, I know they mourn you still."

Muzungu studied her bowl of mush. A frown clouded over her face.

"What is it that troubles you?" asked Tifu.

"Sometimes I wonder."

"About what?"

"Why you did not turn me over to the Leses? They have contact with the outside world and could have given me to the missionaries. They would have found my people."

"We thought about doing that but then decided against it. In a way you were fortunate that the plane crashed so far away from these villages and the Lese did not find you. They would have enslaved you and we do not trust the hands of the missionaries. They have been known to brainwash people into worshiping their God and it has been reported that some of those people are held captive against their will. If Gimiko and the others had not gone hunting that day, you would have either been eaten by animals or died from your injuries. Gimiko says you crawled away from the wreckage before it began to burn. The fire probably kept the animals away until they found you. Because of the rain, only the inside of the plane was burned severely and the people that did not make it out were burned to a crisp. We know that your plane had to have crashed the day of the big thunderstorm because the explosion sounded like thunder and we paid it no mind. When they brought you here the following day, you were frightened of everyone. We worked with you, got you well showed you kindness and soon gained your trust. There was no way we could give you over to uncertain hands."

"Last night I dreamed the dream again. His name is Austin."

"Whose name is Austin?" asked Tifu.

"The man in my dreams. I don't know how I know, but his name is Austin."

Tifu didn't take Muzungu's dreams lightly. She believed in dreams and knew dreams were a controlling force in the life of the Efe. With each of her pregnancies her dreams told her the sex of the child. They even told her of the distinguishing marks each child would have. The dreams told her to say loving words to her mother that she would soon die of a horrible death. A week later one of the villagers was repairing and testing his bow when an arrow struck her through the heart. She died instantly. Then, Gimiko's ancestors came to him in a dream showing him where to find the elephant. So whenever someone mentioned dreams to the Efe, they took them seriously.

"I cannot make much of the dreams other than in your other life this man, Austin, meant something to you."

"Oh, I wish I could remember."

"Does your memory mean that much to you?"

"It didn't before, but the closer I get to becoming Jabusa's wife the more important it is to me. Do you think I have children?"

"I honestly do not. Your stomach is flat; there are no stretch marks and your breast show no signs of suckle. You do not have the look of a mother, my dear. Besides, I do not feel a maternal kindred spirit with you."

Muzungu smiled wearily. She fingered some of the mush into her mouth. Her appetite had left and the mush was tasteless. Her mind was on the reoccurring dreams and what would become of her future.

"When you have finished your flow we will travel to an Efe village that is to the south of us."

"The witchdoctor's village?" asked Muzungu.

"Yes. We will see Yoruba. She will read your dreams. If anyone knows what the dreams mean, she will. I suggest you weave a nice big basket and we will put eggs and meat in it as payment to her. We will leave early that morning. We should be back before Jabusa arrives."

*   *   *

Osun fidgeted with the fishing nets. His mind was on the events of the other day when the Efe people came to their village to trade. The other men's hands moved quickly over the nets. They were looking for damaged links so they could repair them. Tomorrow they would take the boats to the river and fish. Osun was an important figure in the Lese village. He coordinated the hunting expeditions, he said what was going to be planted in the gardens every year, he was the enforcer of order, and the head for the Lese religious sect, and he performed many of the marriages. But the position he was most proud of was his close relationship to the chief and his family. He had the chief's ear and many of the decision made by the chief came from Osun. He hadn't come into the position easily. He had to work many hard years to prove worthy before he was named chief advisor. The advisor that preceded him was exiled from the Lese village when Osun was a young man of 20. For five years after the banishment, the Lese didn't have an advisor. But during those five years Osun was watched carefully. He was faithful and obedient. Many times he went above and beyond the call of duty in obliging the chief and his family. At the age of 25 his faithfulness paid off. He was named advisor to Chief Njau. In two months from now he would have been chief advisor for 41 years.

He'd made his hut a shrine of self-exaltation. All the awards he'd received from the chief were on display. There were spears, masks, armors and drums, each especially made by the tribe's best craftsman, just for Osun. On his arm he wore "The Teeth," a band that had been made out of lions' teeth. He could never be seen without it. The lions' teeth band was the highest token of praise given to Lese men, usually for military reasons in times of war. For a Lese chief to give this to a fellow Lese was synonymous to an American receiving the Congressional Medal of Honor. Very few had received "The Teeth." Throughout the history of the Lese it was recorded that the honor had gone to only 30 others, all long dead now.

Osun could not believe what had happened yesterday. He was still angry, more so at Jabusa than at Muzungu. He would never admit the root of his anger to anyone, not even his wife, for fear that it would get back to Jabusa and the chief. As chief advisor, it was his duty to always and under all circumstances stand behind the chief's final decisions. Chief Njau would have never let the Efe get away with what they had pulled yesterday. They were becoming bold, perhaps because they knew Chief Njau was on his deathbed.

"Times are changing," he said to himself. He worried about Jabusa's reign after the chief died. The Lese Tribe was an organized structure. Osun was proud of it mainly because he'd helped to make it that way. The Lese people were governed by fear. Penalization for crimes committed was severe and it was fear that kept the people obedient to the laws. Since the chief had taken ill, Osun could see the difference in the Lese people's actions. They seemed not to care anymore about their fellow man. They knew Jabusa would not be as harsh as his father had been. He wondered what would become of the Lese people with Jabusa in control. Jabusa did a lot of things he didn't approve of, like spending too much time with his common Lese friends, not being strict enough on offenders of the Lese laws. People were getting away with murder. Just the other day a man was caught stealing eggs from his neighbor. The law called for one of the man's fingers to be chopped off. Instead, Jabusa made the man pay his neighbor back twice as many eggs as he had stolen. Osun thought the penalty wasn't severe enough so he had taken matters in his own hand. The next day he went to the man's house and confiscated one of his goats. He told the man the orders came from the chief and he was not to say a word about it— otherwise his whole hand would be severed. Osun later sold the goat to a fellow villager for a bottle of whisky.

Chief Njau never set foot into the Efes' village, but Osun knew Jabusa was going there every chance he got and he had suspected the reason was a woman. Yesterday's incident confirmed his suspicions. He'd seen how Jabusa pulled Muzungu aside. He handled her like a man would handle his wife on their wedding night—gentle. If Osun were chief, he would have snatched her arm right out of the socket. He also saw the way Jabusa smiled at her during their private conversation and the way she wagged her behind in leaving. There were plenty of women right here in the Lese tribe to fool around with, women who would do anything Jabusa wanted them to. So why was he messing with the likes of an Efe? Maybe it was her strangeness that enticed him. He knew she had her sights on Jabusa, wanted to marry him, become queen, be waited on and live the good life. After all, what woman didn't? But he had hoped Jabusa's firm upbringing would dictate for him to marry another Lese. She had the nerve, thought Osun, to even think she was good enough for Jabusa. If he married her, Osun knew, she would have his ear and would soon become acting advisor. She would be calling the shots and where would that leave him? He saw the brashness in her and it frightened him. She was full of persuasion. All it would take was a year—one year and she'd have the Lese women asking for treatment equal to the men. Two years and the Lese women would be controlling the men. With Muzungu sitting at the feet of the chief, the Efe would be able to come and go as they please. "No way," Osun said. He'd risen from cleaning out chicken coops and goat stalls for other people to put food on his family's table to being a well-respected and handsomely paid dignitary. The Lese people regarded him with respect, mostly out of fear, just the way he wanted them to.

Most of the huts consisted of one large domed room, but the hut he lived in was tri-domed. He had three rooms, a bedroom for him and his wife, a cooking room and a spare room for his children and grandchildren when they came to visit. He had a clay oven built in the cooking room and even a sink with drainage. There was no running water for the sink; it was carried in from the public well located in the center of the village. Still, having it was a handy device for his wife. She didn't have to stand in long lines to wash her dishes. The floors in each room were finished with clay whereas most huts had dirt floors. There were a table and six chairs in the kitchen. The bedrooms had a full-sized bed each. The beds were simply wooden bases with legs underneath to give it height off the floor. They were piled high with furs to make them padded and soft. He'd worked hard to get where he was and there would be a fight if he thought he was going to lose it.

"Oh, I know what you have in mind, Muzungu, but it will not work," he said to himself again.

"What are you saying over there, Osun?" called one of the men.

"I am saying that I will catch the biggest and sneakiest fish of all," he replied with a wicked grin.

*   *   *

The rain the night before had left the morning air thick and muggy when Tifu and Muzungu set out to visit Yoruba, the witch doctor. Tifu hoped Yoruba would be able to help Muzungu with her dreams. They walked for two solid hours before they reached the village. Muzungu had come here a year ago to get medicine for one of the women who had been in labor for three days. The village was five times larger than her village. She remembered thinking how exciting it must be to live around so many people. Other Efes greeted them as they entered the village. Tifu knew many of them and they all were happy to see each other. After conversing for a few minutes, they spotted Yoruba sitting on a stool outside the door of her hut. She was preparing beans for her supper.

"Hello, Yoruba. I am Tifu from the village of…"

"I know who you are," said the old woman. "You are from Gimiko's tribe."

"Yes, I am Gimiko's wife."

Yoruba was more interested in Muzungu than with what Tifu was saying. She studied her carefully. Her eyes froze Muzungu. They were cloudy, still eyes, almost like the eyes of something dead. The pupils did not move on their own but only when Yoruba moved her head to the subject matter did they make contact. The old woman's icy stare sent a chill through Muzungu's body. Her hair was long and standing. It looked as though it had not been combed in years. The teeth she had left in her head were brown with decay. She put the bowl of beans down and pointed a crooked finger at her.

"I know you," she said, "You are the tall stranger from the other world. I met you once before, haven't I?"

Muzungu stepped forward and unconsciously bowed to Yoruba before speaking. "Yes. I came for medicine a year ago."

"Yes, medicine to advance labor. So tell me, how is the little boy getting along with that club foot of his?"

Muzungu was amazed that she would know the child was born with a defect. She was sure no one had told her about it. No one from her village had visited Yoruba's village since the birth. "He is doing well Yoruba."

Yoruba laughed a loud, coarse laugh as she studied Muzungu. "I laugh at your doubt, my child."

"I believe you are who they say you are."

"No, you don't. You stand there wondering about my skills. I admit that I am not the best, but I am better than most. You have come for my services, yes?"

"Yes. I have been having disturbing dreams and I want to find out what they mean. Maybe you can tell me something about my past." Muzungu handed Yoruba the woven basket filled with elephant meat and eggs.

Yoruba smiled and licked her lips. She stood. "Come, let's go inside where it is quieter."

Muzungu and Tifu followed Yoruba inside the dark hut. Yoruba lit candles and asked the women to sit down on a pile of furs. Yoruba sat on the opposite side of them. "Tell me about your dreams."

When Muzungu had finished telling her about the dream, Yoruba took a small cup and shook several small stones from it. She studied the stones momentarily and asked her to place her hands in hers."

Muzungu obediently did as Yoruba asked. The witch doctor looked toward the ceiling and closed her eyes. She started mumbling something neither woman could understand. When she finished, she grabbed a handful of dust off of the ground and threw it in the air. She blew into the cloud of dust, making it scatter all over Muzungu's face. Muzungu began coughing uncontrollably.

"Quiet, child. The Dream God is trying to speak. You mustn't drown him out with your coughing." Yoruba picked up a miniature broom and shook it in the air twice, once to her right and then to her left. She opened her dead eyes and stared into space. "The Dream God tells me that you were once in love with a man with a good heart. He loved you deeply and mourned your death for a long time. But that man is no more the man he was before. His heart has turned to another. He loves this woman, although not as deeply as he loved you. But love intensifies with time. He lives far away. The Dream God tells me that he lives on the other side of the great waters. The god sees people around him. He lives in a place where there are lots of people. Like you, he plans to marry soon. This man has been having the same dreams you now have, but he does not dream as much now. Perhaps because his heart has found love but your heart drifts in search of love. The god says eventually you will find love, but there is no face for the name and no name for the face. You come to me for solutions that you already have the answers for. Someone waits for you. Someone you do not love. The god sees a troubled heart in this person. The god says the decision is yours to make." Yoruba squeezed Muzungu's hands tightly and began shaking violently.

"No!" screamed Muzungu, as she wrenched in pain. "You are hurting me. Let go of my hands."

Yoruba opened her clinched hands. She wore a troubled look.

"What is it?" Tifu asked, frightfully.

"When the Dream God was speaking to me, I picked up another spirit. It was the spirit of warning. It wants me to warn you of an evil person in this world. This person sees the power in you and wants to stop it. You must beware."

"Who?" asked Muzungu.

"You must not let him stop the power."

"Who is this unfavorable person?" asked Tifu.

"They are gone. The god and the spirit are gone."

"But you can't stop now," pleaded Muzungu. "Did he tell you the person's name?"

"He did not tell me. All he said was you must beware, my child."

         *   *   *

Muzungu did not rest that night. She tossed and turned until finally she eased from her bedding and went outside to sit under the stars. She believed she had never felt so lonely in her life. Up until a week ago she felt like fate had dealt her a winning hand. She was feeling like she belonged with the Efe and she no longer felt like a muzungu (stranger). If she had not led Jabusa to believe she would marry him, she would not be in the present predicament. Going to Yoruba was a waste of time. She felt worse now than before. Chills ran over her body as she thought about what Yoruba had said. All of it was disturbing. She had told her a lot of things that meant nothing. She didn't know any more about herself than before seeing Yoruba.

34

The Changing of the Guard

I will bring the blind by a way that they know not; I will lead them in paths that they have not known. I will make darkness light before them and crooked things straight. These things will I do unto them, and not forsake them,

Isaiah 42:16

The day started out just like any other day. The Lese village bustled with busy bodies going about their daily regimen and chores. The beating sounds were similar to the beating of drums. The five women kept perfect synchronized rhythm as they pounded couscous grain, using wooden pestles the size of baseball bats. They were grinding grain in mortars that had been hollowed out of tree-trunks. The young children danced to the beat while the elders who were too old to dance tapped their feet. A few yards away a group of 30 women waded in knee-deep water. They had their skirts tied in knots around their hips as they weeded the rice fields known to the Lese as the "women's crop." The name had been given to the rice fields centuries ago because women were its primary caretakers. Another group of women worked in the gardens harvesting large cabbages the size of basketballs. The size and condition of the Leses' vegetables mesmerized the white traders. Their squashes were so yellow they were almost orange. The sweet potatoes were fat and juicy. The tomatoes were the reddest of reds, large and round. The kernels were so plump on the ears of corn they looked as though they would burst through their shucks. In addition to their perfect appearance, they always tasted delicious. The traders tried on countless occasions to bargain with the Leses for their recipe for growing such perfect vegetables, but the Leses would never give up their fruitful formula of animal manure, fish emulsions and spoiled fruits and vegetables. To do so would almost put an end to their commerce with the traders.

The Leses had become dependent on the goods. The clothes, thong sandals, sweets, cookware and even the mules and donkeys had become necessary ingredients in their lives.

The older men never seemed to work as hard as the women did. They piddled with their arsenals or gathered in the meetinghouse to discuss Lese politics and governing regulations. The laymen of the tribe performed more demanding tasks, such as constructing buildings and making pirogues, mainly for fishing. The Lese life was a comfortable one considering how other nomadic tribes lived. Their way of life had not come easy, though. There had been struggles along the way to becoming self-sufficient and businessmen with the traders. There had been Leses who had formed cliques for the purpose of gaining control. Needless to say, all of them were either ostracized from the village or executed. It had taken several shrewd and wise leaders with warrior skills and courage to get the Leses where they were today. Chief Njau was one of them. Now, most of the Leses who were old enough to be concerned about the future of their tribe watched the actions of Jabusa closely. They knew it was only a matter of time before the old man died and they couldn't help but wonder in what direction he would take them. Many of them expected Jabusa to be wavering in his ruling. They buzzed in Osun's ear, telling him to watch Jabusa and guide him closely. They didn't want to fall to the level of the Efes. *"We will be eating rats and swinging from trees in search of honey"* was the phrase most heard by Osun from the concerned Leses. Osun was in the meetinghouse heading the talks. He was trying to persuade the gathering of men that their lives were about to change.

"We should not be afraid of change, Osun," said Tabar, a 25-year-old.

"You are young and foolish. I tell you that Jabusa will not rule us the way Chief Njau has. He hasn't the skills or knowledge to do so. A weak link will break the chain," said Osun.

"He is his father's child; he was raised properly and taught the Lese ways. They are inscribed on his heart and he will not forget them," said Tabar. Among the men gathered were a group of young men who thought Tabar was speaking logically and agreed verbally with everything he had said.

"The maggot must be smashed before it turns into a pesky fly." Osun slapped the palm of his hand with the other as he spoke.

"Ten years ago when the traders brought us the mules and donkeys, you and the elders did not approve. You all said it would make us lazy," Tabor said. "Ten years later, we are not lazy but more productive and effective. Our village has grown twice the size it was before we acquired the animals. The mules and donkeys carry the tree that is too heavy for us to lift. They aid us in planting and harvesting the gardens. If it were not for the animals we would not have the well in the center of the village providing us with fresh water anytime we want it. We would have to trek back and forth to the river twice a week just for water. You are chief advisor, Osun, not the chief himself."

"What are you implying?" asked Osun angrily.

"You are trying to control matters that are not of your concern. I say let the rulers rule." Tabar stood face to face with Osun. He didn't blink an eye as he stared him down. Osun turned his back to Tabar thinking that would dismiss him from the conversations, but in his heart he knew the young man was right. He reminded him so much of himself when he was that age. He stood on principles those many years ago. Now he wasn't sure what he was standing on; he only hoped for the betterment of the Lese village.

It was noon when the high-pitched scream came from the chief's quarters. The shrill sound brought a halt to everything. People dropped what they were doing and ran toward Chief Njau's dwelling. Jabusa and his mother, Queen Kanya, met them. Queen Kanya cried openly while Jabusa tried to be strong, but his eyes reflected pain and sorrow too. Jabusa stepped down from the dwelling's shaded porch. He stared blankly into the crowd of people.

"Chief Njau is dead," he said dryly. Moans and sobs came from the gathering.

"Mourning will begin at sunset and last for the next 10 days," said Jabusa. He turned and led his mother back inside. There, Jabusa and Queen Kanya would sit with the body until it had been properly embalmed and dressed.

For 10 days the Lese people were not allowed to clean house, wash themselves, slaughter animals, harvest crops, fish or do any of the everyday tasks they usually did. They had to rely solely on the staples already available to them. Most of the villagers knew this day was coming and had prepared for it. The general idea behind mourning was for the whole village to share in the grief. The only communication that was allowed was done in the privacy of their huts. Under no circumstances were teeth to be shown. To show teeth was a gesture of laughing and laughing during the mourning period of a high official was considered mockery in the face of the deceased's family. Penalty for the display of teeth was five days in the village holding cell with only bread and water to eat and drink. For 10 days the spirit of death fell upon the Lese village. The only sounds that could be heard were occasional mourning and the call of the wild forest creatures. A steady trail of people visited Jabusa and his mother, bringing gifts of consolation. The women wore black veils across their face to hide their teeth when they spoke.

Back in the huts children grew restless. They were not allowed to go outside and play. Being confined to the small huts grew thin with them and they released their frustrations by fighting with their siblings. The mourning period was hard on everyone and by the time the ninth day rolled around the people became more tolerant of each other. After sunset on the 10th day they were bursting at the seams with hidden delight. Mourning would be over soon and they could resume their normal lives. The women and men worked diligently slaughtering chickens, goats and steers, preparing them for the funeral feast. On the 11th day they held the funeral.

*   *   *

The Efe were in attendance at Chief Njau's funeral. They stood silently in the background. The four Molokai (*professional mourners*) wore long black robes and ran back and forth among the crowd. They screamed yipping screams and moaned low sorrowful moans. Osun wore the Igbo (*funeral*) mask. He stood at the head of Chief Njau's body. Silent tears streamed from behind the mask gathering under Osun's chin, then dropping onto his white tunic. Chief Njau lay on a table draped in layers of black silk.

The drum could be heard for miles around. The beat, of course, was rhythmic and stirred the emotions of the villagers even more. They swayed and rocked their bodies back and forth in step with the rhythm. The Molokai began dancing around Chief Njau's body. As they danced they sprinkled white powder on the body as a symbol of tears from the ancestors. The Molokai shook miniature straw brooms in Chief Njau's still face and chanted prayers asking their God to receive him into the great beyond. When the drums and dancing stopped, the mighty wail began. Everyone in the village cried, screamed, and yelled. It was a deafening roar and continued for several minutes. After the great wail was over, Chief Njau was placed in an elaborate box made out of ebony wood. Spices, gifts and incense were placed inside the box and he was buried five hundred yards from the village in a cemetery reserved for high-ranking officials and their families. The Efe enjoyed the feast but mainly stayed to themselves. Now that the funeral was over it was time to celebrate the life of a great chief. The villagers danced, sang and play acted the life of a great chief.

Muzungu could not help but notice the white man known to the Lese as "Linus" standing and socializing with the men. His pale white skin made him an oddity as he stood among the dark skins. He wore a khaki shirt and matching pants. His Timberlands were in vast contrast to the Leses' thong sandals. The wide-brimmed hat protected his fair skin from the hot sun. He was tall and lean. His physique caused nostalgia to overcome Muzungu. Something about the man's stature was hauntingly familiar. He seemed relaxed around the Lese. More confusing than that, the Lese accepted him warmly. Muzungu found this very disturbing. They would accept this white man openly and allow him to walk freely around their village as if he was one of them, yet would not let the Efe set foot inside except by invitation.

Muzungu knew the white man had to be a trader. She had heard of them. She had been in the forest for over five years and this was her first time seeing a white person. She knew she had seen them before because just looking at the man was again very familiar. She even knew that the feel of his hair was much different from theirs. She suspected that in her other life she had contact with white people regularly. She felt she should go to Jabusa and offer her condolences, and she would have if the white man had not been so close to where Jabusa was sitting. There was something about the man that made Muzungu feel very uneasy. Linus watched her intently. His eyes followed her every move, examining her carefully. He walked over to Osun and whispered something in his ear, all the while keeping his eyes on Muzungu. Osun looked at Muzungu briefly and frowned at her. He whispered something back to Linus, then walked away to mingle with his villagers.

Linus vaguely recollected that several years back a plane was said to have gone down in these parts. The husband of one of the victims was offering a handsome reward for information leading to the return of his wife. He remembered the amount to be an astronomical $100,000, to be correct, and double that if she was found alive and unharmed. He doubted this was the same woman because the Lese had never mentioned a plane crash and, besides, people in the mainland thought it was a hoax. No African person they knew had that kind of money to offer as reward. If there had been a plane crash, who would be stupid enough to go wandering around in the predatory rain forest? The risk of being killed and eaten was too great. He pulled out a small notebook from his shirt pocket and began writing vigorously. *Muzungu.* He wrote her name carefully. Beside it he wrote its' meaning: *stranger.* He wrote her description: *Very pretty African woman in late twenties or early thirties. Tall and thin with thick long braids. Dark complexion, high cheekbones, large eyes. Moves unbelievably graceful. Appeared in the forest some five years ago. No one knows from where.* Linus stopped writing long enough to take another look at Muzungu. He tipped his hat and smiled at her. Slowly Muzungu raised a cautious hand in greeting. He began writing again: *I don't think she is Lese, without a doubt she is not Efe. I don't believe she belongs here. There is a tame quality about her.* Then on the bottom of the notebook he made a note to check the missing person's bureau when he got back to the mainland. He remembered the camera he kept in the glove compartment of his jeep. A picture of Muzungu might be helpful. He walked back to the main road to retrieve it. He thought there was a slight chance she was the same woman and if so he could surely use the $200,000.

*   *   *

Muzungu had come to the stream to wash pots and some of the few items of clothes the Efe owned. She heard a rustling in the nearby thicket and grabbed the three-foot spear designed especially for the women when they were alone and away from the village. She poked the spear in the bushes, expecting a duiker or some other small game to jump out. Instead she was surprised to find a huge turtle. Muzungu guessed it weighed 70 or 80 pounds and had to be 50 or more years old. Its shell was dark gray with yellow spots. It lifted its head slowly and looked at Muzungu, then continued it's path toward the stream's edge.

"Where do you think you're going?" she teased. "You will make a mighty fine stew for supper tonight." She circled the turtle and grabbed it by its scaly hind legs. She knew better than to try to capture it from the front. She had seen the result of a turtle bite and it wasn't a pretty sight. The turtle was stronger than she thought and slipped easily from her grip. She knew if it made it to the stream he would swim away quickly and she could forget about stew for supper. She aimed the spear at its head and discharged it with all her might. The spear hit the turtle in the head causing little damage. It snapped and hissed at her out of anger. Muzungu took a large step backwards. She looked around for a large stone to smash his head but found nothing. After scolding Muzungu, the turtle headed back toward the stream.

"No way I am letting you go," she said, as she made another attempt to stop it by grabbing its legs. Again the turtle slipped from her grip and snapped more viciously this time. Now it was only a few feet from the stream's edge. Muzungu tried to stop the creature by standing on its back.

"I would not do that if I were you," warned Jabusa, "He is still able to bite you from behind." He startled her and she lost balance and fell to the ground. Jabusa jumped down from the mule and flipped the turtle over on its back. The turtle rocked back and forth as it struggled to gain position on all fours. Jabusa casually walked back to the mule and took the machete from the satchel. He flipped the turtle back over and as quick as lighting brought it down on its neck severing the head from the body. They watched the turtle squirm around on the ground before going completely still. He laughed his robust laugh.

"Has anyone ever told you not to stand on the back of a turtle?"

Muzungu pushed herself off of the ground and began dusting herself off. "I had to stop him, Jabusa. Standing on him was the only thing I could think of at the moment."

"And how were you going to kill him?"

"I would have managed."

"If you were lucky enough to kill him, you could not have carried him, for he is far too heavy. If you had decided to leave him and come back with others to help you, he would not have been here. Either I would have snatched him up," he said amusingly, "or the animals would have gotten to him before you returned."

"Well, that didn't happened, now did it."

"And lucky for you it didn't." Jabusa took some rope from the satchel, bound the turtle with it and strapped it to the mule. Muzungu gathered her washings and packed them neatly inside the pot. Jabusa bent down by the stream and drank some of the cool water, then splashed some in his face. "Come and sit by me." He patted the ground with his hand.

Muzungu eased down beside him. "Thank you for helping me with the turtle. It is my favorite food."

Jabusa was impressed with her gratitude and he smiled at her.

"I am sorry about the death of Chief Njau," she said.

Jabusa looked at her with the smile still on his face. "It warms my heart that you should care."

Muzungu shook her head. "So you are chief now, huh?"

"I am chief and a chief needs a wife in order to run his dominion effectively. You have not given me an answer yet."

Muzungu knew marriage to Jabusa was inevitable. It did not seem like such a bad thing being married to him now. He was not as menacing as she had first thought. She decided that he was halfway decent the day they went to his village to trade. Now she worried about his followers. They were the ones who treated them like dirt. Even at the funeral yesterday, she could feel the cold stares and heard the snickers coming from his people. At the feast when Tifu reached for a piece of meat one of the women forbade her to touch it. The woman plucked a piece of the meat from the bone and dumped it on Tifu's plate. Tifu smiled gratefully and moved on through the serving line. It hurt Muzungu to see one human treating another so rudely. If she were to become Jabusa's wife she would not tolerate such behavior. They were all creatures of the almighty.

"What are you thinking, Malaika?" asked Jabusa.

Muzungu jumped at the word. Deja vu visited her again. She had heard it before. She put her head in her hands as dark images began flashing through her mind. She saw an image of herself and the man in her dream named Austin. The two of them were sitting on a beautiful blanket that had the needlepoint scene of an African village on it. They were feeding the squirrels that had gathered around them.

"Are you all right?" asked Jabusa.

She straightened herself up and tried to focus on their conversation. "Yes, I was wondering about the Lese people. They have a strong dislike for the Efe. I know you loved your father, but I must tell you that I have heard frightening stories about his treatment of the Efe. I can't help but wonder if you are like him."

Jabusa leaned back on his elbows and chuckled. "I want to marry you don't I?"

"But everyone knows that I am not truly Efe, and maybe that makes me just a little better in your eyes."

"Lese men marry Efe women all the time. It is nothing new."

"But tell me the truth, Jabusa. How do the Efe wives fare in your environment?"

Jabusa listened closely to Muzungu as she spoke. He seemed embarrassed after a moment's thought. "Truthfully, I guess their lives could be better."

"You see, Jabusa, that is my point. If I marry you it cannot be expected of me to change my feelings toward my people."

Jabusa looked at her curiously.

"Yes, Jabusa, they are my people and I love them very much. Marrying you would be like marrying the oppressor."

Jabusa let out a weary sigh. "So you are saying that you will not marry me because of our customs and way of life?"

"No, but what I am saying is I will marry you if you promise me to change your way and your people's way of thinking and the cruel treatment that you render to my people."

"Muzungu, you must know this one thing. I hold no hatred in my heart for anyone."

"What about dislike, Jabusa? Do you dislike us? Do you only tolerate us for the sake of trade?"

Jabusa lowered his head. "I know you have seen me come into your village and taunt Gimiko and Suko from time to time, but I truly meant no harm. It was all in fun. And as far as trade, you know that I can be fair. If you are to become my wife, I want you to be happy not sad and worrying about the Efe?"

"My people, Jabusa. You must accept the fact that I regard them as my people."

"O.K. Your people. I promise to regard your people as highly as I regard my own."

Muzungu smiled. "I believe you mean that, Jabusa," she said. "One other thing."

"Yes?"

"How many wives do you intend to have?"

The question caught him off guard and it was a subject he hoped she would not bring up. In Lese and Efe law a vow had to be made before the marriage took place that a man would not take more than one wife. Only then was the marriage bound by that promise.

"Well, I haven't given it much thought yet. Why do you ask?"

"I would not like another woman in your life," she said bluntly. "I prefer not to share you." She did not watch Jabusa's reaction to her statement but kept a straight face and watched the ripples in the stream rolled past them.

"That is all fine and well, but you know a man has needs greater than those of a woman. An extra wife may alleviate my demands on you."

She looked him squarely in the eyes and, without smiling, she said, "I am quite capable of taking care of all your needs, Chief Jabusa."

"If it is your wish to be my only wife, so be it," he said with sincerity.

Jabusa and Muzungu kissed for the first time sitting on the edge of the stream. He pulled her soft body into his muscular one and brushed his lips ever so lightly against hers.

*   *   *

The wedding was planned to take place in two weeks. Each day around noon the children gathered at the village edge and waited impatiently for the sound of hooves and rustling bushes. They squealed with delight at the first sign of Jabusa coming.

"I hear him," they shouted, and the jumping and laughter would begin as Jabusa rode in and began handing candy, usually long thick peppermint sticks, to the children. The day after he and Muzungu had kissed on the edge of the stream he came to the village and brought

Gimiko and Tifu a Billy and a nanny goat as a bride price. Gimiko expected Jabusa's followers to jump out of the bushes laughing at the cruel joke he had played on them. He soon realized that it wasn't a joke. Never in the history of life in the Ituri rain forest had a Lese paid a bride's price for an Efe woman.

The second day he brought five chickens and a rooster. Then on the third day he brought a bundle of thick furs and a bolt of bright red printed cloth. He also extended an invitation for the Efe to come to his village in three days for a pre-wedding feast. There, Muzungu would be introduced to his mother. Muzungu was never one to daydream, but here lately she found herself doing just that. She was excited about the marriage. Her initial opinion had changed about Jabusa. She had seen a gentler, idyllic side of him and she liked it. She recalled Yoruba the witch doctor telling her that she would find love but there was no name for the face. Now, she knew what the old woman meant. Even Yoruba with all her power and wisdom didn't know the person she spoke about was Jabusa. Everything was clear to her now. The burning desire to find out about Austin wasn't as important now. She had even forgotten about the evil person Yoruba had warned her about. The only things she thought about were how to be a good wife to Jabusa and helping to make the Efes' lives better. She knew that as long as she loved him, he in return would love her and the Efe.

Tifu fingered the cloth. "You must make yourself presentable for meeting Jabusa's mother. It will make a nice iro ati bubba (wrap set) and gele (headpiece). My daughter-in-law and I will get started on it immediately."

"That is not necessary, Tifu. I am sure Jabusa is not so superficial as to care what I wear."

"My child, you are so naïve. A man always cares what a woman has on and especially if he is presenting her to his mother. Why do you think he brought the cloth here?" she laughed. Certainly not for us."

*   *   *

Osun listened disapprovingly. He could not believe his ears as Jabusa gave him the orders to carry out for the feast. All of his suspicions were being manifested. This Muzungu was much better than he had given her credit for. Jabusa was doing things for her and her people he had not done for his previous wife. It was shameful and disrespectful to the Lese. He wondered if Queen Kanya knew about Muzungu. If she were anything like Chief Njau, certainly she would not approve. He made a mental note to go to her when Jabusa wasn't around. He would give her all the sordid details about this low-class woman he wanted to marry.

"Chief Jabusa, I just do not understand your actions."

"What is it that you do not understand, Osun?"

"Your wanting to marry this woman!"

"Muzungu. Her name is Muzungu," he corrected.

"Yes, Chief Jabusa, Muzungu," he said meekly. "I think you are still grieving over the death of your father and you are not thinking clearly. You and Queen Kanya should take some time to yourselves. Get away for a while, go to the mainland and visit your mother's cousin that lives there. The change will do you good." Osun smiled his smile of persuasion.

"Osun, you are not in position to think. If I didn't know any better I would think you were against my marrying Muzungu."

"Oh, no, Great Chief!" Osun bowed down before Jabusa in an attempt to lower his rising anger. "I am only concerned with your well being. I—uh—we all worry if you're making the right decision in marrying Muzungu," he chuckled. "After all, she is Efe and there are plenty of beautiful, eligible Lese women. I see the way they look and long after you. They would do anything you want."

"Perhaps I do not want a woman who is just amiable but rather one whose very existence is fueled by bravery and challenge." Jabusa's voice had become very serious and he looked directly into Osun's eyes. "I know the way the Lese feel about the Efe. It is true that we would rather not tolerate them. I remember my father's feeling toward them also, but I have eaten with the Efe and have come to know them as a people.

Other than their lifestyles, they are no different than we are. I now know that my father was wrong."

Osun was shocked to hear the statement coming from Jabusa. Denouncing the teaching, training and ways of one's father was treason, and in Jabusa's case high treason, since his father was chief. His heart was pumping blood of fury now. This could not be. This woman had poisoned Jabusa. She had probably fed him some of her menstruation. He had learned from his mother a long time ago never to eat from strange women because they had the power to cast spells using their blood. That was the only explanation for his abrupt change.

"The Lese people will make an effort to be kinder to the Efe. We will learn to live as brothers. They will be free to come and go when they want, just as we do to them. We will raise our children together. We will become as one."

Still crouched on his knees, Osun bowed his head as if in submission to Jabusa but he was plotting to ruin his plans. He would do whatever it took to keep the Efe out of their lives. He would make it a point to talk to Queen kanya no later than today about the jeopardy this union would bring upon the Lese people and their way of life.

35

Conspiracy

Osun listened eagerly as Linus explained his interest in Muzungu.

"I checked the missing persons bureau and there was a small commuter plane that crashed in this forest over five years ago. The husband of one of the passengers was offering a reward for the whereabouts of his wife. After reading over the file on the woman, this Muzungu fits the description perfectly."

Osun though about what he had just heard.

"This is good," he said, trying to hide his sheer excitement. If Muzungu turned out to be this man's wife, that would be even better. Murder had entered his mind and, if push came to shove, he would kill her. But he'd much prefer her removal this way. Having to kill her would be too risky. He'd have to be extra careful that no one other than himself knew the circumstances involving her death or disappearance. "And how much is the reward?" Osun asked candidly.

"Uh—oh yeah, the husband is offering $50,000 for her safe return." He cleared his throat to help swallow the lie.

Osun watched him shrewdly. "$25,000 each is a lot of money for the both of us. I could do a lot of things with that kind of money. Perhaps even buy myself into chiefdom."

Linus was grateful Osun had not tried to challenge him about the amount. "You're right, Osun, you would make a much better chief than Jabusa and $25,000 is a lot of money to help persuade your people that you should rule them instead of Jabusa. You know that I am a man of my word and will not try to cheat you. We will split it straight down the middle fair and square."

"You will not try to cheat me, for if you do I will kill you." Osun looked half-crazed to the trader and he believed Osun would kill him if he discovered the true amount of the reward money.

"Osun, you and I must keep this secret between us. If people found out about Muzungu's true identity and the reward money, she would become hunted and the chance of our getting the money would grow slim."

"Don't you worry. I will not tell a soul, not even my dear sweet wife. You just do what you have to do to get rid of Muzungu and make us rich. The wedding is scheduled to take place 11 days from now. Jabusa plans a wedding feast tomorrow. I want Muzungu gone before the wedding takes place."

Linus loaded Osun's cart with all the supplies and food items he needed for the feast. He even added extra for good faith.

Osun had found the opportunity to talk with Queen Kanya while Jabusa had gone fishing with some of the Lese men. He was dispirited by what she had told him. "Osun," she had said, "Jabusa has told me all about the tall woman that lives with the Efe. If Chief Njau were still living, I would not have condoned such a union for my son, although these kinds of marriages happen all the time between our men and Efe women." She exhaled and hesitated a little before continuing, "But I see how Jabusa lights up when he speaks of her. I have never seen him so happy, energetic and full of life." She smiled to herself as she remembered the love she shared with Chief Njau. "Love is something irreplaceable; there is no substitute for it and true love comes only once in a lifetime. I know my son loves this woman because he has vowed to me that he will not take another wife while he is married to her. He says she is all he needs. He is much like his father. Chief Njau made that same vow to me. Before he died, he managed to tell me how much he loved me. He didn't care that I was only able to give him one child. He said that if he had it to do all over again he would still choose me." Then Queen Kanya sobbed solemnly in her hands. Osun hated to see her cry. He knew she loved Chief Njau deeply. He had loved him too. They both felt strong about the plight of the Lese people. Both had developed the rules, regulations and the political strongholds that made the Lese tribe the strongest, most organized tribe in the Ituri rain forest. He would miss his dear friend. It seemed to him that he would have to continue the battle alone now since it was clear that he could not count on Jabusa or Queen Kanya.

As Osun guided the donkey-driven cart away from the marketplace and back to his village he marveled at the beauty of the rain forest. It was a blanket of greenery and every now and then a flamingo, peacock or parrot would dart through the sky, adding bursts of rainbow colors to the scenery. Osun loved the forest. It was a paradise. His steps were lively now with hopes that Linus would come through with his promise of ridding them of Muzungu and putting money in his hands.

*   *   *

"Hello, this is Austin and this is Candace. We are unable to take your call at the moment, but if you would please leave your name and number we will get back with you as soon as possible."

"Damn!" screamed Linus. He slammed the phone back into its cradle and picked up the file folder with all the information about Austin. There was another telephone number inside. It was his office number. After three rings Phyllis answered.

"Hello, my name is Linus Snodgrass. I would like to speak to a Mr. Austin Kawissopie."

Phyllis could not help but notice the thick English accent. She didn't think he was related to Austin. He had never mentioned a relative by the name of Linus Snodgrass. "Sir, I'm sorry, but Mr. Kawissopie is not in the office. May I take a message?"

"When do you expect him?"

"Not for a few more days."

"Oh, out of town, huh?"

"Sir, I'm sorry, but I can't say." Phyllis never told anyone when Austin was out of town. People were so misleading and she never knew what they had in mind. "I would be glad to take a message."

"It's very urgent that I speak with Mr. Kawissopie. Look, when he gets in could you please have him call me. Did you get my name?"

"Yes, sir. Linus Snodgrass," she repeated.

"And listen, tell him to only ask for me. If I'm not here, tell him to leave a time when I can return his call." Linus hung up the phone and studied the contents of the folder some more. "She's gotta be the same girl," he said to himself.

*   *   *

They took reluctant steps as Gimiko led them into the Lese village. All around them they saw tables elaborately spread with delicious look-ing foods. The aroma of the food hung heavy in the air and made the Efes' mouths water. They stopped just before reaching the first hut. Muzungu walked past Gimiko and motioned for them to follow her.

"I think we should wait here," said Gimiko.

"It will be all right, trust me." Muzungu walked tall and proud. The dress she wore was breathtaking, fitting her snugly in the waist, hips and round behind. She chose not to wear the headpiece but wore her hair in an upsweep of braids adorned with tiny gold beads. Tifu had made her a strand of red and gold beads to go around her neck. It matched her outfit perfectly. She wore large gold hoop earrings that Suko's wife let her borrow. Jabusa could not take his eyes off her. He smiled as he reached his hand out to receive her, then bowed his head in greeting to Gimiko and his clan. Gimiko and his following bowed back. The Efe children were well behaved and clung to the dress tails of their mothers.

"Mother, I'd like to present to you Muzungu from the Efe tribe."

"Habari *(hello)*, Queen Kanya. Shikamoo *(I touch your feet)*," said Muzungu.

"Marahabaa *(I acknowledge your respect)*." Queen Kanya smiled at Muzungu. She thought she was beautiful. She bowed to Gimiko and the others. This was the closest she had ever come to the Efe people. Other than their size they were no different from the Lese. They both had dark skins, broad noses and full lips and their hair ranged from curly to kinky. They seemed gentle and she was amazed at how loving and orderly they handled their children. A warm feeling immediately overtook her and all the years of prejudice she held in her heart for them melted away. She had never done anything directly to hurt the Efe, but there was a lot she could have done to help them too, and for that she was ashamed. She would learn quickly that prejudice is nothing more than fear of the unknown and that her being afraid of people she knew nothing about made her ignorant. Queen Kanya stepped forward and extended her hand, leading them to the head tables. The feast began with dancing, music and singing. Never before had the Efe experienced such grandeur. The attitudes of the Lese people seemed far removed from their normal snobbish demeanor. The communal bowls were passed around and no one seemed hesitant about eating after the Efe. Queen Kanya sat at one end of the table opposite Jabusa. Gimiko and Tifu sat on either side of her. They talked back and forth to each other like they were old friends. Muzungu sat next to Jabusa. Just to see the Efe interacting positively with the Lese was the happiest day of her life. She had never seen Gimiko and the others laugh and enjoy themselves as they were doing now. She even thought she saw a smile coming from Osun.

The feasting lasted way into the night. The torches and fires lit up the black sky and cast the dancers' shadows against the side of the huts and surrounding trees. Queen Kanya suggested that the Efe spend the night in the meetinghouse since it was so late. Traveling back to their village would be an inconvenience, especially for the little children trying to make the long trip in the dark. Besides she knew they were enjoying themselves playing with the Lese children. Children were wonderful that way; they never saw differences. She wished the transition between the two tribes would be as easy but she doubted it. She knew some of the Lese would embrace the idea of unity and she was grateful for them and hoped their sentiments would prove contagious. The feasting lasted for another hour and then the people grew tired and retreated to their huts. Queen Kanya armed the Efes with blankets and skins to guard against the cool night. She settled them in the meetinghouse where they would rest peacefully; then she retired to her quarters leaving Jabusa and Muzungu sitting side by side under a kombokombo tree.

"Are you happy, Muzungu?" he asked.

"Very happy," she said brushing a blushed cheek against her shoulder. "I never imagined myself this content, Jabusa."

"Then I will see to it that this happiness stays with you for a lifetime. My mother likes you."

"And I like her as well. She showed my people kindness. I appreciate that and I'm sure they do too."

They listened to the distant sounds of the night. The monkeys could be heard communicating and playing among themselves. Occasionally there was the croaking of a bullfrog and the sounds of the crickets though blatant, were also soothing.

"Who are you?"

The question came out of nowhere. Muzungu looked at Jabusa, who was resting his back against the tree bark and staring at the stars. She did not know what answer to give him because she did not know herself. Africans are very conscious and proud of their lineage and usually wear some kind of tribal markings to display their ancestry. Muzungu had nothing to wear. She did not wear the red-dyed circular tattoo on her left ankle like the other Efe did because she felt undeserving. There were no rites-of-passage marks like the female circumcisions or the scarred face. Not even her earlobes gave hint to what tribe she might belong. They contained one simple pierce per ear.

"Jabusa, I do not know who I am. I do not know where I come from or if I have children or a husband, mother or father. Does it matter?"

"It does not," he smiled at her, "Gimiko has told me your story and it is amazing that you cannot remember anything about your past."

"For a long time it bothered me that I did not know, but now since I have the Efe and especially since I have you it does not bother me. The only thing I wish is that I do not have children. I cannot bear the thought of having children somewhere and not being with them to watch them grow or give them hugs and kisses or not being able to tell them I love them. But, I will not think about what I can't change. You and I will start our own past and future."

"I think you must have been a queen or a princess in your other life."

"A queen or princess," she said with mock excitement, "You place me on a pedestal so high that even I cannot reach it."

"You deserve the highest pedestal there is."

"It is good then that I will become your wife. That makes us a perfect match."

"Yes, a perfect match."

Jabusa took her into his arms and kissed her tenderly as the forest creatures' orchestra chorused.

*   *   *

There were five days left before the wedding was to take place. Linus dialed the home number again and still got the answering machine. He was growing impatient. He had to get hold of Austin no later than today. He pushed the receiver button and dialed the office number.

"AFLAME Modeling Agency, This is Phy…"

"Phyllis!"

Immediately, Phyllis recognized the accent and knew it was Linus Snodgrass calling for Austin.

"Phyllis, this is Linus. Look, I hate to keep bothering you but is Mr. Kawissopie back yet?"

"I'm sorry, Mr. Snodgrass he is not in the office."

"I simply have to get hold of him. Can't you do something to put me in touch with him? This is very important."

"Mr. Snodgrass, I would love to help you, but you have to give me more information. I have strict instructions not to interrupt Mr. Kawissopie when he is away on business unless it is an emergency."

"So, he is out of town, huh?"

Phyllis exhaled wearily. "If it would help you to know, yes, sir, he is out of town on business."

"I may be taking a long shot here, but can I ask you something?"

"Yes?"

"Was Mr. Kawissopie ever married to a woman named Maoma Kawissopie?"

The question knocked the breath out of Phyllis. She held the phone tightly. "Y-Y-Y-Yes he was but, Mr. Snodgrass, she was killed in a plane crash some years ago."

"This Maoma, is she about 5 feet 8 inches tall, dark complexion, long hair, large eyes, high cheekbones—a splendid looking woman?"

He was saying is she, as in present tense. Could he mean that she is still alive? Phyllis thought. Impossible. This had to be a joke of some sort. Then she thought about the man's insistent calls. He had called regularly for the past several days. And the urgency in his voice made him sound so convincing. Her heart was beating so fast she had to rest her free hand on her chest to calm it. "Yes, that sounds like her. What are you getting at, Mr. Snodgrass?"

"She is alive!"

"No-no, that can't be!"

"Yes, Phyllis, she is alive and well and living in the Ituri rain forest with a group of African Pygmies about 50 miles from where I sit right now!"

"No, you're mistaken."

"Listen, I have pictures of her. I can fax them to you. Let me have your number and I'll send them right along."

Phyllis gave him the number and waited impatiently by the machine for them to come through.

She looked at the pictures and had to admit that the woman in them had an uncanny resemblance to Maoma.

"Oh my God! I don't believe it." Phyllis rested her head on her desk.

"I think you better believe it, sweetheart, 'cause it's true. Maoma Kawissopie is alive. It's important that you get in touch with Mr. Kawissopie and give him my number."

"O.K. I-I-I'll do it right now. Just stay near the phone. I'm sure he'll be calling soon."

Phyllis hung up the phone and stared into space. Hardin Ferguson walked by and noticed her frightened state. "Phyllis, you all right? You look like you just seen a ghost."

"No, Hardin, I haven't seen a ghost but I think I just talked to someone who has."

*   *   *

"Hello?"

"Candace, this is Phyllis."

"Hi, Phil. How ya doing?" Candace asked.

"May I speak to Austin please?"

"Is everything all right? You sound weird, girl."

"Candace, please put Austin on."

"Oh, O.K."

Candace covered the phone with her hand but Phyllis could hear the muffled words enough to make them out.

"Austin, it's Phyllis on the phone and she doesn't sound too good. I think something is wrong."

Austin took the phone from Candace. "Phyllis, is anything wrong?" Terrible images of his grandmother lying on her deathbed flashed through his mind. Now he wished he'd called more regularly than the once-a-month phone calls.

"Austin, I'm not sure. I just don't know what to make of it all," said a still confused Phyllis. "This man calls several days ago and says his name is Linus Snodgrass and that he must speak to you. He has this thick English accent. At first I thought he was somebody trying to sell something?you know, a solicitor. He would never tell me what it was he wanted with you although I asked each time. I know how you feel about interruptions on your business trips so that's why I didn't?"

"Phyllis, stop babbling and please tell me what is wrong!" he demanded.

"Austin, this man says Maoma is still alive."

There was a deadening silence. Phyllis wasn't sure if Austin was still on the phone.

"Austin?"

Austin laughed unbelievably. "What did you say?"

"This man says that Maoma is alive and well and that she lives only 50 miles from him. He says that she is living with a group of African Pygmies in the Ituri rain forest."

He kept laughing. "That's impossible."

"When he said the part about the African Pygmies, well, I just knew it was a hoax because I always thought African Pygmies were fictitious, but he faxed me a picture with a woman who looks just like Maoma standing with little four-feet-tall people."

"He faxed you a picture?"

"Yes. And he left a number for you to call him back."

"Before I call him back I want to see the picture. It may be a hoax. You remember the reward money I put up. This man maybe a gold-digger. Let me get a fax number from front desk. I'll call you right back."

"Austin, what's going on?" Candace seemed frightened to death as she stared at Austin.

He didn't know how to tell her that Maoma might still be alive. He was just as frightened as she looked. If there ever was a question if he was over Maoma and didn't love her, there wasn't anymore. Deep down inside he knew that if Maoma was alive and there was a choice between her and Candace his heart would lead him to Maoma. For that reason he wished the man was wrong.

"Austin, is Momma Lena all right?"

"Yes, she is fine." Austin ran his hand through her hair and kissed her forehead. "Stay here, Candace. I need to go downstairs for a minute."

"But Austin," she trailed after him as he stepped out of the door.

"Candace, please do as I say."

The clarity of the picture wasn't perfect since it had been faxed twice, but the likeness of the woman was very similar to Maoma's. Austin's index finger traced the outline of Maoma's image. His heart skipped a beat as he remembered the first time he met her. It was in Central Park and she was wearing braids in her hair then. He had loved her from day one. The time they shared together was blissful. It had taken him over five years to get her out of his system and get his life back together; now within a matter of minutes she was back in it. Then there was Candace. She was probably upstairs in their hotel suite going crazy with worry. He had insisted she come on the trip with him to Texas. His trip to Texas was to discuss expanding AFLAME with another smaller ethnic modeling agency there. She didn't really want to come but preferred to stay back in New York and do a TV commercial for Bali underwear. She came because he wanted her to. It would have been so much easier if he had allowed her to stay. He wouldn't have to explain to her what was going on until he had checked everything out. If she hadn't come and this episode turned out to be false, she would never have to know about it. There was no way he could not tell her about Maoma now. Austin dialed Linus Snodgrass' number.

"Hello?"

"Linus Snodgrass?'

"Yes, this is him."

"Austin Kawissopie here. My secretary said you may have some information about my wife?"

"Yes, I do, but first does the reward money still stand?"

"If this woman turns out to be my wife, yes."

"I believe she is the woman you've been looking for, sir."

"Is she being held against her will?"

"No, sir, and I assure you she is fine. Not one hair on her head has been harmed. As a matter of fact she has been well taken care of."

"I don't understand. Why didn't she try to contact me?"

"Out of all due respect, I don't think she could."

"What?"

"Amnesia, sir. When her plane crashed it appears that she had trauma so severe she forgot all she knew of her past. She was the only survivor. They call her Muzungu, that means?"

"I know what it means. I am African and fluent in Swahili."

(Pause)

"This story is too wild to believe."

"I know it sounds like something in the movies, but I'm afraid it's not. She's up there with those people. The first time I laid eyes on her I knew she didn't belong. A cut above, if you know what I mean," he chuckled. "Listen, you gotta get her as quick as possible, Mr. Kawissopie. She's getting married to an African Chief in four days."

*   *   *

When Austin walked through the door he looked like he'd been to hell and back. Candace rushed to him and embraced him. "Austin, honey, what is it?"

Austin flopped down in one of the matching wingback chairs and buried his face in his hands. Candace walked behind the chair and began massaging his shoulders.

"Talk to me, baby, she pleaded.

Austin sat straight up. He grabbed her hands and brought her around to face him. He held her hands tightly. "I need to make a trip to Africa for a few days."

"What! Africa! Why, Austin?'

"Candace, I can't say right now because I'm not sure myself. I just need you to trust me on this."

"But?"

"I know," he placed his finger across her lips. "Hush. I know you're full of questions but I can't give you the answers right now because I don't know them. I'm putting you on a plane back to New York."

"What about you? Aren't you coming?"

"Not right away, but I'll meet you back there in a week or so."

"A week?" she sounded disappointed. "Austin you're scaring me. I've never seen you like this before. What's going on?"

Austin could not tell her, not now, not here away from all her familiar comforts and family. He fixed his eyes on the floor and shook his head.

"Is it your family?"

If he said yes he would be telling the truth; after all, Maoma was family and maybe, just maybe she'd let it go at that for the time being. "Yes, Candace, it is my family. There is a crisis back home. I'm needed there."

"You can tell me," she pleaded. "I'm practically your wife; technically I will be in a month."

Austin wondered if she would become his wife. An hour ago he wanted nothing more. Now, he was full of so many unexplained emotions. If Maoma was still living, that meant he was still married. He silently prayed that he would wake up from this horrific nightmare and pick his life up where it had stopped an hour ago. But Austin would not wake up from this nightmare anytime soon.

*　　　*　　　*

Austin's flight was schedule to reach London around midnight New York time. He promised Candace that he would give her a call then to see how she was holding out. Candace was so occupied with thoughts that she didn't hear the flight attendant ask her if she wanted anything to eat. Candace looked into the face of a pretty redhead with emerald eyes. She knew the girl could tell that she had been crying.

"Will you be eating this afternoon?" she asked again.

"No, thank you. I'm not hungry."

"Perhaps a soda then?"

Candace cut her eyes sharply at the girl. All she wanted was to be left alone. "I don't need anything. Thanks, anyway."

Candace reclined back in her seat and watched the clouds roll by.

*　　　*　　　*

Austin gave the salesman the American Express gold card and watched him rake it through the scanner. He was grateful he'd found a store in London so close to the airport that had the things he needed. The total came to $575.00. The salesman handed the card back to

Austin and began wrapping the clothes he had just purchased. The pair of jeans, khakis and hiking boots would come in handy in the thick African brush. He chose four short-sleeved, button-down camp shirts to wear with the pants. He had sent the clothes he took to Texas back with Candace. He knew they would be useless where he was going.

His mind quickly reverted back to Maoma. If the woman was Maoma, he'd get her checked into a hospital to be evaluated. If she turned out not to be her, he would catch the next plane out of there. He looked at his watch. He had two hours before his flight left. He had forgotten all about the phone call he'd promised Candace several hours ago. He gathered the bags and headed outside to the street where the taxi was waiting to take him back to the airport.

*   *   *

Back in New York, after a night of waiting for Austin to call, Candace lay sleeping on the couch underneath the African blanket with the telephone gripped tightly in her hand.

36

Past versus Present

Osun smacked his wife's behind as she placed a large bowl of eggs and elephant steaks in front of him.

"Ooo," she giggled like an enchanted girl and tried unsuccessfully to dodge the second swipe. "Osun, you came home in a feisty mood last night and it has carried over to this morning. I must warn you that I like it, and if you keep it up I will not let you out to earn a day's pay."

Osun laughed naughtily. "Soon I will not have to work so hard and you will have me all to yourself."

"Wishful thinking. The day I have you to myself is the day you will be too old to satisfy me any longer," she teased.

"I have a surprise in store for you. Soon we will live like kings and queens."

"I have no complaints. We are doing much better than a lot of others."

"But we will do even better. You will not have to fetch water from the well, or work in the gardens. You will rest all day and visit with your grandchildren."

"Ha," she laughed, "you talk foolish, old man. I think the sun has finally gotten to your brains."

Osun looked at his wife more seriously now. "Don't laugh, my dear wife; you will be queen."

"Osun! Osun! Come out," said a voice just outside the hut. Osun pushed himself up from the table and went outside to investigate. The village drunk had come to deliver a message.

"What do you want?" Osun looked at the man as if he were no more than a bug and unworthy of acknowledgment at all. The man was in a drunken state but not so drunk that he would not show reverence to Osun. He half bowed before speaking.

"I'm sorry to bother you, but I have a message from Linus."

The name raised excitement and drew Osun out of his hut. He looked around to make sure no one was watching.

"Linus says he wanted you to know that everything is going well."

Osun laughed and patted the messenger on the back. "Wait here," he told the man, then disappeared into the hut. He came back out carrying a half-pint of whiskey. "Here, take this."

The man was baffled. Never in the history of Osun had he ever given anyone anything other than grief and a hard time.

"Tell no one about the message and I'll see to it that you get a full bottle of whiskey next time."

"Thank you, Osun." The man unscrewed the cap and took a quick drink. "Ahh," he licked his lips at the droplets of whiskey that had escaped his mouth. "I won't, Osun. I won't tell a soul."

*   *   *

It had been exactly 72 hours since Candace got back from Texas. She had not stepped foot outside the apartment in that time but stayed near the phone, waiting for Austin to call. She couldn't understand why she had not heard from him yet. It was totally out of character for him not to keep a promise. She hoped everything was all right. She had called the National Air Traffic Association and there were no reports of a downed plane anywhere. She fed herself excuse after excuse for his not calling—inaccessible telephones, jet lag, his worrying about his family. Truth was, she could not convince herself to believe any of them. She would have found a way to call. Nothing could keep her from it. By that afternoon, Candace was on nerves' end. She found Austin's little black book with the telephone numbers of his family. Her hands shook as she dialed his parents' number.

"Hello?"

"Hello, Mrs. Kawissopie?"

"Yes?"

"This is Candace."

Austin's mom was excited to hear from her. She started speaking Swahili to Momma Lena who was standing nearby. Candace heard Momma Lena rambling off in the background.

"Hello, Candace! What a surprise! Momma Lena says hello. She asked how you are doing?"

"Tell her I am fine and I hope she is."

"Oh, yes, my dear, she is doing well. It is so good to hear your voice. So tell me, How is my son? Is he nearby?"

Candace was shocked at the question. Her words jumbled together and rushed out at once. "What—but—I—I—thought he was there."

Quietness.

"What are you saying, Candace? You don't know where Austin is?"

"He said there was a crisis back home and he had to make a trip there. I have not heard from him in three days. That's why I'm calling!" Candace was eager to get to the bottom of the mystery. Her excitement evoked tears and her voice began to tremble uncontrollably. "He's not there?"

"No, my darling, he is not here."

"Well, where is he?"

"Candace, calm down now. I don't know where he is, but I am sure there is a logical explanation behind his whereabouts." Mrs. Kawissopie tried to sound reassuring.

"What explanation can be logical enough for his fiancée not to know where he is? He lied to me. He said there was a crisis back home and he had to get there. He left three days ago, Mrs. Kawissopie. Are you sure he hasn't been there?" Candace was hysterical now.

"He has not."

"Well, ask Momma Lena if she knows anything!"

"Baby, I assure you she knows nothing. Neither does Mr. Kawissopie, and I doubt if his brother knows anything either."

"But there's a chance he does?" she asked hopefully about his brother's knowledge.

"Candace, I did not say that."

"Ask him for me! Please, Mrs. Kawissopie, ask him if he knows where Austin is!"

"All right dear, I'll give him a call and then call you right back." Mrs. Kawissopie hung up the telephone.

"What is happening, daughter?" asked Momma Lena.

"Candace is trying to locate Austin. It seems that he caught a plane to come here three days ago, but as you know he is not here."

"It is not like Austin to plan a trip home without letting us know beforehand," said Momma Lena.

"Nor is it like him to make fabrications. Austin has always been a truthful person."

"Perhaps he has some wild oats he needs to sow before getting married next month," Momma Lena chuckled.

Mrs. Kawissopie shook her head to disagree. "That is still not like my Austin." She paused after the statement and thought about the situation. "No, Momma Lena, something is wrong."

Candace was a basket case. She had to get out of the apartment, go somewhere, and talk to someone who might know what was going on.

She thought Phyllis might know. She dialed the office then slammed the phone down after realizing it was Saturday and no one was there. She looked up her home number and dialed it. Phyllis's answering machine picked up. Candace left a brief message for her to call. She took a long needed shower, changed into a fresh pair of jeans and tee shirt. She brushed her hair back into a ponytail, grabbed her pocketbook and car keys and headed to her parents' house. This was her last resort. She didn't want them, of all people, to know that there was trouble concerning Austin, but she needed a shoulder to cry on. And since Russell was no longer available, her parents were the next best thing.

*   *   *

Austin tucked the duffel bag between his feet and steadied himself as the old boat traveled up the Ituri River. It seemed to move at a snail's pace. Austin guessed it was 20 or more years old but believed it still had some zip left in it. The skipper began singing an unfamiliar song in thick Swahili dialect after trying unsuccessfully to strike up a conversation with him. Austin wasn't ignoring the man, but his mind was on getting to the town where Linus Snodgrass lived so he could take him to the village. In a few more hours the sun would set and he knew African customs well enough to know that with some tribes the setting of the sun constituted the mark of another day. Austin was racing against time and he knew if he got there after the ceremony, he could not rightfully demand his wife back. He didn't know much about the Efe or Lese people. He didn't know if they were vicious tribesmen or not, but he was prepared to fight for Maoma if he needed to.

"Can't you go any faster?" asked Austin anxiously.

The man pulled out an oversized handkerchief and began wiping the boat's steering wheel affectionately. "This is as fast as we go," he said.

"I know this boat can go faster," argued Austin.

"I didn't say she can't go any faster. This is as fast as I will allow her to go. She is my only source of income and I will not burn her out. Do you know how much it would cost for me to have her fixed if she should break down?"

"No."

"A lot of money, my friend."

Austin didn't consider the man a friend. He wasn't helping him any by slow-poking around.

"Just to replace the motor would cost me more than what I make in a year. So you see, I can't take the chance of tearing her up by going too fast."

"How much do you make in a year's time?" asked Austin.

The man looked at Austin skeptically. "Why you want to know?"

"Just asked, that's all."

The man looked at the fancy watch on Austin's wrist and the top-dollar-hiking boots he had on. This was not an average Joe Blow. He knew Austin had money. He decided to take his chances and tell him his annual income; after all, what could it hurt? "I make $500 a year and that is not much when you have a wife and six kids to feed at home."

"If you can get me to the town before the sun sets, I'll give you $500."

"The man looked Austin up and down before laughing."

Austin pulled five $100 bills out of his pocket and flashed them before the man.

"You are not joking are you?" The man stood open-eyed while anticipating a reply.

"No, I'm not."

*   *   *

The trip had taken three hours by boat; now Austin was standing face to face with Linus Snodgrass. He looked nothing like his name.

Austin expected him to be a short, dumpy, baldheaded, eyeglass-wearing man. But Linus was just the opposite of his expectations. The two men shook hands.

"How was your trip, Mr. Kawissopie?"

"Listen, let's cut through the bull. I want to know where my wife is?"

"Hold your horses. She's not going anywhere. Besides, before I take you up there I need to know a few things, like if you have the money or not."

"Are you crazy? Do you actually think I carry that kind of money around on me?"

"I don't think you're crazy, Mr. Kawissopie, but I don't want you to think that I'm stupid either. Here." He pushed a piece of poorly type-written paper in front of him. Austin sat his duffel bag down and read it. It read: I Austin Kawissopie promised to pay Linus A. Snodgrass the sum of $200,000.00 for the information leading to the safe return of my wife; Maoma Kawissopie.

Austin knew then that the man was in it all for himself. He cared nothing about Maoma's well being. Austin signed the paper and handed it back to Linus. Linus folded the piece of paper and put it in his shirt pocket.

"Let's go Linus."

Linus led him to the jeep. Austin threw his bag in the back and jumped in on the passenger's side. They traveled the only road that would take them to the Lese village. The jeep rocked and jarred as it rode over the rough terrain.

"I can see why you would go through so much trouble to get your wife back. She's a looker, she is. Nothing like those savages she lives with. And you know what? The Lese, that clan she's getting ready to marry into, ain't much better. Although, hear them tell it, they think they some kind of blue-blooded royalty. Nothing but a bunch of bloody apes, the lot of them." No sooner were the words out than he realize what he'd said. "Sorry, bloke. I didn't mean you."

"No need to apologize, Linus, if those are your true sentiments about Africans. I'd much rather know up front who my enemies are."

"Hey, look, I got nothing against you or them. You just really have to see them to know what I'm talking about. No humans should live the way they do. Mud houses, no running water except that well in the middle of the village; everybody eating out of the same bowl using their hands..."

"Communal bowls," Austin corrected him.

"Yeah, well, whatever. And since the Lese look down their noses on the Efe, Lord only knows how they live."

"Seeing that they're apes instead of humans, their lifestyles should be fitting, don't you think, Linus?"

Linus glanced at Austin. He had stuck his foot in his mouth. He wished he could take back what he'd said. He could not afford to upset the man who was going to get him out of the forest and into a life of luxury.

*   *   *

Candace knocked on the door. She could have used the key that Sable insisted on her keeping but she thought it would be in good judgment to knock and wait to be invited in. After all, she didn't live here any-more. Jonah opened the door. His eyes lit up when he saw Candace standing before him.

"Baby girl!" he said, then swept her in his arms and twirled her around. "We thought you were in Texas. When did you get back?"

"Just got back, Daddy." She managed a smile.

Sable heard the commotion and came running into the foyer.

"Is that my baby?' she said. She held her arms opened as she approached her. "Give momma some sugar."

The warm welcome was more than she could bear. The sweet words coming from her parents were the nicest words she'd heard in four days.

She wasn't sure about what was going on with Austin. Wasn't sure about their future. There was a time when she knew he loved her and she felt beyond privilege. Now, she didn't know what his feelings were for her. But one thing she was sure of—she knew the two people standing before her would always love her. She knew they would always be there for her through thick and thin. She felt like a five-year-old child who had just skinned her knees and was trying to find comfort from the one place she knew she could. She fell into her mother's arms and released her tears and sobs.

"Momma!" she cried.

"Baby, what's wrong?"

Jonah rubbed his only daughter's back. A sixth sense told him it was a lovers' spat between her and Austin, but little did he know it was far more than that.

Sable brought a glass of ice tea to Candace and took a seat on the sofa next to her. Jonah sat in an armchair opposite them. Candace wiped her tears and blew her nose before taking a swallow.

"Thanks, Mom."

Sable patted her knee.

"I don't know what I would have done without the two of you to turn to."

"What's going on, Candace?" Jonah took off his glasses and laid them on the end table beside him.

"It's Austin," she said and started crying again.

"You two had a fight, huh? Honey, that's to be expected. You're nervous about the wedding, that's all," said Jonah.

"That's right. I think they call it cold feet." Sable winked at Jonah.

"We didn't have a fight."

"No fight? It's obvious something happened. Look at you. I've never seen you like this before. You look like you haven't eaten or slept in days." Then Sable remembered the time back in high school when Julius broke up with her. She had looked the same way then. Sable hoped this would not be a repeat of the break-up then. She honestly didn't think Candace could handle it without going through a nervous breakdown.

"Austin's is in Africa, Momma. He told me something bad had happened with his family and he had to get to them. I caught a plane home and he left for Africa from Houston. He wouldn't go into details with me about what was wrong. He was supposed to call me at midnight Wednesday but he didn't. I called his family in Dar es Salaam. He was not there and they had not heard from him in weeks. I haven't heard from him yet."

"But I thought you said you just got back in town?" questioned Jonah.

"Daddy, I lied. I thought I could get through the evening without mentioning Austin but when Momma came around the corner talking all that baby talk, I realized that's what I am, a big baby. I couldn't keep the secret to myself any longer. I had to tell someone."

"So you been back all this time and you wouldn't let us know?"

Candace nodded.

"Honey, what have you been doing all this time, sitting by the phone waiting for him to call?"

Candace was ashamed and hung her head without answering.

"I knew it, Aunt Vi knew it, even daddy knew something was fishy about Austin." Sable got up from the sofa and began pacing the floor.

"Now wait a minute, Sable," said Jonah. "You don't know what's going on with the man yet. Stop judging him before you hear both sides of the story."

"I have heard enough to base my opinions, Jonah. A man who's not truthful with the woman he's going to marry in a month can't be trusted. That's the bottom line."

"Well, let's just wait until we know the whole story. When he comes back, he'll enlighten us."

Sable sucked her teeth and rolled her eyes toward the ceiling. "If he comes back!"

"Oh, no, you think he might not come back?" asked Candace, frightfully.

"See what you did, Sable. You done gone and got the girl all worked up again. Sure, he's coming back, baby girl."

"You think so, Daddy?"

"Yeah, baby. He loves you. A fool can see that. You know the man ain't gon' give up his business, house, car and thangs. He'll be back."

Jonah's words were soothing until Sable began talking again.

"Lord, I just feel like falling down crying when I think about how Russell used to love you."

"Momma, please. Don't bring Russell into this."

"Sable!" warned Jonah.

"It's the truth, and y'all know it. Now that boy truly loved you, Candace. He used to come over here many times just to sit and talk with me about you. He never gave up on you. I think you still have a chance with him. He's not married yet, you know."

"That's it!" Candace jumped from the couch and grabbed her purse.

"Where you going?" asked Sable.

"Home!"

"Wait a minute." Sable rushed to her side and threw her arms around Candace, "I'm sorry. You know I didn't mean to say anything to hurt you. You can't go home to that lonely apartment. Stay here with us. At least for tonight. I won't mention Russell again and we can talk about anything under the sun that you want to."

"Your mother's right, Candace. I don't think it's good for you to be alone right now. Your room upstairs is ready."

"Your Daddy just rented 'The Nutty Professor'—you know how he loves Eddie Murphy—and we can pop some popcorn."

"I didn't bring a change of clothes."

"Oh, honey, that's ridiculous. You know I have plenty of things you can wear."

"I don't know," Candace said reluctantly.

"If you're worrying about missing Austin's phone call, don't. He'll know you're here and he has the number."

"Well, I guess."

*   *   *

The sun had just set when Austin and Linus reached the Lese village. Linus took a powerful flashlight from under the driver's seat. He told Austin to wait on the edge in the brush and to keep out of sight while he went in to search for Osun.

"The Lese people are cautious of strangers and don't readily take to them," said Linus, wishing he knew the way to the Efe village himself so he could bypass Osun altogether and keep the money for himself. Plus he didn't want the full amount of the reward disclosed to Osun.

Fifteen minutes later Linus came back with Osun following close behind.

"Mr. Kawissopie, this is Osun. He is the man who will get you your wife back."

"What did you say to him?" asked Osun. "You know my tongue is Swahili."

Austin interrupted; he didn't feel right letting this white man he didn't trust negotiate his wife's safety.

"He said you will be getting my wife."

"So you speak Swahili?"

"Yes."

"It is good that you do." Osun looked at Linus in a threatening way. He wore only a loincloth made of animal skin and thin sandals on his feet. A pouch hung over his left shoulder and a bow over his right. He pulled out a small jar of black paint and began painting his exposed skin.

Austin looked Osun up and down. "What are you doing?" he asked skeptically.

"They must not see me coming," he answered.

"Must not see you coming? What do you plan to do?" Austin asked, growing more anxious by the minute.

Osun didn't answer but worked furiously with the paint.

"Mr. Kawissopie, he will get your wife. He knows what he is doing. We don't trust the Efe people. If they know what's going on, they will never let us take her."

"But I thought you said they were taking good care of her."

"Look, Mr. Kawissopie, I didn't want to upset you over the phone. Truth is, these Efes are nothing more than savages."

"Speak Swahili!" demanded Osun.

"I am telling him that the Efe cannot be trusted," said Linus.

Osun pulled a small blowgun from the pouch and slid a tranquilizer dart into one end.

"What is that?" asked Austin frantically.

"It won't hurt her, just make her sleep for a while."

"No! I don't want you using that on her and I don't know if I want you sneaking in there taking her like that. I feel that if we go in humbly and explain to them the situation we can negotiate her release peacefully."

"There is no negotiating with the Efe," Osun lied.

Austin held up both hands and shook his head profusely. "No-no. What if she is not my wife? Isn't there a way I can see if she is Maoma before you just snatch her?"

"We are risking our lives going in there, you know. Money is not everything. It can't give us back our lives if we are caught and the Efe decide to kill us," said Linus, "We can walk away easily, Mr. Kawissopie. Now what will it be? Get your wife or leave her?"

Austin's heart beat rapidly and he looked from Linus to Osun, who had grown still and indifferent. They seemed prepared to call the whole thing off if he gave them the word. In his heart he wanted their help and knew he needed it. He could not leave without knowing who the woman was. "Yes," he said assuredly, "let's get her."

"All right then," Osun said as he tucked the blowgun back into the pouch. "The automobile will take us to where the road ends. That's about half the way; the other half we will have to walk."

It took 10 minutes to drive to the end of the road and another 30 to walk to the Efe village. The three men sat in the thicket watching the Efe sit around the campfire eating their supper. Austin watched them as they passed the bowls around. He saw the tall women sitting amidst the shorter people. She laughed as one of the men told jokes. Her laughter was familiar, and so was her silhouette against the light of the fire.

"The tall one to the left, is she your wife?" asked Osun.

Austin's mouth was cotton dry as he stared, unbelievingly, at the woman. This had to be a dream he kept telling himself. Here he was in the African rain forest stalking a woman believed to be his long departed wife. The whole notion was absurd. All those years of wanting, wishing and praying to wake up from the nightmare of living without Maoma seemed to be coming true. If he could only touch her he could be sure. His eyes misted over and the lump in his throat grew larger. "It looks like her," he whispered.

"Then we will wait until things settle down, or until she strays away from the crowd," said Osun.

An hour later some of the Efe men drifted into their huts and a few, including Suko, scattered away from the campfire to attend to personal needs. The women gathered the pots and bowls. They carried them to the edge of the circular clearing and stacked them neatly on the ground next to the water barrel.

"Tomorrow you will be the wife of Jabusa," said Tifu.

"This time tomorrow, Jabusa will have you in his strong arms making you feel wonderful things. We will be able to hear your moans all the way here," Suko's wife teased. The women laughed.

"I am sorry to disappoint you all, but since I will be queen I shall act in a dignified manner. You will not get a whimper out of me."

"We heard about Jabusa's big ego; we hear the louder you moan the more gifts he gives," said one of the women.

"Then perhaps you better scream, Muzungu. You know we can use some more chickens and goats," said Tifu.

Loud laughter.

"We will miss you terribly," said another woman,

"No, you won't," said Muzungu. "You are welcome to come see me as often as you like, and I will visit you regularly."

Tifu began washing the pots and bowls. Muzungu took them from her.

"No, Tifu, let me do that. This is my last night with you. You all go to your huts and get some rest. We have a big day tomorrow."

"You are the one who should be getting her rest; we will clean the pots,"

Tifu tried to retrieve the pot but Muzungu turned swiftly so she could not get it. The women began laughing again and Muzungu and Tifu made a little game out of it.

"I am too nervous to sleep. I need to do something to calm my nerves."

"If you wish," said Tifu. She and the other women kissed Muzungu on the cheeks and they each went into their huts.

"In five minutes we will make our move. That will give the others time to settle down," said Osun. "When I blow the dart into her flesh it will feel like an insect bite. She will think nothing of it. Within two minutes she will fall asleep. That's when we must all move quickly. You follow me and we will get her. Do you all understand?" asked Osun.

Linus and Austin nodded their heads. He moved with the stealth of a leopard stalking prey. He stepped through thicket without making a sound. Linus was amazed at how lithe he was and wondered if all Africans had the same ability. Osun crept closer and closer to Muzungu. She was unsuspecting and continued to wash the pots. Osun was less than 20 feet away from her now. He moved slow and smooth in stop-go patterns, blending in with the night. Just as she finished the last pot and turned to carry them back to the campfire, Osun blew the dart through the gun. It hit her in the side of her neck. She dropped the pots and rubbed her hand over the stung spot. She pulled out the dart and looked at it inquisitively, then looked up at the strange, black figure coming toward her. Fear gripped its icy fingers around her heart and she tried to scream but nothing came out. She felt herself growing dizzy and groggy. Everything around her began to twirl. She stumbled toward the nearest hut in search of refuge from the mysterious creature. She became paralyzed and fell to the ground. She stared into the painted black face that hovered over her, and then two more faces appeared. One belonged to the white man she had seen at Chief Njau's funeral and the other one—the other one was crying and it was speaking, speaking to her in the most loving and affectionate way. It was the most beautiful face she thought she had ever seen. It looked like the face of the man in her dreams, the man named Austin. Then everything went blank.

"Hurry!" said Osun as the men tussled over Muzungu.

"No! I will carry her. She is my wife." Austin lifted Muzungu carefully into his arms and began to follow Osun and Linus.

Then the three men heard angry shouts and yells followed by the sound of running feet. "What are you doing?" yelled Suko. "What are you doing with Muzungu. Put her down! Put her down now!"

Osun, Linus and Austin froze in their tracks. They saw the short man's angry look. He bent down and picked up a stone then aimed it at them. Linus smirked at Suko holding the useless stone. He pulled a hidden gun from inside his shirt but, before he could aim it, Suko threw the stone at Linus. The stone struck Linus' wrist causing him to drop the gun. He wrenched in pain as he stared at Suko in disbelief.

The village of Efe came rushing out of their huts. They surrounded the three men.

"What's going on here?" shouted Gimiko. He carried a machete in his hand while the other Efe men were armed with bows, arrows, knives and spears. They all had their weapons raised and aimed at the intruders. Gimiko looked at Osun. He walked over to him and wiped some of the paint off of his face.

"It is Osun!" said Tifu.

"What are you doing here? And why does this man hold Muzungu?"

"This man is Muzungu's husband," said Osun. "He has come to claim her."

Gimiko looked at Austin suspiciously.

"It is true. I am her husband. She was missing in a plane crash about six years ago. I thought she was dead until this man," he nodded toward Linus, "told me about her."

"Put her down!" said Gimiko angrily.

"No, you don't understand. She is my wife. I have come to claim her. I am her husband," Austin said frenetically.

"Put her down!" Gimiko said, more demanding this time. The other Efe men aimed their weapons at Austin. He eased her on the ground but stayed crouched down beside her. Tifu dashed to her side and began attending her. She looked at Austin curiously. She remembered the dreams Muzungu use to tell her about. "What is your name?" she asked him calmly.

"My name is Austin. Austin Kawissopie."

"Then you are the man Muzungu has been dreaming about."

"What?" asked Austin.

"Muzungu has seen your face in her dreams. You are a kind man." Tifu looked over her shoulder at Gimiko. "He is not to be feared; he has a good heart."

The men kept their weapons aimed at them. Gimiko ordered two of his men to go to the Lese village to get Jabusa.

"No!" protested Osun. "You must not bother Jabusa. Can't we settle this ourselves?"

Gimiko could detect that Osun had betrayed Jabusa and was now fearful of his wrath. He never imagined that fate would allow them retribution on Osun. Gimiko enjoyed watching him squirm and now he would give his villagers a chance to reap some revenge. "And how do you propose we do that, Osun?"

"It is quite simple. This man is her true husband. Let him take her. He has come a very long distance to get back what is rightfully his. His faithfulness and diligence to find her after all these years proves his love. Surely you will not come between love, will you, Gimiko?"

"What about Jabusa?" he asked, observing Osun closely. He knew he was not loyal to Jabusa and now he would prove it. "He loves her too."

"Yes, he does, but right is right and…and besides, Jabusa will not make a suitable husband for Muzungu. After a few years he will take other wives, younger wives, and forget all about her. She is better off without him."

"Osun, you are a sorry excuse for a chief advisor. You are Jabusa's worse enemy." He looked down at Muzungu. "What did you do to her?"

"She is not hurt, I swear. It is just a tranquilizer to make her sleep, that's all."

Gimiko nodded at the two men he'd designated to fetch Jabusa. They dashed through the brush and followed the moonlit path to the Lese village.

*   *   *

A loud knock woke Jabusa. He met one of the young Lese warriors at the door.

"What is it that is so important to get me out of my sleep?"

"Chief, these two Efe men say it is most urgent that you come back to their village with them. They say Muzungu is in danger."

Queen Kanya came out of the quarters. "What is it, my son?"

"Muzungu. They say she is in danger." Jabusa dashed back inside and came out with his arsenal strapped around his back, waist and shoulder. He ran to the stable and got three mules, one for himself and two more for the Efe men. They rode out of the village leaving a cloud of dust behind them.

Jabusa and the two Efe men rode into the village. Jabusa saw Linus and Osun sitting on the ground with their hands tied behind their backs. While riding back to the village, the two men had given him as many details as they could. He knew that Osun and two other men, one white, had come into their camp and tried to steal Muzungu away. He was almost certain that the white man the Efe spoke of was Linus. He knew Osun and Linus had formed allegiance. He walked over to Osun and stood over him with one hand on the machete. Osun kept his eyes on the ground. "Chief Jabusa," he began to cry, "I meant you no harm. I was only looking out for your well being."

"How is taking the woman that I love from me looking out for my best interest, Osun?"

"Oh, sir, please don't be angry with me. Try to see things from my perspective. Your plans for unison would have ruined us. All the hard work your father put into making the Lese the most respected people of the whole Ituri forest would have been in vain. One of Chief Njau's last requests was that I keep a close eye on you and steer you in the paths that he had prepared for you. The spirit of Chief Njau will be tormented for eternity if you marry Muzungu."

Jabusa looked at Linus. "You would betray me too?"

"I assure you, Jabusa, I was only trying to help Muzungu. She has a husband. I mean, I would only want the same kind of consideration for myself if I were in her shoes."

"Did Muzungu ask for your help?"

"No, sir, but she has a family."

"Where is this man who claims to be her husband?"

"He is in my hut with Tifu and Muzungu," said Gimiko, while pointing Jabusa in the direction of the hut.

Jabusa entered the hut. He saw Austin sitting by her side holding her hand. Austin looked up at Jabusa as he entered. As a child he remembered his parents taking him to a Masai wedding. Jabusa's chiseled face, strong jaw line and long braids reminded him of the Masai warrior groom. He was quite handsome. He could see how Maoma would be attracted to him. Austin watched him watching Maoma. He wasn't sure of what he was supposed to do or say. He could tell that he was deeply agitated and he didn't want to make matters worse by speaking out of turn or saying something disrespectful to an African chief. But he would gladly fight for Maoma if it came down to that. Tifu caught his eyes and she placed a finger across her lips, meaning for him to stay quiet. Austin was grateful for this kind woman and he made a mental note before he and Maoma left to ask her if there was anything he could do for her or her people.

Tifu bowed her head to him. "She only sleeps, Jabusa. Osun shot her with a tranquilizer dart." Tifu dipped the cloth in the bowl of cool water and wiped Muzungu's forehead with it.

Jabusa shifted his eyes to Austin. "They say you are her husband?"

Austin got up from the dirt floor and extended his hand to Jabusa, but he did not shake it. "Yes, I am. She was taken from me six years ago in a disastrous plane crash. For years I thought she was dead…"

"Why did you wait so long to search for her?" Jabusa cut in.

"I always searched for her, not physically, but I searched. I put out APB's and notices, plus a $200,000 reward for her safe return. I contacted the air traffic controllers for these parts and all they could tell me was that the plane had mysteriously disappeared from the radar. They had no other information. They knew no more than I did."

Jabusa glared at Austin skeptically, "How am I to be sure that you are her husband?"

"But I am." In a desperate state, he searched his pockets for the picture of Maoma he always carried then; he realized he had given the picture to his therapist, Dr. Edwards, on their last visit. He jumped as he remembered the light colored, turtle-shaped birthmark on Maoma's behind. No one but a husband would know such intimate details. "On her backside, there is a birthmark. It is the same color as the white man," he pointed outside to where Linus and Osun sat bound. "She use to tell me the story of how her mother loved to eat turtle stew when she was pregnant with her. She said on the day she was born, her mother craved turtle stew but was unable to get it and that is why she was born with the birthmark of a turtle on her backside. Maoma herself loves turtle stew, too," he added.

Jabusa remembered the other day at the stream when she tried to capture the turtle. She had told him then how much she loved turtle stew, but Jabusa was not swayed easily. "That means nothing. Lots of people eat turtle."

A startled expression came across Tifu's face and she began nodding her head. She looked at Jabusa. "It is true, Chief Jabusa. Muzungu carries the birthmark that this man speaks of."

"Then he has seen it since he's been here!"

"No, Chief Jabusa. Muzungu's clothes have not been removed in his presence."

Jabusa felt threatened even more now. A thought came to his mind. What if Muzungu awakened and saw Austin standing before her? What if his face triggered lost memories and everything came back to her? Worst of all, what if she chose Austin over him. It had taken him so long to get her to trust and accept him? He didn't think she loved him yet but knew in time, with his love and generosity shown to her and her people, she would come to love him. He could not let this man come in here and take the one thing that made his life worth living. If Muzungu was removed from him he knew he would not have the desire to carry on as chief over the Lese people.

He was chief and he had the power to do what he wanted to Austin. He was in his territory making a valid threat. He had the right to protect the interests of his people, and keeping Muzungu was in their best interest whether they knew it or not. He could kill Austin and nothing would be done to him. Nor would the people of the forest criticize him for it. Even though no one had been executed in a while, execution was a way of life in the forest. An execution would probably strengthen the relationship between him and his people. They would respect him more, see that he possessed the strength and courage that his father the great Chief Njau had. Everybody loved a powerful and vengeful chief, he thought. He knew the things they were saying behind his back. This would prove them wrong. Osun would have to die, too. Now he knew it was the reward money that Osun and Linus were after. There was always something about Osun that discomforted him. Now his suspicions were confirmed. Treason was the worst crime a high official could commit. As much as it hurt, he knew it had to be done, because Osun could not be trusted anymore. The white man would have to die too but they would have to make his death appear to be an accident or a disappearance. It had to be in a way that so many questions would not be asked. To kill a white man without justifiable cause could create chaos for his own people. The courts would not consider plotting to take the fiancée of a tribal chief as justifiable cause for execution.

"Get on your feet!" yelled Jabusa to Austin.

Austin slowly got up, keeping his eyes on Maoma. Jabusa pointed his spear at him.

"I didn't come here to fight with you or your people, Chief Jabusa. All I want is what is mine."

"The years have taken away what was yours. Muzungu does not know you anymore. She is happy here; so let it be. I will give you a chance to walk away with your life, but if you are determined to take her then I will have to kill you."

"So you will kill me because I love the same woman as you do? You are a great chief. Do you not have the courage to fight me like a man in the eyes of your people and the Efe people?

Jabusa laughed. "Jabusa fears nothing. I will give you your fight in the presence of the Lese and the Efe."

Austin was relieved. This was what he had hoped for versus being speared through the back or thrown out without a chance for vindication.

Jabusa stormed out of the hut. He walked briskly over to Osun. He stood before him with the machete in one hand and the spear in the other. A large shinny knife dangled at his side. Jabusa always had suspicions about Osun's loyalty. He had heard tales from other Lese about the underhanded things he did behind Chief Njau's back. Jabusa remembered telling his father about the concerns of the people who had come to him in confidence, but Chief Njau had not been interested in what his son had to tell him. He felt that whatever it took for Osun to keep the people in line was good enough for him. Jabusa knew his father had been fond of Osun.

"Oh great chief," he cried, peeking at him and then quickly lowering his head. "I meant you no harm," he said again, "Can't you find it in your heart to forgive me? Please don't be angry with me. You would have done the same thing."

"I would have been loyal to my superior and gone to him and told him of this man who tries to steal his bride! That is what I would have done, Osun!" Jabusa's voice was thunderous, his muscle tensed, and it took all the power he had not to raise the machete and strike the life out of Osun. He looked at Linus, who was a bit more courageous than Osun. He did not look at the ground but kept eye contact with Jabusa.

"Jabusa…"

"Chief Jabusa to you!"

"Yes, yes, Chief Jabusa," he stuttered. "My concern was for this poor man, and when he came to me begging for my help I-I-I just couldn't turn my by back on him. I didn't even know you were engaged to Muzungu. If I had known that I wouldn't…"

"Silence!" he yelled.

Osun cut a murderous look at Linus. He was lying through his teeth. He knew all about the engagement between Jabusa and Muzungu. Osun thought, if he had the nerve to lie right before him then he was probably lying about the amount of the reward money too.

"So tell me that the $200,000 reward money had nothing to do with the two of you abducting Muzungu?"

"Two hundred thousand dollars?" asked Osun.

"Surely you know about the reward money, don't you?"

Osun looked at Linus. His eyes glimmered through the narrow slits his eyelids made. He was determined that he would kill Linus if it was the last thing he did.

37

Home

Sable had gotten up earlier than usual to make the pancakes from scratch. She set the stack of hot pancakes, bacon and eggs on the table.

"Mmm, sure smells good don't it, baby girl?" asked Jonah, trying to lure Candace into eating.

"I'll just have a cup of coffee."

"Candace, you have got to eat. You'll waste away to nothing." Sable put three generous size pancakes on a plate and set them in front of Candace. She added four strips of bacon and raked one third of the eggs she had cooked into her plate.

"Ma!"

"Ma, nothing. You just hush up and eat."

Candace exhaled and took a bite of the pancakes. "They are delicious," she said.

"Buttermilk," said Sable. She and Jonah knew Candace could not resist buttermilk pancakes. Candace dug in ravenously. Jonah winked a conspiratorial eye at Sable as they watched her eat.

"Not hungry, huh?" teased Jonah.

Sable lifted another pancake from the platter with the spatula and was about to put it on Candace's plate.

"No more," she managed to say with her mouth packed with food. "Guess I didn't realize how hungry I was."

"Well, it's just good to know you got something in that stomach of yours. When was the last time you ate?"

"This is my first real meal since I been back. I been eating junk food, you know."

"I'm making barbecue ribs for dinner today. Why don't you come and go to church with us, then come on back here for dinner?"

"No, ma, I got something to do today."

"What? I hope you won't be sitting by the phone waiting on Austin."

Candace got up and took her plate to the sink. She washed her dishes and placed them in the dish-rack. "I really do have something to do," she said as she left Jonah and Sable sitting at the table.

*   *   *

Phyllis Attucks rubbed her bottom and top lip together to distribute the lipstick evenly. She stepped back from the bathroom mirror to get a better view of herself. She smiled at her appearance before exiting the bathroom to retrieve her Bible and pocketbook. Before she could get out of her apartment, the phone rang. She thought it might be Sister Ballard, an elderly church member needing a ride to church. "Hello?"

"Phyllis, this is Candace."

Phyllis knew what Candace wanted. She sympathized with what she was going through and wished Austin had not left her in the dark but explained the whole thing to her. She had grown to love Candace just as she had Maoma. On the other hand, she also sympathized with Austin. She could imagine how difficult the choice would be for him if Maoma were truly alive. "Candace, what a surprise!" she tried to sound impressed. "I was just on my way to church. Can I call you back?" she asked, hoping that a later phone call would buy her time to get her thoughts together.

"Phyllis, this won't take long. Please."

"Candace, I really have to be going; you see, I usher at my church and I can't be late."

"Phyllis, please."

Phyllis sighed. There was no way she could not talk to her now. "O.K., but you'll have to make it quick."

"I feel that you know what's going on. Phyllis, I need to know. I'm going crazy here. I have not heard from Austin since he left. He said he had a family emergency but I called his parents and they know nothing nor have they heard from him. Do you know where he is? Please tell me."

"Candace, I don't want to have to tell you over the phone. Maybe we can meet somewhere."

"Is it that bad?"

"I'm on my way out. I guess I can stop by your place for a while."

"No, you don't have to do that. To be honest with you, I was on my way to your place. I'm only a couple blocks away."

By the time Candace got there, Phyllis had prepared some hot tea. The two of them sat at her kitchen table and Candace braced herself for what she knew would not be pleasant news.

"Candace, prior to my call to Austin, I had been receiving phone calls from a man named Linus Snodgrass. He called several times trying to get in touch with Austin. I wouldn't give him the number or relay the message to Austin because I thought it wasn't important. On Wednesday when he called again, he was desperate and very insistent. I figured if it was that important then he could tell me." Phyllis blew nervously. "Candace, what he told me nearly knocked me off my feet."

"What did he tell you, Phyllis?" she asked it softly, afraid to hear the answer.

"He told me that he thought Maoma was alive and living somewhere in Africa." Phyllis said nothing else but took a sip of her tea and watched Candace closely.

"Alive?" she laughed, "Why, that's impossible. Austin told me she'd been killed in a plane crash years ago. Austin believed him? You mean he actually jumped on a plane to check this bogus story out?"

"Candace, it may not be all that bogus."

Candace looked at Phyllis like she was an alien from outer space."

"What?"

"You see, Maoma's body was never found."

"Never found! What does that have to do with the price of tea in China, huh?"

"Candace, the plane went down in the African rain forest. Supposedly Maoma was found by a tribe of African Pygmies."

Candace began laughing so hard Phyllis though she was on the verge of hysteria. Phyllis jumped from her chair and put her hands on her shoulders to console her.

"Excuse me for laughing, Phyllis, but this story gets wilder by the minute. So you mean to tell me that Austin puts his wife on a plane to go do a shoot for some swimsuit conglomerate of sorts! The plane crashes in the rain forest! Maoma survives the crash! Probably crawls from the plane before it explodes! Manages not to get eaten by animals—because I hear there's a lot of vicious animals on the loose in the African rain forest, Phyllis! Then some African Pygmies just happen by, see her and decide to rescue her?" Candace stopped laughing and her face contorted to anger. She slammed the palm of her hand down on the table, "Give me a break, Phyllis! I mean that story is good enough for one of those daytime soaps."

"The man faxed a picture of Maoma," Phyllis said calmly.

"Where? I want to see it."

Phyllis got her briefcase from the kitchen counter and pulled the faxed photograph from it. She handed it to Candace. "She looks a lot like you."

Candace stared at the picture. If she didn't know any better she would have thought she was the person in the picture. It was clear that the woman did not belong there. She seemed as misplaced as a fish out of water. Candace could see the "fashion model" qualities in her. The delicate way she held her head, the long swan-like neck; even her glance into the camera lens proved that she was accustomed to being photographed. Candace felt nauseous and she grabbed her stomach as she slowly got up from the table. She looked at Phyllis, then studied the picture some more. She tried to find something on the woman in the picture to prove the whole story incredible, but there was nothing. She had seen pictures of Maoma in AFLAME's portfolio archives and this woman was the spitting image. She laid the picture down on the table and took a sip of the tea. She was too distraught to realize that it was sugarless.

Phyllis watched her as she paced the kitchen floor. Candace wondered if she would always be unlucky at love. There had only been three men in her life—Julius, Russell and Austin. Each had a special place in her heart. With Julius, they were both young, inexperienced and the love between them was introductory, tender and sweet. If Julius had asked her to marry him when he finished high school, she would have. She loved him and would have followed him to the moon if it were possible. Then there was Russell. Russell was more than special—he was her friend and she knew he cared deeply for her if not loved her, but she wanted more than a postal worker. If Austin had never come into the picture, the relationship with Russell would have blossomed. The thought of Russell reminded her that his wedding date was coming up very soon. She had to give him credit for trying to win her love. He had never stopped trying until she had given him the final ultimatum. She shook her head at the thought of her thinking he was going to hurt her that day in the flower garden. She remembered his words telling her that he couldn't hurt a fly and that Austin would be the one to do that. She had the sudden urge to call Russell and tell him how wrong she'd been, that he was right and that she didn't think Ophelia was a suitable match for him. She envisioned him picking her up in his strong arms like he use to do and kissing her. Then he'd say something sarcastic and funny, like "Girl, I don't be fronting; you know my love for real." She smiled at Russell's brief revisit and was grateful for the temporary escape from the pain she was feeling over Austin.

"What does this mean, Phyllis?" The tears started again.

"Honey, I don't know."

"He has forgotten about me. He's been gone for four days and he hasn't called. He wants her back, doesn't he?"

"Candace, you know he loves you."

"But he loves her more."

"You have to understand—technically she is his wife and he probably still feels legally responsible for her, even if there is not any passion or devotion left."

"If he loved me, he wouldn't have left me. I'm going home."

"Candace, are you gonna be all right?"

"Sure, I am," she smiled. She walked to the door, then turned around. "I'll be in to work tomorrow. Would you do me a favor, please?"

"Anything."

"Will you call Bali for me and let them know I'm available to do the shoot if they still want me."

"Twila Jackson took the assignment, you know."

"I know, but see if they have room for one more."

"For you, Candace, I'm sure they'll find room." Phyllis's heart was breaking for Candace. If she had the power to make things right again she would. Then, she asked herself, where would right start? Would it start with Austin and Candace's relationship or would it go way back to the beginning before the plane crash? She didn't know. "Wait,

Candace!" she said in a last minute attempt to make the pain a little easier on her. "I've got something you might want." She dug into the briefcase and pulled out a piece of paper. "This is Linus Snodgrass's number. Maybe he can give you some more information."

That afternoon Candace tried calling Linus Snodgrass again. She knew it would be late there but hoped he would answer this time. This was her fifth attempt. She let the phone ring 20 times and got no answer. As soon as she hung up, her phone began to ring. She snatched it off its cradle. "Hello?"

"Candace, you all right?"

"Yes, Ma." She was disappointed but tried not to sound it.

"You know you can come back over here if you want."

"I know, and I appreciate the invite, but I got to get up and go to work in the morning."

"Oh, well, I'm glad you decided to go back. I think it'll be good for you, get your mind off things, you know. Listen, I talked to Shamell in church this morning. I told her what was going on. I hope you don't mind."

"Ma! Why did you do that? I don't want everybody in my business."

"Shamell is not everybody and you know she's just like family. She worries about you just like I do. She sends her love and she wants you to call her."

"O.K., Ma. I'll call."

"When?"

"I don't know when, but I'll get around to it, I promise. Look, Ma, I gotta go. There's someone at the door."

"I didn't hear the doorbell."

"It rang."

"Be careful; look through the peephole first. I don't care how much security you got in that building. Precaution is the best security."

"O.K., gotta go." Click. Candace dialed Austin's parents. A whole day had passed since she talked with Mrs. Kawissopie and it was possible she had heard from Austin by now.

"Hello?"

"Mr. Kawissopie, this is Candace."

"Candace! I heard about everything. Have you heard from Austin yet?"

Candace's heart sank further. She knew they had not heard from him either if Mr. Kawissopie was asking her. "No, sir, I thought you might have."

"No, we have not, and everybody is worried because this is not like Austin."

Candace could hear Mrs. Kawissopie and Momma Lena in the background asking him questions. He tried to carry on two conversations, one in English and the other in Swahili so that Momma Lena could understand.

"Mr. Kawissopie, how far is the Ituri rain forest from there?"

"Quite a ways. Why you want to know, Candace?"

"Because I think that's where Austin is." Then she proceeded to tell them the information she had received from Phyllis.

Mr. Kawissopie was speechless when Candace finished. She had notice that after he translated their conversation, Momma Lena and Mrs. Kawissopie were quiet also. "Are you still there?"

"Yes, Candace. It is such a shock to all of us. She has been alive all this time?"

"I don't know for sure if she really is Maoma. I'm still in the dark here because I haven't heard from Austin. I've tried calling Mr. Snodgrass' number but he is never in. I'm more than worried, Mr. Kawissopie. All kinds of thoughts have crossed my mind. I worry that Austin is being held against his will. Austin is a wealthy man and people may try to take advantage of his fortune."

"We have thought the same thing."

"As soon as I can talk to this Mr. Snodgrass person and get the information on the exact location, I think I'll fly there."

38

True Friends

When Candace woke up in the big king-sized bed the first thing that crossed her mind was the number five. It had been five days since she had last seen and talked with Austin. Mr. Kawissopie had told her to give it a few more days before she boarded a plane to the rain forest of Zaire. He didn't think it was wise for her to go to an unknown place without family or friends to accompany her. She agreed that she would wait until hearing from Linus. Besides, she didn't know exactly where to go to find Austin anyway. She dragged herself out of bed and headed straight for the shower.

*   *   *

From the inside of AFLAME's double glass doors Phyllis watched Candace step off the elevators. She walked the few steps it took to get to the entrance and swung open the doors.

"Hey, girl," greeted Phyllis. Candace was not wearing make-up and Phyllis thought she looked terrible, plus she knew that the emotional upset she was going through didn't help either. Phyllis felt that once

Candace put on her make-up (and she would need a ton of it) she would be camera friendly.

"Hello, Phyllis."

"Were you able to get in touch with Linus Snodgrass?"

"No answer. I tried calling several times, too. I called Austin's parents and told them I was thinking seriously about hopping on a plane and going to the rain forest to find him."

"And?"

"They recommended against it for now. Think I should wait until I talk to this Linus character."

"I think that's wise too," said Phyllis.

"Yeah, well, if I don't hear from him soon, I'm hopping a flight anyway."

Candace was glad she had decided to come in to work. The session temporarily eased her tension and freed her mind from thoughts of Austin. Candace noticed that everyone was especially nice to her. They spoke softly, smiled a lot and refrained from mentioning Austin's name. She'd seen a couple of models whispering to each other and stealing glances at her. Sympathy was the one thing she didn't want. It only grabbed her by the ankles and pulled her down deeper into depression. When the session was over she went to the dressing room to change back into her clothes.

"What's up?" said a voice behind her. She looked around to see Twila. Candace had hoped she could avoid Twila or anyone else for that matter. She wasn't in the mood to divulge her business.

"Hello, Twila, how's it going?"

"Look like to me I should be asking you that question."

Candace didn't say anything. She hoped Twila would see that she wasn't in the mood to talk and move on.

"Heard 'bout Austin skipping out on you."

Candace exhaled and rolled her eyes toward the ceiling.

"You don't need to get uptight about it, partner," Twila chuckled. "I was just asking. Probably ain't nothing but a little lovers' spat anyway."

"Twila, I'm really not in the mood O.K?"

"I don't meant to sweat you, Candace. I was just asking cause I'm concern, that's all."

Candace took off the Bali bra and slipped her tee shirt over her head.

"What you need is something to get your mind off Austin."

"And what would that something be, Twila?"

Twila pulled out a small plastic bag from her pants pocket. There were two white rocks inside. She shook it in front of Candace's face.

"What're you doing?" Candace knew what she was doing and couldn't believe she had the audacity to offer her crack cocaine.

"Girl, don't be acting all Saintified and Holy Ghost filled. This what you need right here to free your mind."

"No, Twila, I don't need that!" Candace picked up her shoulder bag and walked past her. Twila grabbed her arm. "I'm sorry. I forgot you not into this. I just hate to see a sister suffering that's all. I know how much you loved Austin. Rejection can be a mother, can't it?" she said provocatively.

"Rejection? Who rejected who, Twila?" Candace snapped back angrily.

Twila held up both hands and backed away. "Damn, Candace. Chill, girl. I ain't trying to raise your blood pressure. I just wanna tell you about the party at Madam Yvonne's house this Friday night. You oughta come and go. It'll help get your mind off things."

"No," she said and continued to walk on.

"Ain't gon' be no drugs there, if that's what you scared of. You know Madam don't go for that."

"No, thanks, got other things to do."

"Other things like what? Austin ain't here. You gon' sit home holding your hands and being a good little girl? I bet you one thing, wherever Austin is he ain't sitting idle. If you change your mind, you know where she lives."

Candace left the dressing room thinking seriously about what she had just said.

*　　　　*　　　　*

Muzungu felt as though she had been hit in the head with a rock. She opened her eyes and saw Tifu sitting by her side.

"Take it easy, Muzungu."

"My head. It pains me something awful."

"Yes, I know," said Tifu. She pushed Muzungu back down on the pallet of skins. Muzungu saw the daylight filter in through the hut's door. "What happen and why am I here resting in the middle of the day? She only remembered being teased by the women about her upcoming marriage. Then they left for bed and she began washing the pots at the water barrel. She bolted up from her slumber position. "It is my wedding day! Why am I here? Why does my head throb?"

"Here, drink this." Tifu put a cup of strong smelling herbal tea up to her mouth. "This will ease the pain."

Muzungu took a sip of the bitter tea. "What happened?"

"Just rest for now, Muzungu."

Muzungu remembered the pain she felt in the side of her neck and then pulling out the dart. She remembered falling to the ground and seeing the faces hovered over her. She closed her eyes and saw the frightening black face, the white face and the kind face that had been crying. Her eyes popped opened and she looked at Tifu in terror. She lifted herself up again. Tifu tried to push her back down but Muzungu pushed her out of the way. "He is here!" she said hysterically. Tifu knew she was speaking of Austin, but she wanted to tell her as gently as possible what awaited her outside the hut.

"No, Muzungu!" Tifu tried to overpower her but she was no match for Muzungu's size and frenzied state of mind. Muzungu pushed Tifu to a far corner of the hut, got out of bed and stumbled outside. The light of the sun blinded her at first and she held her hands over her eyes to shield them from its brightness. Tifu jumped up from the dirt floor and tried to pull Muzungu back inside.

"She is awake! yelled Tifu.

Austin, Jabusa and the Efe men stood over Osun and Linus. They turned around to see Muzungu stumbling out of the hut. Muzungu saw the Efe men. In addition to her throbbing head, her body was stiff and she couldn't think clearly, but she was alert enough to notice Jabusa standing amidst them. She smiled at him. Then she noticed the other tall figure stepping out of the huddle and coming toward her in slow motion. Her smile melted away as she looked puzzled at the man.

"M-a-a-o-o-m-m-a!" The words left his mouth, reaching her in slow motion too.

It seemed as though the man was calling her but she didn't recognize the name. She saw the commotion of bodies behind him. Two of the Efe men caught him but he shook them off and continued toward her at a faster pace now. Then Jabusa started yelling for him to stop. When Austin got close enough, Muzungu recognized his face.

"Austin," she said softly but loud enough for him to hear it.

"You know me! Yes, I am Austin! Yes, Maoma it's me—your husband. I have finally found you, Malaika." He reached out to take her in his arms but before he could Muzungu collapsed to the ground. The shock of seeing him was too great and she fainted.

"Bind him!" ordered Jabusa.

The Efe men surrounded Austin. They struggled with him for five full minutes before they were able to subdue him. He was tied to a tree next to Linus and Osun.

"She is my wife! What are you going to do, kill me? Do you think that will stop her love for me? All you will do is make her resent you! She has seen me already! She knows I am here!" He yelled continuously.

Jabusa was crouched down beside Muzungu. He tried to ignore Austin's words, but he knew he was speaking the truth. "Shut him up, gag him, do something!"

Suko stuffed a cotton rag in his mouth. Neither he nor the other Efe people held any animosity toward Austin. When Tifu had said he was a kind man with a good heart, they believed her and from that point they regarded him such. Austin looked into Suko's eyes and he could tell that the young man did not feel comfortable at what he was doing to him. Austin tried to tell him with his eyes that he understood and did not hold it against him.

Muzungu began to come around. She looked into Jabusa's face. Tifu was at her side too. Everything was happening so fast. She thought she had seen Austin but quickly decided that could not be right. The events of the night before came rushing back into memory again. She looked at Tifu then back at Jabusa. She lifted herself up and saw Osun and the white man tied to a tree. Her thinking was becoming clearer now. She inhaled a deep breath of air. It wasn't a dream after all. "What is happening?" she looked from Jabusa to Tifu.

"Let me tell her, Chief Jabusa. I know Muzungu better than any of us here." As soon as she had spoken the words she looked briefly at Austin tied against the tree and knew she was wrong. It was Austin who knew her better than anyone. Jabusa saw her glance at Austin and he too looked briefly at the man who rightfully had claim to Muzungu. His heart began to break. He knew losing her was inevitable. Time, distance and even the loss of memory could not erase true love. He was a warrior chief who had been reduced to a mere brokenhearted man. Tears filled his eyes but he blinked them back, refusing to blemish the reputation of a warrior chief. If Chief Njau had still been alive and saw his only son cry over a woman, it would have shamed him deeply. He considered himself a man in every sense of the word, but the pain he felt was bringing him to the realization that there is no such thing as iron men. Even his father, as great as he was, had to have had something in his life he felt so passionately about that it reduced him to tears. Although he had never seen him cry, he believed at some point he had. Jabusa listened quietly as Tifu explained everything to Muzungu.

When Tifu finished, Muzungu got up and walked over to Austin. She took the stuffed rag out of his mouth. "Untie him," she said gently. Suko looked at Jabusa, who was watching Muzungu intently. He nodded his head at Suko, who pulled the knife from his side pouch and sliced the thick vines that held Austin captive. Muzungu raised her hands and touched Austin's face. The touch was welcoming, and Austin reciprocated by kissing her hands. Then they both sobbed like babies.

"Is it really you?" she asked through her tears.

"Yes, Maoma, it is really me. I searched so long for you. I never accepted your death and had constant dreams of you. I prayed many nights for God to wake me from the nightmare I was living."

"I can't believe it is you, Austin."

Austin took her in his arms and hugged her tightly and she hugged him back. "There is so much I want to tell you," Austin said, "Do you remember our lives in New York?"

Maoma nodded. "Bits and pieces of my past with you have been trying to resurface but I could never put the pieces together in a complete picture. Yes, Austin, now I remember New York, the apartment, AFLAME, the modeling." She looked surprised, "Oh!" She put her hands on her face, "I remember the children," she looked at him. "My third-grade class at the school. That explains why I have such a fondness for children."

"Yes, you taught at MLK Elementary."

"And I remember Central Park and Sunday picnics with you. I remember Phyllis, Momma Lena, your brother and parents." She kept on telling him the things she remembered. She talked a mile a minute and was fighting the tears and sobs to get the words out audibly. "I remember the plane crash," she said slowly and with great effort. She paused and stared off into the thick forest of trees. The scene re-enacted in her mind and her eyes fixed on an imaginary airplane dropping from the sky. "At first the ride was smooth, then the plane started shaking. I heard one of the pilots talking on the radio. He was calling for help. He said the plane had lost an engine. He couldn't get a response. For some reason he had flown off course and was too far out of range. He yelled back at us to pull the pillows down and cover our heads. We did as told. The plane started descending and we could feel the belly of the plane scraping against the treetops. Everybody started screaming and crying. There was a lady in the back praying for God to save her. Then the plane turned upside down. There was this very hard hit and a loud explosion. I knew we had crashed then. After the crash I remember thinking that it wasn't so bad and that we had all survived it but, then…"

Austin knew she was struggling to get the story out. "Maoma, that's O.K. You don't have to continue." He thought about his own therapy and how traumatic the loss of her had been for him. He knew she would need therapy and that one of the main things the therapist would want her to do was talk about the ordeal, but he would not pressure her now. He made a mental note to call Dr. Edwards and set up an appointment for her.

"No, Austin I want to; I need to."

Austin smiled and rubbed the top of her hand with his palms.

"I looked around and there were bodies everywhere. They were bloody, twisted and mingled together. A severed arm was lying on my lap. I screamed and brushed it off of me. Then there was another explosion and I thought somebody or something was pushing me forward, but it was the impact of the explosion. It had blown me out of the plane before the fire engulfed it. I tried to crawl as far away from the plane as I could because I thought it would blow again. It was raining and the ground was muddy and slippery. It was hard to move around. That's when I must have passed out because the next thing I remembered was waking up to find Tifu by my bedside attending me."

Austin enclosed her in his arms again. "You are going to be all right now. No harm will ever come to you again."

Jabusa watched the two of them embrace each other. He saw the tender and loving way she looked at Austin. She had never looked at him that way. He knew all of this could have been avoided if only Osun was loyal to him. It was supposed to be his wedding day, and he was watching the woman he loved cuddle in another man's arms. He stormed over to Osun. He pulled out an arrow from the bag that hung over his shoulder and began whipping him with it. Osun's cries were loud and shameful.

"Please don't kill me, Chief Jabusa! I am so sorry!"

"No, I will not kill you just yet. I assure you though, you will die. It will be a painful and slow death. You think I am a weak chief. Too impotent to rule the Lese people. You have spread this poison throughout my village. I know of your secret meeting with the elders. Do you think I am so moronic that I do not keep up with the activity that goes on in my village?"

Muzungu knew Osun was treacherous. She knew Jabusa had no more use for him than a maggot, but she could not allow him to die at the hands of Jabusa. She pulled away from Austin.

"No, Jabusa!" Muzungu's voice was soothing to Jabusa's ears. "Don't kill him," she said. She shifted her eyes to Osun. She remembered the words from Yoruba, the witch doctor. She'd warned her against an evil person who was trying to hurt her. Now she knew that person was Osun. She knew that if Osun had his way it would take nothing for him to kill her. Still she could not stoop to his level.

"Why do you want to save the life of a man who would do this to us? I have no use for him."

"To take his life will not make the situation go away. What's done is done. You are too good to kill another human being, Jabusa. Do you want to have the blood of this man on your hands?"

Osun was grateful that Muzungu had come to his rescue. "Oh, thank you, Muzungu, for sparing me."

"Osun, my objective is not so much to save you but to save Jabusa from becoming like you."

"Your life is spared Osun, only because Muzungu requested it," said Jabusa.

Osun showered Muzungu and Jabusa with thanks.

Jabusa stepped behind the tree and cut the vines from around their hands. "You are to pack up your wife, children and grandchildren and leave the Lese village. If I ever see your face or any of your family's faces again, I will order you all killed."

"Yes, Chief Jabusa, and thank you for sparing me."

"The same thing goes for you, Linus. I will order the Lese to kill you on sight. Our trade agreement is no more."

"I want my money, Mr. Kawissopie. I got you your wife." He pulled the folded piece of paper Austin had signed earlier from his shirt pocket. "This piece of paper is legal document that you owe me $200,000."

Jabusa snatched the piece of paper from Linus' hand and tore it into bits. Nothing is owed to you. The sparing of your life is your payment. Now go!"

Osun and Linus backed away from Jabusa and the Efe. Osun knew the both of them were lucky indeed. It was not the custom of the Lese to leave an enemy alive. When they got to the thicket's edge they did an about-face and ran into the forest. Jabusa looked at Muzungu as she stood beside Austin. He knew which one of them she would choose, but he had to hear it from her. "Muzungu." His voice was deep and resounding. The sound of it brought back memories of the day at the stream when he had called her name. It was commanding and had stopped her in her tracks.

"This is our wedding day. My people have prepared for the wedding feast." He held out his hand for her to take it. Muzungu dropped her head.

"I cannot, Jabusa. I am already married."

Jabusa wore a tough exterior and tried to act indifferent to Muzungu's decision to go with Austin. Muzungu knew he was hurting. He didn't ask her if she loved Austin or promise her the sun and moon. He kept a stern face. He took one last look at Muzungu before turning and walking away.

"I beg your forgiveness," she said.

Without acknowledging her apology he climbed on the back of his mule and galloped back down the narrow path that had brought him there.

*   *   *

Austin spent the next two days with Muzungu and the Efe people. They showed him the best hospitality they could offer. They tried to keep a positive attitude about Muzungu's leaving but they were finding it hard to accept. The children clung to her like little magnets. They expressed their feelings truthfully, as children often do. They were sorry that she would be leaving them but had come to accept her marriage to Jabusa because she had promised them that she would visit them twice weekly and expected for them to visit her too. But when they learned she would be going far away and traveling over the great waters, they became concerned and some of them even cried.

"I promise to come back and see you," she said to the children.

"When?" asked an older child.

"I will try to come back in a year's time."

"That's too long!" wailed a five-year old boy.

"No, it's not. You will see how fast a year goes by and I will be back here with loads of presents for you."

"Will you bring us toys?" asked the five-year old.

Muzungu's heart broke. The only toys they knew were the wood-carved toys made by the Efe men. She smiled at the thought of the younger boys playing with a shiny bright red fire engine and the girls cuddling a soft doll with movable eyes and limbs. It didn't take a lot to please them and they never asked for too much. For the rest of her life she would always have a special place in her heart for the Efe, especially the children. She pulled the five-year-old boy in her arms and planted a kiss on top of his head. "Do you know what a bicycle is?" she asked amusingly, and looking from child to child to include them too.

"Yes, one of the Lese men has one," said the five-year old.

"Yes!" she laughed, and then praised the child by clapping her hands. "You are so smart. Well, what about a wagon? Do you know what that is?"

"Yes!" said another child, jumping up and down and finding the question/answer session quite interesting. "You can carry things in it."

"That's right, you can carry things in it. But, wagons are best for carrying children." She nodded her head as she spoke.

"But wagons are for carrying things like wood, food and water from the stream," said a larger child.

"Yes, you can use it for that too, but the main purpose for bicycles and wagons are to provide fun for children like you."

The children looked on in awe.

"And if you all promise me that you will be good, when I come back to see you I will bring you these things. I will also bring dolls and candy and all the honey you can eat in a lifetime. I will bring you blankets softer than those of the Lese." Her eyes widened as she told them about the shoes with rubber bottoms. "I will bring you real shoes. Shoes that will protect your feet and make you run and jump as fast and high as the duiker."

"What about as fast as the leopard?" asked the five-year old.

"Even faster than the leopard!" She hugged the child and planted another kiss on his head. The other children crowded around her. They threw their arms around her and the ones who were not able to hug her reached through the bodies of children just to touch a part of her. They whispered "I love you's" to Muzungu.

"We will miss you," said the five-year-old.

"Yes, we will miss you," said the others in unison.

Muzungu was beyond words. Her emotions had overtaken her and all she could do was cry.

*   *   *

Candace dialed Linus Snodgrass's number for the umpteenth time. She slowly keyed in the numbers and after each one she prayed that he would be there. She held her breath and closed her eyes tight.

"Hello?" said the English voice.

"Hello!" Candace almost screamed the greeting into the receiver out of excitement. "Is this Mr. Snodgrass?"

"Who wants to know?" he said sourly, still stewing from being cheated out of the $200,000 that he felt was rightly his.

"My name is Candace. Candace Brooks, and I'm calling from New York. I was told that you might have information on the whereabouts of an Austin Kawissopie."

Linus was resting back in his worn vinyl swivel chair and had his feet propped on a desk that hadn't been properly dusted in months. Austin's name made him spring forward and once again dollar signs started dancing before his eyes. "Yes, ma'am I do know where he is, but now that information is top secret. I just can't give it out to anyone."

"I'm not just anyone, sir. I'm his fiancé."

This was too good to be true, he thought. He begin smiling from ear to ear. The woman sounded green, yet ripe enough for the picking. "His fiancé, huh?"

"Yes, sir, and he left here on last Wednesday night and I haven't heard from him since. There is something terribly wrong. It's not like him to go away without letting anyone know where he is. Can you please help me?"

"Well, seeing that he's your fiancé, I guess I can but it ain't gon' be cheap ma'am."

"What do you mean?"

"I mean the where-a-bouts of your soon-to-be husband is classified information. No one s'pose to know where he is. I could be endangering Mr. Kawissopie and myself by giving you that information."

"But sir, I'm almost his wife," she begged.

The thought of getting paid had Linus bursting at the seams with expectation. "How much money you got?" he asked bluntly. Linus wanted out of the Rain Forest. The Lese were his main source of income and without their business he couldn't turn a profit. Besides the order for any Lese to kill him on sight and Osun's threat were reasons enough to flee. He didn't like the idea of looking over his shoulder afraid that a Lese or Osun would kill him.

"Sir?"

"The information you're wanting don't come cheap. If I'm gon' risk my life by telling you where Austin is, then I need something for my troubles."

"Is he being held ransom?"

"Look, I'm not giving you any information without payment."

"I got some money but not a lot, Mr. Snodgrass."

"I want fifty grand."

"It would take me a while to get that kind of money. I would have to liquidate my assets."

"What do you mean?"

"It's tied up in stocks, bonds and CD's. I just can't go in the bank and demand it instantly."

"How much you got then?"

"I can get you $20,000."

Linus couldn't wait. He had to move fast before Austin and Muzungu got out of there. He knew Candace was going to be disappointed with the outcome. Your fiancé brings his wife home, I mean, who wouldn't. But that wasn't his problem. All he cared about was getting his hands on some fast money and getting as far away from this neck of the woods as possible. "Well, the twenty will have to do then," he said, half-disappointed. "I tell you what you do. Get the twenty grand and have it wired to me in exactly three hours. If I don't get the money by then, the deal is off. You got that?"

Candace picked up a pen and began writing on a scratch pad. "Yes, sir, I got it."

"Now, here's the deal." Linus proceeded to give her the instructions for wiring him the money.

*   *   *

Candace twisted the key in the lock and rushed inside. Everything had gone as planned and she was feeling a little easier because of it. She threw her shoulder bag on the couch and rushed to the phone to dial Linus.

"Hello?"

"Did you get it?" she asked anxiously.

"I got the money right here in my hand. You did good, Candace," he said, while clearing his few possessions out of his desk drawer and throwing them into a duffel bag. The $20,000 was a far cry from what he had originally planned, but it would help to give him a start on a new life in a more civilized place.

"Where can I find him, Mr. Snodgrass?"

Linus laugh a sinister laugh that sent a chill up Candace's spine. The pit of her stomach dropped and she knew then that she had made a grave mistake by sending the money to him.

"You ain't gonna like what I got to tell you, sweet'eart."

"I paid you the money. I did what you asked. Now I want to know what's happened to Austin. Is he dead?"

"He's far from being dead, but I tell you one thing—after the way he double-crossed me I'd like to kill him. He promised me money for finding his long departed wife for him. I found her and he didn't keep his end of the bargain."

"What?" Candace realized the story Phyllis had told her was true.

"That's right, girlie. It seems that your lover boy already has a wife." He laughed some more.

"No!"

"Yes! They call her Muzungu and she has been living up in the woods with them grungy Pygmy people." Linus was finding the whole situation hilarious. He began laughing even harder. "I got an idea," he said with a note of exhilaration. "You can move here too and still marry Austin," he said sarcastically. "They allow that sort of thing in tribal society. You know, its called polygamy."

"No!" Candace said louder. "He loves me. He said he did. He wouldn't…"

"Look, Candace, I don't know you from the next Joann Blow, but let me give you a word of advice. Count yourself lucky and get as far away from that creep as you can. Find yourself somebody that truly loves you."

"Where is he?" she demanded.

"Look, kid, I told you. This man has the woman he wants. He was about to give his life up there for her. Now doesn't that tell you anything?"

"Where is he?" she asked again, this time more determined to get an answer.

Linus sighed before giving her exact location of Austin's whereabouts.

*   *   *

"I'm terribly sorry, ma'am, but if you are not the authorized user of this credit card we cannot book the flight for you. Get me cash or a credit card with your name on it or one that has authorization for your use," said the airline reservations.

"I am trying to tell you, Miss, that I have money but I can't get my hands on it right now. It's all tied up. As far as the credit card goes, it belongs to my fiancé who happens to be in Africa. That's why I need to get there. I use his card all the time and I've never had trouble before. I don't understand why you're trying to give me a hard time about it."

"It is corporate procedure not to allow someone to use another person's credit card without their authorization. I'm not about to take the chance of losing my job by booking this flight."

"Let me speak to your supervisor!" Candace shouted. There was a line of impatient people standing behind her.

"Ma'am, I have to take care of the people waiting in line. Will you step aside and wait over there. My supervisor will be with you shortly."

"No, I will not! My needs are just as important as theirs are! I know my rights and will not permit you to treat me this way! You obviously have never heard that the customer is always right."

The reservations clerk pushed a button underneath the counter and within a minute a security guard was there.

"What's going on here?" he asked

"I've got a line of people waiting. I asked Ms. Brooks to please wait over there until someone with more expertise can help her but she refuses."

"Ma'am, I'm gonna have to ask you to step over there, please? We have to keep the line moving," the guard said. Candace knew she had no choice but to eat crow and move to the side. She felt the stares of people in the terminal. She was hot with humiliation. She felt the tears well up in her eyes. She wiped them away as they rolled over the bottom lids.

The guard looked at her sympathetically. "It won't be long, ma'am. Someone will be here to help you."

The supervisor told Candace the same thing that the reservations clerk had. Candace walked out of the airport. If only she had not wired Linus the money before getting the information, she would be on her way to Africa.

*   *   *

Austin and Maoma left the Efe village riding on the backs of the two mules Jabusa left for the Efe. Suko escorted them on the three-hour trip to the main road, where they would hitch hike a ride to the Ituri River's edge. From there, they'd wait for the next boat to come and carry them to Joopa, the nearest town. Maoma watched Suko from the rear window of the jeep until he turned into a tiny dot in the road.

The boat ride back across the Ituri was long and tiresome yet remarkable to Maoma. She marveled at the sights and sounds of the forest. Some of the scenery was breathtakingly beautiful and some frightening. The boat sailed under shadows that darkened their passage and made everything seem haunted. That was when the trees seemed to reach their twisted limbs toward her and the leaves released whispers of wind that summoned her to stay. She saw a python looped over a crooked limb. It sent chills up her spine and she quickly averted her eyes downward to the body of water only to see what looked like a floating log. But, after looking closer she recognized the log to be a crocodile. She cuddled closer to Austin as he tightened his protective arms around her. She could not believe that for six years she had been confined to a 50-mile radius. The Efe were not big on exploring outside their natural habitat, and for that reason her six-year isolation with them was never questioned.

When they reached the town of Joopa, the man transporting them was nice enough to take them to the Riverfront Hotel, the town's only lodging place. Austin paid him well and thanked him for his kindness. The front desk clerk gave Austin and Maoma the nicest double room in the hotel and still it did not measure up to the worst hotel Austin had ever stayed in State-side. There was a basin in the sleeping section of the room and the bathroom was only large enough for a shower stall and toilet. Austin left Maoma to shower and rest while he went in search for suitable clothes for her. The rags she wore were clean but they were faded, worn and barely covered her. He had planned to take her to dinner later that evening at a café located across the street from the hotel. He wanted her to look nice for the occasion and to have traveling clothes for the trip back to New York. When they had walked into the township earlier that day, the citizens stared at Maoma with her animal skin moccasins and rags that barely covered her. She looked to them exactly like what she had become—a nomad from the forest.

He had made reservations for them to leave Joopa tomorrow via commuter plane to the capital city of Kinshasa. From Kinshasa they would fly on to Algeria, where they would spend half a day. They would later fly to Paris, and 24 hours later would arrive in New York City. Austin picked out undergarments, three long dashikis and two pairs of slippers, a gold pair and a black pair.

The sales clerk thanked Austin and helped him tuck the packages under his arm. Austin smiled at the woman and turned to walk away. Before he got to the store's doorway, he stopped in his tracks. "Candace!" he said. The packages began dropping one by one from his arms. The clerk rushed from behind the counter to assist him.

"Sir, is anything wrong?"

Austin stared off into space. He looked at the woman as if seeing her for the first time.

"Sir?"

The events of the past week played through his mind. He remembered Candace crying when he put her on the plane. She was asking for more information and he only gave her little white lies. He remembered telling her he would give her a call around midnight that night, but he had forgotten. He buried his face in his hands.

"Are you feeling well? Do you need to rest?" The woman guided Austin to a nearby chair and sat him down. "Let me get you a drink of water." She rushed to the back of the store and disappeared behind a pair of curtains. Seconds later she emerged with a cup of cool water. Austin took it and gulped it down.

"Thank you," he said hoarsely. He looked around the tiny shop frantically.

"Sir?"

"Is there a phone?"

"Yes, it's in the back."

"I need to make an emergency phone call to the United States. I'll pay you up front." He reached into his pants pocket and pulled out his wallet. He plucked two $20 bills from inside and handed them to the woman. "This should cover the call."

The woman quickly took the $40 and tucked it into her bosom. She led him to the back room behind the curtains.

The answering machine came on and Austin heard the voices of a one-time jubilant couple. "Oh, Candace! I'm so sorry. I promised to call you a week ago but things happened and I couldn't—I—I" He paused, then sighed heavily before continuing. "We have to talk. When you get in, give me a call. I don't have the number where I am right now, but ask the operator to connect you to Joopa, The Democratic Republic of the Congo." he spelled the town for her, "I'm staying at the Riverfront Hotel. There aren't any phones in the rooms, so you may have to hold while they come and get me. Oh, Candace, I'm so sorry." He eased the receiver down on the cradle. There was no easy way to tell her that she needed to clear her things out of the apartment within the next three days, that their relationship was over, and that he was bringing his wife back home.

*   *   *

Maoma looked like a different person when Austin escorted her out to dinner that evening. She was beautiful in the clothes he brought for her. The dashiki reached down to her ankels. It had two slits in the sides, revealing her long beautiful legs. The shoes were a perfect fit and she was impressed that Austin remembered her size. The couple sat opposite each other at a small round dinner table in a back corner of the café. Austin listened as Maoma described her life with the Efe. She told him the loneliness she felt at first, not knowing who she was or where she came from. She talked about the terrifying dreams with the vultures and the most recent dreams with him in them. She was amazed to learn that Austin dreamed of vultures, too.

She told him how she prayed that the man in her dreams would find her and make things right. She told him about her visit to Yoruba, the witch doctor, and how she had warned her about an evil person in the forest who turned out to be Osun. When she talked of the fond memories, her face lit up and her laughter bubbled over like champagne in a glass. She told him about the elephant hunt and the time one of the Efe children caught a wild monkey and brought it to the village. The child was determined to make the monkey a pet, but that was before it destroyed almost everything in the village. She talked of marriages, births and deaths. Some events were naturally sadder than others, but she was optimistic as she spoke of each episode affectionately.

"I am so glad that I found you. I can't even begin to tell you how my life has been without you. I prayed too, Maoma, and God has answered my plea. He has put us together again." He lifted her hand and kissed it tenderly. Maoma smiled a reticent smile.

"I see you still have your healthy appetite," she said, eyeing his plate. Austin looked down at his plate. There were remnants of a hearty meal. He had ordered an inch-thick T-bone steak, one quarter of a baked chicken, steamed squash, pan bread and two thick slices of pumpkin and yam cake.

"I eat in great abundance only when I am happy," Austin laughed.

"I am flattered that you waited for me all these years. Most men would have remarried after the first year of their wife's death. I'm surprised you didn't."

The statement brought Candace back to mind and he remembered she would be calling later on. Maoma had to know, and he decided he wouldn't spare her the details. He cleared his throat. "Maoma?"

"Yes, Austin?"

"There was someone else."

Maoma looked at him and Austin could see the understanding in her eyes. That was one of the many things he loved about her. She was slow to judge, patient and forgiving to a fault. He squeezed her hands as if trying to find strength and support to go on. "Her name was Candace— I mean her name is Candace. Candace Brooks."

"Is?"

"Is meaning that I haven't told her that you're still alive. Everything happened so fast. When I got the phone call several days ago, I was in Texas on business. She was with me. I couldn't tell her right then and there. In my heart I knew if you were alive I would choose you. I wanted to make sure it wasn't a hoax first. I didn't want to worry her needlessly."

"What excuse did you give her for flying halfway around the world?" she asked sincerely.

"I told her that it was family matters and that I would explain it to her when I returned."

Maoma looked sad for Candace.

"I know what you're thinking, Maoma. But this is something that couldn't be avoided. God knows, if I knew what the outcome was going to be I never would have gotten involved with her. Broken hearts are a fact of life. Candace is young, smart and beautiful. I am sure she will heal and find the person that is meant for her.

"Do you love her?"

"Yes, I love her. We were engaged to be married next month, but my love for her doesn't even come close to what I feel for you. If you believe in soul mates, then you must know that you're mine."

"Oh, Austin, that poor girl. I can imagine the anxieties she's going through right now not knowing exactly what's going on." Maoma shook her head wearily, "Oh, God, and the pain she will feel when she knows the whole story."

"Heartbreak is the worst pain a person can experience. I know because I've been there. I survived and so will she," said Austin, "I will do all I can to help her get through this."

Maoma concentrated on the statement. She could not identify with the pain of heartbreak because she had forgotten the love they had those six years ago. Now she remembered it and knew how rich it had been, but things were not the same anymore, since Jabusa.

She had grown wiser living among the Efe and had learned that life's simple pleasures were the things that made you happy. She had all of that with the Efe and the first time she thought she loved Jabusa was at the elephant-meat trade. He had proved his love by giving her all the things she'd asked for. He had made a statement to his people on that day that the Efe should be treated with the same kind of regard they expected for themselves. The statement proved to the Efe what they had dared not challenge in all the years of Lese and Efe life in the forest. Jabusa's statement said that they were as good as the Lese or any other people that walked the face of the earth. After that day, Muzungu noticed that the Efe walked a littler taller. All it had taken was respect from the man who would become chief.

It was on the stream's edge when they kissed for the first time that she knew she loved him. As she sat before Austin she thought of the strong, emotionless, tough man who had won her heart. She pictured him withdrawn and sitting in the darkness of his quarters. Her arms ached and she wanted to cover him with them. She rubbed her hands over her arms and pretended she was holding Jabusa and rubbing away the hurt and pain she had caused him. She imagined Jabusa's muscles relaxing and him turning back into the sensitive, caring man he had become. Then she thought about the Efe. She wondered how her absence would affect their relationship with the Lese. Would it continue to improve or worsen? She suspected the latter.

"Are you cold?" asked Austin.

His voice broke her meditation and Jabusa slipped from her consoling arms back into the dark corners of his dwelling. Maoma released her hands from around her arms. "No, just tense I guess."

"Everything is going to be fine once we get back to New York. The apartment is exactly the same as when we were married. Do you remember how we use to curl up on the floor watching TV?"

Maoma smiled. "Yes and your favorite shows were westerns."

"They are still my favorite, and you had a fondness for them too."

"Gary Cooper, Randolph Scott and John Wayne," she chuckled.

"There is so much that I want to share with you," he said, "but I will remain patient until you are ready too."

Maoma knew Austin wanted to make love to her. He'd tried twice at the Efe village and then again when they checked into the hotel. She told him she needed more time and asked him to be patient. Now, after realizing how much she missed Jabusa, Tifu, and the Efe children, all the time in the world would not make her ready to accept Austin back into her life the way he wanted her. If she went back to New York with him she would be living a lie and she would have constant, agonizing thoughts of the people she left behind. Austin wanted her world and his world to merge into one big unified cradle of matrimony, but that could not happen because the years they spent apart had made a new person out of her. It had brainwashed her into thinking and acting like the forest people and she had grown to love their way of life. She remembered the morning rush hours, the crush of the subway getting to work, and when she got there, the rebellious children she tried to teach. The children were a different breed compared to the Efe children—even the Lese children. The forest produced genuinely respectful and obedient children. Some of the American children she remembered were almost a lost cause because they were not receiving the proper basics from home. She remembered the racism she encountered daily, the suffering of the aged, the young, the sick and the poor. She remembered the political pressures of the nation as a whole. She was ashamed to live in a country so wealthy yet with citizens dying from starvation and disease. She could not go back to the complexity of her old life. She could not leave the paradise of the forest, for its tranquility ran through her veins like the blood that sustained her very life. Her world and Austin's world could not unify. Their worlds would only collide and cause every connective tissue that made her the decent person she was to shatter into pieces. So many pieces that all the king's horses and all the king's men would not be able to piece her together again.

39

No Fool a Third Time

They walked casually back to the hotel room. Austin had complimented Maoma a thousand times on how fantastic she looked and just before he opened the door to their hotel room she allowed him to plant a kiss on her lips. Once inside he tried to take it even further by caressing her and running his hands over her breasts, but she pulled away. He looked at her, questioning.

"Maoma, what's wrong?" he asked, anticipating the same answer she had given him since their reunion; she needed more time. Instead, she closed her eyes and Austin knew she was about to say something he did not want to hear.

"Maoma, sweetheart?" he coaxed.

"I'm not sure" was all she said, hoping that would be enough and Austin would get the message without her having to spell it out to him. But she should have known better, for she knew Austin was the type to get the ifs, ands and buts out of every situation. If the result did not suit him, he would try another approach until it did.

"Not sure?" He released her completely and ran his hand through his hair. "Not sure about what?"

"I've lived in the forest so long. I'm not sure if I can readjust to urban living…"

A knock at the door interrupted her sentence and she was grateful for it. Austin opened the door to find the desk clerk standing before him.

"Mr. Kawissopie, you have a long-distance phone call at the front desk."

"Thank you. I'll be down in a second." Austin knew it was Candace calling. Her timing was bad. He was put between a rock and a hard place, not knowing exactly what Maoma meant. "Maoma." He went to her and rubbed her shoulders. "I understand you're frightened about our life resuming, but I assure you everything will be fine. Like I said before, I'm willing to wait for you however long it takes. Just, just don't disappoint me," he said. "I'll be right back." He closed the door gently behind him.

Maoma stared at the inside of the door. She had a choice—to disappoint one or the other. There was so much to gain for so many people, including herself, if she stayed in the forest. If she went to New York, only one person would be satisfied. Austin. If she had known it was Candace on the phone downstairs, she would have insisted that Austin spare the girl and mention nothing about their reunion. That way he could pick up their relationship where it had left off.

*   *   *

Austin cleared his throat before answering. "Hello?"

"Austin!" Candace was highly excited and before she could get the second syllable of his name out she began crying.

"Oh, Candace, I'm so sorry. I forgot to call you like I promised. So much has been happening."

"Austin, please tell me what's going on. I've been hearing so many stories I-I-don't know what to believe. I'm losing my mind here. Please tell me that you love me! Please tell me!"

"Candace." Austin's voice was calm and demanding, "Calm down. We need to get through this, but we won't be able to if you're hysterical."

"But I talked to Phyllis and she told me that Maoma is alive and you're there to see about her! Phyllis gave me Linus Snodgrass' number and I called him and he said the same thing! Is it true? Austin, please tell me that it's not true!"

"Candace," he said calmly again.

"Austin, tell me that it is not true!" she demanded.

"Candace, baby, please let's not make this hard on us." His voice broke and he began crying too.

"Tell me that it's not true, I said!"

Austin said nothing, but she could hear him crying. Candace's knees buckled underneath her and she crumpled to the floor. The worst was coming. She knew he was dumping her. She felt herself unraveling like yarn from an old worn sweater. She pushed herself off the living room floor and walked into the bedroom where they'd spent many wonderful nights wrapped in each other's arms, depleted after hours of lovemaking. She grabbed Momma Lena's blanket off the bed and began rubbing it as thought it was a magic lantern and would grant the one wish she needed.

"What happened to the love, Austin? You said you would always love me."

"Candace, I do love you, more than you'll ever know…"

"Well, you have a strange way of showing it!" she screamed.

"I know you're hurting and so am I, but these things that are happening are out of my control. If I could change things back to the way they were, I would."

"You lying son of a bitch!" she sobbed.

Austin was shocked momentarily and realized she was acting normal under the circumstances. He didn't want to see her this way and wished of a way to ease the pain.

"You never stopped loving her. You told me I had changed all that. You said I was the reason you wanted to love again. You promised to marry me and that you would always be here for me. I'm a fool!"

"Oh, Candace baby, no! You're no fool!"

"I should have picked up on it that night after Blacktravaganza when we got in the fight and I called Maoma's name. You told me to never call her name again. That was a sign right then and I failed to recognize it. I never should have come back to your sorry ass," *sob*, "Should have kept going all the way back to Russell. He never lied to me. He never did." *sob*.

"Candace, please don't cry on me. Whatever you need I'll get it for you; you just name it."

"I need you, Austin. That's what I need. Can you get me that?"

"Candace, I-I'm so very sorry."

Candace plucked a Kleenex from the dispenser on the nightstand and blew her nose. She cleared her throat and wiped her eyes. "O.K. I've got to get a hold of myself," she said, "I know this is all a bad dream and if it's not we can work something out." Candace was desperately trying to hold on to the best thing she had ever known. "Austin, are you really going through with this? What about the wedding plans? We've got over a hundred guests coming to my parents' house in less than a month. What am I going to tell them?"

"If you want me to I'll send letters to everyone explaining the situation. I'll take total blame. You won't have to worry about that."

"Yeah, right, like that's the least you can do!" Candace began crying again. This was no joke. It was not the twilight zone. It wasn't even a dream. Austin wasn't coming back to her. She wondered what she had done so terrible in her life to warrant this. She ate all her vegetables when she was a little girl. She washed behind her ears, said her prayers nightly, even asked God to bless the whole wide world. She gave food to stray animals and helped little old ladies with their grocery bags. She was average when it came to parental obedience, so why in heaven's name was she paying the price to the piper? A solid minute passed without either of them saying anything.

"When are you coming home?" she asked casually, as if the previous conversation had never transpired.

"We should be there in about three days."

"We," she chuckled. "Well, I'll be out of your way. There won't be any indication that I ever existed."

"I'm sorry, Candace."

"Oh, yeah. I almost forgot."

"Yes, Candace?"

"You owe me $20,000."

"Certainly, Candace. If you need $20,000, it's yours…"

"No, partner! I didn't say I needed $20,000; I said you owe me $20,000. You see, that's how much Linus Snodgrass charged me before he released the information you should have given me days ago." Candace slammed the telephone down. She ran into the living room and grabbed a priceless porcelain figurine from one of the end tables. She raised it in the air with the intention of smashing it against the stone fireplace. Then she heard it just as plain as night and day. It was the voice of Aunt Elvira. *Baby, stop that foolishness. Ain't no cause for you to break up the man's thangs just cause he following his heart. You can't control love bit more'n you can control the rain that God sends from the sky. I know you hurting but you'll be all right. Yo' time coming. Just trust Aunt Vi, yo' time coming."* Candace eased the figurine back on the end table. She flopped down on the sofa and gave herself a good cry.

*   *   *

Austin could not believe what Maoma was saying. She wanted to go back to the rain forest. She didn't want to go to New York. She said she would feel like a caged bird if she tried to live there. She wanted to remain free among people who weren't pretentious. Said she had grown accustomed to the fresh air and the pure foods and nature itself. Said the forest was like drugs and she couldn't get enough of it. Said she had taken the Efe as her family, Gimiko and Tifu as the brother and sister she had never had and the Efe children as the children she one day hoped to have.

Austin knew there was more to it than what she was saying. "And what do you take Jabusa as? He is the true reason why you do not want to leave, isn't he?"

"I have never lied to you, Austin, and I don't intend to start now. Yes, I have grown quite accustomed to Jabusa."

"Are you sure the word is accustomed?" Austin asked with an air of sarcasm.

"I love him, Austin," she said bluntly. "I have led you on enough already. It is time for me to be truthful. Go back to Candace and heal her wounds. She loves you and you love her…"

"You don't know what you're saying, Maoma. You can't mean that you want to go back up there. Look how you were living. Think about all the things you will have if you come back with me. The best food, clothes and living quarters. You used to want to move to the suburbs. We can do that it you still want, and—and children. We can have a house full…"

"No, Austin. I don't want the clothes and houses and all the other superficial things. I need simplicity and wholesomeness, something much more precious than material wealth."

"What about me?" Austin sounded puerile as he asked the question. Maoma's heart pained for him, but what she was doing was for Jabusa, the Efe and her own survival and sanity.

"I do love you, Austin, and I always will, but it's not the same love we used to have." She looked tenderly into his sad eyes. "Go back to Candace and beg her forgiveness. Tell her what she needs to hear, even if it is a lie. Tell her that she is the one you truly love. Tell her you made a choice between her and me and you chose her. I have faith that she will make you happy and give you a beautiful life."

Austin rested his head in Maoma's lap and she rubbed his tight hair the same way she used to do some six years ago.

On the day Austin's commuter flight was scheduled to leave for Kinshasa the same man who took him to the forest and brought him and Maoma back to Joopa escorted Maoma home. She took with her three large duffel bags filled with tennis shoes, clothes and toys for the children and a few items for the Efe adults, all compliments of Austin. She wore one of the dashikis Austin had brought for her and the gold shoes. Austin stood on the pier of the river's edge and watch Maoma sail out of his life forever. She waved to him and blew occasional kisses until he was out of sight. Austin smiled for the first time since she had broken the news to him that she would not be returning to New York. The pain he was feeling was bitter, but there was sweetness about it too. The sweetness was in knowing that Maoma was alive and well and very much loved.

*   *   *

When Muzungu walked into the Lese village, like a chain reaction, the normal noise of the daily activities stopped. The women stopped beating couscous grains, the children stopped playing their games of tag, and old men sitting under palm trees stopped their chatter and laughter. Muzungu walked through the center of the village smiling and slightly bowing her head to everyone she met. The Lese villagers bowed submissively to her. They knew she was returning to Jabusa and to take her rightful seat on the throne. She walked up to the chief's quarters looking like a radiant queen in the new clothes Austin had bought her.

"Jabusa?" She called his name delicately, unsure how he would receive her after her betrayal of his love.

The sound of his name was as sweet as the rich honey the Efe men brought from the forest. It sent a tingle up his spine and reminded him of the euphoria he would never have with Muzungu. Jabusa thought he was dreaming. He had sent one of his men to the Efe village two days ago to see if she had really left. The man came back with news that she had. Jabusa retreated to his quarters, where he remained until this very moment. He inched to the door daring to think that the voice was coming from Muzungu. He drew back the bamboo hanging and was face to face with her. His heart skipped a beat and he blinked his eyelids tightly to see if the apparition would disappear. She bowed on her knees to him.

"My chief, I ask your forgiveness for my unwise decision to leave. I was in a state of confusion and ask that you will accept me back into you good graces." She remained bowed with her eyes on the floor. She felt Jabusa's strong grip seize her and pull her into his arms. He kissed her fervently, then whispered in her ear. "There is nothing to forgive. Nakupenda, Malaika. Welcome home."

*   *   *

It was the sadness of the occasion that caused the three of them to move around like robots. Jonah and Sable helped Candace pack her belongings, mostly clothes, into boxes and suitcases. Austin's apartment was quiet except for the sound of footsteps marching back and forth across the marble foyer, taking boxes down to the cars. Every 15 minutes Sable asked Candace if she was all right. Candace nodded her head without uttering a sound. When the last item was packed, Candace took the spare key Austin had given her off her key ring and laid it on the coffee table beside the engagement ring. She took one last look around the apartment. She remembered the times they had wrestled on the floor, giggling and laughing until one of them cried uncle, and the times they curled up on the leather sofa listening to the soft jazz sounds from Earl

Klugh, Kenny G or their favorite, Jerald Daemyon. She stepped out of the apartment and into the hallway. She paid silent homage to the fond memories she was leaving behind before closing the door.

At six o'clock that evening Candace thought she would go crazy with worry, and Sable's constant coddling wasn't helping either. She remembered the party at Madam Yvonne's and thought that might be just what she needed. She stretched out across the bed and catnapped until it was time to get ready for the party.

Candace put on a black spandex mini skirt and matching midriff halter-top. She paraded in front of the mirror, watching her sleek, shapely figure. She pulled the barrette from her ponytail and her hair fell down around her shoulders. She didn't bother to comb it but instead jostled it to giver herself a sassy look. Her hair made the perfect statement with the outfit. She put an extra layer of mascara and eyeliner on. She chose a dark plum lipstick and coated her lips heavy with it. She slipped on a pair of three-inch heels making her look like an amazon. If Austin cared anything about her, he would not approve of her appearance. She was sure that when he got back to the office his cohorts would be more than eager to tell him how she had dressed. She sprayed Bijan on every inch of her body, so much that she smelled loud and cheap. The heavy fumes drifted out of the bedroom and down the stairs. They would be watching her every move tonight, she thought, and she would give them something to tell Austin. She wanted Austin to know that he was the one responsible for her abrupt change, her downfall. She had to make him hurt as deeply as she was and if hurting herself was the only way to get back at him, so be it. Candace walked into the kitchen where Jonah and Sable were playing a game of Scrabble. "I'm going out," she said, nonchalantly.

Sable looked at her watch. It read 10:00 p.m. She twisted around to look at Candace. She pulled her glasses down from her face. "Candace, where in the world are you going dressed like that?"

Jonah laid the timer down horizontally so the grains of salt would stop his minute from running out. "Lord, have mercy, girl," he laughed. "You going to a costume party or something?"

"Yeah, daddy," she lied and was grateful for the quick excuse Jonah had just given her. She walked in a little further and yanked open the refrigerator door. She took out the carton of orange juice and drank straight from the carton.

Sable turned back around to the game. "Who's having a party? You sure you feel up to it?" asked Sable, content with the explanation for her outrageous dress.

"Madam Yvonne."

Sable twisted back around and gave Candace a more serious stare. "Why would you want to party with Austin's friends, seeing that you're done with him?"

"They're my friends, too."

"But I thought you didn't like them that much. You've always tried to keep your distance from Austin's staff in the past." Sable's eyes were acute and Candace felt they were reading her real intentions. She knew Sable didn't buy the "bored need to get out of the house bit."

"What is this, Momma, 21 questions?" she snapped.

"There's no need to get so defensive, Candace Renee. I just asked a simple question that's all."

"I'm sorry, I'm just on edge," she said, after realizing she was acting like a horse's behind. "You know, I'm thinking this party is just what I need to help me get through this thing. I'm sorry for snapping."

"Candace, I know what you're going through is pretty tough and you shouldn't act like you're not hurting. You need to express your emotions thoroughly, and if that means moping around and giving yourself a good cry now and then, do it. What I'm trying to say is, there're right ways and wrong ways to vent your frustrations. I don't want you doing anything you'll be sorry for down the road."

Candace walked over to Sable and wrapped her arms around her shoulders. She planted a soft kiss on her cheek, "I know, Mom. Look, don't wait up for me."

"You be careful," said Jonah.

*   *   *

Austin's fingers shook nervously as he dialed his telephone number. He had practice a dozen times what he was going to say to Candace. He would tell her exactly what Maoma had told him—that he had made a mistake thinking he stilled loved her, that he had gotten love confused with what he thought was still his obligation. He would apologize a thousand times to the 10th power of course, and hope she bought it. The answering machine picked up. Austin's instinct was to hang up. He envisioned Candace standing by the phone listening to him trying to explain his irrational actions and then laughing at him. But, before he could will his hand to ease the receiver back onto the hook, his voice slipped out. "Hello, Candace. If you're still there, please pick up. If you don't want to talk to me, that's O.K. too, I understand, but just listen to what I have to say. I'm so sorry for all the pain I caused you. I want you to know that I still love you as much as I always have. And-and I want you to know there is no one else that can take your place." There was a pause, "Not even Maoma. You see, I realize that I have fallen out of love with her and in love with you. But it took my seeing her face to face before I was able to know that. Maoma has changed. She is not the same person I knew years ago and, even if she was, I know now that I would still want you. It's you that I need in my life. I just want you to know that I'm on my way home, without Maoma. So if you're there, pick up! Pick up, Malaika!" Austin sighed long and heavy into the receiver. "I'm at a stopover in Paris. My flight arrives at Kennedy around 7:30 tomorrow evening. I hope to see you when I step off the plane. Bye-bye, my love."

Austin sat on his hotel room bed with his fingers crossed. He prayed that a reconciliation was not too late.

*   *   *

The party was wild and Candace knew instinctively that she didn't belong there. The cigarette smoke was so thick you could cut it with a knife. In a far corner of the room she spotted Madam Yvonne, a drink in one hand and a cigarette in the other. As usual she was the center of attraction, alluring both men and women. She was all glamour as she took baby puffs from the cigarette and blew the smoke into ringlets that drifted over head. She looked up long enough to see Candace standing at the door.

"Excuse me," she said and made her way toward her. Madame Yvonne was all teeth, Diana Ross-style, as she approached her. Out of all the personnel at AFLAME, Madame Yvonne and Phyllis were the ones Candace liked most. Phyllis was down-to-earth and had a heart of gold and Madame Yvonne was truthful and fair. When she saw talent she cultivated it until it bloomed into a beautiful flower. And, thanks to her, Candace had become a rose. Candace knew fate was on her side the night of Blacktravangza when Twila took ill. If it wasn't for her letting her model the swimwear and wedding attire she would still be a nobody. The other models, especially Twila, thought Madam Yvonne had vagina envy and purposely gave them a hard time because she could never be the woman they were. "Hello, darling, it's so good to see you. My, don't you look snazzy." Madame Yvonne kissed Candace lightly on the cheeks. She guided her to a corner that was virtually void of people. "I heard about Maoma still being alive."

Candace knew the leak had to have come from Phyllis. She only hoped she wasn't going around telling everyone.

"It's such a tragedy, dear, because you two were so close and you made a striking couple, but you're doing the right thing by getting out and mingling with folks. I always say there's more than one fish in the sea and, honey, the way you look those fish will be jumping out of the water to bite your bait."

Candace appeared as though she wanted to speak, but the hurt and shame stifled her words. Madame Yvonne patted her hand. "I know, child. Been there, done that. Broken hearts happen to the best of us, but we bounce back, don't we?" she said, then winked a quick eye at her. "What you need is a drink, baby." She raised her hand to a handsome young man who was watching her every move. He looked to be no more than 25. He smiled as he approached Madame, who imitated a cat as she brushed her left shoulder against the young man's broad chest and purred something in his ear to make him blush openly. It was obvious that the two had an affair of sorts going on. "Candace, I'd like for you to meet Reginald Cundiff. Reginald, this is Candace Brooks. She's one of AFLAME's top models." Reginald shook Candace's hand. His looks could kill and he was definitely model quality. He moved like a man who knew how to charm women.

"Hey, Candy! How you doing?" He rushed the words out. "Yeah, I remember seeing her picture in Ebony. She was modeling some jeans. Yeah, girl, you was fly." He talked in first person/second person tenses.

Candace thought that the young man's looks would take him far but certainly not his communication skills. Madame Yvonne rolled her eyes downward and scratched the back of her Carole Channing wig. Candace could tell that her toy-boy's English skills embarrassed her.

"Uh, yes, baby," said Madame Yvonne, "now you remember what we talked about, don't you?" She sounded like a mother reminding her child the importance of social graces. "It's better for you to be seen and not heard. You never know who may be watching you."

"Oh," he chortled, "I almost forgot. It won't happen again."

Candace suspected his "behind the scenes auditions" with Madam Yvonne were to assure himself a spot as an AFLAME model.

"Candace here needs a drink. What would you like, baby?"

"A gin and tonic would be fine."

"A gin and tonic. Ain't that kinda' strong for you, child?" Madame asked out of concern.

"No, I drink it all the time."

"Mmm, go 'head with your grown self then." She waved her hand for Reginald to get the drink.

"All right. A gin and tonic it is." Reginald headed toward the bar. Madame Yvonne's eyes met Candace's and they snickered simultaneously.

"Well, what can I say. I have a weakness for young taut flesh, especially when it comes in a package like that. He wants to model," she said, watching him walk away from them, "He's got potential, don't you think?"

"A lot," said Candace while looking at the fine young man walk away to retrieve her drink.

"Just needs to be cultivated, but I'm working on it, added Madame."

"I suspected as much," said Candace, and they laughed again.

When Reginald came back with the drink, Madame told Candace to make herself at home. She slipped her arm under Reginald's and guided him into the mass of guests.

Candace sipped on the drink. She knew most of the people at the party but was reluctant to mingle for fear that they would start asking questions. Sooner or later they would find out that Austin had dumped her for Maoma. She thought about her career with AFLAME and knew resignation was inevitable. There was no way she could work for Austin now that she was no longer the apple of his eye. New York, for that matter, had suddenly lost its luster. She thought about Germanton, North Carolina, her little hometown. It was serene and opposite the frenzied lifestyle of New York. She wondered what her childhood friends were like now. She could probably rekindle friendships with them if they were still there. Aunt Vi was gone, but granddaddy Wilson was still there. And the house she grew up in was just sitting idle now that her parents were back together. There wouldn't be a house payment she would have to make nor would she have to buy furnishings. She had enough money put aside to last her awhile in the event she wasn't able to find a job right away. She could put her journalism degree to use at one of the many TV or radio stations in the North Carolina Triad area. She decided she would research the market and start sending out resumes no later than next week.

She had come to the party with the intentions of showing off. The possibility of even hooking up with Twila and letting her turn her on to some dope had even entered her mind, but standing among the so-called "beautiful people" didn't fascinate her anymore. She was reminded of how she was dressed and although she fit in she was suddenly ashamed. Ashamed that she would let one person cause her to regard herself as less than what she was. It was time to go home. She would grieve over her sorrows but not by alcohol, drugs or self-degradation. She would grieve the old-fashioned way. She would have herself a good cry and cry as long as it took to get Austin out of her system and in the process she would prepare to get on with her life. Candace eased the drink down on an end table and dismissed herself from the apartment.

*   *   *

When Austin clicked on the light, its rays caught a glimmer of the ring's diamond. It sparkled brilliantly, casting a miniature ray of rainbow. Austin closed the door behind him and dumped his bags on the floor. He picked up the ring and the spare key he had given to Candace. He was not surprised that she had left them. He walked into the bedroom to see if the message he left for her had been retrieved. The light on the machine blinked once. He pushed the button and heard himself. He thought that if she had gotten the message, she wouldn't have left. He felt better thinking that there was still a chance for them. He wanted to call Torryville but decided to wait until first thing in the morning. Austin pushed the ring over the knuckle of his little finger and reclined back on the bed. He was tired from jet lag and fell asleep almost instantly.

That next morning Austin woke up with a good feeling in his heart. He got up; showered and made himself a light breakfast of toast and coffee. He dialed Candace's parents' house but got the answering machine. He opted not to leave a message. That would be too impersonal after all that had happened. He decided he would go into the office and catch up on the past week's occurrences, and then take a drive out to Torryville.

40

Goodness and Mercy Shall Follow

Jonah opened the heavy oak door and was caught off guard by the sight of Austin standing on the other side. Jonah had never been a violent man, but just the sight of Austin made him want to swing punches at him. Jonah could not imagine what would possess him to show up at their house. He could see guilt written all over his face.

"Mr. Brooks, there has been a terrible misunderstanding. Please let me explain…"

"Explain? Jonah asked furiously, "I think you've already explained yourself quite clearly. You told my daughter to get lost…"

"Those weren't my words!"

"I don't care what your exact words were, the meaning was the same. Now you got the nerve to show up here at my door?"

"If you would just let me see Candace, I can clear up all of this."

"Hell, no, man! Candace don't want to see you no more! She got plans for her life and they don't include you!"

"Shouldn't Candace be the one to make that decision?"

"She already made it!" Jonah yelled. The commotion drew Sable to the front door.

"Jonah, what's going on out there?" She was equally shocked to see Austin and a fury swept over her as well. "What are you doing here?" she asked coldly.

"I just want to explain some things to Candace."

"Mr. Kawissopie, the best thing for you to do is leave. Candace has had a very rough time of all this and if you care for her at all you wouldn't put her through any more."

"You don't understand…"

Jonah stepped past the threshold and began shoving Austin. "Get off my porch! Just get the hell off my property!"

"I'm not going anywhere until I see Candace."

Jonah pushed him again and Austin stumbled backwards and tumbled down the steps. Jonah stepped down off the porch and positioned his fists boxer style. Sable appreciated Jonah for being the man of the house and protecting his women, but she was frightened now and thought the situation had gotten out of hand. She feared that someone would get hurt.

"You want some more of this?" Jonah asked, weaving and bobbing like Muhammad Ali. Austin pushed himself off the ground.

"Stop it!" yelled Candace. She had heard the disturbance and come out to investigate. She stood behind Sable on the porch. Jonah took a step back but kept his eyes on Austin and his clenched fists up ready for defense.

"Go back in the house, Candace, I got everything under control," ordered Jonah. Sable grabbed Candace by her shoulders as she passed her and proceeded to step off the porch.

"Honey, go back inside. There's nothing you need to say to him," added Sable.

"Why are you here, Austin?" Candace asked.

"I love you, Ca..." before Austin could complete his sentence Jonah interrupted.

"What you take my daughter for, a fool?"

"Daddy, please. Just go inside and take Momma with you."

"Naw, baby girl. His ass needs kicking.

"But honey, you're making a mistake. Can't you see what he's doing?" said Sable.

"He's trying to dangle you like a yo-yo, baby girl," added Jonah. Candace wiggled out of Sable's grip and walked down off the porch. "Daddy, I can handle this. Now go on."

Jonah eased his arms down and he and Sable reluctantly walked back inside.

"I left you a message on the machine, but I guess you had already left. I was trying to tell you not to leave, that I made a mistake."

"A mistake?"

"I know what you're thinking."

"Austin, how can you mistake love?"

"Candace, I thought I was still in love with Maoma, but I was wrong. She's changed; I've changed."

"Where is Maoma?"

"She stayed."

Candace looked at him suspiciously and she was curious as to why Maoma didn't come back with Austin. "Why?" she asked, detecting a note of disappointment on his face.

"She has grown accustomed to the life she is now living."

Austin was giving her one-sentence answers, which was not his style. He had always expounded thoroughly on any question or statement given him except, of course, anything pertaining to Maoma. Candace believed that she still had to speak easy when mentioning her.

"So, when did you realize you didn't love her, before she decided not to come back with you or after?"

"Does it matter?"

"Not really," she said, keeping herself distant from him.

"Oh, Candace, you don't know how glad I am to hear that. I have worried so that you wouldn't accept me back into your life." He reached for her, but she took a step back. "But I thought you said it didn't matter?"

"Austin, it doesn't matter. Don't interpret it the wrong way. I don't want you back into my life anymore."

The statement knocked the wind out of Austin's sail. "You don't mean that."

"Yes, I do." She began shaking her head. "I love you like I've loved no other man and I thought what we had was good. Better than good. Spectacular. The problem is that I love you more than you could ever love me and, Austin, that's not enough."

"So what are you saying? That you want to give up everything we've built together?"

"I don't want to give it up. I have no choice."

"Of course, you have a choice Candace. You're not making sense."

"You see, Austin, I could never play second fiddle."

"You won't be playing second fiddle."

"I've always played second fiddle, even when Maoma was dead. You loved her memory more than you loved me. Now that she is alive, you will always wish in your heart she had come back to you. Me, on the other hand, I'll be living in fear that she will come back and if that happens," she paused, "well, we both know what you'll do."

"What? You think I'll drop you like a hot potato?"

"It's been known to happen." She was straightforward, "The thing is this, Austin. I need to have faith in the man I intend to spend the rest of my life with. I've lost all faith in you." She thought about Russell and how devoted he had been to her. She now knew that Russell was the kind of man she needed. But as far as Russell, it was too late for him. She truly hoped he would have a good life with Ophelia. "Now can you honestly look me in the eye and tell me if Maoma tires of the forest life and decides she wants you back that you won't take her?"

"Is that what you're worrying about?"

"You didn't answer my question."

"That won't happen, Candace."

"Answer my question truthfully, Austin."

"All I know is what I want for us. I can't answer what might happen years from now any more than you can assure me that you will always love me."

Candace smiled a tensed smile as she ran both hands through her hair. "You've just answered my question."

"What about your career? How can you still work for AFLAME and see me on a daily basis and not want to continue our relationship?"

"Modeling is great, but I don't think I want to do that anymore. It's lost its flavor with me."

"No, Candace, you're making drastic decisions. AFLAME needs you and you need AFLAME. You've always wanted to be a model. Not many people get that chance."

Candace choked back her tears. "You're right, but I think I want to try my hand at journalism. Besides, I'm tired of New York. I've decided that it's too fast for me. I want to go back home and start over. Breathe some good, clean fresh air. Be around decent, honest folks." The statement was meant to hurt him. "Yeah. I think there is a better life for me back in North Carolina."

"Don't do this to us."

"I'm not the one who terminated what we had."

Austin was becoming frantic. He was losing her. "Don't decide right away. Why don't we discuss it over dinner? Do you remember our first date? We went to Arthur's. We can go there again if you like. You remember how we danced and laughed and the next day we made love. It was beautiful. Candace, don't throw all of that away," he pleaded. "I don't know what I would do without you."

"You will continue to work at AFLAME and be the dashing, debonair man that you are. You will meet the woman that's perfect for you and you will get on with your life. You'll do just fine." Austin grabbed her hands as she was backing away. She lifted them to her lips and kissed his hands lightly. "Good bye, Austin. Remember that I truly do love you." She pulled her hands away and ran into the house. She took one last look at him before closing the heavy oak doors behind her.

She had just closed an excruciating chapter in her life that she hoped she'd never have to relive. The pain she felt was like no other she had experienced. Not even her breakup with Julius years ago could compare, not even the divorce her parents had put her through as a child, or the loss of her grandmother and Aunt Elvira. But she had found in herself the strength to turn her back on an addictive love that she felt would be her future demise. She had found confidence in herself and that confidence generated a greater self-love and self-respect.

Aunt Elvira's voice came to her again. This time it wasn't in the forceful, critical tone it had been the day in Austin's apartment, but instead it was a faint, soothing whisper. It told her that her time was coming and in the meantime to draw her strength from the 23rd Psalm. She remembered how Grandmother Loretta and Aunt Elvira use to cite the 23rd chapter of Psalm whenever they faced adversities. They both had said there were powers in the scriptures. Candace began climbing the stairs to her room, where she would have another good cry. With each step she cited the verses.

"The Lord is my shepherd; I shall not want" step

He maketh me to lie down in green pastures" step

He leadeth me beside the still waters" step

He restoreth my soul: He leadeth me in the paths of righteousness for his name's sake" step

Yea, though I walk through the valley of the shadow of death, I will fear no evil" step for thou art with me; thy rod and thy staff they comfort me" step Thou preparest a table before me in the presence of mine enemies: thou anoinest my head with oil; my cup runneth over" step

Surely goodness and mercy shall follow me all the days of my life and I will dwell in the house of the Lord forever." step.

She turned the doorknob to her room and entered. She thought her world and Austin's world would come together as one, but instead their worlds collided—head on. The good thing was, the collision had not been fatal. She would survive and become stronger because of it. Yes, she would wait on her time to come, because she was worth it.

Epilogue

The Rain Forest

Gimiko led his tribe through the thick foliage. The mules were loaded down with good things from the forest. The larger children pulled the smaller ones in the three shiny red wagons. They were on their second pair of sneakers, compliments of Austin, and had mastered the act of walking and running in them. The Efe men teased the women about their weight gain, mainly due to all the candy bars and jars of honey Austin had sent as well. They moved with speed and excitement as they made their way to the Lese village. They were going to see their Lese friends, but most of all they were going to see Muzungu. The children were especially excited because it had been several weeks since they had last seen her and they missed her terribly. They understood that she was weak and confined to bed. Tifu brought along a honey jar filled with goat milk, chicken stock and boiled herbal leaves she'd picked from the forest. It was a cure-all remedy handed down through generations. She would sit by Muzungu's side and lift her head as she poured the good medicine in her. She hoped Queen Kanya and the other elder women were taking care of her.

The Efe continued to travel until the canopy of trees thinned and the sunlight filtered through. The children began squealing with delight. They knew they were only a few feet away from Muzungu. Tifu smiled at their enthusiasm but feared the noise would be too much for Muzungu.

"You must be quiet, children," Tifu warned. "The noise is not good for Muzungu. I know you're all excited, but you must contain yourselves."

The forces of habit made Gimiko stop on the village edge. Suko looked at his father and knew that the years of oppression inflicted upon them by the Lese had caused him to stop and wait for an invitation.

"Jabusa said we are always welcome here," Suko reminded him. It was then that Gimiko proceeded into the village. Queen Kanya met the clan at the door of the chief's quarters. She opened her arms to greet them. Tifu was the first to receive her embrace.

"Muzungu is resting quietly now. She has been asking for you, Tifu. I know she will be happy to see you all."

Tifu held up the jar of medicine. "I made this for her. One sip and she will feel like new."

"Is that Tifu I hear?" Muzungu's frail and weak voice flowed through the thick clay walls of the house. Queen Kanya ushered Tifu and the others in. Jabusa sat at the head of Muzungu's bed. He unwrapped the bundle he held in his arms. Tifu, Gimiko and the adults smiled at the beautiful brown baby boy. The children ooed and ahhed at the baby as they crowded around Jabusa. Tifu patted Muzungu's hand. "He is a fine little warrior. You have done well. Muzungu looked all around her. All she could see was love. From time to time she did think about Austin and how he was doing. She hoped he had been able to reconcile with Candace.

Looking at the precious little boy was confirmation that she had made the right decision in staying. Her journey had been a long, tough one, but she would do it all over in a heartbeat if it meant keeping the joy she now possessed.

Germanton, North Carolina

Candace wore a relaxed pair of jean shorts and a simple low neck knit top. She had been wearing her hair in a Halle Berry style cut for almost a year. She found that the shorter hair style made her look more professional in front of the TV camera when she was delivering portions of the news as an investigative reporter, and her male counterparts seemed to take her more serious with short hair. Candace heaped another pile of spaghetti on Russell's plate. He licked his thumb and let his eyes follow her every move.

"What cha looking at?" she teased.

"I like what I see."

"Well, thank you kindly, Mr. Ingram. She eased down in the chair beside him and he leaned over and kissed her lips.

"What was that for?"

"For letting me come visit you."

"You know you're always welcome here."

"I hope you mean that."

"You know I do."

"I'm not sorry for how things turned out," he said

"What do you mean?"

"You know, your misfortunes with Austin."

"Oh, that."

"Yeah, that dude tried to steal my baby from me, but God don't like ugly. Don't get me wrong now, 'cause I'm sorry for the pain he caused you, but not for nothing else. I saw right through that dude first time I laid eyes on him."

"Seems that you weren't the only one."

"If things hadn't happened the way they did, I probably wouldn't be sitting here now."

"Do you ever hear from Ophelia?"

"Nope."

"You say that so nonchalantly."

"How am I suppose to say it, with feeling? We were never a match anyway. When I broke it off with her a month before the wedding, she told me that she suspected something was wrong. I don't think she really loved me anyway. She was infatuated with the idea of getting married more than anything. When I told her I couldn't go through with it, she didn't cry and carry on like women usually do. It's ironic how we both thought the other was married and living happy lives."

"Yeah, it is."

"If I hadn't called your mother to see how she was doing, I never would have known."

Candace chuckled, "I'm surprised she didn't call you sooner to give you the 411. You know she's always liked you."

"What can I say? I'm a likable kind of guy."

"Yes, you are." This time it was Candace who leaned over and kissed him.

"Listen, what would you think about my moving south?"

"Come on, Russell, don't play with me now."

"No, I'm serious. I put in for a transfer with the postal service and it looks like it might come through."

"You would do that?" she asked, Skeptical.

"You know how I feel about you, Candace. You're my everything."

Candace smiled, "I think I would like that, Russell. I think I would like that very much." Candace cocked her head to the side as she heard Aunt Vi's voice once again. It simply said, "See, I told ya."

Book Club Discussion Questions

1. On a scale of 1–10, how realistic would you say "Colliding Worlds" is?

2. Have you ever been in a situation similar to any of the characters? If yes, how so?

3. As a parent, how can you relate to Sable and Jonah's role?

4. Parallel the prejudices you've experience in America or your country to those of the Efe and Lese Tribes.

    4a.) Discuss what you feel would be a good solution to ending those prejudices.

5. Do you feel spousal abuse is more prevalent among white-collar or blue-collar professionals?

6. Was "Colliding Worlds" an enjoyable read?

About the Author

Vivian Bivins is a graduate of Winston-Salem State University and works for the Forsyth County School System. She is married to Sammie Lee Bivins, Jr. They have two daughters, Samantha and Senora. She lives in Winston-Salem, North Carolina. Vivian is currently at work on her second novel.

Vivian Bivins would love to hear your comments about Colliding Worlds. You may contact her at Samasase@aol.com